The CHAMPION of BARÉSH

STAR WORLD FRONTIER

BOOK 1

SUSAN GRANT

Copyright © 2016 Susan Grant
ISBN: 978-1-940200-28-6
Edited by: Mary Moran
Cover design and Interior format by The Killion Group, Inc.

Even with many layers of editing, mistakes can slip through. If you encounter typos in this book, please send them to Susan Grant at
www.susangrant.com/contact

A desperate woman in need of a miracle—
A bad-boy prince in need of redemption

She was playing with fire...

Jemm Aves battles to keep her dreams alive on a dead-end world. Working for the mines by day, she's a successful bajha player at night, disguised as a male to be allowed to compete in the colony's dangerous underworld where club owners will go to extremes to retain the best players. Every win puts her one small step closer to her goal: saving enough to escape Barésh with her family. When a nobleman from one of the galaxy's elite families recruits her to be a star player for his team, it's because he doesn't know her secret. Her ruse proves to be her most perilous game yet when it puts both their lives—and her heart—at risk.

Prince Charming he was not...

Prince Klark is eager to reverse his reputation as the black sheep of the Vedla clan, a family as famous for its wealth and power as it is for being a bastion of male-dominated tradition. If his bajha team can win the galactic title, it would go a long way toward restoring the family honor that his misdeeds tarnished. He travels to Barésh to track down an amateur who's risen to the top of the seedy world of street bajha, offering the commoner a chance of a lifetime: a way off that reeking space rock for good. But his new player comes with a scandalous secret that turns his plans and his beliefs upside down. He sets out to win a very different prize—his champion's reluctant heart.

RITA-winner Susan Grant is back with an all-new, stand-alone tale of two improbable lovers, their daring secret, and the gamble destined to alter the course of their worlds forever.

OTHER BOOKS BY *NEW YORK TIMES* BESTSELLING AUTHOR SUSAN GRANT

Anthologies
Mission: Christmas (featuring "Snowbound with a Prince")
Mysteria (featuring "Mortal in Mysteria")
Mysteria Lane (featuring "The Nanny from Hell")
Mysteria Nights (combines the *Mysteria* and *Mysteria Lane* anthologies)

Make sure you don't miss my next book. Sign up for my new release email list at **www.susangrant.com.**

ACKNOWLEDGEMENTS:

Jill Sardella, I dedicate this book to you. You never gave up on me. Your awesome nagging was just what I needed, when I needed it.

Thank you to my incredible team: Barbara, Carolyn, Chris, Corey, Debbie, George, Heather, Jill, Julie, Karen, Liz, Melisse, and Melissa, and a few other precious souls (you know who you are). You all are amazing. I feel so blessed to have your help. It allows me to focus on what I love most—creating stories.

CHAPTER ONE

Barésh

Jemm Aves's brother tied a blindfold over her eyes to the sound of the crowd cheering for her quick end. "This is it," he said. "No turning back."

"I know. I'm fine, Nico. I'm doing this." For a moment, Jemm thought the loud rhythmic thumping was her heartbeat but the people in the arena were stomping their boots. It was a rough crowd; they were drinking hard and chanting threats. They wanted blood.

"Aye. Try to last as long as ya can." Nico's hands shook as he checked the seals and fasteners of her jumpsuit to make sure there was no skin showing. Contact with bare flesh with even the tip of an active sens-sword caused excruciating pain. At the settings used in back-alley bajha matches such as this one, accidental contact with the blunt weapon could cause a burn, seizure, or worse. This crowd wanted the worst.

Unlike her opponent's protective bajha suit, hers was dingy and patched, originally used by her father and custom-made for his larger frame. It was good that the shock-resistant fabric hung so loosely on her. She was a twenty-four-year-old woman trying to pass for a teenage boy in a bar full of laborers who liked to think they were still able to tell the difference.

Not that there weren't some females in the audience, but none competed in bajha. Not here on Barésh, this backwater frontier world, or anywhere else in the galaxy. It wasn't forbidden, exactly, but to her knowledge no lass had ever dared try. Bajha was a game of the ancients, based on instinct and intuition. It was also a rich man's sport, beloved by the *Vash Nadah*, the unimaginably wealthy and privileged royal families who ruled the galaxy. They used their tamer version of bajha as a path to a higher state of consciousness. But for Jemm, it was a lifeline, a way out for her family.

The crowd's stomping grew so loud that the concrete floor beneath her boots shook. With each breath, she almost choked on air thick with the reek of urine, sweat, and "swank", the chemical cocktail that put nearly as many Baréshtis in the grave as the trillidium mines.

"Jemm, quit fidgeting." Nico adjusted her hood over a skin-tight cap that hid her scalp and flattened her hair. He wanted Jemm to cut her hair short, but she had refused. The tail of her long, thick braid was channeled between her shoulder blades, her street clothes layered on top. The shapeless bajha suit covered all of it like a painter's tarp, yet she sensed her little brother's unease in the way his fingers fussed over her.

The boisterous horde did not scare him; this was his world—these rowdy drinking holes—his escape. Bringing his sister into that world to play bajha? Well, that probably had him a little concerned.

"They'll see a lad and not a lass. I know it. We've got expectation bias on our side," she said in hopes of easing his jumpy nerves—and hers.

"Expectation...what?" Facts gleaned from book knowledge tended to defeat him. Their father had hungered for education, as did Jemm, but Nico craved things she would rather not think about.

"It means we see what we expect to see. No one *expects* to see a lass dressed in full bajha gear," she plucked at her jumpsuit, "so they won't see one."

"Let's hope they don't," Nico muttered with a last yank on her hood.

The refs would call the match if they discovered the trickery and levy a gaming fine they could not afford. The consequences of that would be disastrous. That was the real risk she and Nico took embarking on this insane scheme.

What about their mother, her health failing? And little Button? The child was Jemm's responsibility now. What would happen to her if they got into trouble? Their household slept with a real roof over their heads unlike so many others. Nico had not been able to work in years, but Jemm held a steady job, a good one—by Baréshti standards. Employment working for the mines but not in the mines was considered a "fancy gig". Was it selfish to want more?

She and Nico argued these doubts over and over again in the weeks leading up to today. They desperately needed the money, that much was true, but entering the seething, sometimes violent world of back-alley bajha? Disguised as a male?

It was her idea, but Nico went right along with it. No surprise there. How did she expect him to talk sense into her when he was always looking for ways to improve their situation with get-rich-quick schemes?

It's just one match. One round fought with a local champ before being eliminated. It would earn her a piece of the betting pool divided between the amateur challengers afterward. The longer she lasted against the champ, the bigger her share. She had no illusions about taking this any farther than that. She was a grown woman with obligations and a family to support.

A family that depends on you to be the responsible adult who doesn't spend nights in north-city fight clubs.

What was she thinking? Her skin tingled with perspiration.

Nico's hand tightened on her upper arm. "Listen up. We watched this champ. Studied him. We know how he fights. All ya have to do is stay with him as long as ya can."

She nodded. "I got this."

"Aye, ya do." He squeezed her arm. "Now, go out there and earn us some silver."

Suddenly the chaos ebbed enough for a voice from center stage to reach her ears. "Happy Eighthnight, my friends!" The announcer had arrived, bellowing out his greetings.

No turning back.

Nico lifted her blindfold the smallest distance necessary to allow her a peek at the spectacle. "We call him Bounce."

Jemm couldn't help grinning. While not overweight, Bounce was shiny, short, and very round. He was a little bouncy ball of a man with soft, puffy jowls framing his lips that hinted at the kind of meals of which she and her family could only dream. The profits the club raked in from hosting these matches kept the announcer well fed and living an enviable quality of life. Cleverly, most bars held bajha games on Eighthnight, which was both payday and the evening before the lightest workday of the week. Since this particular north-city dive was favored by mineworkers—trill rats—the place was packed. Naturally, the sport was as popular on Barésh as it was in the rest of the galaxy. But in the colony Eighthnight betting was tainted with an air of desperation that took bajha to a whole new and frenzied level.

"Welcome home to Rumble, and the finest games you'll find in the colony!" Bounce roared to thundering approval. "Tonight, five challengers will attempt to unseat the reigning champion, one of them a newcomer!"

Jemm stood taller as laughter and jeers drowned out Bounce's voice.

"Join me in welcoming back *your* champion of champions! The undefeated... The unconquerable..."—a pause for dramatic effect—"the Bla-aaaaack Hole of Barésh!"

Hole strutted to center stage with an exaggerated, slow-motion gait. Every week it was the same: the champ sent a slate of hopefuls to their defeat. With odds so predictably in his favor the gamblers wagered not on who would win or lose, but how long a hopeful lasted. Flash-jewels set in his teeth and revealed by his grin were cosmetic luxuries. No one wore black in the ring, but he did. Fitting perfectly, his unconventional outfit was a calculated intimidation tactic for the competition. The suit followed his musculature, clinging to powerful thighs.

What a show-off. It made her want to last long enough to force him to catch his breath, and maybe catch a few licks from her sens-sword.

"First to take up the challenge tonight is our newcomer!"

Nico snapped her blindfold back in place. As the hot spotlight found Jemm, she could picture the announcer checking his notes before he finally shouted out her stage name, "Sea Kestrel! Step into the ring!"

The crowd reacted with mocking howls and disbelieving hoots: "What kind of name is that? Who is this sucker?" Some made bird cries to taunt her. Even Nico had urged her to use a different ring name, initially.

But it was the nickname her father gave her. His dream was to see her fly strong and free, far from this desolate rock, like the fabled raptor itself, but he died before he had the chance to take his family off-world. *May I live up to the name, Da.* Her spine tingled as she closed her hands around the thick grip of her sens-sword.

Nico checked her hood and blindfold again. Then he released her to a pair of referees who also inspected her regulation eye covering and the setting on her sens-sword before she was allowed in the ring. Somewhere on the other side Black Hole allowed his blindfold and weapon to be checked. Then they were left alone.

Her pulse quickened, and her lips formed a small smile. It was one thing to watch bajha, to practice sparring, or to listen to Nico's accounts of club matches, but to be in the ring for real was an incredible rush. The joy of the heart-pounding moment expanded like a ball of fire in her chest, along with the dread of being found out and expelled from the ring.

Quiet your mind. Hefting her sens-sword in her hands, she found the familiar weight comforting as the raucous bedlam died down. She slowed her spinning thoughts and steadied herself in a way only her father had been able to understand.

A deep sense of peace stole over her. Everyone knew the goal of the game was to seek out, tag an opponent and register a hit on the chest plate without the aid of the usual five senses. To target Hole, Jemm had to find him first, using her intuition. Reaching out with her mind, she unfurled her awareness like a net, spinning, fanning out. *You must listen...*

"But not with your ears," Da would explain when she was a small girl sitting, rapt, on his knee, his bajha suit unfastened at the neck after a match, the very suit that protected her now. "You don't need your eyes to see, Jemm. The neurons in your body will guide you to your target. Let your senses show you the way."

The champion loomed into her consciousness. With no build-up at all, he charged toward her with all the bluntness of a runaway ore hauler.

She sidestepped him, leaving him to lurch into the space where he had been certain he would find her. The crowd screamed with boos and cheers, ignoring or ignorant of the rules that bajha be played in silence.

"Last as long as ya can," Nico had told her, but Black Hole was not reading from the same playbook. His impatience to defeat her in the opening seconds of the match was as obvious as a drunkard's footsteps on broken floorboards. She and Nico had watched some of his matches to study his fighting style. He liked to use his size and speed to take opponents out quickly. Typically, his stamina waned in later bouts, allowing challengers to last longer against him. No such luck for her tonight. She was first up, and Black Hole was fresh and ready to pound an upstart into a coma.

A thud of a boot, his sens-sword jabbing, Hole lunged in for the kill. Spinning away from his thrust, she raked her sens-sword over his backside. His involuntary grunt of surprise gave away his location.

You make it easy when I can hear ya, Hole.

The crowd's thunderous, disbelieving reaction faded to near silence as the fighters circled each other, sens-swords at the ready, close enough for her to smell his acrid stink of fear. He knew what he was up against now, aye. Not only was she not going down easily, she had enough skill to taunt him.

She hadn't set out to humiliate him, but she couldn't help it. He was so ridiculously overconfident! An inner, devilish sense of showmanship tempted her to dish out another whack on the rump, but overconfidence would be no more flattering on her than it was on him.

Play the way you were taught.

The champ left nothing in reserve as he angrily tracked her around the ring. She danced backward, keeping out of reach, partly to last longer and earn a larger prize and partly to goad him into attacking before he was fully ready.

Come and get me, Hole.

He glided into her space but this time she stood her ground. Their sens-swords clashed as she parried him, energy fizzing, heating her chin. Her sens-sword's edge skittered along his before she slid home, burying the tip in the center of his chest plate.

The force of impact traveled up her extended arms, a cascade of snapping sparks filling the air between them. Bursts of energy jolted her, and she tasted the tang of it on her tongue.

All around her raged the crowd's reaction. Her eardrums buzzed with the sheer volume of it. Gasping, she pulled her sens-sword back, disarming it, and then sank to one knee, her head lowered humbly as was the protocol in bajha.

Holy crat. She won.

She *won!*

Triumph swelled inside her.

Bounce grabbed her by the scruff of her neck and shouted for the referees. "Check his blindfold! Check him now!"

Before the refs reached her, she forced herself to slow her breathing to keep from exhibiting any of the triumph she felt inside. Finding nothing amiss with her blindfold, they untied it and held it up to the light to check for thin spots or pinholes in the fabric, all reasons to declare the win invalid. Finally, a ref reported, "No evidence of cheating. The win stands."

In the blaze of the spotlight, Jemm was still processing the incredible turn of events when Bounce's spongy hand snatched her wrist and thrust her arm in the air, yanking her to her feet. "We have a new champion! Seeeeeeeea Kestrel!"

That was when it finally registered that the sound coming from the audience was not cheering. It was angry shouting.

"Jackpot!" A spectator crowed in the midst of it. "Forty to one. How do ya like them odds, ya dozers? I'm rich—!" Someone's fist caught him in the jaw.

Throughout the arena fights broke out, quenching the sporadic celebrations like cold water dumped on molten rocks. None of the miners had placed wagers tonight expecting to lose, and not a single one of them was interested in hearing the good news of the few who had bet against the champ. Already security guards were storming the stands, armed with shock batons. A miner leaped down to the ring floor, pursued by a small gang focused on finishing the fight.

Where was Nico? It looked like they were going to have to fight their way out of here to wherever they would collect the winnings. That was what people like them had to do. Just as the galaxy's elite possessed an inborn sense of entitlement, the Baréshti lower class were hardwired to fight. They fought their way into the world and fought against being taken from it, fighting every day in between.

"Come to the office." Bounce grabbed a fistful of her bajha suit to steer her toward an exit between the stands but she dug in her heels.

"Wait!" she croaked in the lowest, most masculine voice she could manage. "My manager…" She struggled not to drop her sens-sword or have her hood ripped off by all the jostling. A pair of wiry security guards with mean eyes and batons in their gloved hands worked at keeping the throng away from them.

"Here! I'm here." Her brother plowed his way toward her, sporting a bruised cheek and a split lip. His eyes sparkled with excitement, a grin making dimples in his cheeks that she could not recall seeing since he was a boy. Pumping his fist in the air, he somehow had the good sense not to shout out her name. "By the dome, ya did it! You won!"

It was still sinking in. "I know, I know." *Holy crat!*

"Get back!" Security guards muscled Nico backward. One of the men jammed a baton in his stomach, causing him to double over. The other raised his baton to strike the back of Nico's skull.

No! Jemm tore free of Bounce, armed her sens-sword and slapped it against the guard's hamstrings. A strangled shriek. The guard's knees buckled, his baton falling, and he went down like a bag of rocks. She pivoted to the other guard, aiming her sens-sword at his heart.

The guard's startled gaze swung from Jemm, who faced him in full-on, nostrils-flaring, eyes-narrowed attack mode, to the much smaller shock-baton in his fist. He absorbed the sight of his partner writhing on the arena floor with saliva foaming between his lips. Then his gaze snapped back to the player who had just taken down the longest-running bajha champion in Rumble's history.

He released Nico.

Jemm hooked her brother's arm in hers while the guard helped his partner stand on wobbly legs. "You okay?" Jemm whispered.

"I'm good." Her brother winced a little as he rubbed his belly. "Are ya *crattin'* crazy, though? It's a capital offense to attack someone with a sens-sword."

"Do ya really think they're gonna arrest their new champ, Nico? I'm aware of the laws, but I'd have cooked his brains if he hurt ya."

"Aye," he said ruefully. "I know."

"Both of you lads, this way." Bounce propelled them through a doorway and down a narrow, stuffy corridor. Here, the turmoil was somewhat muffled.

Nico took her by the arm, yanking her closer for privacy. "Let's talk about the rematch. Right now no one knows if you're a fluke or the real deal. If ya face Black Hole again, and put him on his ass—again—they'll know. The betting will be through the dome!"

Jemm choked out a laugh of disbelief. Talk about putting the ore-trailer before the tug. "Let's get paid for this match first."

"Oh, we will. I promise you. Rumble's owner's got plenty of silver to spare. He made his fortune from bajha betting."

She shrugged, not caring about some aristo's good luck. She was more concerned with getting paid and leaving Rumble before they got rumbled themselves.

"Migel Arran owns ten or eleven clubs. He offers lucrative player contracts; some of the best in the colony."

"How'd we jump from talking about a rematch to playing under contract?"

The announcer, living up to his name, bounced along ahead of them, clearing a channel through a stream of security team members flowing past in the opposite direction, rushing toward the brawl. She forced her voice lower. "This is dangerous talk, Nic. A rematch is one thing, but signing a contract? The more exposure, the greater the chances we'll get caught."

"What about expectation ballast?" he countered.

"*Bias.* Anyway, the plan was to play one match. One."

"That was before you blew Black Hole out of the ring. I knew you'd do well, and you knew, too, but holy, craggin' crat—"

"I know," she breathed, giddy with incredulity. Taking down the champion was as unexpected as the powerful sense of freedom and control that buoyed her the moment she stepped into the ring. The exhilaration of playing the sport she loved in actual competition was a heady new rush, and she wanted more. Then she remembered that someone in their family needed to act like a responsible adult. Needed to keep a roof over their heads and food on the table. Bajha, no matter how thrilling, could prove extremely temporary. "I have a job."

"It pays crap."

"Our family depends on that 'crap job'," she snapped, feeling a hot rush of anger.

Nico's hands came up. His gaze held such shame it was hard to stay irritated with him.

"You ready to go in?" Bounce was waiting for them by the doorway to what Jemm guessed was the office. He waved a hand at them and pointed inside.

Nico held up a finger. "As soon as I'm done conferring with my player."

Jemm dragged the back of her glove over her eyes to wipe away the stinging perspiration. Her hair was soaked under the knit cap she did not dare remove. The exertion of the match raised her core body temperature, which was still rising like a runaway chemical reaction.

"Let me handle things in there," said Nico. "It's not that you can't, but I know what to say. If you do talk, talk like a fella."

"I'll try not to talk at all." She rechecked the safety setting on her sens-sword and followed her brother down the hall.

Bounce ushered them into a dim and smoky back office. It smelled like someone somewhere had smoked hallucivapes, cigarettes stuffed with a potent, concentrated form of swank. Foul stuff that. It dizzied her.

A member of Rumble's security team lowered a heavy bar over the office door, further isolating them from the brawl outside. Other hefty guards milled around, eyeing them.

"Great Mother..." Bounce sagged against the nearest wall and mopped his shiny forehead with a square of fabric pulled from his suit pocket. "What a night!"

Nico's eyes went wide at the plush surroundings in the office, and then he quickly blinked the awe away. "No time to be lollygaggin' around, Bounce. It's time to pay up."

"You'll be fairly compensated, I assure you," someone said from the other side of the room. A man dressed in some of the finest clothing Jemm had ever seen lounged behind a desk. The wall at his back had an array of screens with varying views of the bajha ring and Rumble's ever-busy bar. On the desk was a fancy bottle of liquor, a personal communicator, and his spit-shined black boots crossed one over the other. "I'd just about lost hope that some amateur would topple that blowhard Black Hole. Then you show up, a skinny kid in a shabby suit. Will wonders never cease?"

Lazily, the man slid his feet off the desk and sauntered over to Jemm. Judging by his ordinary eye color—more brown than golden—and commonplace dark blond hair, he was not noble-born. Yet, he carried himself with the arrogant swagger of the aristos who lived within walled compounds. The colony elites seldom passed through Jemm's life. When they did, it was in tantalizing glimpses as they whooshed past in flycars, or went about their privileged lives mostly insulated from the fumes and filth and unceasing pandemonium of Barésh. Now here was a man who had modeled himself after them in almost every detail. Expensive nano-light tattoos decorated his throat and cast enough of a glow to make rainbow patterns on his high, starched, pristine white collar. Something iridescent coated his hair, an oil or wax, and his eyebrows, too. Was that pure trillidium threaded through micro-holes ringing his left ear from top to the lobe? It was the stuff that starships were made of, and must have cost him dearly.

The owner's chin lowered, his expression amused, probably at the way Jemm and Nico gaped at him in wonder. "Migel Arran," he said. "Welcome to my club, and congratulations on your win, son." If someone was smoking hallucivapes it was not him. His eyes were too clear for that vice, too shrewd. He shifted that appraising gaze to Nico. "I assume you're the manager?"

"Aye. Manager, trainer, promoter." Nico's voice sang with pride. "Nico Aves is the name."

"Well, Mr. Aves, manager-trainer-promoter, your player handled himself admirably in the ring tonight. It's been a long time since we saw this much talent in an amateur."

Bounce's jowls flapped as he nodded in agreement. "A very long time."

Nico gestured at Jemm. "Talent like that doesn't come for free, ya know. About that compensation you mentioned—we're here to collect our winnings. A mighty big share, too."

Jemm winced as Arran's eyes flashed with something at odds with his pleasant expression. Her brother deserved a pat on the back for the tough-guy act he was putting on, but she hoped he didn't push it too far. Arran could very well toss them out in the street with *no money*, and there would not be a thing they could do about it. But Jemm doubted Arran would do that. If he was smart enough to become this rich and powerful, it meant he knew enough to want to woo talented newcomers, not chase them away. In the next instant the owner proved her right by snapping his fingers to summon one of the staff. "Bring something cold for our VIP guests." Then to Bounce, he said, "Get something for the manager's split lip."

Bounce brought Nico a wet towel wrapped around ice, which Nico gladly applied to the bruises on his face.

"Sit down, please," Arran said, motioning to two chairs arranged in front of his desk. "Make yourselves comfortable."

It's easier to negotiate when the other party has their guard down, Jemm thought, hoping her brother realized that, too. If Arran tagged her as a trill-rat bumpkin won over by a few kind deeds, he was mistaken.

"We're fine as we are," Nico said, tossing aside the wet rag, in no mood to delay getting paid.

"The cash box, as well," Arran told Bounce in a more private tone.

"Your refreshments." A staff member handed them each a bottle made from real glass. Vapor from the deep orange liquid wafted toward Jemm. She cradled the bottle between her gloved hands, sniffing at the contents. The fruity, floral scent made her mouth water.

Arran smiled. "Pure, unadulterated, genuine Siennan citrus juice."

Jemm's attempt to sip the beverage extra slowly to make it last failed with the first taste. The juice was so heavenly good and her dehydration so raw that she drained the inverted bottle within seconds, stifling a small burp with the back of her glove. Nico slipped the empty bottle into his pocket to bring home, and Jemm followed his lead. Glass was dear in their neighborhood. Ma could use the bottles for many things.

It took two guards with two separate key devices to unlock the cash box, while Bounce hovered nearby. The lid whirred open to reveal a compartment filled with more money than she had ever seen in one place: credits in the full range of denominations from pale blue to gold to black. Her stomach did a cartwheel as Arran removed a silver card. Oh, the worries that single silver would ease: the broken window, her mother's medicine, a new pair of shoes and better food for Button...

Arran pointed the credit at Jemm. Swiftly, she extinguished the yearning in her face and in her eyes for the money before he could glimpse it. "Your winner's share," he said and offered them the money.

Jemm thought she saw her brother's hand tremble as he pocketed the silver. "Now I know ya gonna want to hold a rematch, Mr. Arran. A contest of champions, if ya will. How about a little more incentive for my player here to make that happen?"

"A contest of champions, indeed. I like the way you think, Mr. Aves." Again, the bar owner dipped his hand into the cash box. Between his fingers he held up four more credits, pointing them at Jemm. "Sea Kestrel, these will be yours for the rematch next week, regardless of the outcome. That's simply for showing up to play. You and Black Hole will go at it again. If you win a second time, let's just say there's more where these came from. Money won't be a problem for you any longer. I pay my club's players very handsomely."

"Under contract?" Nico asked, eyes narrowing.

"If young Sea Kestrel here defeats Black Hole again, many opportunities will arise." Arran stacked the four silvers in a neat pile, leaving them front and center on his desk as a reminder of his offer—their take if they returned. "I look forward to doing business with you both next week. I don't like no-shows." His gaze found Nico's. "Do we have an understanding, Mr. Aves?"

"Aye, we'll be here." Nico accepted Arran's forearm-gripping shake in the way that the colony elites liked to do, as if one's word alone was not enough. Nico's dingy glove with its cut-off fingers rested for a few seconds in stark contrast to the sleeve of Arran's clean and costly suit.

"Excellent." Arran pivoted to Jemm and reached for her gloved hand. As she extended her arm, the glass juice bottle clinked against one of the rubber seams in her pocket. The owner's gaze followed the sound, but he said nothing.

Shame prickled inside at the condescendingly charitable way he turned a blind eye to the deed. It was not like her to pilfer the bottle in plain sight like one of the furtive little cave-scampers that snatched fallen crumbs from miners' food sacks—only to end up crushed under a boot. She was willing to disguise herself for the chance to help her family, but she was not a common thief. But, if she returned the bottle now, it would put Nico in the awkward position of having to follow her lead—or not. She let it be. After years of looking out for him, she was used to giving him a break.

Jemm was taller than many men on Barésh. When she straightened to grasp Arran's offered arm, she had at least an inch on him. She took hold of his forearm confidently, like she was grabbing for the wheel of her tug. But he did not release her like he had Nico. The urge to yank her arm away flitted through her. "Son, we need to talk about your ring name. Sea Kestrel? What kind of name is that?"

"It's a type of bird from a far-off world," Nico explained. "It hunts at sea."

Arran waved away the explanation with a flick of his hand. "Come up with a ring name that better represents your abilities. Something more robust, with more…panache and something to which the citizens of this rock can relate. There are neither flying birds nor any seas on Barésh."

"Or black holes," Jemm rasped, annoyance making it easy to deepen her tone.

Arran chuckled. "This entire colony is a black hole."

Something heavy slammed against the outside of one of the office walls, maybe the thud of a body and then the sharper rap of a baton. The bank of screens above the desk displayed brawls throughout the club. "Great Mother," Arran growled, stalking over to the screens, hands on his lean hips. "Is security from the other clubs on the way?"

A burly guard with a comm in his hand answered, "They've just arrived, sir."

"Good. I want this club under control. Bounce—show our guests safely out."

"Take the stairs to roof level, lads," Bounce instructed. "Cross over to the warehouse next door. The bridge will take ya to where you won't get hurt."

They clambered up metal stairs and burst outside, a heavy, rusted door slamming behind them with a resounding boom. In the shadow of a hulking storage barrel, Nico grabbed her, giving her shoulders a shake. "A whole silver!" They hugged like children, giddy and breathless. "Four more waiting for us, Jemm!"

He whooped, and Jemm laughed, covering his mouth. "Shush."

"Why? I want to shout it out to this entire slag heap."

"And bring on a gang of alley pirates to steal our silver away?" She stripped off her bajha suit to reveal her street clothes underneath. Hopping on one foot, she tugged off the flexible rubber boots, then her cap. Her long braid whipped free, her scalp cooling in the night air. "We have to keep this to ourselves. Not even Ma can know. Especially Ma. Nico! Are you listening?"

"Aye, I won't say anything. How about we go out and celebrate?"

Exhaustion seemed to be caving in on her. She had worked all day and tomorrow would be a repeat. "I've got to get up before dome-rise, Nic. Long day ahead."

"I'll have you back home in no time flat."

"I'll *always* have work in the morning," she reminded him. "How's that gonna fit with your plan of me playing bajha at night? I need to sleep at some point." Or risk an accident that would injure her or others she worked with.

"We'll figure it out, Jemm. We will."

"Another thing, inside ya were talking about playing under contract. Is that a good idea, to commit ourselves like that?"

"We don't have to commit to Arran."

"I mean Arran or *anyone*. Once, when I was small, I heard Da and Ma arguing. Something about his contract with a club or a bar, and about there being players who ended up indentured to club owners." The memory darted away before she could grasp it. "Ma was upset."

"Of course she was. She hates bajha."

"Aye, but why? Did ya ever wonder? She forbade me to play, you know."

Nico waved away her question. "You can be an independent contractor. How's that? I'll book your gigs. I'll manage all the details." His voice gained excitement as he went on. "With me as your manager you wouldn't have to worry about any of it. Are ya in, Jemm?" His bruised lips curved into a grin as his eyes pleaded with her, his face so alive.

When did she last see him this way? The old Nico. Not since the accident did he show this much passion about something. It made her heart ache.

"All right," she conceded. "Aye."

He punched the air. "Yes!"

She wanted to caution him that her agreement was conditional; it did not mean she had promised anything beyond the rematch with Black Hole. But Nico was already light-years away, lost in his fantasies, his big ideas, about money not yet earned. Meanwhile all she could think about was next week's match looming closer with each breath. How odd that terror and hope could blend together so thoroughly that they became one impossible emotion.

Expelling a breath, she rolled her gear and the senssword in the fabric of her jumpsuit, forming a bundle to carry home. "I'm not changing my ring name."

"No. Why would ya?" Nico sobered some. "It was Da's pet name for ya. He'd be so proud to see ya use it while playing the sport he loved."

"I think so, too." She brushed the backs of her fingers across his cheek. His open, friendly face was so much like their mother's, minus the hollow cheeks and pallid skin. But his hazel eyes were rimmed in green and tinted a golden hue in the center like hers. Like their Da's eyes. "Let's go home."

They took off into the night, racing across the rooftops toward the clustered, conical buildings of the old city silhouetted against a star-filled dome. The dome, like the city, came alive after sundown. With each rapid rotation of the colony, diminutive moons rose and set like the components of an ancient time clock. Day after day, night after night, never changing, it was a scene as familiar as the back of her hand. Yet, tonight, for the first time in her life, the entire world seemed new and all things possible. She could even believe that nothing would stop her dreams from coming true.

CHAPTER TWO

Eireya

A door chime, soft but persistent, floated through an apartment fit for a prince: a suite of rooms carved out of a palace that was without argument the most expensive real estate in the galaxy. The origins of the Vedla ancestral home predated the Trade Federation itself, which for the past eleven thousand years had unified a vast league of worlds. But in the "time before" the Vedlas had ruled for so many eons that they became overconfident, lazy, and careless. It took losing the throne and an ensuing massacre that reduced them to only three survivors to wake them up to their failings. But they overcame them and helped reunite and stabilize the galaxy after the Great War with the help of seven other clans. Now there were eight kings instead of one; together they were known as the *Vash Nadah*: "pious warriors" in the language of the Ancients. The eight royal families sustained a popular and benevolent government, but the idea of having to share power still grated on the Vedla psyche like sand between the toes.

While the other seven clans chose harsh and forbidding worlds on which to live—to set the example of sacrifice—at least the Vedlas were able to return to soft and lovely Eireya after expelling the ruthless warlords who took up residence during the Dark Years. Some said echoes of that inconceivable violation whispered through the palace halls to this day. They warned: *Never allow complacency. Be vigilant in all things.* This was the Vedla credo. But on this fine morning, ancient whispers did not invade Prince Klark Vedla's awareness; a blasted door chime did.

A visitor at this early hour? Klark exhaled through his nose as he stowed his sens-sword in its beautifully engraved, antique case. For what purpose would someone disturb him other than to exasperate him? His after-workout refreshment had already been delivered discreetly while he was absent from his quarters, and he was not aware of any appointments. This was his private time; this dawn hour was his favorite part of the day, which he kept free from palace drivel. Any staffers who did not want to deal with the consequences of souring his mood would know better than to disturb him right after he finished bajha practice.

His muscles might be sore and spent but his mind remained as becalmed as the sea at sunrise, a soul-deep quiet that he not only cherished but *needed*, and that never seemed to last long enough once the lights in the arena came up. He wanted no visitors violating his rapidly receding sense of peace. Great Mother, was that too much to ask?

Unfastening his bajha suit to the waist, he poured a glass of an icy ion and botanically infused beverage. Custom-matched to his body chemistry by the family physician, the drink was further personalized to his taste in the palace kitchens.

"Con, open windows," he told the suite's controller. A wall of glass panels retracted and disappeared. The scents of fresh-cut lawn and the sea drifted in from the terrace. Beyond, a vast ocean sparkled under an equally endless fair-weather sky. It looked, deceptively, like freedom. But Klark knew better.

He might not wear a surgically implanted locator in his neck any longer but the force-shield the palace security detail had erected all around his quarters was still in place. When he was first sentenced to house arrest they had briefed him that while the shield would not cause him any injury, a breach would alert security in an instant and initiate a warning on monitors all through the palace.

Klark knew how to escape in other ways. He closed his eyes, casting his senses outward, farther and farther, until he fancied he had reached the edge of...everything. There he probed with the very fingertips of his thoughts, looking for the key, sensing that something wonderful existed beyond his reach that he could never manage to grasp.

Then the keening, spirited call of a sea kestrel beckoned him back.

He opened his eyes in time to catch a glimpse of the native raptor hovering before it dove and soared low over the water. Gray, gold, and black glinted on spread wings as it glided away. Standing there, his boots rooted on the thick, flawless black slab floor, he watched the bird until it vanished from sight. Part of him yearned to fly off with it.

Then a second ring of the door chime dragged him back to reality with all the force of a hard landing. Simultaneously, he felt a vibration in his pocket, ending once and for all his post-bajha quietude.

The buzzing narrowed the possibilities of who dared disturb him at this hour. It was neither a servant nor a lowly palace advisor. That left only family or someone of enough rank to have access to his private comm. In that case, he supposed he ought to answer the door.

Klark turned his back to the sea and refilled his glass. "Con, show alcove." A holo-display floating above his desk illuminated. Six of the king's senior councilmen dressed in traditional black suits, capes, and boots waited outside. They were the very last people to whom he wanted to speak.

"Why are they here, Con?" he asked the room controller. "To make certain I still am?"

"Please repeat your request," intoned the female voice.

Klark frowned. "Rhetorical question. Display bajha scores." Watching his team ascend through the galactic league rankings was always a mood lifter. Although it was still the preseason and most of his players were participating in the annual goodwill tour of the Eireyan worlds, the exhibition matches boosted his hopes that this would be the best season in years. In what was probably the most difficult part of his detention, he had not been allowed to attend any matches in person. It had turned him into an absentee owner.

He remembered the councilmen waiting at his door. "Con, allow entry," he grumbled.

The doors to his suite whooshed open. The men bowed deeply, fists thumping on their chests as Klark regarded them with annoyance, his partially undone bajha exposing a black T-shirt underneath, the weeping glass gripped in his hand. "Rise," he said.

One gentleman stepped toward him and stopped, the fabric of his cape swirling in an eddy around his boots. His five compatriots remained clustered together near the doors like a school of minnows that feared being eaten after wandering into the deep. "Your Highness," he greeted.

"Councilman Toren," Klark acknowledged. Palace gossip often recounted the stern councilman's handsome appearance when he was a younger man; his charisma broke the hearts of numerous ladies at court. But the years had thinned his coppery skin, making his features razor-sharp. His eyebrows grew so long and feathery that Klark's brother, Ché, had dubbed him "The Goth-hawk" after a species of raptor in the Eireyan highlands. The councilman was a contemporary of their father the king, his closest advisor and lifelong confidant. Klark recalled the days of having an advisor, but the last he had heard the man was serving out a life sentence on a remote penal colony. "To what do I owe this unexpected pleasure?" he said in the coldest possible tone.

Anyone else in the government would have stuttered in the crosshairs of Klark's frigid regard—the infamous Vedla stare—but Toren knew the family far too long to be affected. "I bring good news, Your Highness. The terms of your house arrest have been met. Your incarceration has ended."

The news sparked both relief and disbelief. Keeping his reaction hidden behind a "bajha-face", Klark shifted his focus to the time displayed on the viewscreen. "That's sixteen weeks, three days, eighteen hours and forty-four standard Eireyan minutes early."

Toren's eyes crinkled. "I knew you'd be eager to have this over and done with."

"Don't read into it," Klark retorted dryly. "I'm a Vedla. Attention to detail is born and bred in us."

Toren addressed the other councilmen. "You are dismissed."

The men pounded their fists to their chests with hearty thuds, bowing to Klark as they stepped backward. Once they were gone, Toren switched to the more personable tone of someone who had known Klark since he was toddling around in nappies. "I thought you would be pleased to learn of the shortened sentence."

Klark wandered over to a plush pale blue, gray, and cream rug to set his glass on the showpiece of his quarters: a low, large table of transparent, petrified sap encasing myriad creatures trapped inside it. According to family lore, the block of amber was excavated from an uninhabited forested world that vaporized soon after when its parent star went supernova. The table was commissioned many thousands of years ago by a Vedla ancestor with questionable taste. Klark had been terrified of the piece as a child. It caused him untold nightmares. Yet, it was the first item he had chosen when as a boy he was relocated from the nursery to his own apartment. He spent more than a few brooding moments since considering the bizarre creatures frozen within the depths of the amber. The sight of their gaping maws usually convinced him that any upset was trivial in comparison to being trapped in amber for all eternity. Although sometimes circumstances made him feel like he was.

"Of course, I am pleased, Toren. Who wouldn't be after so many months locked up?" Well, notwithstanding the time he escaped only to end up accused of trying to assassinate his brother's fiancée. Certainly, he could see how some would think him capable of such a nefarious plot, given his history of taking family politics into his own hands; but in that incident, at least, he was innocent—although he did violate the terms of his original punishment. "I simply did not expect my sentence to be commuted. I don't exactly qualify for time off for good behavior."

Toren's lips compressed as if he wanted to agree aloud, but then thought better of it. "Both the B'kah Crown Prince Ian and your brother, Crown Prince Ché, negotiated the details. The heart of the matter is that the decision was made. You're free to come and go as you please."

Free to go *where*? And do what? The rest of his life loomed suddenly in front of him like a stranger's shadow, long and dark. He turned his back to Toren and looked out the windows. "Why has my brother not given me the good news himself?"

"Prince Ché is still on his honeymoon."

"Yes, of course." It had been several standard months since his elder brother, the Vedla crown prince, had gone off to vacation with his new bride, which to Klark seemed an ungodly length of time to spend with any one person, let alone the same female. But since Ché was so visibly in love it seemed reasonable. Still, Ché had a comm at his disposal, did he not? He used it while away to remain in contact with their father about various official matters. He would have known of the reduction in Klark's sentence before Toren did. He had crusaded for it, after all. Yet, he was too busy to call…

Klark frowned at the gorgeous view outside. "And my father?" Why press for an explanation for the silence? What did he hope to prove? The absence of messages from the two highest-ranking Vedlas was a message in itself: he had been sidelined. He had always known the day would come. In the not too distant future his elder brother and his bride would produce heirs and Klark would be further bounced down the royal rungs. As third or fourth and so on in line for the throne, he would no longer be needed as he was now. Unless the unspeakable were to occur and all perished. He had always found it rather macabre that he was expected to spend the rest of his days being on standby for something he never wanted to happen, but it was indeed his duty. He had just never given any thought about what to do in the meantime.

He fisted his hands behind his back, trying to catch up to what Toren was telling him. "His Majesty is immersed in official duties at the Wheel."

"Ah. Yes." One bright spot in all this was that as the number-two son Klark would never have to spend tedious days governing the Trade Federation on an ancient space station shoulder to shoulder with representatives of the other clans. The thought was even less appealing than having to marry to keep the bloodlines going. Such were benefits of being the spare and not the heir. There were beautiful and talented courtesans at Klark's beck and call anytime he desired some bed sport; fine dining and expensive liquor were only a snap of his fingers away. Life was an unending party for a young bachelor with limitless wealth. At least on paper it was supposed to be. It had long since become rather dull.

"His Majesty did mention that he was very pleased with the decision to end your sentence early," Toren said.

"He expects that..." The man stopped himself. "He hopes you are pleased as well."

"Rubbish. What were you going to say, Councilman?"

"I imagine His Majesty will prefer to convey his thoughts in person."

"But since he is otherwise engaged you can pass them along."

Toren obeyed with a single nod. "His Majesty is confident you'll exercise better judgment going forward, now that you've served your time and have had the time to ponder your actions. Good judgment comes from experience, and experience comes from making bad decisions."

Klark stared at Toren. He could envision those words being uttered by the man he resembled physically and strove to emulate. King Rorrik Vedla had a well-deserved reputation as a taskmaster of the Treatise of Trade, the holy document that was the moral bedrock of their society. His traditionalist values and his desire for Vedla superiority drove his every action. Then Klark brought dishonor down on them all, leaving their family reputation in shambles.

For as long as he could remember, he had been striving for his father's approval. Now the prospect seemed more elusive than ever.

Klark set his jaw. "His Majesty can be assured that further bad decisions are not on my calendar."

"Speaking of calendars, what are your plans, Your Highness, now that you're free?" A master of tact, Toren turned chipper. "A long vacation, perhaps?"

"A vacation?" Klark scoffed.

"Why not? Certainly, you've had your fill of being at the palace by now. Where in the galaxy have you wanted to visit? Now's the time."

Klark started to answer then let his breath exit. The question quite frankly stumped him. Then Toren's attention swerved to the viewscreen and a clip of the final moments of an exhibition match on Inaresh Station. "Ah. Yonson Skeet. Our leading scorer," Klark said.

Both men uttered a shout, seeing a replay of the winning strike. Klark pumped his fists in a quick, controlled jab, as if he held the sens-sword in his own hands. "Beautiful move, beautifully played." Next, Skeet was shown waving to a packed arena before the vid switched to the athlete being interviewed, his humble charm on full display. Audiences loved the fellow. Out on the goodwill tour, Skeet drew large crowds eager for the chance to meet him. Females all but threw themselves at the single athlete. He was as skilled in the public arena as he was in the bajha one, making Klark damned glad Skeet was his.

"We're doing superbly, are we not?" Toren said. "I know the hand you've had in it all, bringing the team to this level. Well done, Your Highness. Talk at the Wheel is that we have a chance at making it into the finals."

"Finals, bah. Nothing less than winning the Galactic Cup will do."

"Snatched back from those B'kahs." Toren's eyes twinkled. "Now that would be fine, indeed."

"It's still the preseason, of course. There are many months to go, and much work yet to do, but the players are strong. Skeet, Xirri, G'Zanna, and others."

"How strong?" A female voice rang out as clear as a prayer bell. Before Klark realized what was happening, his youngest sister had glided though the open doors into his suite. She lifted his sens-sword from its case, holding it out in front of her, her silken slippers planted wide.

"Not very strong, I don't think. This sword is not at all heavy—"

"Kat, put it away," Klark scolded, but she aimed it at him with mischief in her eyes. "Katjian. *Now*. Bajha is not for princesses."

Klark and Ché had at turns caused their parents angst, but he swore that the youngest of the four Vedla siblings was going to prove his parents' undoing; she was nowhere near as quiet and compliant as her elder sister.

Pouting, Katjian replaced the sens-sword. Councilman Toren used the moment tactfully to end his visit. He bowed to Klark, "Good day, Your Highness." Then he did the same for Katjian. "And to you, Your Highness."

"Con, secure the doors," Klark called out after Toren exited the suite. His quarters felt more like a busy starport than a private apartment the way visitors were coming and going. Turning, he lifted a brow at his baby sister.

Sunlight pouring into the suite lit up the braids of the princess's ornately woven hair and turned them fiery red blonde. She was fairer in coloring than both Ché and Klark but still undeniably *Vash* in appearance with her tawny skin and pale golden eyes. Of his two sisters, she was the prettier, although both girls' beauty turned heads. Ten standard years younger than he was, at seventeen she would be married off within a few years to live out her life on her husband's homeworld.

"Why isn't it?"

"Why isn't what?" Klark held back from snatching the sens-sword away, closing the case only after she had rested the sens-sword properly in its brackets with a dose of respect he did not expect.

"Why isn't bajha for princesses?"

How did she think of such questions? "Because it isn't for females."

"But *why*?"

"Bajha is no ordinary sport. It is a path for noblemen to reach a higher state of consciousness," he added, certain another "why?" was forthcoming. Her persistence was legendary in the family. Katjian had been tagging along after him and Ché since she had learned to walk. A governess was always racing after her to snatch her back in those younger years. She pestered him less now that she was older and busy with the various and sundry things royal *Vash* woman kept busy with. Sometimes he missed her heartfelt attempts to be part of his life, but she must follow the path set for her, as did all the Vedlas. "We practice bajha to improve intuition, instinct, and discipline. Such are a warrior's essential skills that a man can put to use in all areas of his life."

"That's stupid." Katjian dragged a fingertip along the rim of the case. "No man is actually a warrior anymore. They just play at being one."

"Not *play*. Hone. Refine. If we do not practice the art of the warrior, we lose it. To lose such skills is to invite catastrophe. Kat, you're a Vedla; you should know this more than anyone. It was our family that allowed the warlords to topple our ancestral throne. Our family's failings at leadership that sent the galaxy into the Dark Years. It was a complete collapse of civilization." It was not out of the ordinary for his family to discuss events that occurred eleven thousand years ago as if they had happened yesterday.

"I know all that." Katjian's eyes flashed with a certain, glowering vexation that reminded him a little too much of his own. "I may be a female but I can read. I read the Treatise of Trade. I know our family history."

"Our *unique* history. Our ancestors survived near-extinction, a focused effort to murder every last one of us." There was no question their clan's blood was superior to all the rest. Those purist views led him to take action in support of his family that went awry. In some circles, Vedla circles, he was considered a hero. Most everyone else saw him as a menace. Granted, he went too far, and both he and his family paid the price, but other clans simply did not grasp what it meant to be a Vedla. "Passed down from generation to generation is our need to keep our clout intact so that no one will ever again become powerful enough to harm us. Never allow complacency. Be—"

"Vigilant in all things," she finished reciting for him. "I know."

"It's why we Vedla men must never again let down our guard."

"Or Vedla women. If the pregnant Queen Keera and young Prince Chéya did not escape the warlords, there would be no Vedlas at all. Likely no *Vash Nadah*, either."

He acknowledged that truth with a nod. Like her, he was well-versed in the Treatise of Trade. "From a woman's body comes life. Because of this, she must be protected, respected, worshipped. This is what the Great Mother expects *of men*, has always expected of men. She is a female deity, after all, overseeing the mortal world and that of the Ever After. From Her womb sprang the original civilization that spawned all humankind."

"I see that you are determined to turn this into a history lesson, dear brother, and thus it is pointless to continue this discussion. There is nothing in the Treatise of Trade that forbids women from becoming warriors. I know. I've looked."

"The very idea of a female competing in bajha is ludicrous. Would you wear men's clothing? Would you train to be a warrior rather than a wife and mother?"

Her wide eyes considered each outrageous possibility for seconds too long. "No," she replied quietly. Then she seemed to waver. "I don't know."

"What do you mean, you don't know? How can you not know?" How much time had she spent talking to Ilana, their brother's Earth-born wife? Earth, the newest addition to the Trade Federation, was an unorthodox world that had shaken up their ancient society in myriad ways. Now one of their unconventional citizens was family. To his surprise, he had grown fond of Ilana; she was courageous and full of life, and yet disciplined when she needed to be—a good match for his brother. But, fearing what Katjian would say, he did not ask the question. Better to run damage control than try to reverse what was already done. "We've entered an era of change. It has rocked the values of the *Vash Nadah*, this we know. But, by the heavens, Katjian, if we Vedlas don't uphold some semblance of normalcy and remain the guardians of tradition, who will?"

"That's why I came to you today and no one else, Klark." She made a face, then gazed up at him with shimmering golden eyes. "Please convince me my feelings are wrong. Because if anyone can do that, it's you."

"What feelings?" he asked. "What are you talking about?"

"I don't want to disobey Mother or Father; I don't want to make them unhappy, but…" She sighed. "I have no real say about anything in my life—and I hate it. I feel trapped."

It took his breath away that she dared to confide such a damning secret with him, knowing how rigid his beliefs were, how traditional, and the great lengths to which he was willing to go to safeguard their family's reputation. He was blasted lucky to have gotten off with only house arrest after trying to prevent a *Vash* princess, Ché's original betrothed, from marrying another man—a non-*Vash-Nadah* man from Earth. Klark's interference nearly cost the pair their lives. Although he had never intended for that to happen, he would have faced execution if it had. All was now forgiven, but not forgotten.

In the face of his silence, Katjian kept going, "I think Ché must have felt trapped, too, because he went to Earth and fell in love with Ilana."

"No, Kat. Ché complied with what was expected of him—"

"But—"

"Creatively, I'll give you that—but nonetheless he did."

"What about you?" She frowned up at him.

He reared back. "What about me?"

"Sometimes when I'm watching you and you don't know I am, I can see in your face that you feel trapped, too. Just like the rest of us. We Vedla offspring are nothing more than fish wriggling in a net."

"What foolishness is this? Fish wriggling in a net?" *Like a creature entombed in amber for all eternity.* He somehow kept his gaze away from the table of fossils and focused on his sister's expectant, upturned face. "Kat, you know better than to try to interpret my foul moods."

Or read into Ché's unorthodox actions. Klark loved his brother with all his heart, but the crown prince of their clan should be a faultless, shining example for them all.

"First of all, a mindless, netted fish is in an involuntary state; ours is a voluntary one," he offered, trying to imbue his words with a cheerful tone.

Convince me, she had pleaded with him moments earlier, and he was already marching down the road to failure. He must change her view, somehow, or bear the responsibility of the consequences. He could not help thinking of Tee'ah, the Dar princess, who had fled an impending unwanted marriage and nearly got herself killed in the process. Not all of those near-misses could be blamed on Klark's actions. Katjian might be tempted to run away and risk her life as well unless he redoubled his efforts to be a good example for her, a model *Vash,* and to not flirt with the limits of conventional behavior like their elder brother had. Especially now that he was aware of how closely his youngest sister watched him.

His entire family depended on him to set the standard.

From the depths of his mind he pulled out the best explanation he could conjure—the one he had secretly used to preserve his own sanity in his darker hours. "We're not netted. We're swimming, actually."

"Swimming..." *Is that the best you can do?* A single, lifted brow asked that question of him as she folded her arms over her chest. She was far too young to wear such a cynical expression.

"We respect the sea because of its power. To survive in the sea, we must learn to work with it, and not against it. For instance, if a riptide pulls us in an undesired direction, we know not to panic and fight the current lest we risk exhausting ourselves before we can make it back to shore. Our ancestry is like the sea. It's stronger than we are; it requires us to think before we act. Find a way to embrace who you are, Kat, and what you are. Find a way to...stay afloat."

"You always know what to say." She wound her arms around him and squeezed, her cheek nestled against his chest. A stiff and awkward moment ticked by before he relented and hugged her back, stunned by her trust and adoration despite all his misdeeds the past year. Something inside him softened in the warmth of her unconditional love. At the same time that softening exposed a weakness in him. Softness led to complacency, and complacency led to catastrophe. Family history bore that out.

A chirping tone rang out from the direction of his desk where his viewscreen flashed with an incoming call. Now what? The morning had turned into a ceaseless parade of interruptions. He gave his sister's hands a squeeze as he unwrapped her. "We will talk more another time. Don't do anything rash in the meantime. Come to me first before you consider," he hunted for words of tact, "anything irreversible. Do we agree?"

"Yes," she said. "I promise."

He hesitated a few seconds more before letting go of her hands, as if she were a vase that almost tumbled off a shelf, a priceless piece he did not dare release until he was sure it was back in place. While she seemed somewhat pacified, he was not quite sure if he had helped or made things worse. "Be off with you. I need to take this call."

But Katjian trotted behind him as he strode over to his desk and opened the screen to a familiar face. Her curious eyes brightened. "Oh, look! It's Yonson Skeet. He's adorable."

Adorable? "He's the captain of Team Eireya, our pro bajha team."

"I know," she all but sighed.

"Leave it, Kat." The last thing he needed was his little sister swooning over bajha players.

What was Skeet up to, calling him out of the blue? He and the rest of the team were busy with the annual tour: playing exhibition matches, granting interviews, kissing babies. "Mr. Skeet. It's good to be able to congratulate you face-to-face on your fine match yesterday. Well done!"

"Thank you, sir. Please excuse the interruption." Klark had always insisted on less formal modes of address from his players. He wanted to encourage a brotherhood of athletes, not a court full of simpering supporters. Skeet's head bowed briefly before his attention veered toward Katjian and her sweetly demure smile.

It's a trick, Skeet, Klark wanted to say. *Don't fall victim.*

"Your Highness," the player said with awestruck solemnity in his tone, not something Klark often saw in Skeet. Then his gaze returned to Klark. "Sir, you need to see this vid."

"Appropriate viewing material for the princess, I assume."

"Oh, yes. That is, if the princess likes watching bajha."

"I do," she breathed.

Klark rolled his eyes. "Go ahead."

The image switched to a shaky, poorly lit feed of two men without headgear gripping sens-swords. They were playing blindfolded in what looked to be a bar with no barrier separating the audience from the players. The masses were practically in the ring with them, making all manner of vulgar noises, the lit ends of hallucivapes twinkling like blue stars in the stands.

He tried to cover Katjian's eyes, but she ducked, staring in half-horrified, half-delighted wonder. What had he done, letting her stay and watch? "This is what amateur street bajha looks like, Kat. Back-door bar betting in its lowest, most inglorious form. It's an absolute insult to the game, and not what I play or what our league plays." He angrily swiveled back to Skeet. "Why am I being subjected to this slop—?" His question died in his throat. "Never mind…"

It was suddenly obvious why Yonson Skeet had blown through protocol to show him this vid. In an incongruous scene, an amateur wearing a cap instead of safety headgear and cloaked in a comically baggy bajha suit displayed elegant poise and damn-near perfect moves while engaging his opponent. Somehow this player was able to exhibit the highest standards of the sport, despite being in the epicenter of a revolting tempest of drunken madness.

Skeet's voice came over vid's noise. "Pretty unexpected, yes?"

"Indeed." Klark leaned over his desk, hands flat on the surface to better watch the amateur track and dispense with his opponent, all with a pro's confidence and humility. It was highly unusual to see the latter in a street player. Arrogance had no place in the sport, but in the street leagues it was known to be celebrated. "What focus he must have, what discipline, to be able to play so well in such utterly appalling conditions."

All too soon guards came at the camera, batons waving, and the feed went black. "Tell me how you came by this footage, Yonson."

"A buddy of mine is a freighter pilot. He and his crew were on-surface for an overnight. They go out for a few drinks, and there's this bajha match going on. Street bajha. You know the kind, crazy back-alley stuff. But there's this player—and he's good, really good. Apparently, a couple of weeks ago, this same kid took down the reigning champ in less time than you can throw back a shot of Mandarian whiskey. My friend figured I'd be entertained by the whole thing so he recorded as much as he could before security put a stop to it." Skeet shot a glance behind him then lowered his voice. "It's gone viral here on tour. All the coaches are buzzing about it. They're saying that amateur ought to be drafted right out of the bar into the pros. How about Team Eireya, Prince Klark?"

"I can't deny that's an intriguing proposal. But you know commoners aren't raised playing bajha the way we are. And a street player?" Klark shook his head. "It's usually doomed to fail." Transitioning from competing in bars and impromptu arenas to the lightproof, soundproof arenas of the pros most often proved insurmountable, although the mid-leagues did sign such amateurs on occasion. "Perhaps a single commoner every one or two generations is capable of competing at the lofty level of the galactic league, Skeet."

"Maybe he's one of them."

"Hmm." Klark rubbed his index finger across his chin and played the vid again, watching this time without a thick veil of skepticism coloring his judgment. The amateur looked even better the second time around. A tingle curled up his spine. What if this player was a true diamond in the rough, and Klark was the one to polish that gem to greatness? What if such an addition generated much-needed excitement and grassroots support and pushed Team Eireya up over the last hurdle to winning the Galactic Cup. Was there a better way to buff his family's reputation back to its once-glorious shine?

Then he reminded himself this was a street-bajha player.

Klark pushed up from the desk. "What else, if anything, is known about him?"

"Only that he came out of nowhere a few weeks back. Goes by the ring name Sea Kestrel."

"Sea Kestrel, eh?" His favorite creature. If that wasn't a sign, what was?

"Since you can't travel, sir, I can have the tour ship make a temporary stop. I'll track the kid down, invite him on board, and play a few practice matches with him. I'll let you know what I think."

"Actually, my travel ban is lifted. Regardless, I will not have one of my top players traipsing around grubby bars choking on hallucivape smoke. I'll send a couple of scouts."

Skeet visibly deflated. Then, like the tenacious athlete he was, he rallied. "With all due respect, sir, I think a pro should accompany the scouts. It's still preseason. The tour schedule has slack built in. I've got the time. Besides, who cares about a little smoke or a grubby bar? I'm not made of glass, you know." He smiled, and that smile was not aimed at Klark alone.

Klark noted with dismay the effect Skeet's infamous charm was having on his sister. Her expression had gone soft, her eyes dreamy. He shot her a warning glance, which she completely disregarded, but Skeet noticed. His focus snapped back to Klark and stayed there this time. "What do you say, sir? Can I go?"

Klark exhaled. "It's a harmless boondoggle, I suppose. It makes sense to see how the amateur performs against a top-tier player before going through all the expense and bother of transporting him off-world. Since you had the initiative to bring this to my attention, you might as well bear some responsibility for seeing if this Sea Kestrel has any ability beyond looking good on camera."

"With pleasure, sir." Skeet appeared eager for the adventure.

Klark rather envied him. "Where is this ghastly establishment by the way?"

"Out in the frontier. On one of the fringe-world mining colonies. Barésh, they call it."

Klark choked down a curse to keep it from reaching his sister's ears. Barésh? Of all places. "Yes, I know it. I was there once, I'm sorry to say." While on an ill-fated scheme that not only cost him his freedom but damaged his family's formerly stellar reputation. "You don't want to go to that reeking space rock, Yonson. Trust me on that. I'll allow you to back out gracefully. Just say the word."

The man laughed. "All I hear in those words is the challenge."

"That you would, wouldn't you?" Klark glanced at the frozen image of the amateur, on one knee, head bowed. He felt that tingle again, his gut telling him to pursue this. Moreover, there would be no lasting harm sending Skeet to check out the amateur. He was already out and about traveling on tour. "Very well. It appears that Mission Sea Kestrel is on."

After sending his sister on her way, Klark settled into his routine of having his luncheon brought to his balcony to be served alfresco. Today the chef prepared plump, lavender prawns with minced sea spirals in a spicy fish broth, served with triangles of flat bread that were baked perfectly with soft puffy centers and crispy edges. It was one of his favorite dishes, yet he consumed it almost robotically, purely out of habit, while he reviewed Skeet's vid that he had uploaded to his tablet. The more he watched, the more he saw the potential in the street player's raw talent and the less he felt like delegating the recruitment process to others.

What if there were complications? Yonson may not be made of glass, as he liked to put it, but street bajha had a corrupt and violent underside. There were tales of bar owners and managers who went to great lengths to protect and keep their best players, conspiring to hide them from anyone else who might woo them away. More, although Skeet assumed that their rivals hadn't gotten wind of any details, Klark could not assume scouts representing other teams would stay away once word leaked out. The mere thought got his competitive juices flowing. If that long-shot amateur was capable of competing at the professional level, it would be for Klark's team and no other. But how could he guarantee that if he stayed home?

On the other hand, he was supposed to be on his best behavior and exercising good judgment until his wrongdoings faded in everyone's memories. Returning to one of the more notorious locales of his aborted scheme was not the best decision.

Klark drummed his fingertips on the table. Then he called out, "Con, send someone to collect my plates."

"Summoning galley attendant," the disembodied female voice replied.

Klark folded his napkin into a precise square and placed it to the right of his bowl. Taking his tablet with him, he stood. At nearly eye level a pair of kestrels soared past, a mated pair. He paused at the balustrade to enjoy the aerial acrobatics as they hunted for fish, looking a lot like bajha played in the sky. It never ceased to fascinate him how two individual creatures could maintain such a singular, focused resolve. Seemingly on instinct alone, each one trusted that the other would be at their side. *Two equal halves that together are greater than one.* With an inexplicable, soul-deep regret, he realized it was the kind of bond he was not destined to experience.

Then he frowned. Waxing poetic about mated birds, was he? What on Eireya was wrong with him? It must be his lovesick teenaged sister Katjian's fault.

He shifted his glare to scores of scavenger gulls cawing and tussling with each other. Now, that was more like it. The scavengers reminded him more of the world of chaotic human communication he was used to. They wheeled above a trawler chugging toward shore, loaded with bounty for the communal evening meal at the palace. Fishing boats had followed the identical course day after day for a dizzying number of centuries, undoubtedly beset upon by a similar cloud of gulls.

In another familiar daily sight, a solitary figure came into view along the shore path, dressed as always in a severe, neck-to-boots charcoal-gray outfit.

"Ah. Uncle Yul. Right on schedule." Klark's mouth pulled into a deeper scowl at the sight of King Rorrik's younger and only brother. The grim bachelor prince hiked along the shore every afternoon after lunch, passing below Klark's balcony so reliably that he could set his timepiece to it. Uncle Yul was not as unsettling as the table of entombed, extinct creatures, but ran a close second.

Wisely, a palace gardener driving a cart laden with cuttings gave the man a wide berth.

"Go, Ché! Go!" Two giggling boys scrambled into a gardener's cart left unattended, the elder taking the steering wheel, and off they went.

In a heartbeat, the memory pulled Klark back to the joy-filled days of being a youngster here, how he and Ché used to hijack the carts from under the gardeners' noses. They would ride, riding all through the manicured grounds and sometimes the beach until they had either crashed or were caught. Ché always took the blame, because he was older and insisted on being the one to talk their way out of it.

"How dare you allow Ché to bear the responsibility for your antics while you stand by silently like a disgraceful little coward?"

The warm memory vanished like the sun behind a cloud, replaced with one of Uncle Yul dragging Klark away by the arm for a "private discussion". How old was Klark when that happened? No more than four or five. It was the only time they ever were alone. To this day he could not remember where exactly on the palace grounds the drubbing took place—only that Uncle Yul had been seething and Klark was so stricken at being the sole focus of that fury that all his mind retained of the moment were the words his uncle hurled, each one landing like a gut punch. *"Is this the way you want others to see you? Is it? Spineless, gutless, unworthy of the Vedla name? You are the second son, boy. Can you not grasp what this means? You have but one duty in this life—one! And that is to protect your elder brother, the crown prince. No matter what he does, what he says, no matter where he goes, you're accountable for it. Next time trouble finds the two of you, you are to bear the brunt of it. If you ever bring shame to this family by doing otherwise, you will answer to me. Now, go! I'll be watching you,"* he shouted as *Klark fled.*

Klark released the railing after realizing he had been gripping it as if his life depended on it. Standing there, opening and closing a cramped hand, he used his bajha skills to settle down. *Damn you, Uncle Yul.* To this day, he avoided his uncle's knowing, judging eyes, but there was only so much one could do to escape relatives at the palace.

Toren was right—he needed to get away for a while.

But not for the aimless vacation he and everyone else expected of him. He would schedule a starship of his own and rendezvous with the goodwill tour. Together with Skeet and Xirri they would run that amateur through the paces.

For the first time in a very long while Klark felt the prickle of genuine anticipation. Like Skeet, he enjoyed a challenge almost as much as he enjoyed winning.

Going over in his mind the arrangements to be made, his mind churning with ideas, he spun on his heel to walk inside—and collided with a cloud of perfume, soft skin, and silken hair.

Fingernails scraped down his arm, lips brushing the side of his throat. "Greetings, Your Highness."

Klark moved the woman back to arm's length, then dropped his hands from her sun-warm shoulders. She was undressed more than she was dressed in a pale green netted creation fastened loosely to various piercings of gold body jewelry and leaving little of her perfect figure to the imagination. "Why are you here?"

Her mint-green eyes, a synthetic shade, searched his face with bemusement. "It's Thirdday."

"Thirdday." He gave his head a shake. "Yes, yes, of course." With his thoughts on the Barésh-based amateur, he had forgotten all about his standing appointment with this courtesan, whom he allowed to enter his quarters the same day every week when a kitchen server arrived to tidy up. To their right, a galley boy was discreetly gathering up the last of the dirty dishes. Inside waited Klark's bedchamber where he would have normally taken a few hours' pleasure with the woman, or anywhere else around the suite her nimble fingers led him. "Your services are not needed today," he said. "You may go."

He allowed her to precede him indoors then waved her toward the exit. The woman blinked as if she could not believe she had been so speedily dismissed. "A massage instead, Your Highness? A perfect salve for sore muscles. Or perhaps a relaxing shampoo?"

"I require nothing of you. Please cover up and go."

"As you wish, Your Highness." She bowed humbly, her jewelry tinkling as her fragrant hair spilled over one shoulder. His loins had little reaction at the sight of her bejeweled breasts swinging freely behind the netting.

I'll train that amateur myself, he was already thinking as he returned to his desk, a holo-keyboard appearing with an eager swipe of his finger. Certainly, he could send the others in his stead—a prince was nothing else if not a master of delegation—but he wanted control of this project, this labor of love. His ode to his love of the sport.

In the next moment, he wondered if he had lost his mind. A commoner amateur had little hope of panning out to be a worthy player, after all.

But what if?

Indeed, what the hell if? If Team Eireya were to win the galactic title, it would go a long way toward erasing his recent stumbles, allowing him to start the process of restoring the family reputation that he had tarnished. How could he not take this opportunity? Even if it meant a journey back to Barésh, that stinking pit of humanity, to track down an aptly named and elusive Sea Kestrel with enough raw talent to be worth the trouble. Or, so he hoped.

CHAPTER THREE

L et's get this show on the road, you dozers. We're burning daylight." Jemm stalked around the tug before starting her fifth and final delivery of the day, inspecting the vehicle for broken parts, thumping her gloved fist on a bumper here, smoothing her palm over a dented panel there, even though the loaders were still hard at work stowing the last canisters of ore in the trailer. The men's muscled, sweating bodies swayed in unison as they hoisted and stacked the heavy tubes. They were running late, way late—today of all days, the one time she needed to be *on* time.

Just my luck. She circled back around to the front bumper, shaking grit from her goggles before sliding them up and over her forehead. Squinting upward at the dome, she tried to gauge how much actual light was left. "The sun's as false as a miner's hopes," went the saying. Sunshine on Barésh was as manufactured as the domed sky, but it ruled the rhythm of life on the mining colony. Luckily the same dome that made their home habitable and protected everyone from the icy reaches and radiation of space also brightened and darkened on a schedule that never varied. Her great-grandfather's timepiece, which she inherited from her father, was a heavy, familiar weight around her wrist. It had been broken for a long while now. Years. There never was enough money to get it fixed. Now that she had stocked up on food with her bajha winnings and paid to fix the broken window, even putting away a little extra for emergencies in the crock hidden beneath the apartment floor, she could finally rationalize paying someone to make the wristwatch function again, a luxury she missed having. Not that it would have told a different truth than the sun, less than a hand's span from disappearing below the horizon.

In the fading light she could already make out the faint glow of Barésh City. It was the latest she had ever left with a load, and from the farthest smelter, too. No driver planned on having to cross the badlands after dome-set.

Jemm checked that her sidearm was fitted property in her holster and then zipped her leathers to her chin. She swung herself up into the driver's seat and drummed restless fingers on her knees. "Let's go! Pick it up. I gotta get on the road."

Grumbles and curses told her the men were moving as fast as they could. The lead was immune to her glare as he sauntered around the front of the tug with a tablet containing a form to be signed off by her and eventually the receiver at the docks. "You're mighty itchy to get rollin', lass."

"Ya think?" She took the tablet and stylus. "It'll be dome-set before we know it, Arik. You're taking way too long."

"Am I?" Arik's glove wrapped around the open door's frame. His sleeve was hiked up, revealing a nice rounded biceps. His teeth were clean and straight but his lean frame revealed the cumulative hazards of his job. Where there weren't scars on his body there were tattoos, or both. "Ya never complained before," he drawled, his tone reflecting the mischievous, flirtatious glint in his eyes. "I thought ya liked it long and slow."

She shot him a darkly amused look. "Not if it's gonna put me behind schedule."

"Ya might feel different if ya took up with me again."

"Why would I? No good came of the first time."

"Not true. Some good came of it." His lower lip sported tattooed stripes that formed a fan shape when he grinned. "Good memories."

She smiled in spite of herself. "Aye. A few." Then she switched her concentration to the weight-and-balance document displayed on the tablet. Arik was a good man. He just was not the right man. There probably wasn't one. She had long ago stopped bothering to look.

One of the loaders signaled Arik with a sharp whistle. Then Arik nodded at her. "You're good to go, tugger. The trill's all on."

"My weight gauge reads way past max, but here in the paperwork it says I'm hauling a normal load. Look."

"Insurance," he explained.

"Insurance? What do you mean? For what?"

"Accidental loss."

As her stylus hovered above the signature line, she glared at him. "How am I supposed to sign off on this? It's incorrect."

"Look, Jemm, it's not my call. It's come down from the foreman. Every late-day haul from now on is gonna be this way. You got valuable trill going between the smelters and the processors, and too many sticky fingers in-between grabbing what they can. Blasted scurries and plains pirates, they're getting bolder all the time. This way anything lost to those rock-roaches will be skimmed off the top, not eaten out of the authorized load."

"So, let me get this straight—the mine bosses are padding loads to buffer against black market losses. Like this won't show up on an audit?"

He shrugged. "They've always cooked the books, Jemm. Nothing's changed but the method. Ya gonna sign off or not?"

"Crat, Arik." She angrily scrawled her signature on the screen and thrust it back into his hands. Not that she had a choice. It was transport the trill or lose her job.

Resentment strangled her like fingers wrapped around her throat. The only thing worse than feeling powerless was being forced to compromise her principles. But the mine bosses were very good at using desperation as leverage; they knew their workers would do what they asked because the alternative was that bad.

It only hardened her resolve to get off this slagheap for good. She didn't know where she would take her family, but anywhere was better than here. Da had said so. He died before he could realize that dream, but she had kept it alive, painstakingly saving up, most times only a few coins a week, to purchase one-way tickets for her, Ma, Button, and Nico in steerage on a starship bound for as far away as she could afford. It might be decades before she had enough to get them off-world, but she refused to let that fact demoralize her. It was why she had cooked up the bajha playing idea in the first place. At the rate she and Nico were earning silvers, she would be able to reduce the wait time considerably. And now, all of it had been put at risk.

By the simple act of signing for the load, an incorrect load, she was now complicit in the trickery going on. If the bosses found out about it, she would never have to answer to the charge. The lead loaders would be blamed, and the tug drivers too. Then she would be fired by some upper-class cog who would never know what it felt like to go to bed hungry, all because those who ran the mines cared more about looking good to their boss, some pampered *Vash* overlord light years away.

Calm yourself. Everyone's depending on you.

She tapped into a deeper resolve, her dogged determination not to be pulled off course, and took a steadying breath before fitting her goggles over her eyes. Out on the barren plains, the shadows were lengthening like streaks of grime on a wet wall. She needed to leave—an hour ago.

She thrust her boot against the accelerator, her thumb on the start switch, and the tug rumbled to life. "Time for me to roll."

Arik poked his head into the cab. "Your engine sounds a bit rough to my ears, lass."

"It's fine."

"You can always say it ain't, though. A mechanical problem would delay ya overnight. You could then take the load out at dawn—a normal load, not a padded one. Owing to your late start, it might be a wee bit safer, all the way around. If ya know what I mean."

"Arik…" She saw now what he was trying to do for her: offering her the option of lying about the tug's mechanical condition to protect her from the doctored paperwork and the coming darkness.

But there was no way she could take him up on it. Nico was at this very second waiting for her in the city, wondering where she was.

Arik mistook her frown for something else. He poked a thumb at the other loaders who were heading back to their barracks for the night. "A solo bunk, don't ya fret." He pressed a gloved hand to his heart. "Without me trying to share it with ya. A noble sacrifice on my part, true, but I'm a giver that way."

She laughed. "Aye. Ya are. And many thanks for your kindness. But I've got to get back to the city tonight. I can't be late."

He pretended to frown. "What's his name?"

She rolled her eyes. "Like I have time to run around."

"Then why run back at all? What's there for ya?"

Everything. The chance to make my dreams come true. "It's a family thing. I promised I'd be there." It was the closest she could veer to the truth of Nico booking her a gig in a new bar. After three weeks of Eighthnight successes they had both agreed she could fit in a midweek match. Miguel Arran would not be happy about the idea, but that was his problem; they hadn't signed an exclusive. But, the new bar owner wouldn't be very happy, either, if she showed up late. No, she couldn't tell Arik any of that.

He would never believe it anyway.

"Aye, then, Jemm. See ya next time, tugger. A safe drive to ya." He winked then saluted her with the tablet in his hand then walked off to bellow orders to the other loaders. Their voices drowned in the rumble of the engine as she carefully rolled forward toward the city and the setting sun.

With the extra weight she was hauling, the tug felt sluggish and slow to pick up speed. Far ahead of her she could make out the lights and the dust kicked up from another tug, a straggler like her, heading home from one of the closer-in smelters. Soon it had sped away and she was all alone.

She wasn't afraid. Unlike everyone she knew, she actually liked being alone. Back in the city, life was lived elbow to elbow, a stinking, shouting, shoving existence. Chaos. Out here, the solitude quieted her thoughts much like the inner peace she found in bajha.

Dusk was kind to Barésh, disguising the colony's flaws the way shadows camouflaged the tired eyes and pockmarked skin of a bottom-tier sex server advertising her wares from the darkness of an alcove. Even the ugly brown, ever-present smog had transformed into a warm glow that gilded the skyline. But soon enough, as she drew ever closer to the processing plant, reality would reappear, detail by squalid detail, and the city would once

again be all she could see and smell and hear. But for
now, she was free of it.

From the seat of her tug, she watched the horizon
extinguish the sun, and felt the air chill. In all the years of
ore hauling, she had crossed the badlands after dome-set
only once before. She remembered being surprised by
how beautiful it was, and it was no different this time
around. The dome lost its opaqueness, becoming star-
filled. The whirl of heavenly bodies was eye-catching in
the middle of the city center but out here on the darkened
plains it left her in a state of humbled awe.

The Old City looked especially magical with its
unique buildings shaped like upside-down funnels
converging in pointy, silvered caps, one of them the roof
over her family's apartment. They were the oldest
structures on Barésh, predating the Trade Federation and
constructed by the same ancients who built the dome. The
long-vanished race possessed technology that was
responsible for the wormholes the starships traveled, the
handheld comms that allowed the privileged to call
anywhere in the galaxy in real-time for a chat, and many
other wonders Da had taught her about.

She could sure use one of those fancy comms now to
let her brother know where she was. She was rolling
along at a virtual crawl compared to usual. Could she
coax a bit more speed out of the overloaded tug? The
engine rumbled evenly, despite the strain of extra cargo.
All the readings were within limits. "We're all gonna
have to work a little harder tonight," she said, goosing the
throttle.

The engine did not seem to mind. The oil temperature
crept toward redline but she would keep an eye on it. So
far, so good.

Nico was probably at the bar by now. She could
picture him waiting outside for her, a vape pinched
between his fingers, the other hand buried in his pocket,
his shoulders hunched. Everything was more difficult for

Nico when he was sober, his pain sharper, even after all this time. But they had a standing agreement: no alcohol until after her last match of the night. He had kept his end of the deal for weeks, had not complained, taking his role as manager and promoter seriously. Both of them were stoked by her unbroken string of wins. She would not let him down tonight.

Hang on, Nic. Almost there.

It was full dark now. Grit swirled in her headlights. She squinted ahead, watching for large rocks and potholes, one hand on the wheel, the canisters of ore clanking in the trailer. She was ready to think she had made it to the city limits without a glitch when there was a flash in the dual cones of her headlights.

Something solid had darted across her high beams.

A prickle of apprehension told her that she was no longer alone. A half a heartbeat later a pack of small beings spilled out of the darkness and swarmed in front of the tug.

CHAPTER FOUR

Jemm yanked on the emergency brake, steering into the skid, the trailer swinging too wildly for the weight. Somehow she got it stopped without losing the load.

A rock struck the windshield with a bang. The hardened glass did not break but she jerked back all the same. She drew out her sidearm, standing up in the cab to flip on the overhead floodlight switch in the ceiling. It illuminated a gang of children, some who looked as young as three standard years old. They surrounded the tug, pelting it with rocks, while the older ones were hanging on to an ore canister, trying to pry it loose from the trailer.

Scurries.

"Be off with ya!" she yelled outside like an irritated mother. "Git! Now. Or I'll shoot your little heads off!"

A rock half the size of her fist whipped through the open side window and hit her in the right arm. Her leathers blunted the impact but it still smarted. She fired a warning shot toward the trailer to protect the ore. A stream of green-white plasma hit the ground right where she wanted it. The burst was impressive and would get anyone's attention. The outer ring of scurries scattered like rock-roaches, but the main cluster remained in place, intent on worrying the canister loose like a bad tooth. Before the orange glow of molten sand had extinguished, the scurries she had spooked had returned to help the others. They seemed fearless.

Or, maybe they were merely desperate, like her.

Another rock sang past her head, and she ducked. As a tugger, it was her responsibility to protect the load. It did not matter if she was firing at plains pirates or scurries; she was paid to defend the trill.

She hunkered down, tracking the red laser sight across the bustling little bodies. "That was a warning shot! Next one's for real." In the crosshairs she saw some of the small, smudged faces up close. Hungry little kids, dressed in rags.

"Crat," she muttered. "Craggin' crat."

Jemm knew that the scurries were gangs of feral children and orphans, but the reality had not hit until seeing them in the flesh. They were so small. So young.

Your instructions are clear: shoot to kill.

A sick feeling made her gut clench as the scurries tipped the canister out of the trailer. Culled from the herd, it hit the ground with a resounding bang. The lid was quickly unscrewed. Trill spilled out, silver chips the size of ketta-cat paws scattering over the rocky ground.

The children squealed like someone had thrown candy.

No one was hurling rocks at her anymore. They were filling their pockets and little sacks with as much of the extremely heavy ore their tiny bodies could carry. One of the youngest girls tucked her hair behind an ear as she bent over to pick up a chip, her eyes round with delight as she snatched her prize.

She's just a little girl. Jemm's chest squeezed tight. If circumstances were different, that could be her child. Anyone's baby. It could be Button out here.

Jemm gripped her weapon, two-handed, her finger on the trigger. She was to exterminate any and all ore thieves on sight. Company orders. The directive felt like a knife pressed to her throat. Yet, in her failure to act, she might as well be daring the mine bosses who held sway over nearly every aspect of her life to go ahead and finish her off.

"I can't," she whispered. *I won't.*

She refused to murder children.

The decision was like a release of pressure off her soul. Air escaped her lungs as she sank heavily into the driver's seat, her weapon in her lap, her body quaking as the miniature pirates scurried away into the night.

People. People everywhere, pushing, shoving, fighting, shouting, offering all manner of vices for sale, barter, or trade. As Klark made his way with Skeet and Xirri from the docks to the area known by the locals as Central City, he felt more like a fish swimming upstream in a polluted, debris-clogged river than a gentleman going out for the evening.

The tour ship had dropped the two players off before continuing on to other already scheduled worlds. It gave the pros a few days to spend with Klark.

He tracked down the bar where Sea Kestrel was scheduled to play. It was not a long walk, and he could have hired a hovercar to drop them off near the bar. But, he knew better than to flaunt his means, especially when his goal for the trip depended on discretion. Although woolen cloaks worn over plain trousers tucked into dull black boots in most circumstances would not attract attention, Klark was aware that he and his companions nonetheless stood out on these streets.

He pressed the sleeve of his cloak to his nose, if only to reassure himself, with the residual scent of soap, that clean laundry still existed. The air smelled even worse than he remembered: a foul cocktail of sweat, dust, overworked machinery, and something putrid, either human waste or rotting food, or both. That he was parsing out the colony's stench into its individual components was the surest sign yet that he had lost his mind when he decided to return. *Oh, my Sea Kestrel, you had better be worth it.*

"We'd blend in better if we hadn't showered for a month," Skeet stated, having picked up on his thoughts. "Don't they ever bathe? There's got to be running water if they want it. There's power, obviously. Look around. They've got downtown lit up like a carnival."

"Now do you see why I offered you gentlemen a last chance out?"

Skeet laughed. "We'll know who to blame if this turns out to be for naught."

"Sea Kestrel?" Xirri asked, slinging a playful arm over his teammate's shoulders. "Or you, Skeet?" They tussled briefly before parting.

As the two athletes chatted and laughed, he felt as if he were observing the scene through meter-thick observation glass; he could watch but was unable to participate.

Not unable—merely unsure how to join in. Such lighthearted behavior was a concept foreign to Klark. He had never before traveled in the company of friends, and not since boyhood had he cavorted in any fashion, not even with Ché. The responsibility of being Vedla born and bred was too heavy a weight on their shoulders, although after Uncle Yul's rebuke, much of the fun was leached out of frolicking with his elder brother, anyway. As the years went on, Klark had simply fallen out of practice when it came to feeling carefree. Yet, he already felt unusually lighter in spirit for having stepped outside his usual boundaries.

Even if it was on Barésh.

They rounded a corner and navigated through the grating din of a street full of virtual reality arcades. Every one of the arcades was packed to overflowing with patrons willing to part with their precious coins for a temporary escape.

"Poor clods. Who can blame them?" Xirri looked openly appalled by the spectacle. "If I had to live here, I'd be right there with them, plugging in and tuning out."

"I'm ready to pay to play right now," Skeet grumbled.

"Luckily, here we are," Klark said. He held out an arm to stop his players in front of the entrance to the bar. Narrow Margin was a working-class establishment, not bottom-rung but not a place frequented by wealthier citizens either. Outside, banners boasted of tonight's bajha matches: *Bajha Nightly! The Best Players and the Best Odds in the Colony!*

"Narrow Margin, eh? Fitting name." Skeet smirked as they pushed through the door and elbowed their way to a reserved table overlooking the ring that a bribe had gained them. "There isn't enough room to inhale."

"Just as well," Klark said dryly. "I don't recommend breathing any more than you have to." Despite a ventilation system working so hard it sounded like it was wheezing its last gasps, the stench of vapes, liquor, and body odor in such confined surroundings was quite unpleasant. Yet, it did not seem right to mock the locals for their hygiene when it was clear the situation for many of them was quite dire. Where were the Earth-dwellers? It was his impression that Earth would take charge of mopping things up now that they wore the mantle of supervising the frontier's fringe worlds. The newest member of the Trade Federation had certainly whined loudly enough about wanting the responsibility after members of their government witnessed the wretched conditions on Barésh. The *Vash* bore the full blame for centuries of neglect, it was true, revealing a flaw they were striving to correct in their culture, but if there was any justice in the galaxy, the Earth-dwellers would be able to improve the lives of those who lived here. After all, these miners performed an important job: The Trade Federation needed trillidium.

Klark held up three fingers at a bar server. "Ale, please."

Half listening to Skeet and Xirri, he perused the surroundings as they stood at the table to await the commencement of the evening's sport. He noted details that were important to surviving a visit to Barésh or anywhere else. *Be vigilant in all things.* The tables were bolted to the floor. There were no chairs whatsoever. They were undoubtedly viewed more as potential weapons in a bar fight than a comfortable landing spot for anyone's rear-end. A makeshift bajha ring served double duty as a dance floor. Electronic music boomed, a relentless pounding, like a bad headache; yet a few drunken souls were moving to the beat. He tried to fathom what it must be like to compete in bajha in the midst of all the noise.

"He usually plays on Eighthnights only, fellas," someone said from directly behind him. "But tonight's your lucky night."

Klark pivoted toward the voice. "Are you speaking to me?"

"Aye. All three of you. It's why ya came here, right? To bet on Sea Kestrel."

Their silence did not deter the man a whit. He called out to other nearby patrons. "He's a-comin'. Don't ya fear. Stay right where ya are." He splayed his hands as if that might dissuade anyone from walking out, although the rowdy crowd showed little sign of desiring to do so. "Running a little behind schedule, he is, aye, but go on— all of you—drink up while ya wait!"

Perfectly timed, the drinks arrived. Klark lifted a plastic cup to take a sip of his ale (that was actually surprisingly good) as he observed the man chatter on. He appeared younger than Klark and the players, but something in his eyes looked far older. A ragged scar bisected his left eyebrow on an otherwise pleasant face. An easy grin made him seem even more approachable, and within moments he struck up a warm rapport with several tables of revelers. Like Skeet, this man knew how to get by on his charm.

There was little else he was getting by on, judging by the shabby clothes on his back. A thick woolen sweater with hacked-off sleeves covered a shirt with a collar limned with grime. Both garments were patched more than they were whole, but each and every repair was sewn with small, careful stitches. His fingerless gloves revealed scabbed and swollen knuckles on his right hand. He had been in a recent fight. Yet, here he was, coaxing them to purchase drinks while clearly still sober himself. "Have ya tried the ale yet?" the man was saying to anyone still willing to listen to him. "Tastiest in the colony. Go on, you won't be disappointed."

"Do you work for the club?" Xirri asked somewhat doubtfully.

"No. I'm here for Sea Kestrel, like you."

Klark gestured to a spot between him and Xirri. "Join us." The chap had several things going for him: he was friendly, he did not stink, and someone cared enough about him to mend his clothes. "Allow me to buy you an ale."

Having a local with them would provide further camouflage as to their intentions here. The man wavered, an inner battle seeming to contort his brow as he contemplated the cups of ale. He wanted it, but he gave his head a shake. "I thank you, but I've gotta meet an associate here very soon." He lowered his voice, winking conspiratorially. "But take my advice—for sure money, there ain't none better than Sea Kestrel. Go on and wager all you've got, fellas. You won't lose." His eyes radiated a glint of hunger, a certain desperation, as he once again tried to will them into staying put.

"We have no intention of going anywhere," Klark assured him. "Nor do I expect to lose." His wager was one of a very different sort, however: betting Sea Kestrel would not turn down the opportunity to train if it meant a chance of playing professionally. The manager might prove a harder shell to crack, however, especially if faced with losing a player who had proved to be a great moneymaker. In that, Klark's limitless wealth would have to do the talking.

"To a successful evening," he said and turned back to his players. They clinked their cups together in anticipation of the match to come.

When Jemm finally arrived at the fight club, she found Nico waiting for her in the back alley. Her knit cap was pulled tight over her hair, covering her ears and eyebrows. Her bajha gear was stowed in the bag she wore slung crosswise over her body by its strap. She was still dressed in her leathers, but her sidearm was under lock and key back at the processing plant. Working-class Baréshtis were not allowed to carry guns.

Before she could say a word, Nico launched into scolding her. "I started out waiting for you at home, like we planned. Ma wasn't happy you didn't show for dinner."

Her stomach grumbled at the thought of food. "Did ya bring any leftovers?"

His double blink told her he had not thought of it.

Nothing she could do about it now. She was almost too tired to care. While she prided herself on her fitness, the result of years of pitching in to help load her trailer with ore, the drama on the plains had knocked the stuffing out of her. She had to drain the heavy canister of trill so she could drag it back into the trailer solo. Then she scraped up the spilled ore, handful by gloved handful, loading everything back where it belonged, all while racing against time and keeping an eye out for more brigands.

"Sorry, Nic. It couldn't be helped. I was beset upon by scurries." Stiffly, she lifted the gear bag over her head. The bruise on her upper arm fired out blasts of pain with each beat of her heart. At first it had been isolated to her upper arm, and numb where the rock had struck flesh, but now the pain radiated down the bone clear to her wrist. She flexed her hand, working her fingers. Icing the wound was the answer, but while the frozen chips were not as dear as chips of trill, she would have to throw good money away to buy some. Besides, there was no time for that now, anyway. She would live. "Stinking little grubs made off with a quarter canister of ore."

"You came in short? Ah, Jemm. Now what? We can't afford any trouble. We've got obligations now."

She almost snorted. As if obligations did not already rule her life. "Don't get your pants in a wad, Nico. No one at the processor noticed. They were unloading the trailer before I shut down the tug."

"What am I supposed to tell Migel Arran if ya get thrown in the brig?" he asked as if he had not heard her, punching one hand inside the other as he stalked back and forth. "He's not the only one, Jemm. Half the club owners I know are begging me to arrange matches in their bars. If Sea Kestrel can't be relied on, soon no one will want to talk to me, and there goes our money. Poof! Gone."

"Listen to ya! You're not fretting because I had to battle pirates, or even that I might be fired. No, you're worried because in the brig I wouldn't be able to play bajha. What a rotten inconvenience that would be, losing your only player."

"You ain't my only player no more," he shot back just as angrily.

The moment went as silent as a moment could be on Barésh. In the background, Jemm could hear the muted hubbub from inside the bar and, from somewhere farther away, a shriek of pleasure or pain. But loudest of all was the thump of her heart kicking in outrage against her ribs.

"Aye, I've added another player to my roster, and soon I'll add another," Nico said, puffing up some. "Now that I've got the silvers to spend on training them."

"The last I checked we didn't have so much money that we could afford to be giving it away." Her chilly tone swept past him without ruffling a hair on his pretty little head. He was too busy sharing his ambitious plans to become the most sought-after manager in the colony.

"I've got to invest back in the company, Jemm. I'm a businessman now. Don't ya worry; there'll be more coming in for us both, and it'll keep on coming because you'll keep on winning. Soon we'll be trill rats no more." At that, his eyes shone, and his smile sparkled.

The sight of him so cheerful sucked the fury out of her. "You dozer," she muttered. He had gone and done it again, wrenching her heart by summoning the Nico Aves of old. The Nico she and Ma had missed and grieved for years and thought was gone for good.

Sighing, she pushed past him to go inside and change clothes. Her sore arm bumped up against his, but she made sure no hint of the vivid bolt of pain appeared in her face.

One of Nico's requirements for her to play in a club was a private dressing room. This bar had generously offered their utility closet. Complete with a mop and bucket. She kicked them out of the way. A quick look around to make sure no one was nearby to witness her transformation, and then she ducked inside.

Nico grabbed the door handle so she could not shut him out. "Look, Jemm. Being a manager is no easy job. When ya didn't show I had to hurry back here to do damage control. You think it was easy to keep the crowd from running off? Socializing and telling them you'd be worth the wait. It's what I had to do to keep this from turning into a disaster, while you were off—"

"I'm here now, right?" She shut the door in his face and unzipped her leathers with an angry yank. She could not suffer him acting affronted anymore, as if the jarring incident on the plains had personally inconvenienced *him*. She stripped down to her black, company-issue long johns worn under the leathers. The high-tech absorbent fabric would be put to good use under her bajha suit.

"Jemm?"

Silently, she counted to three. "What?"

"It might not seem like it sometimes, but I do worry about ya." His tone gentled. "I'm sorry. I know you're good at what you do, the driving. I also know the mine bosses are heartless bastards. Whatever happened today, I hope it goes no further. Because it won't matter if you're innocent; you'll still be found at fault."

Like Nico was the day he lost Kish, his wife and best friend.

She pressed her lips together, her hand flat on the closed door as if she had touched it to her brother's cheek. "Some rules changed—in the drivers' favor. I think I'll be all right."

"Good, because there are scouts here. Here in Narrow Margin. From the pros."

The galactic league. She cracked the door to the broom closet and peeked out. "How do you know?"

"I saw them come up the street from the direction of the docks, looking around all disgusted and determined, like they were digging for something valuable they lost in the trash. Then they walk into Narrow Margin, a middling fight club, and settle in for the evening—on a

Sixthnight? It ain't no coincidence, Jemm. They're here to see you."

Her insides flipped. "How would they know about me?"

"Word of mouth. A lot of folks come and go with the ore trade, as ya know. Could be one of them saw you compete, and took word off-world."

If only... "This story's getting more farfetched the longer you go on," she scoffed.

"Farfetched, but true all the same." Nico thrust his chin out. "One of them is *Vash Nadah*."

She went still. A *Vash Nadah?* They were descendants of the clans that saved the human race and founded the Trade Federation. Royals. Now one of those godlike beings was going to watch her play bajha.

Not gods. Upper class was upper class, and none of the elites deserved her awe. "How do ya know they're not from here? We don't know every cog in the compound."

"Ya know it when ya see the real thing, Jemm. He ain't a mongrel like most of what we've got here. He's from worlds afar."

"Worlds afar..." She savored the words aloud, letting them melt on her tongue like the heavenly and expensive treat ice cream she had tasted but once.

He sighed with dramatic exasperation. "Jemm, if your eyes get any wider, they'll fall out. Get changed. They're about to start the games."

She pushed the door shut. Scouts! Were they really here to see her? Was there a chance they would offer her the opportunity to play off-world? It would be the answer to all her dreams, and those of her father before her. She could get her family off-world and not have to wait decades to do it.

And if they found out she was a female? What then?

Nerves kicked her pulse higher.

Quiet your mind. No fretting about what might be; it was time to play. Her job was to play a few matches tonight, win them, and that was all. Taking into account the current, battered state of her body and mind, that alone would prove challenging enough.

She felt herself calming as she drew on her bajha suit, sleeve by sleeve, leg by leg, a cherished ritual. It was a salve for the outside world. Always had been. Bending to secure her boots, she closed each fastener with respect. *I'll need ya here with me tonight, Da.*

More than she ever had.

The bar owner had shrewdly saved the best for last, forcing Klark to suffer through ten laughably bad amateur matches, with the top three winners slated to play against Sea Kestrel. Yet, he found himself enjoying the farce, entertained all the while by the derogatory, running commentary by Raff Xirri and Yonson Skeet, two of the most celebrated pro players in the galaxy. Fortunately, no one seemed to recognize them. The patrons no more expected to encounter sports celebrities in a back-alley fight club than they did a prince. The poor lighting and hovering vape smoke further helped cloak them in anonymity.

Finally, the lights flashed as the announcer took his place in the center of the ring. The star attraction's matches were imminent.

Sea Kestrel. Klark felt the player's presence in the club before he saw him. He used his mind as much as his eyes to scan the perimeter of the bajha ring, his body taut with a heady and unaccustomed sense of anticipation. Then he finally found him.

In the gap between a pair of tattered purple-sequined curtains stood a young man engulfed in a patched, gray-with-age bajha suit too large for his slender body. Despite the crowd's riotous whistling and cheering, Sea Kestrel's attention remained fixed on the announcer. His face was almost ethereal, one could even say feminine—youth being the reason for that softness, of course.

"At last," Klark said under his breath. His unknown, backwater, street-bajha gem in the rough.

"Yer drinks, fellas." As a barmaid sloshed three more cups of ale onto the table, clearing away their empties, a man appeared at the amateur's side with a blindfold, fastening it around his hood while leaning in close to confer with the player. It was none other than the friendly chap who had coaxed them to stay and drink up earlier. He was Sea Kestrel's manager! Klark let out a surprised chuckle.

"And now, lassies and fellas, Narrow Margin, home of the best bajha under the dome, presents the indomitable, the incredible, the rising star…Sea Kestrel!"

As the announcer bellowed out the introduction and the crowd reacted with foot-stomping cheers, Sea Kestrel did not storm the ring like the rest of the amateurs had done before him. Instead, he bowed his head, appearing to reach inside for calm as he gripped his sens-sword in two hands. Seconds ticked by before he finally strode with mature and measured confidence into the ring.

A tingle along Klark's spine argued that this gamble would not be for naught, that something could—and would—come of it. This moment heralded a new beginning, which was something he sorely needed.

"He's injured," Skeet said.

Klark jerked his head around. "How can you tell?"

"Watch his right arm. He's favoring it."

Sea Kestrel and his opponent submitted to the ref's inspection of their blindfolds and sens-sword settings before they took their positions in the ring. Based on Skeet's observation, Klark took note of how Sea Kestrel wielded his sens-sword. He had seen enough injuries in bajha players to know that Skeet had called this one correctly. Sure enough, the amateur was using his left arm to take some of the load off his right, the elbow of which he kept tucked close to his rib cage like a broken wing.

Klark had pondered solutions to various contingencies when going over this plan, but he had not considered anything happening to Sea Kestrel before he could get to him. It drove home the fact that nothing on Barésh was secure, particularly someone's wellbeing. He took an extra deep swallow of ale.

Any evidence of injury melted away as the young amateur met his opponents one by one, allowing each of them the chance to engage him long enough to entertain the crowd—and, no doubt, as a show of mercy for the lesser players' egos—before sending the fellows to their defeat. When it was over, Sea Kestrel dropped to one knee, head bowed humbly, as the last match was decided in his favor.

"Bravo," Klark said, clapping.

Skeet was grinning from ear to ear. "So he was worth the trouble to come here, then."

"Indeed. He certainly possesses an innate sense of showmanship. In fact, he reminds me a lot of you, Yonson."

That the amateur had the strength and wits to do it while injured solidified Klark's opinion that the player's mental discipline was extraordinary. But would those considerable skills translate to the rules and expectations of the pros? That remained the million-credit question.

It was high time he found out the equally valuable answer.

"Gentlemen, let's settle the bill and go introduce ourselves to our fine young player." Klark gathered up his cloak and glanced toward the back of the club, where he hoped a pair of shabby, sequined drapes represented the last barrier to the culmination of his journey here.

CHAPTER FIVE

Jemm peered through the backstage curtains, hoping for a glimpse of the off-worlders. All she saw was smoke, strobe lights, and too many milling bodies. "How do we know they ain't slavers, pretending to be scouts?" she had asked Nico after the match.

"They ain't slavers," he assured her.

"You don't know for sure."

"Aye, I do. I know how to judge a man. They offered to buy me a drink, and didn't even know who I was."

He was probably right. One thing was certain—she had sensed something out there under the spotlight that was new to her. Not the typical blunt-force attention of an audience or the intentions of an opponent, but the feeling of being observed with a nonthreatening focus as distinct and bright as a searchlight beam in the night. It confused her. It would have distracted her if she had let it.

Then she got hold of herself. If she had sensed anything at all, it was probably wishful thinking. Scouts for the galactic league, in Barésh City, in a bar on a Sixthnight, to see her? Anything that sounded that much like a fairy tale probably was.

She let the curtains fall together. "I've got another dawn run tomorrow. I need sleep, and I'm starving." When she was this hungry, she got angry. "Hangry," the loaders at work called it, and often tempted her with morsels from their food sacks to keep her from protesting too much about loading delays. "Wait—is that food ya got there?"

Nico came toward her, his arms full of supplies. "Aye. Or something like it." He handed her a jug of water, a hand towel, and a protein stick, which she snatched out of his hand, tearing off a bite. "I watched them watch you the entire time. They're keener for you than we are for them. I predict they'll want to see more of ya. Now, wait here. I'll go get our cut." He frowned at her. "I mean it, Jemm. Stay right here. Don't change clothes, and *do not* go home." He held up a finger for emphasis.

"I want this as much as you do, Nico."

Nodding, with a vape dangling from his lower lip, he stepped away to retrieve their winnings from Narrow Margin's owner. He claimed her open distaste for the club owners was bad for business, so she had been letting him take care of it. She much preferred having a few solo moments to savor the inner peace left from bajha before it faded altogether.

Leaning against a wall, she pressed the towel to her face then looped it over her neck. It was stuffy backstage. Nico lighting up a vape had not helped any. By now her hair was drenched under her knit cap. Her exhaustion was so all-consuming she was tempted to curl up and sleep where she stood, despite the relentless pounding ache in her arm. Tipping her head back, she emptied the water jug with deep, greedy swallows.

"There you are!" called out an accented voice she knew was not of this colony.

She almost dropped the jug, dregs of water splattering on her boots, as three clean, well-dressed men glided one by one between the parted curtains like flycars through the mist. Clean and well-fed they were, aye, but these were no typical Baréshti compound cogs; they were as physically fit as Arik and the other loaders.

And tall. She was not a petite woman, standing as tall or taller than many Baréshti males, but these strangers towered over her by at least a head.

The first visitor backstage wore a grin that creased his friendly face from one cheek to the other. He was blond and good-looking in the boyish way her brother was, but in peak physical condition. A wholesome Nico, if such a thing were possible. "That was some mighty fine playing," he said, one corner of his mouth denting a cheek with the kind of dimple girls loved.

A second off-worlder joined him. He was also everyday blond but darker with angular features and flared dark brows over a pair of miss-nothing golden-brown eyes. "You played an excellent set of matches. Despite the lack of competition."

"The *competition*, if this boob wants to call it that, was pathetic," the Nico lookalike laughed. "But blasted entertaining."

Their cocky grins reminded her of what she was used to seeing in the ore loaders. It gave her a thread of familiarity to grasp onto as the two looked her up and down with respect and instant camaraderie. With one difference.

Always when meeting strange men for the first time, even other tug drivers or loaders, she had come to expect some degree of sexual appraisal. A woman working in a man's world learned to ignore it, as long as it did not interfere with her job. Yet, there was not one speck of carnal interest in the gaze of these off-worlders. It meant her disguise was working. They assumed she was male like them.

"I'm Yonson Skeet," the Nico twin said, poking a thumb at his chest. "And this sluggish half-wit is Raff Xirri. We play for Team Eireya. We stopped in to see you along with our esteemed team owner." Skeet turned to look over his shoulder, his voice muted and far more respectful. "Sir Klark Vedla."

Jemm's gaze lifted to the third off-worlder. With a cloak draped over the crook of an arm, he stood exactly two paces behind the pros, as if to observe the exchange rather than be a part of it. While all three men wore aristo-quality clothing, this man's dark brown trousers and shirt were impeccably tailored, designed to pay homage to an athletic build—the spread of his shoulders, narrow hips, long muscular legs—without flaunting it. Not even Migel Arran's wardrobe could match the attention to detail. His hair was warm and tawny like his skin, but did nothing to counteract his coldness, an impression accentuated by a long perfect nose, high cheekbones, and a firm jaw—features that looked so sculpted and hard they could be made from bronzed stone. It distracted from his good looks and left her with the sense of a rigid, downright grim fella.

Until he stepped forward to greet her, his mouth breaking into a glorious smile that melted his demeanor like a match held to wax. "Ah, Sea Kestrel. What can I say? Well done. Very well done." He spoke with a dignified brogue that was as sweet and smooth as melted ice cream.

Vaguely, she knew she was expected to say something in return, but all she could do was track that smile to where it ended, glinting in his arresting pale gold eyes. *Vash Nadah* eyes.

From worlds afar…

Something tickled her chin. That was when she realized she had been gaping at the off-worlders the entire time with water dribbling from her parted lips. She dashed her sleeve across her mouth and chin.

"That's one way to use a bajha suit," said, Yonson Skeet, the wholesome Nico lookalike. "As a bib!" He and his teammate guffawed at the insult, and she found herself back in familiar territory. Her mostly male fellow tug drivers and the loaders showed affection the same way, shooting disparaging zingers at each other the way some females blew kisses.

The *Vash* owned the team. Who could own a whole team? Who had that kind of money? The thought was dizzying. It seemed ridiculous now that she had fretted the men might be slavers masquerading as scouts. This nobleman did not need to force players to compete. He could buy them, bribe them, wine and dine them.

"You impressed me, Sea Kestrel," the *Vash* said. "I expected you might, but not to this degree," he said, pure enchantment lighting up his gaze.

Her heart skipped a beat.

She had always wondered what it would be like, seeing a fella so captivated with her that his eyes alone would be enough to make her catch her breath. To be a lass on the receiving end of that kind of heart-stopping, center-of-his-world regard would be something indeed. Da looked at Ma that way when Jemm was small, before everything went bad.

Except that there was only one reason this man regarded her with such interest and passion. He assumed she was a street-bajha player with a knack for wielding a sens-sword that he as a team owner might be interested in recruiting.

A *male* street bajha player.

She took a few cerebral steps back. It would not do to gawk at a man who thought she was a lad. "Thank you," she croaked in her deepest, gruffest voice.

Sir Vedla's face also closed off and reverted to a grim façade. She hoped it was because he realized it was more befitting his status, not because having a teenage lad ogling him made him uncomfortable. "The barkeep gave me ice," he said, steady and aloof. In his left hand was a small, wet, fabric-wrapped bag.

"Ice?" She sounded silly, husking out the word in her "boy" voice. "What for?" Now she sounded defensive as well.

"You were favoring your right arm during the match. You weren't as of a few weeks ago. How recent is your injury?"

Holy crat. He noticed? Unlike her brother.

Nico had returned to her side in a cloud of vape smoke. "You're hurt?" His eyes narrowed when she shook her head and said nothing. He tossed his vape on the floor and crushed the plastic shell with the heel of his boot then smiled at the men. "Nico Aves is the name, fellas. We met earlier."

"Indeed we did," Klark said pleasantly. "You're the manager, I see."

"Manager, promoter, and coach of this fine player, Sea Kestrel." Her brother stuck out a hand wrapped in a glove so greasy that if she were the *Vash* she would have hesitated to shake it, too.

Nico chuckled. "Don't worry, I ain't contagious. Not yet anyway." He took Sir Vedla by the arm in the way Migel Arran had taken his all those weeks ago, then offered the same greeting to the pair of pro players. How easily her chameleon of a brother could move between worlds, whereas Jemm felt the most at ease when she was alone, driving in her tug or lost in practicing bajha.

"What happened to your player?" the *Vash* asked with a hint of accusation, as if he were the one tasked with protecting her and not Nico.

Nico turned to Jemm. "What happened to you?"

Memories of her encounter with the scurries pelted her like the rocks they had thrown. She tucked her painful arm closer to her side as if to shield both her thoughts and the injury from the men's prying eyes. Like the stray yipwags of the colony, she instinctively knew to keep any wounds secret, whether they were on the inside or the out. On Barésh, hiding weakness was a matter of survival. "It's just a bump."

"Yeah? I pull and tear enough body parts to know it's more than a bump," Skeet argued.

The *Vash* nodded. "As do we all. Unfasten your suit so I can take a look at you."

Undress for him? *Crag me.* Jemm's fingers clamped around the ends of the towel as if grasping a comforting hand. "That ain't necessary."

"Aye, it ain't," Nico spoke up. "I'll treat Sea Kestrel later, if he requires treating."

Jemm nodded. "Aye, he will."

The players exchanged questioning looks. The *Vash* appeared unhappy about her refusal. Sir Vedla was used to getting his way. "What is your given name?" he asked.

"Kes," she replied as she and Nico had rehearsed.

"Kes. The most minor of injuries can ground a player if not caught early. Have you seen a physician?"

"Here we don't call doctors for every little pinch or scratch." Not when you were forced to decide between eating and medical care. *Like Ma.* But she was certain that choice was one these off-worlders had never been forced to make.

"I see. Well, I came here to talk about a proposition, but holding an ice pack makes it rather difficult. Why don't you take it?"

The ice pack dripped water onto the floor, drumming out a tempting beat. Although she kept her expression as blank as possible, she had the sneaking suspicion Sir Vedla had guessed her longing for the ice.

"Whether you need it or not," he added. He dipped his chin, their eyes locking. Beneath that smooth, chilly surface, there was a man trying his hardest to do a kind act.

Mumbling her thanks, she took the ice pack, moved aside the towel and unfastened the top two fasteners of her suit to slide the bag into place inside her sleeve.

Hunching her shoulder to make room, she was careful to give no indication how much that movement hurt. With the chance of a lifetime within her reach, she could not risk the impression that she was damaged goods.

Nico piped up. "Well, that's settled. Let's talk about that proposition you mentioned."

"Ah, yes, that." The *Vash*'s aloofness again fell away with the change in subject, segueing into boyish enthusiasm. "It should be clear why I am here," he told her in his exquisite accent. "I feel that with enough practice and desire you have the potential to move beyond street bajha. That's not something I say lightly. Thus, I'd like to offer you the invitation to train with us for a few days, here on Barésh—my ship—the goal being an opportunity to try out for Team Eireya. The galactic league."

There it was. The door opening. Everything she had ever wanted was summed up in those three words. Jemm stared hard at the grimy floor for a second or two, trying to contain the joy swelling in her chest. Her bajha skills formed the perfect emotional armor, so by the time she was able to look up at the *Vash* again, she was composed.

Except, his pale gaze had observed it all. He acknowledged her reaction with the slightest of satisfied nods, then turned to Nico, offering him a white card embedded with tiny red lights and the word *SECURITY* in black letters. "You two will need this to access the secure area of the docks tomorrow."

Nico squinted at the card, pretending he knew how to read. "That is all fine and good, but our time don't come for free, fellas. If Sea Kestrel is with you, he can't play matches for me. And that means a stoppage in my income stream." He wiggled callused fingers. "How about a little earnest money to motivate me to add this to our busy schedule?"

"I fully intended to compensate you," Sir Vedla said, and reached inside his cloak.

"And, on Eighthnight he's all mine. We have a standing engagement at Rumble, a North City fight club, the day after tomorrow. Until anything is signed, I have to stick with my player's prior engagements."

"Of course."

It was an advantage that Nico had the guts and the gall to speak up to these noblemen. Nothing seemed to rattle him. But when Sir Vedla opened his money holder and counted out a single gold card Nico's swallow was audible.

"Will that do, Mr. Aves?"

Her brother remained silent as he contemplated the credit. A gold card was equivalent to a couple of months' worth of players' cuts—at least!

"It will do, won't it, Nic?" Jemm broke in, her scowl leaving him no choice but to accept what the team owner had offered. Overconfidence was no good in the ring, and greed had no place in negotiations, not when they involved her. She could not afford to let Nico's brashness to chase away these scouts and the biggest chance she had ever had all because he wanted to haggle over a few extra credits.

"Aye. It'll do." Nico slipped the gold into his pocket.

"My ship is berthed at Star Tube J," the *Vash* said. "I'll see you there in the morning."

"I have to work," she said.

"Je—" Nico almost blurted out her real name, but her glare stopped him. If that glare were a physical thing, he would have suffered a life-threatening injury.

She dropped her voice to a whisper. "I can't not show up to my job, Nico. This ain't no sure thing yet."

"You're either all in or all out."

"I'll be all in when I'm actually in."

"You gotta be all in to get there."

She shook her head. "I ain't quitting my job."

By now the three men were leaning in to overhear their intense, whispered conversation. She turned and they popped back upright. "Sir Vedla, I work every day but Firstday. I'm usually done by dome-set. I'll come to your ship as soon as I get off."

"Do what you must, but come ready to train hard. There'll be no accommodations. If you are up to snuff, you'll be signed. But I'll warn you, few street bajha players can adapt to league rules."

"Well, I can. And I will," she said fiercely. There was no other option. To fail was to condemn herself to Barésh for untold years longer, working for a company that expected her to kill children.

She had the feeling he saw more of her struggle than she wanted anyone—especially him—to know. She tore her focus from those perceptive golden eyes and cleared her throat.

"That's the can-do attitude we like to see, Kes." Skeet chucked her on the arm, her good arm. "I'll be rooting for you."

Xirri smiled. "See ya tomorrow, bud."

Sir Vedla pivoted on the heel of one of his expensive boots and strode with his players out of the club.

As soon as they were gone, Jemm turned to her brother and grabbed him by the arm. "A lass, playing for the galactic league. Are we crazy?" Her stomach flip-flopped from hope to dread. "He's a team owner, Nic. Messing with an elite of that stature, do ya know how dangerous this is?" She would rather face down a mine boss than be caught lying to the *Vash Nadah*.

"There's nothing false about your playing. That's what he saw, that's what he wants. Mark my words, it's gonna be the best decision he ever made." He pushed her toward the utility closet. "Now go get changed. You've got a big day tomorrow."

Tomorrow! Dome help her. Jemm packed her gear and donned her street clothes, joining Nico outside in the alleyway behind the club. Her hair was brushed out and swinging free, her leather jacket unzipped, the cool air blissful on her company-issue undershirt. She held her injured arm close to her body. The ice had helped some, but not enough. She hoped it did not put tomorrow's practice in jeopardy.

Nico took her gear bag from her to sling over his shoulder. "Here. Drink up." The cobblestones were slick with dew. Her boots skidded on some night slime as she paused to drink from the water jug Nico had refilled for her. Her timepiece slid heavily from her wrist to her hiked-up sleeve as she tipped her head back to guzzle from the jug. She did not pause until she had finally taken her fill, expelling an appreciative gust of air. Nico waved a handful of silvers at her, the precious gold credit tucked safely away, his eyes scrunched with happiness. "I'll buy you dinner. A big dinner. All you can eat. There's a place up the block. I've never gotten sick from the food there. Not once."

The mere mention of food made her knees weak and her stomach growl. "Don't tempt me."

"C'mon. You know you want to. And ya deserve it."

After this insane day, she deserved to burrow into her bed and go unconscious for a few hours, too, before she had to leave for another long day of ore hauling. What if the scurries came at her tomorrow for another go, thinking she was an easy mark because she had not fought them off? How long until the bosses got suspicious at the loss of ore?

Her shoulders sagged.

"Crat, Jemm. You ain't been yourself tonight." Her brother cornered her, his voice careful. "What's wrong? Don't tell me it's nothing, like your arm."

"I almost had to shoot those kids," she mumbled. "The scurries."

"But you didn't."

"But I could have. Then what? I'd be no different than them—the bosses."

"You never would have killed a child, Jemm. You've got a real conscience. You always do what's right."

She had not done "right" accepting the fraudulent load Arik had dispatched her with. But if she hadn't gone along with the scam, she would have ended up having to explain what happened to that quarter canister of trill. At the very least, she would be held responsible for the loss due to carelessness, because if she did not defend the load with deadly force, then she had given it away like candy. At the worst, they would accuse her of pilfering it for herself, owing to the lack of any evidence to the contrary. "I don't want to become one of them, Nic. The longer I stay here, the more I think I might. That's why I've got to get out. I've got to get all of us out."

"C'mere." Nico gathered her into a hug.

She sagged into the warm, vape-scented comfort that was Nico, her cheek resting on his thick, scratchy sweater.

"You ain't ever gonna be like one of them upper-class cogs," he told her. "It just ain't in ya." Then he went rigid, grabbing a fistful of her hair at the base of her skull to pull her close, his other hand landing on her bottom.

"Nico! What the hell—?" Her protest was muffled against his chest.

"Pretend ya like it. It's them scouts—the pros and the *Vash*." He cursed. "They're back, and headed this way."

CHAPTER SIX

D on't say nothing," Nico warned. "Nothing at
all."
Jemm's pulse boomed like the detonations
of ore-charges. She let her hair spill forward to
camouflage her face from the off-worlders. The crunch of
several pairs of boots on grit came from only about
twenty steps away. "Nico, glad to find you still here."
Even without a view of the voice's owner, she knew that
lovely brogue belonged to the *Vash*. "I'm looking for Sea
Kestrel."

Her timepiece slid around her wrist she dragged her
palms down Nico's sweater and pretended to nuzzle the
side of his neck. "Cut me loose before they get too
close," she whispered. "Make it believable, or we're done
for."

He nodded. "Run along now, darlin'! I've got business
to attend to." He moved her backward and gave her a pat
on the bottom for good measure.

She used a flirtatious hair toss to keep her face hidden
before she turned her back to the off-worlders and
sashayed off, hoping they would act like men and fix
their attention on her swaying rear-end instead of the fact

they had not gotten a good look at her. She felt their gazes following her all the way to where she disappeared around the corner a half block away. She stopped there, her blood roaring in her ears. *Craggin' crat.*

"Who was that?" she heard Skeet ask in an admiring tone.

"My girlfriend, Jemm. She's a good lass, she is."

Jemm? Was he crazy? "It takes some truth to make a lie believable," went the saying. Her brother had taken that advice to heart.

"Kes has already gone home, fellas." Nico herded Sir Vedla and the two pro players back to Narrow Margin's back entrance. A group of drunken miners stumbled past behind Jemm, their loud conversation making it impossible to hear what was being said as the *Vash* stopped to hand something to Nico. Then goodbyes were said.

But before Sir Vedla made it back inside the club a sex server stopped him. Her hands were all over him as she tried to separate him from his companions. Despite the weak light, the contrast between this aristocrat from the stars and the thin, dirty, scantily dressed young woman curling around him like oily hallucivape smoke was obvious.

Breathless, Nico careened around the corner. "Crag me. That was close," he said.

"Too close." Jemm peeked around the corner again. Despite how far the sex worker was beneath Sir Vedla's lofty station, he refused her advances without visible disgust or disrespect. It took two tries before he was able to disentangle himself from her and disappear with his players inside, leaving the girl to gaze after him in awe.

Then it hit Jemm that she was standing there doing exactly the same thing.

Xirri made a low whistle as Klark herded his players back through the bar. "That's some sweet piece Nico's got on his arm."

"Did you see that walk of hers?" Skeet lifted his brows at them.

Klark kept quiet. Of course he had noticed the way the woman carried herself. What man wouldn't? She was tall, confident, dressed from chin to boots in black leather, and she knew exactly what she was doing when she undulated away. Leaving him to gawk at her tight ass and incredible hair—long, wavy strands that ranged from reddish brown to amber to the palest blonde that he could all too easily picture tousled after some bed sport. Too bad it had hidden her face. He would have liked to know if her features were as captivating as the rest of her. But all that aside, her laudable physical attributes were not what had left him both drawn to and puzzled by her. It was her scent.

A light, clean musk—only a faint, fleeting trace, yet it was enough to register as familiar. Then it vanished before he could sort out why.

He knew that scent.

Klark discarded the thought. It must be the bad air fooling his normally dead-on nose. Or, maybe the ale he drank had scrambled his wits. Whatever it was, he hoped that with a good night's rest he would be back to himself in the morning.

"Look at you, sis, all dreamy-like."

"What do ya mean?" Jemm dragged a hand over her face, as if one could wipe off traces of wonder like badlands grit.

"You're all agog at those off-worlders," Nico teased as they took off in the direction of the old city. "Well, they want you, too. The owner does—for his team."

Her insides cartwheeled at the thought. "Wouldn't that be something. Eh, Nico? What did they want? I saw the *Vash* give you something."

"Aye, it's for—" He stopped hard, glanced left, then yanked her close. "Whoa. We've got visitors. Don't turn around."

"The off-worlders again?"

"No. Keep moving."

Her heart sank. "Alley pirates?" She thought of the gold card in Nico's pocket. A gold! It would be devastating to lose it. Luckily there were other people out on the street. Usually, alley pirates operated in the dark and isolated maze of narrow alleyways that Baréshtis used as shortcuts.

His grip tightened. "No. Migel Arran's toadies. Persistent rotters. They came looking for me the other day, but I outmaneuvered them."

"Why didn't ya tell me?"

"I can handle Arran, that's why."

She matched his long strides, the back of her neck prickling. "It's because I played in Narrow Margin tonight."

"Aye. And this is how Arran means to communicate his dislike of the matter." Nico pulled her into another hard right turn, taking them in the opposite direction of home, knowing that leading Arran's gangsters to the apartment would be a terrible mistake. It left her feeling like a plains-bunny in the badlands, zigzagging to shake off predators before reaching the burrow.

To her dismay, they ended up in North City, her brother's swank-soaked stomping grounds and where she had beaten Black Hole a month ago in Rumble, one of Arran's clubs. Nico knew the district like the back of his hand, whereas what Jemm knew of the area she would rather forget. In the bad times following Kish's death, she would go from bar to bar to track him down and bring him home, hoping that when she found him, he would be alive.

"In here." Nico pushed through a door to a stairwell, pulling her along behind him. They clambered up the narrow staircase. The steps were uneven, littered with spent vapes. It smelled like rotted food, urine, and exhaust fumes. From behind one of the closed doors came the muffled, frantic sounds of a couple having sex.

"Oh, that's nice. I hope ya know where you're going."

He answered with a withering look.

She let him propel her along, trying to fight an increasing sense of hopelessness. *I'll never escape this place.*

It was like being stuck in a bad dream; it started out with so much hope tonight, meeting Sir Vedla and his pros, being invited to train. Now she was on the run, running in circles, unable to get back home, Nico pulling her farther into his world with every step until she would finally be in too deep to get out.

"Nico. We can't run all night."

"We're not." A moment later they emerged out on the rooftop. Moons swirled overhead, obscured by thicker than usual smog. It tinged everything brown. Nico backtracked, finding another staircase that led back down to street level but on the other side of the building. He looked both ways before he led her back into the crowds. It was a normal throng for the late hour. Jemm scoured the crowds, examining the faces of passersby. No one stood out as threatening. "They're gone, eh?"

"Aye. Shook 'em loose again." Downright proud of himself, Nico grinned.

"Eventually, we're gonna have to deal with Arran," Jemm said. "Avoiding his messengers is just prolonging the inevitable."

"I'll talk to him on Eighthnight, like I meant to all along."

They walked the rest of the way home in tense silence.

Up, up the dark, dank, spiral staircase they climbed until they reached the seventeenth floor, the pointy tip-top of the building where the odors of raw sewage, burned cooking grease, and mildew were not as strong. Nico dug in his pocket. "The esteemed owner of Team Eireya wanted ya to have this. A salve for your arm, he said." He dropped a small tube into her hand. "He seems a good fella. They were on the way back to the docks when Skeet remembered he had some on him, and your *Vash* made them walk all the way back to give it to ya."

"*My* Vash?" She lifted a brow at him then squinted at the tube. "Anti-inflammatory," she read. An upper-class potion. It was good that the team owner thought enough of her to go through the trouble to get her the healing salve. He definitely was not what she had expected. Apparently not all elites were like the ones who ran Barésh.

Jemm slid the tube in her pocket before unfastening her work boots and setting the heavy things just inside the door. "Go clean up before Ma sees ya."

Nico headed to the washroom while she tiptoed across the tiled floor in her socks, shrugging off her jacket as she went. It was warm inside, the air close, smelling like soap, hot wax, and the fading aromas from an earlier meal, a good meal. Better food was one of the side benefits of a scheme so fraught with risk.

Jemm followed her nose to the kitchen. The main, octagonal room followed the interior shape of the cone-shaped building. A small dirty window punctuated each wall except for one sparkling clean window she had purchased with her first bajha winnings. It allowed a sweeping view of the old city.

Curtains could be pulled closed to separate three bedroom areas and the cramped washroom from the living area. Only one bedroom had its barrier up, where her mother and Button slept.

After a day that was equal parts wonderful and horrible it was good to be home. In the kitchen, she rinsed off her face and hands. Her parents had always insisted on good hygiene even though filth reigned on Barésh. But then they were very lucky to live in the old city in a building with plumbing that worked (more often than not). Jemm gazed down at the small tube of salve cupped in her hand. It had come from far away, concocted by some chemist in the *Vash's* employ. Then she looked at her arm. There was a large lump where the rock had impacted bone and muscle. The skin was not broken but badly bruised, a colorful blotch of red, purple, and blue that would only get worse. Gingerly, she rubbed a film of cream over the lump. Right away, the pain began to subside.

Not because her skin grew numb, but due to the cream acting on the injury itself. It was a nano-salve. Microscopic computers, her father had explained, helping her to learn as much science as a child could absorb. Jemm examined her ointment-moistened fingertips as if she stood a chance of seeing the wee machines at work. Oh, the wondrous things the Baréshti upper class and the rest of the galaxy had at their disposal that the workers here did not. The miracle medicines that could make her mother well again. Would the *Vash* have anything on his ship for Ma? He must. Desperation pushed aside any reservations Jemm had about being cheeky enough to ask a man who owed her nothing.

A paper-wrapped bundle sat on the counter. Inside was a loaf of yeast bread. Jemm inhaled the intoxicating scent before using a knife to slice off two hunks, one for her and one for Nico.

"I bought fresh pen-fowl at the night market. I'll cook ya both some." Her mother's voice ended in a muffled cough as she emerged from the bedroom.

"Ma, you didn't have to wait up for us."

Her mother waved a hand. Candlelight flattered her jaw-length wavy hair: dark red at the roots lightening to blonde at the ends, exactly the same shade as Jemm's. Traces of the beauty she once was battled fatigue for precedence on her perpetually careworn face as she moved about the kitchen. "I'm assuming you're hungry."

"Starving," Jemm mumbled, her mouth full of bread.

"There's jam, too." Ma removed a small crock filled with a deep purple mash from the cold box.

Jemm slathered it on the bread. "This near-jam smells like the real thing."

"It is real."

"From fruit? No, Ma. Save it for our Button." Jemm started to scrape the jam off the bread. "She's growing, and needs the vitamins. I can make do."

Ma stilled her hand. "There's enough." She bent over, coughing, a deep and phlegmy hack, her hands convulsing on the countertop. Jemm started toward her but her mother waved her off. "Sit. Eat your bread."

Jemm sat at the battered wooden table that never failed to conjure memories of better days: her parents, Jemm, Nico as a small boy with his best friend Kish at his side, sitting around the table, laughing and sharing the meager meals that Ma could somehow fool them into thinking were feasts. "I'm sorry I missed dinner with you and Button. I had a late run."

Ma's doubting glance at the gear bag laying by Jemm's stocking feet and a disapproving twist of her lips made Jemm feel guiltier for the sin of omission. She was dying to tell Ma all about the wild events of the evening: talking to off-worlders, one of them a real *Vash*, and how it was the first real chance they had at new lives. But she had the feeling her mother would take to the idea that Jemm was selling sexual favors better than hearing the news she was playing street bajha, and for reasons her mother stubbornly refused to share.

"How's our Button?"

"As well as a young'un can be with no one but an old woman to care for her all day. No Ma around. No Da." Her mother stifled a cough as she lit the stove and heated some oil in a pan until it rippled with heat.

"You're not old, Ma. Things are gonna get better. I'm gonna get us out of here. I swear it."

Her mother's lips thinned as she sprinkled diced vegetables and spices into the oil. The bits sizzled and popped, releasing a delicious aroma. "You're sounding like your Da now. 'Get us out of here,'" she muttered. "He used to tell me that, weaving his fanciful stories. Look where it got him." She waved the spatula at Jemm. "It put him in the grave, it did."

Jemm knew better than to argue. Ma was sure to come around once the prospect of leaving was a real event and not the unrealized dream of a husband she had never forgiven for dying and leaving her.

When the vegetables had browned, Ma tossed in several slices of fresh pen-fowl, once a rare luxury for the family, now a few-times-a-week dish, stirring the thick, pink slices with a spatula until they turned white, the skin crispy with browned edges. Jemm's mouth watered. "Smell's like heaven, Ma."

Nico stomped into the kitchen. "By the dome, Nico," Jemm said in a stage whisper. "The whole city will hear ya. Not to mention Button."

The shine in his eyes told her he had grabbed himself a swig or two of cheap whiskey from the bottle he kept under his nightstand. A whiff of his breath confirmed it.

A yowl preceded a brown spotted ketta-cat leaping through a cat door. Ditsi scampered to Nico, purring and rubbing against his legs, knowing he would pass her scraps under the table.

Nico almost tripped over the creature as he trudged over to a chair and sat in it. Ma fussed over him, fixing his plate, handing him a fork and napkin. Then she served

Jemm and settled down at the table to work on mending while they ate.

"Mum-mum!" A wisp of a little girl in pajamas came shooting out from behind a bedroom curtain. Her blonde hair was messy from her pillow, one hand gripping the arm of a stuffed doll Ma had made for her. She scrambled up into Jemm's leather-clad lap, a squirming armful of warm, gangly limbs. Snuggling close, her cheek pillowed by Jemm's breasts, she stuck her thumb in her mouth and let out a contented sigh. Jemm kept one arm around her as she ate with the other.

"She misses ya when you work so late," Ma said, unhappy about it.

"Mum-mum's sorry when that happens, right, Button?" She kissed the child's silky hair, pressing her lips to her warm little head. It brought back thoughts of the scurries, which caused her to hold Button extra tight. "I always miss ya. You know that, right?" She felt the little girl's head bob.

Now that Jemm would be training with the off-worlders her schedule would only get worse. "I'll be late again the next few nights, Ma. I have...some things to do after work."

Secrets new and old sat between them like unwelcome guests.

"I'll save ya dinner."

"That's all right, Ma. I'll be eating in the city." On a starship. If only she could tell her.

Ma's needle jabbed at her mending. She coughed, her frail shoulders rocking.

"Ma, go to bed," Nico said. "It's late. We'll clean up."

"And put Button to bed," Jemm added.

With the back of her hand pressed to her mouth, the woman nodded, and left for her bedroom, her muffled coughing coming from behind the curtains.

"She's getting worse," Jemm said. "That potion she gets at the market doesn't help anymore. We can afford better treatment now."

"Aye, but she won't spend the money."

"We can use that gold card in your pocket to get her a doctor."

"No compound doc is gonna come into the city to treat a trill rat. Besides, to Ma, it's blood money. She would rather die than benefit from street bajha."

Jemm exhaled. "I'm sure she knows where the extra money is coming from. She says nothing because it means better food and clothing for Button."

At that, Nico's hands curled into fists on top of the table. Jemm made a face at his gloves. "Why do you keep wearing those dirty old gloves when there's money to buy a new pair?"

"Why do ya wear that timepiece? It doesn't work."

"It was Da's. And I mean to get it repaired."

He turned his hands over, looking at them with those old-soul eyes that never seemed to fit his boyish face. "These are what I was wearing when Kish got killed. If I wash 'em, it's like washing off her."

Jemm's breath caught. It was like he had reached inside her chest and squeezed her heart. She slid her hand over one of Nico's battered gloves and twined her fingers with his. They sat in silence, their dinner plates picked clean. Button's breathing was slower and deeper now, her lips slack around her thumb. She had fallen asleep.

"I'll meet ya tomorrow at the processing plant when ya get off work," Nico said finally. "I know a place where you can change clothes."

"Aye." She pushed back from the table, shifting a floppy Button from her lap to her hip. Ditsi darted out from under the table and leaped through the cat door, heeding the call back to the night now that her belly was full. Jemm hitched Button higher in her arms. "Would you like to put your daughter to bed?"

Nico shook his head.

If only he would hold on to his daughter as fiercely as he did his gloves. Even a gesture as small and kind as feeding Button a few scraps off his plate like he did for the ketta-cat would give Jemm hope he would act like a real father one day. But ever since Kish was killed he had steered clear of the mines—and their baby. "I will if your arm hurts," he mumbled.

Her arm.

She stopped in her tracks, yanked up her sleeve. The discolored bruise was almost gone, as was the swelling. "I don't feel it anymore. That salve, it's all but healed it." Her next thought was for their mother. "If these off-worlders have miracle medicines for sore arms, they might have something to help Ma's cough. I'm gonna ask."

"The better you fight tomorrow, the more likely they will be to help."

"Aye, I know it."

When she at long last made it to her bed, despite her bone-exhaustion, she could not fall asleep. On her side, she looked out the dirty window, and thought of the building's open midsection five floors below, the enormous round terrace supported by columns with trill cores. Other daughters had learned to hang laundry to dry on the racks placed there, but her father brought her to the midlevel to watch him practice bajha. Eventually, she joined in, and those were the best of days, playing bajha, falling in love with the sport and soaking in his excited praise as she improved. They would be out there for hours at a time, Da using the broken-off handle of a shovel to train her to wield his sens-sword, the expanse of the city spread out beneath them, the edge only one blindfolded misstep away. All the while, he would tell her stories of the galaxy and its history, of pirates and kings, of the boggling array of creatures and merchandise from myriad worlds. It was where he taught her to read, to work with numbers, to think for herself. To dream.

"You are never to touch those things!"

The memory of her mother's grief-laden voice ripped into the blissful images. The cry reverberated in Jemm's mind with as much sharpness as it did that day on the terrace, when Ma discovered her wearing her father's bajha suit, the fabric billowing around Jemm's small body. Even now, lying in bed some fourteen standard years later, that moment remained vivid: the sens-sword gripped in her hands, Jemm frozen to the spot, as if she had been caught standing over a dead body with the murder weapon still in her hands.

Her father's dead body, judging by her mother's reaction. *"I swear, I'll burn all of it before the day's done!"*

"No, Ma! Please. They're Da's."

"Your Da is dead. *You'll end up the same way if you're wanting to play...that game."*

Bajha. Ma could not bring herself to utter the word. Not then. Not now. It was as if she blamed the sport for Da's death, but her father died of an infection from a broken leg he suffered in an accident in the mines. Jemm watched him die, bit by bit, day by day, burning up with fever, until it seemed a mercy when he finally breathed his last.

The bajha suit might not have his scent anymore but as long as Jemm had his boots, his suit, and his sens-sword, the spirit of Conrenn Aves would live on. Maybe that realization convinced her mother to relent on her threat to burn the gear. But it came with a caveat. *"You're never to use these things again. Do ya hear me, girl? I forbid it."*

Because it seemed to hurt her mother so, Jemm did give up bajha. It was like losing her Da all over again. At eleven years old, she sneaked out on the terrace to practice a year later, on the anniversary of his death, just once, seeking the joy, peace, and centeredness that only bajha could bring her. That one taste was not enough. She snuck out again the next week to practice. Soon she was doing it all the time. She had never set out to lie to Ma or, eventually, flat-out disobey her. It just happened to end up that way.

Her father—ring name: Badlands Fire—had dreamed of going pro but never had the chance. He had wanted to make a better life for the family, but never could. Now, it was up to her to do it. Once, bajha was only an escape from the hell that was Barésh. Now it was far more. What she needed to do now, she would do for her Da. After all, he was the one who taught her to dream in the first place.

"You're either all in or all out."

Jemm pushed upright and swung her legs off the mattress. Nico was right. There could be nothing halfway about this.

She combed her fingers through her hair that was still a wee bit damp from her shower. How pretty the strands were, how soft Then she reached for her pocketknife on the bedside table.

"All in," she murmured. Then she lifted the knife, held her breath, and sliced through the first thick hank of hair.

In the fading light the next day, Jemm walked with brisk, purposeful strides to the docks. She was dressed in full bajha gear. Under her suit a thick, reinforced padded work vest masked the fact that she had breasts, which she had further bound underneath the vest with some spare fabric. She wasn't big on top, never longed to be, thank you very much, but it was best everything was tamped down, nice and neat.

Nico was chatty, giving her all sorts of playing advice she did not need, but it made him feel important and it kept her mind off what she was about to do.

Ahead the docks loomed. Twenty-four years on Barésh and Jemm had never set foot beyond the outer secure area, let alone the docking tubes that led to actual starships. The closer they got to the port, the more the street widened—to allow truck travel—and the better the surface was beneath their boots. Most colonists walking this close to the docks had reasons for being here, and so it was no surprise seeing the curious glances and some suspicious stares thrown their way. A flycar whooshed by, slowing, the upper-class occupants behind shadowed windows wanting to have a look at them. Jemm's fingers lifted involuntarily to her hacked-off hair. Some tufts wanted to spring straight up; others swirled into waves. It left her earlobes and neck exposed. But haircuts were commonplace. Maybe the sight of a fully suited-up bajha player got them to wondering about her. After all, she was a long way from the nearest club. That, and Nico's ragged-around-the-edges appearance and tough-guy swagger did not hide the fact that they were a pair of trill rats loose in an area reserved for compound cogs, elites, and crews from the docked vessels.

Like the trio of starpilots, two males and female, who crossed the street in clean, crisp indigo-blue uniforms with silver trim. *From worlds afar.* Jemm gazed with awe at the woman, and instinctively tried to meet her gaze, to give her a sisterly nod, as one female working in a mostly man's world might do to acknowledge another. But the woman starpilot looked right through Jemm. Of course, she would. They headed for the lone virtual reality arcade in the area, probably in an attempt to pass some dead time and avoid downtown while doing it; Barésh could be intimidating to the uninitiated.

Jemm and Nico slowed to allow a truck to pull off the street and park in front of the arcade. Three men jumped out to unload it. One bald, sinewy fella had so many tattoos decorating his scalp it looked like a helmet. He opened the tailgate and withdrew some rope as the driver, a huge brute sporting a red beard with knotted ends, charged around the truck, headed straight for Nico. "You've got some nerve, Aves!"

"Run!" Nico's shout ricocheted off the buildings as he shoved Jemm out of the way. Then Red Beard grabbed Nico and threw him up against the closest wall.

CHAPTER SEVEN

Nico hit the arcade's façade so hard it knocked off some loose plaster. A light overhead smashed to the sidewalk, glass tinkling, but the patrons inside went on playing, wearing goggles with twinkling lights and headphones.

"This is from Migel Arran—with love, mate." With one hand wrapped in Nico's sweater, Red Beard drove his fist into Nico's face and plowed another punch into his gut. "And that's from me, for making me chase you around the city all week."

Jemm yanked open the zipper on her gear bag. It was a capital offense in the colony to use a sens-sword as a weapon, but that was moot at the moment. She had to save her brother's life.

But Nico climbed back to his feet and lunged at Red Beard. Another group of pristine starship crewmembers cruised up the street. They saw the commotion and did a quick about-face.

"Now, now. What ya trying to do with that, lad?" A pair of arms cinched around Jemm as tight as bands of trill, yanking her backward into a hard body and pinning her arms flush to her ribs.

She bucked and twisted. "What the crag. Get off me, you rotter."

Her attacker caught her using her thumb to arm her sens-sword and kneed it out of her hands. It skidded across the concrete, bright bursts of violet energy fizzing and snapping as the baton-blade collided with bits of glass and plaster.

"Never allow an opponent to take your sens-sword away, Jemm. It's the most unforgivable gaffe in the sport of bajha." Her father's words boomed like detonations in her ears. Her face blazed with shame.

"Get off!" She slammed her boot heel hard onto a foot. But the boot was made of thick, expensive leather, and it was like she had touched him with a feather. Body armor made it difficult to find another place to land a kick.

"Be still!" He jerked her sideways, clamped a hand over her nose and mouth, cutting off her breathing. Black spots filled her vision and she almost passed out. He removed his hand and awareness flowed back like fresh water into an ore pit. "That's better," his swank-scented voice said in her ear. "We're not supposed to hurt ya, lad. But if ya don't listen, I'll make sure your manager never walks again."

The man was large enough to make good on his promise, and something in his tone told her he would be happy to. The gangster with the head tattoos circled Nico and Red Beard, holding the coil of rope. Bot-rope. Built to obey verbal orders, its flexible trill core made it unbreakable.

Dear dome. What were they planning to do to Nico? They were large men dressed in black body armor and heavy leather, steel-toe boots. They might be armed, as well, sponsored by their boss who earned the right to carry by circumstance of birth.

Nico spat blood on the pavement. "Right nice to hear that Migel Arran loves me so much. Who can blame him? It's my bubbly charm." Red Beard's punches should have

knocked him out cold, but he was on his feet. Her brother
was somehow able to take more punishment than anyone
she knew, even having the wits to argue with charm.
"I've got a love note of my own to send. Tell him if he
wants Sea Kestrel playing Eighthnights at Rumble, the
weeknights are mine. We ain't bound by contract, and
Arran knows it."

"His rules aren't up for debate, Aves."

"We ain't bound by his rules," Jemm spoke up. "If he
thinks he can control us by force and threats, he can find
himself another champ."

That drew Red Beard's attention the way dropped
crumbs drew cave-scampers. "Ooh. A battle of wills
between Sea Kestrel and Migel Arran, eh? We'll see
who'll win that war, won't we?" Red Beard hustled over
to her, moving close enough for her to smell the faint
odor of swank on his breath. That was all she needed—
another coward who substituted the chemicals for
courage.

She kept her face impassive as he lifted a lock of hair
off her forehead. "Youth. So fleeting. Especially on
Barésh." He examined her as if looking for places to land
future blows. It was how these things went if you defied
those with power. The second encounter was always
worse. A third was most always fatal. "Arran's got a spot
saved for you in the prison league if your manager
decides to ignore the rules. Young lad like you?" He
winked, making a clicking sound with his tongue. "You'll
be a sweet piece of meat amongst all those hardened
criminals, won't ya?"

The thought of being discovered as a female behind
bars made Jemm shiver. That she did and Red Beard
noticed left a bitter taste of hatred in her mouth. It would
not matter whether or not she was guilty of any crime if
someone like Migel Arran wanted her arrested. Nico had
talked before of bajha matches played by prisoners who
arrived in chains and left the same way. Penal ships

transported them from planet to planet, and system to system, where they would dock at settlements, stage matches for money and move on. Convict players who died along the way were replaced by an endless supply of petty criminals in the frontier.

"Aye, Sea Kestrel, torn apart by the big bad carnivores. Nothing left but feathers." The other gangsters burst into laughter. "Let him go," Red Beard growled and walked away, wiping her brother's blood off his knuckles with a rag.

Set free, Jemm almost staggered, but used her innate balance to catch herself with a graceful step forward. The man who had held her walked into view. "Poor birdie," he said with a wheezy chuckle. "Tweet! Tweet!" Red sparkly lights implanted in his teeth made his mouth look as if it were filled with fresh blood. The red reflected light in his eyes was ghoulish as he waggled his elbows like a pen-fowl. "Chickey, chickey!"

Red Beard was back in Nico's face. "Arran wants you to know it's not only Narrow Margin you gotta give up to keep the peace. It's Ore's Head, too. It's no secret ya got matches scheduled there with your other players."

Nico appeared as jarred by the warning as Jemm was surprised by it. "Is that so?" he managed, but he sounded less plucky now.

"Aye. Don't make Arran send me back for ya, Aves. I won't be so lenient next time." Red Beard turned to her next. "I'll be betting on you this Eighthnight, Sea Kestrel. I expect to win like always."

People scattered as the trio returned to their truck and drove off.

Jemm retrieved her sens-sword and ran to Nico. Blood stained his best sweater, the one he had chosen to impress the off-worlders tonight, and his collar was torn. More mending work for Ma. On his forehead was an ugly lump. Blotches under his eyes were already turning purple. "It's broken," she murmured and touched her towel to his swollen bloody nose.

"It ain't the first time." Grunting, he used the wall next to them to keep his balance as he straightened. "On the bright side, no cracked ribs. Arran, that stinking cog. Sending his goon-cogs to rough me up. Talk about nerve!"

She swallowed, trying to work moisture into her mouth, her voice measured despite her entire body shaking with adrenaline. "What are we gonna do, Nico? Arran means to control us."

"He can't stop me with a busted nose and a few sore ribs."

"He'll have ya killed and me shipped off to the prison league."

Nico gave a pained laugh. "Jemm. This is street bajha. This kind of thing, it happens all the time. It's only posturing. Part of the game."

"Some game." But this was Nico's world, one she had never fully understood. It was dangerous and volatile and why she had to get him out of here before it caught up to him. "What's Ore's Head? A club?"

"Aye. I leased it."

At her first attempt to reply, no sound came out. "You leased a club. *Leased.*"

"I'm leasing to own, actually."

"By the dome," Jemm croaked. "And you were meaning to tell me when?"

"It makes better sense than renting since I'm building my own team of players. They need somewhere to practice. How Arran found out already, I've no idea."

"You're supposed to be managing our money."

"I am! Eventually, I'll own that club. I'll use the profits to buy more clubs. I'll be more powerful than Migel Arran one day."

She could not meet his animated eyes. The harder she worked to get her dream of a brother off-world, the harder he seemed to try to stay here. She glanced toward the docks. "They're probably wondering where we are."

"You go on alone, Jemm. We'll meet here later and I'll walk ya home."

"You're coming with me."

"No, I ain't. Go on. You can handle anything they'll throw at ya."

"I know that, but—"

He spread his hands. "How's it gonna look, you showing with me like this?"

The air went out of her in a weary sigh. He was right. The sight of him beaten up would not impress the off-worlders. She used the corner of the soiled towel to wipe away a smear of blood from his cheek. "You're a good manager, Nico. I've not said it enough."

"You've not said it at all," he corrected with a crooked grin.

"I should have. I wouldn't have made it this far without your help. Whatever happens tonight, know that any failures on my part weren't because of you."

"Ah, Jemm. You won't need me there to convince them you're the champ they've been waiting for. Mark my words."

The look they exchanged held so much hope, but it was tempered with the knowledge that most of the time on Barésh dreams never reached orbital velocity.

Then Nico turned away to light up a vape, and Jemm resumed the walk to the docks as if the terrible interruption had not happened, as if prison leagues and clubs leased with Button's lunch money had not been discussed. All of it had to be buried. Only the next few hours mattered.

Where the dome curved to the ground was a portal wide enough for the road to pass through and tall enough to accommodate large trucks. Through the opening blew a steady breeze of cool, dry air, telling of a difference in air pressure between the city and the docks beyond. The port proper was a hubbub of trucks uploading supplies and unloading ore, but as she left the busy area behind, the passage narrowed into a transparent tunnel that branched off into other tubes, each with starships clamped on to their ends like kits suckling on a teat.

The tubes were for travelers and tradesmen to transition from Barésh's habitation dome to the vessels that would transport them anywhere they wanted in the known galaxy. Her eager steps carried her into a land of giants. The great ships gleamed in the starlight and floodlights, their massive landing truncheons firmly planted on the gritty surface outside. Other craft hovered in stationary orbits far overhead, requiring shuttles to reach them.

Arriving at Star Tube J, she found a checkpoint staffed by a couple of security guards passing the time playing cards. Behind them waited Sir Vedla's craft. Like its owner, *Chéya's Resolute* was sleek and hard, and luxurious in the way the other working ships were not. The ship's name was painted in Federation Basic as all vessels' names were, but underneath the name was a line of exotic characters in a fluid font she guessed was the ancient language of his homeworld. His family went all the way back to the earliest days of recorded history, chronicled in the Treatise of Trade itself, the most important document in the galaxy. In contrast, her family history could pretty much be summed up by the bajha suit she wore.

She ran a hand over her suit, the patchwork of repairs, the oldest of which were stitched carefully, her mother's tiny stitches made with love for her husband. The later repairs after Jemm took over wearing the suit in secret and was forced to do any mending herself were rough and uneven. It was no secret she drove tugs a lot better than she could sew.

She cleared her throat. The dozers looked up, their faces immediately showing wariness and then mocking curiosity. She squared her shoulders, acting like she belonged here, and deserved to be here, and thrust out a hand with the security card Sir Vedla had given her. From there, it all went downhill.

CHAPTER EIGHT

Klark drummed impatient fingers on his thigh. His focus swung between watching Skeet and Xirri drill to the viewscreen linked to the security camera at the top of the gangway to the ship.

Was Sea Kestrel going to show or not? His mind concocted all sorts of disastrous directions the evening could take. Was his favorable opinion of the manager correct? The man was young, eager, clever, but also streetwise and slum-smart. While Klark trusted his instincts, there was always the possibility he had erred giving the man the gold credit. Nico Aves could very well pocket it and, along with Sea Kestrel, disappear, never to be seen again.

No. Deep down he knew otherwise. The player would be here. The fiery hope he saw in Sea Kestrel's eyes matched what he felt about this venture. His underdog, his diamond in the rough, wanted this chance as much as he wanted to offer it to him—*and* the amateur seemed to possess the pluck and determination to defy his manager-handler if need be.

But if not? Klark drained a glass of ion-infused water then frowned. The thought of returning to the palace and abandoning this venture was too disheartening too consider.

"Your Highness."

Klark practically jumped out of his chair at the voice. One of his starpilots was centered in the viewscreen. "I have Barésh port security on the flight-deck comm. They say they've apprehended a bandit trying to sneak aboard our vessel."

"A bandit?" The gangway vid feed displayed nothing but the empty ramp in the glow of a floodlight. "Where?"

"They've detained him at the checkpoint. But they wanted to inform us of the fact before taking him into custody. Because if it is a bandit, Your Highness, according to their description he's dressed for bajha."

Damnation. Klark pushed to his feet. "That's Sea Kestrel."

"Shall I send you the checkpoint vid feed?"

"Yes. By all means."

Skeet and Xirri emerged from the ring, towels looped around the necks only to laugh in incredulous delight as they joined Klark in staring at a soundless vid of Sea Kestrel resisting what appeared to be an attempt by port security officers to frisk him.

Kes stood taller than both men, but the balance of power was not in his favor. A surge of protectiveness set Klark's blood to boiling. "This is completely, unequivocally unacceptable."

With his starpilot hot on his heels, he pounded down the gangway and into the star tube, driven by a pure need to safeguard both his plans to repair and boost his family's standing in the Trade Federation and the street player on which all those plans hinged.

"I said, put your hands out!" The guard held a set of handcuffs to slap on Jemm.

She was smart enough to keep her arms pressed to her sides. "What for? I didn't do nothing."

The leader of the two shook his head. "What about that gear ya got there, lad? You didn't come by it honestly."

"Aye, I did. It's mine. My father gave it to me."

"That's another charge against you. It's a capital offense in this colony to use a sens-sword."

"It ain't against the law for playing bajha. I told ya, that's why I'm here."

"A bajha match on a starship?"

True that it sounded unreal to have a starship with a fight ring, but a *Vash Nadah* could have anything they wanted, wherever they wanted. "Call Sir Vedla if ya don't believe me."

"That won't be necessary. I am here." The *Vash* stormed toward Jemm and the cluster of security cogs. Charcoal-gray workout pants covered his long legs; a shirt of the same hi-tech material molded to the musculature of his arms and chest. Behind him was a starpilot, resplendent in a crisp indigo-blue flight suit with sparkling silver piping and matching silver wings on his left chest. They looked like avenging gods compared to the dozers manning the checkpoint. It was like summoning a rescue from the Ever After itself. All that was missing were the trumpets and billowing clouds.

Sir Vedla's terrifying gold eyes were searing hot with fury, yet at the same time he came across as chillingly calm when he stopped in front of her. "Are you all right? Have they harmed you?"

"I don't know what they would've done, sir. But I'm fine." Her voice, forced deeper, came out husky as she wiped a damp hand on her thigh.

He whirled on the guards. "What is the meaning of this?"

The men peeled away from him like sheet metal under the heat of a blowtorch. "We caught this trill rat trying to sneak into Star Tube J, and he's armed," the lead offered with weak bravado.

"That's a sens-sword, and he's no bandit. Moreover, he was not sneaking. He's a well-known bajha player in this colony. Invited—by me—for an exhibition match."

"I did not realize that, sir."

"Obviously. There has been an abysmal failure of common sense here. Who is your supervisor?"

"Ardo-Illy Heddad," the man mumbled.

"Note that," Sir Vedla told his starpilot.

"Already done, My Lord."

My Lord? The manners of the elite were as foreign to her as the rest of this new life of which she was getting a tiny taste. If "lord" and "sir" were used interchangeably, she would soon find out.

"Kes, if you would like to add any additional infractions to the growing list of grievous offenses, now's the time." Sir Vedla's concerned gaze smoothed over her like warm hands. "You've got bruises in the shape of fingers on your jaw."

From the gangster who had almost smothered her. Jemm swallowed hard.

"Which one of these men did this to you?"

She shook her head. "It wasn't them."

"Who then?"

"That's another story."

"I look forward to hearing it."

Jemm did not look forward to telling it.

The *Vash* gave the security cogs an icy glare. "This is not the last you will hear of this." Then he motioned with his chin to Jemm. "Let's go."

He did not so much as walk with them as he did lead the way. In a few long strides he had left her and the starpilot behind. Then, realizing they were not with him, he turned. A regal brow lifted as he waited for them to catch up.

"About those checkpoint guards, Sir Vedla," Jemm said, trying not to sound so breathless. "Those fellas are only security cogs. If ya report them to their boss, they'll be fired."

"And deserve to be."

"Aye, maybe, but if they're like a lot of people in the colony, they won't have a backup plan. Their families could starve—or worse, will have to work down in the pits. No one wants to go there."

Sir Vedla glanced sideways at her in surprise. A furrow had formed between his brows. "What are you saying? I should dismiss filing a complaint?"

"Aye. I'm to blame for the trouble. I didn't have the kind of ID they wanted."

"You didn't need it. I logged in all the pertinent information last night. It should have been sufficient. This is Barésh, for heaven's sake. You'd think it was the Wheel the way they're so uptight about security."

The Wheel was the seat of government for the Trade Federation that ruled the entire galaxy. He tossed around the name as if it were nothing. "Still, they wouldn't have expected someone like me to show up here."

He seemed to consider her, and what she had asked of him. "Kuentin," he said after a moment. "Hold off contacting anyone about the security guards. For now."

"As you wish, My Lord."

"Firing fools is one thing. Causing starvation is quite another," Sir Vedla explained, frowning. "That is not right."

"You don't know Barésh, then," she said under her breath.

But he heard her. "The laws of the Trade Federation are supposed to protect every citizen, no matter what an individual's personal wealth. This is the foundation of the Treatise of Trade. My ancestors fought and died for the rights of all people. Something needs to be done if those laws aren't being followed here." Vexation gave his tone a sharper edge. "Where is Earth in all this? They certainly complained loudly enough about wanting to manage their own neighborhood. King Romlijhian B'kah gave his blessing to naming Earth as sovereign administrator of the frontier. It's more power than any planet other than a *Vash* homeworld has ever held. But have you seen any Earth-dwellers around?"

Jemm shook her head. "I wouldn't know what one looked like."

"If they'd shown half the interest in helping the frontier as they do marrying into the *Vash Nadah,* Barésh might not have the problems you've described. But that's a political debate best saved for another day." He swiped his card at Tube J's entry. The gate slid open. "Next time you come, that's all you have to do."

"If I can get past the checkpoint."

"Oh, you will. Trust me on that." He hesitated, seeming to sniff the air.

"What?" Nervously, she hoped the soap she had used wasn't too sweet-smelling and thus not boyish enough. It was all they had in the apartment.

He shook his head. "Nothing. I thought I... It's not important. How is your arm, by the way?"

"The salve you gave me healed it."

He made a sound of relief in his throat. "I expected I'd have to summon a physician."

"They don't treat mineworkers."

"What? Why not?"

"Mostly because we can't afford it. We have access to potions for most ailments at the markets."

"They would not have dared to refuse my request, no matter whom I wanted seen." His lips compressed with disapproval. "I don't see how your colony's physicians can justify hiding behind compound walls, barricaded from the masses they're bound by oath to treat."

"Because there's more money to be made taking care of the rich and powerful." He must know that. Everyone did. Why did he seem so surprised? Despite what Sir Vedla might think was right or wrong, on Barésh Trade Federation law had never applied to anyone but the elites. She had heard of Earth, but their involvement remained just another unconfirmed rumor. Barésh had no champion. "So, there's no physician on your ship?"

"No. A trip of this short length didn't necessitate one. Several staff members are trained in first aid, however." As if sensing there was more to her question, he looked her over. "Why?"

She cleared her throat. "Just curious." She wasn't going to ask him to help Ma until she accomplished what she had come here to do: play bajha to the best of her ability.

"I see you traveled here dressed in full gear, Kes. That isn't necessary, either. There is a locker room and showers on board my ship for your use."

None of which she would be using. On this ship she would need to hold fast to both her wits and her clothing.

"Where is your manager, by the way? Nico?"

"He...couldn't make it."

"Couldn't make it? I'm surprised Nico is absent when he seemed so eager to participate last night." He glanced with renewed concern at her jaw. "Does it by chance have anything to do with the bruises on your face?"

He was too perceptive. "We ran into a scheduling conflict," she hedged.

Sir Vedla made a sound in his throat that was amused and annoyed at the same time. "You hold up quite well under interrogation, Kes."

"You'll soon learn to give Lord Vedla the information he desires." Kuentin the starpilot's grin conveyed patience, even affection, toward his master. "The players' welfare matters to him, and not only in the arena."

"Kuentin is right." The *Vash* eyed her as they paused at the top of the gangway. "I take care of my own. However, you didn't answer my question."

She tried to form the best answer. "We had a conflict of interest with the owner of the club where I fight on Eighthnights. Nico had to stay behind because of it."

She could tell her answer had not satisfied him. Worse, it had generated both his curiosity and concern. But by then they were climbing up the gangway with a hollow cacophony of boots clanging against metal and rivets. The hatch hissed open and they entered the ship.

Vast banks of electronics filled the area to her right—the flight deck, complete with a pair of seats in front of joysticks, from where the ship was controlled by the pilots. Myriad crisp and tiny lights glowed like miniature stars. A huge window in the nose of the vessel framed a view of the docks but would show the expanse of open space when underway. Seats of pristine real leather were placed here and there, harnesses limp without bodies to fill them.

Her first glimpse of the interior of a starship. She hoped it was not her last. It was better than anything she had imagined. To the left, a corridor reached deeper into the vessel. Before she could absorb more of the amazing sight, a different starpilot greeted them.

"You're Kes," he said with a friendly smile. "Commander Belkar here. Welcome." He peered behind her. "Weren't there going to be two of you?"

"Aye. My manager couldn't make it."

"Scheduling conflict, apparently," a skeptical Sir Vedla said dryly.

A younger man about Nico's age approached. "Lord Vedla, Mr. Skeet and Mr. Xirri have inquired about the evening meal. Shall I prepare the dining hall?"

"Yes, please. We will dine after practice."

Jemm's first thought was that there would be a good meal in her near future. Her second was that the starship was large enough to contain a dining hall and an arena. Sir Vedla seemed to take pleasure in her marveling gaze. *"Chéya's Resolute* is used frequently for team travel. There are twenty separate bedroom quarters, a generous galley, dining room, gym, pool and, yes, a bajha arena. Regulation size, but with limited seating. Come, I will show you."

He strode away. This time she knew she had to hurry to keep up. The ship buzzed with a palpable humming energy, not the manic desperation that was all she had ever known. There were more people around than she had expected, all of them going somewhere with purpose. Sir Vedla, or Lord Vedla, whatever he was, probably did not tolerate any lollygaggers.

Her guess was that he was not much older than she was, a few years at most. Yet, he was so comfortable being in command, and in this life of being waited on hand and foot, having won the hereditary jackpot of being wealthy beyond imagination. In spite of all that good fortune, he seemed to bear the burden of what he was on his shoulders, constantly reeling himself back from smiles, laughter, or teasing, as if there was only a limited amount of time in life to be spent on lightheartedness, and he was required to budget those moments. Whatever his responsibilities were—and they must extend beyond his bajha team—she sensed they weighed him down like a ballast.

Her life could not be more different. As a working class lass and her family's sole income earner, her biggest worry was survival. Making sure there was enough money for food, being able to afford running water to the apartment, or where the family would turn if she got injured or sick like Da had. His death forced her to enter the workforce at thirteen after they had exhausted the last of his bajha earnings. Those were the stark responsibilities she knew too well and learned to bear far too young. Sir Vedla might as well be another species with the kinds of concerns he bore daily, compared to her. Yet, he had crossed the great divide between them to offer her this incredible opportunity.

A man hurried by with an armful of towels. Another carried a tray of bottled drinks, frost still sheeting off the glass. By the dome, Vedla had brought a club's worth of server staff with him.

"Hydrate," he said and snatched two bottles from the server's tray, handing her one. She drank in the sight of the cold bottle with her eyes, remembering when she and Nico pilfered the ones Migel Arran had offered only a few short weeks ago. She would not dare repeat that gaffe.

Clutching the drink, Jemm followed him deeper into the ship. The air was as fresh and clean as out in the tubes, but it held the scents of many more things: cooked food, leather furniture, a tart and fruity cleaning solution, a faint acrid odor generated by the ship's equipment...

And the *Vash*. His scent wafted behind him: a masculine mix of clean clothing, aristo soap, and the heady scent of his exertion. She liked his smell.

No, Jemm...

Focus.

Think like a lad.

"Skeet and Xirri are in the ring, drilling," Sir Vedla explained as he walked a few strides ahead of her in the narrow corridor. "They've been participating in our yearly goodwill tour these last few weeks. Team Eireya brings bajha to the fans as way to thank them. I borrowed the players, if you will, to assist me in your tryout, but they'll return to the tour late tomorrow to act as public relations superstars." He slowed a bit, allowing her to walk at his side. "There's a lot more to being a pro than you might realize. But you're not in this alone. If I sign you, I'll be around to help bring you up to speed. Most new players need some assistance learning to deal with the public. They become instant galactic celebrities, after all, and are exposed to all the temptations that come with it."

Fooling Sir Vedla was one thing, but if she were lucky enough to become a pro, she would have to dupe the entire Trade Federation while touring countless worlds and meeting untold number of people. Dome help her.

"If I wasn't confident in you, you would not be here," he continued. "My team is only as strong as its players. I've set my sights on Team Eireya winning the Galactic Cup, and I will do whatever it takes to make that happen."

She snapped her focus away from the many shipboard marvels around her to consider the *Vash* once more. His declaration reflected the same, all-consuming hunger for a dream that she recognized in herself. Their dreams intersected. It made them allies. If she succeeded, he did, too.

"Here we are," he said and brushed his fingers over a lighted square, causing a glass door as thick as her arm to swoosh silently out of their way. "The arena."

Almost three-hundred-sixty degrees of glass surrounded the large space. One half was dedicated to an outside view. The other half looked over a pristine arena with white walls and floor.

"Kes!"

"Sea Kestrel."

The cheerful voices of Skeet and Xirri yanked her focus to the ring. They were both suited up, their expressions friendly as they welcomed her.

"You're in the ring first, Raff." The *Vash* turned to her next. "Ready your sens-sword."

She was still marveling at the regulation-quality arena when his order woke her up to what she had come here to do. The white-walled, featureless chamber was silent. Only a few scuff marks on the ring's white padded surface hinted that it was used for anything other than display. Three rows of spectator seats rose up from the floor, situated outside a transparent wall encasing the ring.

Sir Vedla rapped his knuckles against it. "Nanocrylic. This is what differentiates the arenas used in regulation play. "It is a material infused with nanobots, microscopic robots, that give it the ability to display what's inside—in the ring—to the audience sitting on the outside, even in the complete absence of light. Because, also unlike the bajha you're used to, we play in the complete absence of light. Headgear, but no blindfolds. No eye covering whatsoever. The nanocrylic also shields the players from outside sounds. Yes, you'll play in total silence. All this leaves the players to rely on their remaining senses. Intuition, instinct, are what elevates one player over another. Intuition can be sharpened, but if it's not there, if it's not born in a person, it cannot be developed."

"Regulation play is much more difficult than what you're used to," Xirri remarked to her as he buffed his already flawless sens-sword with a cloth. "Hearing your opponent stomping around on wood floors, peeking through blindfolds, you're used to taking advantage of all the inputs while you play. Here, we have none of that."

Jemm glared at him. "There's no peeking allowed." Did he think that was how she won the matches? "Sounds, aye. But seeing thorough the blindfolds is cheating. Cheating will get ya expelled from the match—and from bajha for good. One offense and you're gone. The refs check our blindfolds after our managers do."

Skeet bent over to fasten the tops of his boots. "All Raff means is that your learning curve may be pretty steep."

"So, don't feel bad when I whoop you," Xirri added in her ear with a daring grin as he sauntered past, his lean, athletic body filled with confidence and covered with an immaculate and expensive bajha suit.

With her sens-sword gripped in frayed, worn-out gloves, Jemm followed him into the ring. No emotion crossed the studied calm of her face.

"Raff—catch." Sir Vedla tossed Xirri a blindfold.

"What's this for, sir?" the pro asked, startled.

"If we've a street bajha player as our guest, we might as well warm up with a game of street bajha."

"What?" Xirri looked to Skeet for help, but his team captain was laughing too hard.

"It'll take more than blindfolds," Jemm argued. "We'll need noise, like loud music and people—talking, cheering, stomping. But we need an audience for that."

"Great idea!" Skeet grinned. "We can import the crowd from the arcade across the street from the docks."

"Negative," Sir Vedla said. "Con," he called out. "Summon all crewmembers not involved with official duties or who aren't on required rest to the arena."

"Summoning all off-duty nonessential crewmembers," the controller droned in reply.

Skeet laughed harder. Xirri spread his hands. "Sir."

"Don't whine, Xirri," Skeet said. "It's not attractive."

Xirri mouthed something foul at his teammate, Jemm guessed, then lifted the flexible helmet worn for regulation play over his head. "I'll take that." Sir Vedla reached for the helmet.

"Now I know you're kicking me to the curb, sir," Xirri said with a laugh. "You're going to let a street bajha player melt the hair off my head."

"Not at all. You'll both play with sens-swords at level one." Then the *Vash* spoke to the ceiling. "Con, play Bonali strings quartet, third orchestration." A melody came over the sound system that caused pleasure to suffuse Sir Vedla's face. "That should do nicely."

Jemm choked down a laugh. "If ya want to put a babe to sleep, maybe. In that case ya might as well not have anything."

"It's one of his favorites," Xirri said under his breath.

"Perhaps," Sir Vedla conceded. "But not, apparently, the appropriate choice here. What music do you suggest, Kes?"

"Thump. That's what's played in all the bars and clubs. It's digital. You heard it last night. It goes thump, thump, thump."

Xirri clutched his chest. "Like your heartbeat right before you flatline."

"The songs differ depending what tune is layered on top of the base beat. They lower it for the matches, but not too much. In case anyone wants to dance."

"I couldn't tell with all the booing and ketta-cat calling," Sir Vedla said dryly. "Controller, search archives for thump music."

"Searching...searching. I have found one selection of thump music. It is a sample. It is seventeen seconds in length. Shall I play it?"

"Not long enough. Whew!" Xirri said.

"Con," Sir Vedla said. "Play sample selection of thump music. Infinite repeat." His lips quirked in the barest of smiles. "Survivable decibel level."

"I do not understand: survivable decibel level."

"Level five, please," he told the controller. The music began.

By now, members of the crew were filing in. Skeet waved them in. "Come one and all. Take a seat anywhere. Tonight only, free admission."

Xirri gaped at the spectacle then rolled his eyes. "Sir, you're not really serious about having us play with the lights up and all this noise."

"Of course I am. How else will I simulate street bajha? You're an excellent player, Raff. One of my best. A little distraction is nothing you can't handle."

Klark tried to imagine thump music coming through the palace speakers. What would Uncle Yul think? The mere thought generated a laugh. When did he let out an honest laugh while at the palace? Not often. Here, far from home, he was enjoying himself, and had been since arriving on Barésh, despite some of the unsavory qualities that made this rock, well, Barésh. It was all a far cry from the dry, dull, all-too similar days at the palace.

"I need my blindfold inspected."

He glanced over at Sea Kestrel's voice. "Yonson, take a look at Raff's blindfold. I'll see to Kes." He walked over to the amateur and cinched the blindfold tighter. To check for snugness, he ran his fingertips along the edge where it followed the contours of the player's head: nape, temples, and cheekbones.

Sea Kestrel went rigid. Klark paused. It was clear the young player was averse to being touched, even in such a benign way. If beatings were a part of his life, it was understandable. The idea of someone manhandling Sea Kestrel rekindled his anger upon seeing the faint fingerprint-shaped bruises, again conjuring protective instincts he never knew he had. Kes might not feel like sharing the details, but Klark would learn what they were. He would know everything about Sea Kestrel in due time.

He finished up. "All seems to be in order, Kes. I don't feel gaps anywhere."

Only when he removed his hands and stepped back did Sea Kestrel's gloves come up to recheck the blindfold. "Aye. That feels right."

"Excellent," Klark said above the music. "Usually we say 'lights' when we want a match to start. In this case, I'll say 'commence' when it's time to begin. Or, rather, I'll shout it."

"This is hardly noise, sir."

"The others here might disagree, including me. It does give you an advantage over Raff Xirri, something few bajha players in the galaxy can boast. Don't let him intimidate you. Try to last as long as you can. That's all I ask."

Kes seemed to stand a little taller. "That's what Nico told me the night I played against Black Hole. My first match."

"You never played before that?" It did not seem plausible. Surely he had misheard.

"Not in any kind of competition, no." A shrug. "But I've practiced bajha almost all my life. My Da taught me."

Incredible, Klark thought. That much talent in raw material form, begging for him to refine it. He could not wait to get started, and hoped the fates gave him the opportunity.

Skeet gave Klark a pointed index finger upward to signal that he had secured Xirri's blindfold. At least the player now wore a cocky grin in reaction to the situation into which Klark had thrown him.

Xirri moved closer to Sea Kestrel. "Nervous?" Klark overheard his player asking the amateur.

"Aye. A bit."

"I won't be too hard on you," Xirri said kindly, but the edge in the pro's tone told Klark the true story. Xirri had a lot of talent and a passion to win that no make-believe street bajha match had a chance of extinguishing. Kes would have to be able to handle anything he dished out. Weakness had no place in the pro circuit.

"Let's hear some noise!" To the pounding beat, Skeet walked around the arena, waving his hands, goading Klark's starship crew into cheers and applause—and to stomp their feet to the thumping music. "Come on, folks. Is that the best you can do?"

The crew gave a weak imitation of a real Baréshti crowd, and the music was more annoying than loud, but there was enough disturbance to simulate a street bajha match. Without the gods-awful stink.

"Players!" Klark raised his fist. The noise ebbed some in anticipation of what was to come. Both Xirri and Sea Kestrel lifted their sens-swords a few inches above the playing surface, their boots placed at shoulder width. Their bodies might be motionless, poised, but they were reaching out with their minds, already beginning the hunt, even though the match had not yet formally begun. The pause seemed to last forever and carry with it the weight of destiny, of fate. Then he arced his fist downward. "Commence!"

CHAPTER NINE

In the first seconds of the match something hit Jemm on the shoulder. Other items showered her, bouncing off her with the airiness of wadded-up paper. Something crunched under her boot with the consistency of a disposal cup. The crew was lobbing trash into the ring.

In a real fight club, throwing anything into the ring would get a spectator in trouble, likely booted from the audience and beaten up out back, but these off-worlders deserved credit for trying so hard to imitate a street bajha match.

"They're throwing stuff," she heard Xirri complain. "Skeet is a dead man. I'll tell you that." But, with the match underway, she was not of the mind to chitchat.

She glided backward and away. The regulation playing floor was spongy, distracting her for a moment, but she willed her pulse to slow, and her breathing followed suit. With her sens-sword gripped in steady hands, she let her awareness fan out. Out, out...farther and farther...swirling like a net cast over the surface of an infinite sea.

Like Da had taught her.

Xirri's annoyance at the debris pelting them lingered along with his irritation at the cheers and clapping, but then he vanished also.

Panic sparked as she searched for him. *Quiet your mind. He'll sense you.* Step by sidestep, she circled the pro, pushing everything else out of her mind that was not directly related to this match, this opponent. This moment.

She reached out, searching for him. Xirri was good— lightyears better than any of her challengers in the clubs. No wonder he was a pro.

Suddenly, he lunged at her from an unexpected direction. She whirled away, her back arching, as Xirri passed by all too close. And then he was gone.

Another barrage of trash flew into the ring. Xirri did not like the flying garbage, and most of it was aimed at him. She had never endured a trash shower while playing, but she was used to tuning out distractions. Not so Raff Xirri. A ball of paper ricocheted off his body, hitting her in the chin, letting her know he was close by. His exasperation sputtered like the glowing end of a vape in a dark cave.

She shifted her weight, stepped backward, her boots soundlessly padding. She didn't even breathe as she arced her sens-sword around to where she had sensed him last. Her arms came up, hyper-awareness leading her swing. Her sens-sword slapped sideways on his chest plate, energy pulsing faintly, but not registering as a hit. Sloppy—body hits were frowned upon by the league. But it allowed her to sense the backwash of the pro's surprise…the echo of his heartbeat. Then, grunting silently, she twisted her arms, angled her wrists to bring the blunt tip of the sens-sword home. Xirri parried, but her sens-sword slid past his to impact his chest plate, vibrating from her hands to her teeth. A valid hit.

She dropped to one knee, head bowed, her breaths coming in pants, sweat trickling down one temple.

Slowly she came back to the real world, surfacing bit by bit, until she felt herself being pulled to her feet by a hand wrapped around her wrist.

The first thing she heard was Sir Vedla's clipped but triumphant cheer, his hands clapping together. The first thing she saw was Skeet's bright white grin as he yanked off her blindfold. He laughed heartily, teasing his teammate. "Sea Kestrel beat you, Raff Xirri! He finished you like last night's dinner. This is what happens when you get cocky." To Jemm, he said, "You defeated your first pro. Good job."

Disarming her weapon, she glanced sheepishly at Xirri. He had definitely been the main target of the projectiles, most likely Skeet's.

"No fair! It was a hostile audience. They were throwing rubbish at me." With an amused grin, Xirri strode over to Jemm and grasped her arm, their gloves wrapping hard around each other's wrists. A well-regarded pro had been taken down by a dive-bar sword-swinger, but his smile gave no hint that he felt bad about it. "Things will go a little different for you in the rematch," he warned with a dangerous glitter in his eyes, "when we play the way *I* play the game."

"Not yet." Sir Vedla pointed to her. "Kes, hydrate, then return to the ring. Yonson, you're up next. This time with official league rules."

The service staff were already busy clearing the playing surface of trash.

As Jemm drank her fill, dashing the back of her glove across her lips, the *Vash* rattled off what she could expect with Skeet in the arena. "Yes, I'm throwing you into the fire with my captain, without your having a full understanding of the game rules, or the experience, of course, but we all know you can play bajha. Now it's time to measure how much your performance degrades without the cues you're used to."

Few street-bajha players were able to adapt to league rules—he had warned her about that just yesterday. If she wanted to be the exception, she had better concentrate on his every word. It might make the difference between winning the opportunity to go pro, or returning home, her hopes dashed by a missed chance.

"What I will do now is simulate what you can expect. I'm not going to actually play, but offer a quick lesson. First, check that your sens-sword is switched off." Sir Vedla pulled his long-sleeved overshirt over his head, stripping down to a lighter weight black T-shirt underneath. The briefest glimpse of ripped abs, a flat belly, smooth, tawny skin with no body art, no scars, no roadmap of a lifetime of hardships, before he wadded up the heavier shirt and tossed it aside. His body was as hard and unforgiving as his face, but with a brutal sleekness, as if he were made of skin, sinew, muscle, and nothing else. He was a deadly weapon on legs tempered with an air of bred-in arrogance. His physical appearance was at odds with his kindness to her. The disparity was fascinating.

He walked up to her with a helmet and lowered it over her head. "It's not custom, of course, but how does it feel?"

Seeing the Team Eireya logo—a simple graphic of a bird of prey, its wings spread—on the black headgear was surreal and also thrilling. She had seen images of league pros in full regalia, and thought they looked badass. The helmet weighed almost nothing yet covered her entire skull and the upper half of her face. She followed the edges with her glove, and pressed down on the top to make sure it was fitted firmly to her head. Cutouts left her ears and eyes exposed. A guard shielded the bridge of her nose. Only her mouth and chin remained unprotected. But as in street bajha, hitting bare flesh, whether by accident or on purpose, was a sign of a sloppy, second-rate player and a sure way to suffer ridicule and be expelled from the sport. "Good," she replied. The helmet would be one more distraction to ignore in a long list of them, but she was ready. Aye, and eager to go up against Yonson Skeet next, no matter what the outcome might be.

"Excellent." Sir Vedla donned a pair of glasses. "These eye shields are light enhancers that will allow me to see you, but you will not be able to see me. In the way non-players know to see, that is. Shall we begin?"

She made sure her weapon was disarmed then closed her hands around the grip. "Aye."

He called out, "Lights!"

The darkness was immediate. She had never experienced darkness so complete, so suffocating. It was said the deepest caves were like this: lightless, airless death traps. She pulled in a breath on instinct as her mind needed to make sure an atmosphere still existed.

"Don't be jarred by the absence of light. That same place your mind already goes during play is still there. It doesn't change with silence and the dark. In fact, it may intensify."

Sir Vedla moved away, but his presence, her awareness of him, did not fade. He remained present like the heat of a blaze did even when you were not next to the fire.

"Bajha dates back to prehistory, to the very ancients who created all we know, birthed by the Great Mother Herself. It has always been a game of warriors, and it still is. Always will be. The practice of bajha helps us attain a higher state of consciousness. It develops our intuition and instinct to their full potential. This is how a man becomes the greatest warrior possible, a worthy protector, and an exceptional and memorable lover."

Crag me. The *Vash* used bajha to perfect his skills in bed? It brought a whole new meaning to thrust and parry, not to mention sparks. *Quiet your mind.* In the next breath she crushed her reaction to that bombshell, which was nothing like anything her father had told her about the sport.

"In competitive bajha the goal, of course, is to hunt an opponent. To track him, and tag him." Sir Vedla's voice had come from a different direction than she expected. But even as that thought registered, she sensed that he had moved again.

Jemm stared wide-eyed into the all-encompassing blackness, her heartbeat an accompaniment to Sir Vedla's voice. "As bajha players, we use our somatosensory system daily as everyone else does, using the five senses to perceive the world around us. In bajha, the absence of the usual five senses forces us to rely more on scents, the blood coursing through our veins, the hair on our body, and even taste. But in bajha, we rely on our neurons, too. They're specialized cells, the smallest component of our nervous system. With them we can see...but not with our eyes. We can listen, but..."

"Not with our ears," Jemm said under her breath along with him, hearing her father's patient voice teaching her.

"Neurons allow us to see and to hear, to feel and to taste. In the dark, they will point to your prey."

He had moved again, but she was better able to follow him as her mind settled, her awareness reaching out. "Where am I, Kes?"

She paused, felt, *sensed*, and poked a glove in his direction.

"Yes! Excellent. Most would point to the last place they heard my voice, but you waited to detect me, and found me. Think of that mindfulness as a fishnet, how you would cast it out over the sea."

Spinning, fanning out over a blue, blue sea, the net bejeweled with droplets of water. Her father's words echoed in her mind from across the years, bringing with it the images she always imagined while playing. "It's what my father told me, too. He played bajha. He taught me about the in-between that not everyone can sense. He also compared it to a sea. In bajha, you dive into the in-between to keep your opponent from finding you."

"Yes, exactly. You said your father played? He doesn't anymore?" His voice was nearer now. Interest had lured him close.

"He died when I was a child. He was a mine mechanic. There was a collapse in the caves. It shattered his leg. A few days later the fever took him."

"Fever. Great Mother. I'm aghast to hear that a man can die from an infection a mere fifteen-minute walk from starships capable of light-speed travel."

She felt his horror-struck sympathy like a physical touch. "Aye, it's true."

"How did he know about seas? Was he from the off-worlds?"

"No. He learned from being told, like me. Also at the arcades. He watched vids and told me about them."

"So, you never saw a sea. Your father never saw a sea. Yet, he was able to teach the concept, and you have excelled to extraordinary levels employing it. Incredible." There was a brief, deep, and contemplative gap in the conversation. Then, he said, "I think you're ready to play Mr. Skeet. Lights!"

The illumination came up slowly, allowing her eyes to adjust. Sir Vedla removed his glasses. Yonson Skeet joined them in the ring. "You gave Sea Kestrel all the secrets to defeating me, eh, sir? Just don't share anything with Team Sienna, Kes. That's the B'kah's team." He was busy fastening the neck clasps of his beautiful bajha suit, his outfit as clean and bright as his broad grin that dimpled both cheeks. A galactic celebrity. His boyish charm was disarming, the kind of demeanor designed to make a person let down their guard.

It would not work on her. This was the match that mattered, and Skeet had no intention of letting her win it. Not that she expected to, but there would be no allowances like there were with Xirri, no handicapping the game. Skeet's reputation as the captain of a pro team, and his ego, was on the line if she beat him at his own game. Despite all of it, she had to fight to win.

They took their places, headgear on, blindfolds off. She worked to rein in her runaway heartbeat and screaming nerves as all her dreams and doubts came crashing together at once.

I'm ready, Da. Guide me.

"Lights!" Sir Vedla shouted, and plunged the ring into darkness. But the word "lights" did not have a chance to fade in her ears before Yonson Skeet came at her, fast and hard.

CHAPTER TEN

Jemm barely evaded Skeet's swing and almost did
not make it out of his way before his sens-sword
skittered along her left hip, hissing, but far from
her chest plate.

She almost stumbled in her haste to put distance
between them, both mental and physical. This was
Skeet's domain, and he made sure she heard that loud and
clear from the first seconds of the match.

As she fought to regain her poise and take control as
she was long accustomed to doing, Skeet used his sens-
sword to swat her backside. The cog! Body hits were
considered fouls and poor sportsmanship in regulation
play. He wanted to unbalance her and steal her
composure. But she held her emotions in check with as
steely a grip as she did her sens-sword.

She reeled away and swatted him back, feeling
exhilaration return.

Silence.

No cheering or laughing. No thunderous stomping.
Just her rough breathing and pounding heartbeat she was
so desperate to keep muted. It was unnerving not hearing
the crowd's reaction. It hit her then that she loved the

cheers and noise as much as she did the sport itself. She had come to expect hearing the crowd's reaction to her moves. Without it she was alone with her opponent.

Jemm glided away from the pro, away…away, diving deep as if into a body of water, imagining tiny streams of vanishing bubbles the only trace of her presence left behind. By the time Skeet would sense that trace, she would be where he would not find her.

But Skeet followed her in and out of the infinite place that only bajha players and a few other lucky souls knew well. It brought back a poignant memory of playing bajha with her father. *He's as good as Da.* A blur of swordplay, bursts of air, an almost blurted-out curse from her, the stealthy padding of Skeet's boots against the cushioned floor. It went on and on, the longest and most rigorous match she had ever played.

Yonson Skeet kept command of the contest from beginning to almost the end, when he appeared to her, unexpectedly, for a fraction of a breath. His lingering scent, the heat of his skin, and she knew she had him, those racing seconds that felt like forever as she felt him coming about, his sens-sword whooshing through the air, a well-planted boot, and then her shock as his sens-sword landed in the center of her chest, mocking any prospect she had held of tagging him.

Sparks heated her face and blazed in the darkness, but Skeet kept pressing forward, forcing her to skip backward, making his victory over her a chest-pounding, primitive roar of a statement, the aggressive, bajha version of ripping out and eating an enemy's heart.

"Lights!"

The illumination came up slowly yet was somehow blinding. Blinking, gasping, Jemm fell to one knee, her head bowed, the taste of defeat on her tongue for the first time.

She fought the crushing weight of disappointment that settled on her chest and squeezed her heart, putting an uncomfortable pressure behind her tired eyes. She had thought she might do all right, but he had defeated her so soundly, grinding her under his heel and then some. Only a fool would think she could have risen straight out of the back-alley bajha circuit to compete with the pros. A fool like her. With dreams always too big to be feasible. Ma and Button would never know what she almost won for them, but Nico would.

She peeled off her gloves, but wore her pride in the set of her shoulders and her composure in measured breaths as a pair of boots appeared in from of her. "I want to thank ya for the opportunity to try out, Sir Vedla," she said, as deeply as she could manage with her disappointment squeezing her throat. On one knee, she looked up at the *Vash* with a cheerful smile, even though it was not what she felt on the inside. It was good to be gracious, even though she would never see this magnificent man again, his starship, his players, or crew.

Sir Vedla reached for her hand and pulled her to her feet. His golden eyes were as warm as dome-rise on the badlands. "You think I'm sending you home without an offer?" he purred in his smooth brogue.

She tugged off her helmet and tried to make sense of the bewilderment in his eyes. "I know the kind of players ya need for your team. I'm flattered ya thought I had a chance, though."

"I have every intention of inviting you to play for Team Eireya, Kes. I thought that much was obvious."

It took every ounce of restraint not to let loose and scream. "You do?"

"Of course! I could not be more pleased. You played an excellent match—against my best player. In fact, for a moment there at the end I thought you had him. It had me on the edge of my seat. Oh, and when you slapped him back..." Sir Vedla clapped his hands. "Bravo."

Skeet laughed. "Whose side are you on, sir?" he pretended to complain.

"Your first time with regulation rules, too. It could not have gone better. You exceeded every expectation. Well done, Kes. Truly. Well done."

It was a blur after that, the genuine congratulations and pats on the back from the two pros, the thanks from members of the crew who had stayed for the entertainment, all while so many thoughts tumbled through her head. Would she train here? Or, away? If it was away, she would have to tell her supervisor. They would fire her, of course, and her feelings on that were a jumble of relief and nerves. What about Ma and Button? What would she tell them? How long before she would be able to have them join her? And Nico... She loved her brother but if he had access to all the money she would be paid while she was gone, well, he could be a wee bit too free-spending. She would need to make arrangements with Sir Vedla to make sure the family had what it needed while she was away. She would ask him to leave out a percentage so Nico did not have access to all of it, and go off knowing that her family was taken care of until they were reunited.

She was so immersed in her thoughts that she did not realize she had followed the men into the locker room until Xirri started shrugging off his boots and bajha suit, and then his underclothing as he walked, bare-bottomed to the showers. All three men had been exercising most of the day and now were eager to clean up for dinner.

"You're probably hungry," she heard the *Vash* say. He was stripping off his clothing also.

"I'm hungry, aye." As much as she wanted to take advantage of her disguise to see how closely he measured up to her preconceived notions, she didn't take a gander. She was better than that. Wasn't she? She pretended to adjust the strap of her gear bag that she had dropped onto a bench made from a slab of polished real tree wood.

"Help yourself to the showers, then. Afterward, we will dine and discuss the rest of the details."

She nodded, not trusting her voice, and unzipped her bag to fetch her towel. It was covered in Nico's dried blood. She yanked the zipper closed before anyone noticed.

The sound of bare feet padding on the soft floor circled around to her. The *Vash* was naked—to the waist, she realized with a peek lower, and he was incredible: lean and muscled, broad in shoulder and chest, narrowing to tight hips and a skin-tight pair of black undershorts leaving hopelessly little to the imagination.

She had used less effort moving a canister weighed down with ore than it took to drag her eyes from that body.

"Towels," the *Vash* said, pointing to a tall pile of perfect, fluffy, clean white towels. She chose one and breathed in the fragrance of expensive soap, wishing she could take one home for Ma, then scoured her cropped hair with the towel until the ends stood up.

"I'll use the sink to wash up."

"No shower? If you need a change of clothing, there's more than enough here for you."

She needed privacy more than she needed a change of clothing. "No, I'm right fine, sir."

"I see. If that's what you prefer." But before the *Vash* departed for the showers, he paused to look at her for a moment as if she was something that needed figuring out. She just hoped he did not think on that too hard.

CHAPTER ELEVEN

T he dining table boasted more food than Jemm had ever seen in one place in her lifetime. Food on platters, food on plates, on forks, in spoons, in cups and bowls. It was all she could do to keep from salivating like a yipwag, one of the furry, wet-nosed, tail-wagging street scavengers that sometimes ended up in miners' stewpots.

All the men had showered, shaved, and dressed for dinner in fresh clothing: crisp high-collared shirts unbuttoned at the neck with sleeves extending to their wrists and tails tucked into crisp, pressed trousers. They looked so handsome and urbane. In contrast, she wore her old bajha suit, which she had unfastened to her waist, with the padded vest providing cover for her female curves. In her only nod to "dressing for dinner", she had combed her hair away from her face. It made her look even younger and, she hoped, more boyish.

A server moved over to her after he had attended to the *Vash*. The man arranged a clean plate and cutlery in front of her, and draped a napkin on her lap. "Enjoy your dinner, sir."

She had never been called "sir" before, or any sort of respectful gender-specific title. Nor had she ever attended a dinner like this, or sampled most of the food items in front of her. The firsts were piling up faster than trill chips in a collection vat.

Skeet patted his hard, flat belly. "The roast is spectacular tonight."

"Everything's spectacular when traveling with the team owner," Xirri said, his muscled arms flexing as he cut into some sort of exotic vegetable she did not recognize. It squirted amber juice onto his plate. He speared a piece of meat with a fork, rubbing it in the juice to make a gravy. Jemm all but followed it into his mouth with her gaze. "Kes. Hello? Are you going to eat, son, or just stare?" he said, his earnest eyes pinching with laughter.

With a fork she speared a small slice of roast on the platter. The piece dribbled juice and browned bits of meat as she lifted it. The aroma was so heady and rich, she was sure she would die of pleasure before she could transport the slice from the platter to her plate.

Xirri chewed as he gestured with his fork. "These roast tubers are insane with that gravy."

"There's lowberry gel for the meat," Skeet suggested. "Go easy on the rip-radish, though. It's hot. Spicy hot."

Sir Vedla offered her a roll from yet another a plate. "As light as air," he said.

Finally, Jemm got samples of everything on her plate. "By the dome," she muttered under her breath with her first taste of a morsel of meat. It was so delicious that she shuddered. The rip-radish was indeed spicy, but she enjoyed the heat. She forked a roast tuber next, moving a chunk in slow, deliberate circles in a puddle of gravy before bringing it to her lips, using her pointed tongue to catch an errant drip before savoring a bite. Then she felt eyes on her, and looked up to catch Sir Vedla observing her with dark eyes and the strangest expression. Doubt? Bewilderment?

Mortified, she almost dropped her fork. Had she given herself away with feminine mannerisms? Whatever his thoughts, he kept them well-cloaked as he went back to cutting his meat. "I'm pleased you like the efforts of my chef," he said with flawless poise.

"I never met a food I didn't like, sir."

"Excellent, because tonight we have a special treat in store. Ah. Here it is now."

A server entered the dining room with a large platter, setting it down in the center of the table with pride. "As you requested, My Lord."

Arranged on a bed of crushed ice in the center of a yellow fringe of citrus slices were dozens of glistening pale purple, spotted nuggets about the size of her thumb.

"Marvelous," Sir Vedla said, rubbing his hands together. "Kes, I thought you might enjoy a specialty from Eireya, my homeworld. Meat and tubers can appeal only for so long, after all."

Rustling sounds came from the ice. Her eyes widened. Hands flat on the table, she leaned forward, sure her ears were playing tricks on her. "They're moving."

"As fresh as can be, yes," Sir Vedla said. "Shoal dabs are a species of crab found in the warm shallows of the seas on my homeworld. They have no shells. The meat is quite mild, buttery and slightly sweet. They're very good simmered in a fish stew, or pan fried and salted, but they're at their peak of flavor fresh, like this." He reached for the platter with a pair of tongs. A shoal dab dropped and scampered sideways across the table.

Skeet crushed it with a plate. "I hate when they do that."

"A waste of a dab, Yonson." Sir Vedla speared another with his fork. The thing wiggled on the prongs until he popped it into his mouth and chewed.

"Crag me," Jemm blurted, to the players' laughter.

Even Sir Vedla laughed at her shock, his grin broad and real. She watched him, transfixed. He was a different person when he laughed. In the next moment he seemed to catch himself, and his levity faded to a polite, cordial, close-lipped smile. It was as if returning to this neutral stance was as much a trained habit as a two-handed grip on a sens-sword.

If only he were a trill rat like her instead of an aristo, because his stuffiness was a dare of the worst kind. The man begged to be shaken up a bit. Begged! Aye, she would start by mussing his perfect hair and rumpling his perfect clothes so he would blend in better when she took him out dancing: thump music—nice and loud—them grinding close to the beat, sweating, laughing, shouting above the noise, with enough ale to quench their thirst and weaken his inhibitions. Afterward, she would spirit him away someplace private. By the time she was done with him, he would know what it was like to have a little fun.

The mental image warmed her all over. She extinguished it immediately. Acting like a young man meant she had to think like one too. Revealing even a whiff of attraction for the owner of Team Eireya would poke holes in the still-thick layer of expectation bias protecting her.

"Your turn, Kes." Sir Vedla's eyes sparkled with the dare. "You said you never met a food you didn't like."

"I never met a food that tried to run away." With tongs, she transferred a few shoal dabs to her plate. They were weakening. One dragged itself to the rim. She nudged it back to huddle with the rest of the doomed. She felt the eyes of the men on her as well as the beady, black eyes-on-stalks of the dabs as she selected her first victim. She had never seen a sea creature in person, never touched or smelled one. Now she was about to eat one.

Holding her breath, she stabbed at one. It skidded out from under the tines of her fork. It was more solid than she had expected. She cursed and tried again, keeping her prey corralled with her knife.

Both Skeet and Xirri were laughing, and even the server had stopped to watch. Sir Vedla's lips twitched with amusement behind the rim of the bottle he held to his mouth. "I thought you had more predatory instinct in you than that, Kes."

Jemm speared it this time. Refusing to look at it before carrying it into her mouth, she bit down once before swallowing it almost whole. She felt it descend all the way down her throat to her stomach. Then, with a few big gulps of the sweet beverage in the bottle, she made sure it stayed there, in case the thing tried to reverse course.

"Well?" Sir Vedla asked.

"If I ever have the chance to experience the sea, I think it would taste and feel the way the shoal dab tasted and felt—cold and fresh."

Pleasure suffused his features. "You'll have the opportunity to visit the sea before too long. At the end of the playing season the entire team is invited to Eireya. The reality of the sea cannot compare to what you saw in the arcades."

"It's a week you won't forget," Skeet assured her.

Jemm was certain she would never forget this meal, let alone dipping her toes in a real ocean.

The server arrived to collect the dirty plates. It would not be right to ask to take any scraps home, but, oh, how she would have loved to see Button's eyes when the shoal dabs were brought out, to hear her sweet giggles. "It was the best meal I ever ate, all of it was, but don't tell my Ma I said so. Although with ingredients like this to work with, I think she'd give your chef a run for his money. I wish Nico could have been here." It slipped out before she thought about the consequences of reminding Sir Vedla of his absence.

"Ah, Nico." He leaned back in his chair, tapping his fingers together, a relaxed enough posture on the surface but she sensed inner tension coiling like a heavy spring. "So, remind me why your manager isn't here. Some sort of trouble with a club?"

"Migel Arran, who owns Rumble, where I play Eighthnights, didn't like that I fought at Narrow Margin last night. He wants an exclusive. We refuse to give it. He sent a few of his thugs to try to change our minds. They caught up to us outside the docks—threats, intimidation, the usual crat."

His eyes flickered darkly. "Threats? Intimidation?"

"They beat Nico up and threatened to send me to the prison league."

Sir Vedla looked like a predator that someone had poked with a sharp stick. "Is that how you came by the bruising on your jaw?"

"Aye. One of Arran's gangster cogs. He said they had orders not to hurt me, but I know they would. They said if I fought back, they'd make sure Nico didn't walk again." She swallowed, her throat thickening with fear all over again. "I'm worried about Nico, because he ain't worried about them."

The furrow was back between his brows. "Where is he now?"

"He stayed behind in town to wait for me. We didn't want ya to see his condition and label us trouble, and maybe I'd lose the chance to try out."

Sir Vedla listened to her story with a tight-lipped frown "The chance of that was zero."

"Nico says it's just posturing—that it's normal in street bajha. But I still worry about him all the same. Migel Arran's a crattin' double-crosser and a bully, an arrogant cog coward of the worst sort. I'd rather spit on a silver than accept another from him, if ya want to know." She took a heated breath.

"Tell us how you really feel, Kes." Xirri's eyes were shining as Skeet looked on with no small amount of awe.

Sir Vedla pressed his fingertips together, bringing them to his chin. "Your status as Team Eireya's newest recruit won't allow for much free time in the coming days, and soon we will depart for further training. That's reason enough to terminate your agreement with Arran."

"Aye, but Nico's got other players on his roster now. He wants to build his presence, something Arran doesn't want him to do. Even if Arran accepts me going pro, my brother's still at risk."

"Your brother..." Sir Vedla said. "I'd wondered, seeing a resemblance. The eye color. Green with the gold hue at the center. Unusual and striking." Then he blinked and gave his head a shake, his jaw hardening. "Protecting one's family must always be a priority." He called out, "Con, summon a hovercar," then pushed up from his chair. The players shoved back their chairs and stood. Following their lead, Jemm shot to her feet. "For safety's sake, I'll see you and your brother driven home tonight."

CHAPTER TWELVE

The hovercar glided up the street leading away
from the docks. A yellow-orange pinprick of a
glow bobbed in the shadows under the
overhang of a building. "There he is," Kes said, pointing.

They pulled up to a forlorn soul leaning against the
crumbling wall, shoulders hunched against the dampness.

Nico aimed a cagey glare at the one-way windows of
the vehicle, his vape pinched between his fingers, smoke
curling into the damp night air. "How do I open this so he
can see us?" Kes tapped on the window rapid-fire. But
Klark was already leaning across the seat to touch the
control, sending the panel sliding lower.

"Get in," Kes said in a deep, stern tone, then laughed
seeing Nico's startled double-take.

"By the crattin' dome," Nico said, tossing the vape
over his shoulder. "This beats walking any day." With a
broad grin, he climbed inside and craned his neck to take
in every inch of the luxurious interior. The odors of
sweat, vapes, blood, and liquor entered with him. The
bruises and swelling on his face did not mask the wonder
Klark saw there.

"Sir Vedla gave me this salve, Nico. For your face, and anywhere else they got ya—"

The man made a derisive noise in his throat. "I don't need no potions—but I thank ya all the same. I'll heal the old-fashioned way."

"You might have a point," Klark said. "The ointment would take down the swelling, but if your nose is broken, it may need to be set before any cartilage fuses."

Nico snorted then winced at the pain of doing so, his eyes watering. "I've broken it before. It'll heal without any fussing."

Kes slipped the tube back in her pocket. "Look at us, Nic. Did ya ever imagine we'd be in a flycar?"

Nico shifted his lopsided grin to Kes. "The owner of Team Eireya wouldn't be giving us a ride back to the city if he wasn't planning on signing ya."

Kes smiled back. "It ain't official yet, we'll do the signing tomorrow when you can be there, but the offer's been made and I'd like to accept."

As the two Baréshtis hugged, Klark absorbed the happy sight. It made him look forward to meeting Migel Arran even more. "First, a detour. It won't take long."

One of his bodyguards was at the wheel. He acknowledged Klark's verbal signal with a shared glance in the rearview mirror and then they were on the way to their first destination. While Klark was well-versed in nearly every known form of martial arts, bringing a Vedla bodyguard along as backup made sense. He wanted to keep his newest player safe from a man who had already demonstrated violence—a grave mistake he would soon learn.

"You can make as many detours as ya like; I'm just along for the ride," Nico said. He had stretched out in the plush leather seat as if he had been riding in speeders all his life.

Soon the streets grew more crowded, the people and buildings cruder, the stench outside detectable even with the vehicle's filtered air. "Ah, North City," Nico said. "There's Rumble. Where all this began." His brows came up when the hovercar stopped in front of the bar. "You planning on going in? I don't think I'm Arran's man of the moment."

Kes searched Klark's face with a worried narrowing of the eyes. "This ain't a good idea."

"If you'd rather wait behind in the hovercar, I prefer it—"

"Not a chance," the siblings argued.

"It was me who was playing here," Kes said. "I should handle him."

"I'll allow you to formally end your agreement, such as it is, but if there's any handling to be done, I'm best positioned for the task."

Kes frowned. "Ya don't know how it works on Barésh. Arran won't forget his threats against Nico just because ya asked him to. He'll wait until we've gone away and hunt him down."

"Psshh." Nico waved a hand. "I ain't afraid of that cog."

"Ya should be," Kes replied sharply.

Klark picked up on Sea Kestrel's fear with bajha-honed awareness. It coiled around his heart and sat cold in the pit of his stomach. It only stoked his desire to modify the club owner's behavior. "You're wrong when you say I don't know Barésh. I've been here before. I've been in your arcades, and in your bars."

"You were? When?" The player's face was a cavalcade of reactions to the news, not the least of which were disbelief, nosiness, and flat-out surprise. "Why?"

"That," he said, "is not important now." The tale of almost-murder and mayhem that led him to Barésh was not one he wished to share with the young and innocent Sea Kestrel, even though the player could very well be an integral part of repairing the damage he had caused his family. "Taking Migel Arran down a few rungs is. You'd be amazed at the power of a few well-placed connections in a colony of this size. I happen to have those connections. They'll make fine leverage when I convince Mr. Arran of the folly of flaunting his measly power."

"His power may seem measly to you, but here he's a powerful man."

Nico frowned at an angry Kes. "We've got a genuine *Vash Nadah* on our side now. What could go wrong?"

They piled out of the hovercar. Miners clustered around the vehicle, a few jerking back curious hands with a yelp after Klark's bodyguard, Voowen, engaged the security field.

"His office is in the back," Nico said. He and Klark flanked Sea Kestrel with Voowen bringing up the rear as they pushed through the hard-drinking crowd of miners, many of whom still wore the day's cave grit on their faces. The thumping music was deafening. Pungent hallucivape smoke hung thickly in the air. He tried to imagine Sea Kestrel walking in here to compete in bajha for the first time.

"Sea Kestrel!" Shouts reverberated above the chaos. Cups of ale were raised. "You on tonight? It ain't Eighthnight, but I ain't complaining!"

"Not tonight, fellas," Kes called back with a friendly wave. It was clear the player was popular in the club.

"In here." Nico pushed open a door at the rear of the club. A hallway led to an open office door situated near the back. A partially undressed woman teetered on spindly heels as she left the office, adjusting lacy black garters with her thumbs before applying a coat of silver lip color. A few other staff members idled.

"Gentlemen, how can I help you?" A short, round man separated from the group. The plush flesh of his jowls fluttered with each word. There was a hint of a scowl when he recognized Nico, followed by fretful concern upon seeing the man's wounds. He flashed a brief but nervous smile at Kes. But he brightened seeing Klark, knowing what he was. "Welcome to our fine establishment, good sir."

"That's Bounce," Nico said, poking a thumb at the little man. "He's the announcer here. Hey, Bounce, is your boss in?"

"Certainly!" The man did seem to bounce along as his little legs carried him on ahead and into the office. "They got to ya, eh?" Klark heard Bounce mumble to Nico under his breath. "Sorry, mate."

Nico glared back. "It ain't gonna stop me."

The owner's office was a fairly large space but stuffy and cluttered. Bounce waved a number of muscular security guards out of their way. A desk commanded the space below a vid feed of the club. Klark could not see who sat in the chair. His view was blocked by the soles of a pair of men's boots propped on the desk and the naked woman who sat astride that pair of legs.

Kes swore under his breath and turned his gaze to his boots. Nico touched his brother's arm as if to apologize. The player had seemed flustered in the locker room earlier, as well, not wanting to undress. Either the youth had been sheltered at home, or he was unusually modest. Whatever the reason, Xirri and Skeet had made it their goal to take care of that innocence pretty quickly. It pricked every protective instinct Klark had to think of Kes being sullied by what the team had planned for him, but boys will be boys. Only the highborn were introduced to sex by experienced pleasure servers, as Klark was.

"Mr. Arran, there is a very important gentleman here to see you," Bounce called out with cheer.

The female threw an annoyed then suddenly very interested glance over her bare shoulder at Klark. A face peeked sideways around her, male hands landing on her hips—Arran's hands, Klark presumed. "What the bloody hell—?" Then recognition of his visitor's status cut off the verbal explosion.

The boots scraped off the desk, spilling the naked female to the floor. She gathered up pieces of clothing, seemingly more out of possession than any interest in modesty. Arran stood, adjusting his trousers, his smile faltering the instant he realized Nico and his bajha champ were part of the group. The collection of color-shifting tattoos on his neck was as ostentatious as his high-collared shirt and hair pomade. All of it was in style, apparently, but Klark did not give a whit about galactic fashion trends. It was the trillidium piercing Arran's left ear that was unique to Barésh and took the whole look over the top.

Arran came around his desk, a telling glance at Nico's battered face before offering his hand to Klark. "Migel Arran at your service. To what do I owe this honor, My Lord?"

Klark kept his hands folded neatly at the small of his back.

Arran's face fell a second before his hand did. Those blasted illuminated tattoos. They made it hard to read everything in his intelligent eyes, but the man did appear to sense something was amiss. "Lord Vedla." Klark gestured to his companions. "You already know Sea Kestrel and Nico Aves."

"Yes," Arran said with another uneasy glance at Nico's battered face that provided the answer to whether he had ordered the attack. "Good to see you both again. How may I help you, Lord Vedla?"

"I understand Sea Kestrel appears here on Eighthnights. However, I have signed Sea Kestrel to play as a pro for Team Eireya. His new obligations necessitate a permanent schedule change. He will no longer be able to play for your club."

Migel Arran sat down hard on the edge of his desk. "Team Eireya." His gaze shifted to Kes. "Well. Isn't that something? Congratulations are due, Sea Kestrel." He smiled. "If it doesn't work out, come home—after all this you're sure to be in high demand in the colony," he joked.

Kes's face remained stony. His eyes were fiery and full of hate, but his voice was steady. "If ya got any problem with this good news, now's the time for us to talk about it."

"Problem? Quite the contrary," Arran said pleasantly. "In this business, champs come and go. I'll be sorry to lose you, Sea Kestrel. You were one of my best. But, there are enough players and clubs to go around in this colony."

"Your mouth is telling me one thing, Mr. Arran, but your gangsters and their fists were telling quite another at the docks tonight. Look at my brother's face. Look."

People seemed to come out of the ornate woodwork to observe the exchange between the champ and the owner: several sex servers, a bar server, security guards, and Bounce.

"A misunderstanding, Sea Kestrel. Clearly," Arran said, waving away a few concerned guards.

Kes told Klark, "I heard his gangsters say that Arran sent them."

"I heard it, too," Nico said.

Arran took a breath and exhaled. "My men were looking out for my interests in the city. It's what I pay them to do. It looks like things went too far, however, and for that I do apologize. But, Lord Vedla, understand that this is part and parcel of street-bajha culture. Jockeying for the best players."

"By killing my manager?" Kes argued. "By sending me to the prison league?"

Klark quieted Kes with a touch on the arm. "If I may have a word in private with you, Mr. Arran," he murmured so coldly that a shudder ran through Arran's body and his face turned as pale as sea foam against his starched collar. He itched to snatch that prissy collar in his fists and shove the man backward against the nearby wall, but if he had learned anything from his blunders the past few years, it was self-control.

Arran waved his hovering guards away with a flick of his hand. His his throat bobbed as he faced the full power of the Vedla glare. "My Lord."

Klark's heartbeat made a hollow sound in his ears that competed with the thump music outside in the bar. Sea Kestrel was more than his diamond in the rough, his slum-bred secret weapon; Kes was the answer to lifting his team's standing and his family's at the same time. But all of it could have been destroyed on a whim with one word from this self-important, rock-sucking, backwater bully. "If you ever again lay one hand, either your own or through your orders, on any member of the Aves family. Or if you take action to negatively impact Mr. Aves's right to advance his other players in any club he desires..." Klark mentally twisted his knuckles in Arran's collar, imagining the man's face turning purple. "Colony-Marshal Vrent will shut down your establishments faster than you can use your middling station to bully helpless colonists. You will never earn another credit from a club until the day you die. Of course, there's always work to be found in the mines, I'm told."

Arran's pupils shrank at that. "You have my word. I won't hinder Nico Aves in any way."

"Do you understand what a man of my status and connections can do if you choose to break your word?"

"Yes, Lord Vedla. Completely." Arran's voice was hoarse, as if he had sensed Klark's desire to choke the living daylights out of him. "There's more than enough room for the two of us in this city."

"Do ya really know the Colony-Marshal?" Nico asked Klark when they returned to the hovercar. Kes gaped at him with the same amazement.

"He knows me," Klark replied. Every once in a while his infamy was an advantage.

On the way home, they approached a cluster of activity surrounding a large white tent lit by floodlights. Jemm twisted around in the seat to get a better view. "What in the dome is going on out there?" A line of people stretched out from it and wound around the corner. Red and black letters dominated one side of the tent. Below those was an emblem emblazoned with red squiggles and a silhouette of a human form with blocky alien runes she didn't recognize. Another banner contained words in Federation Basic. "Doctors without Borders?"

Nico laughed. "That ain't no name for a club. The Ore's Head is right around the corner though; the club I'm leasing."

She threw him a sideways glare. "Not a club. The sign on that tent." As they drove closer, she read, *All clinics and vehicles are weapons-free zones.* As if regular Baréshtis walked around with pistols.

"Earth-dwellers," Sir Vedla said, his mouth taking a downturn, his tone flat. "It seems they have decided to get involved in your colony, after all. It may be a very good thing. They are an industrious people, after all, despite their outsized ambitions. They can help the Baréshtis. Great Mother knows, the Federation has failed you."

"Slow down," Jemm told the driver. Rolling down the window, she leaned out to see. The colonists waiting in line appeared to be more ragtag than usual. Many had coughs like Ma, with lung disease being prevalent on Barésh, thanks to mine work and pollution. Others looked to be suffering with the usual chronic conditions like rashes and sores or colds. Still others sported fresh wounds in need of mending. Her heart clenched at the sight of all the sick children. Some stood with their parents, clinging to hands; others lay limp in strong arms. She had never seen so many ailing little ones gathered together at once.

Then she noticed the suspicious, even defiant looks aimed in her direction. The flycar labeled her as rich, a cog from the compound. She was no longer a mineworker in their eyes; she was an elite, one *of them*—the upper class. Maybe they feared she would scuttle whatever was unfolding. "Stop the flycar."

Jemm opened the door and jumped out, and Nico followed. "What's going on?" she asked the crowd.

One man took in the sight of her and deemed her to be another trill rat. "They be Earth-dwellers, lads," he said.

"They've come to give us medical care," answered another, holding the hand of an emaciated little boy with hollow eyes. "For free."

"Free?" Jemm frowned at the tent, trying to figure out the catch.

"Aye. They're here to treat all that needs it," the woman standing with him said.

"For anyone?" Jemm immediately thought of Ma.

"Aye, not just upper class." The woman's eyes narrowed with fear and distrust at a point somewhere over Jemm's shoulder.

Jemm pivoted her head and spotted the *Vash* leaning against the hood of the flycar as he waited for her, arms folded over his chest. He acknowledged her notice with a slight tip of his head, but let her be, although she was certain he would intervene in an instant if he sensed she was in any danger. But his mere presence was ominous to those in line.

He could not help appearing insolent. Arrogance was bred into him—eleven thousand years worth of breeding. His standoffish expression grew dark as a pair of off-worlders made their way toward them, seeing to people in the line, pulling some out, directing others elsewhere.

Earth-dwellers.

Everyone in line stared at the pair of Earth-dwellers and their exotic appearance. Their white-and-red jumpsuits sported the same emblem as the tents, but other runes on their uniforms were unreadable.

The female held a tablet and the man a device that he touched to foreheads then read the digits from a tiny screen to his companion, who then recorded the information. She had pale skin with pink cheeks, shiny black hair in curls, and blue eyes.

Black hair and blue eyes—Jemm had never seen anyone with that coloring. Her associate was as startling and wondrous as she was. The man's complexion was on the opposite end of the spectrum, his skin a rich brown. He was older, completely bald, his scalp as dark and shiny as a kuu-nut. But his brows and beard sprouted gray hair. It was rare to see Baréshtis with dark facial hair, and rarer still for any fella to have enough to form a beard like this man from Earth. The Trade Federation was a fair-haired, darker-eyed civilization overall, except for the highborn *Vash*, conspicuous for their pale eyes and tawny hair and skin. But even they had only golden hair to shave from their jaws.

The Earth-dweller aimed a friendly finger at Nico, his eyes sympathetic. "You with face injury—go last place in line," he said, his accent thick. When Nico stood in place, the man apologized. "My sorry. Many people you. Too few us."

"No, that's all right," Nico said. "I don't—"

"We hope more…personnel here soon. My bad Basic, your language. Will learn, but Doctor Randall will know more. CJ!" he called out to her. Looking stressed, the female held up her index finger and mouthed words in an unfamiliar language while she kneeled in front of the skinny little boy, who appeared so frightened by the sight of her that tears trickled down his sunken cheeks.

"You are doctors?" Jemm asked.

"I am nurse—physician's assistant. We are three doctors and three nurses here. Too few." He exhaled, and, despite a concerned glance at Nico's battered face, was itching to return to the others in more desperate need. "We no think so many in need."

Jemm thought of the medicine Sir Vedla had given her for Ma earlier that was for infections and inflammation, but not for anything worse, which was what she feared. But it was all they had on board. Jemm spoke up before the Earthman moved on. "I'd like my mother to come here. How long will ya be around?"

"Here for good. In tent, until we make something more…" He seemed to search for the right word.

"A more permanent structure," the female doctor walked with purpose over to Nico, her black curls bouncing. She looked very young to be in such a position of authority. "Jesus. What happened to you?"

"It ain't nothing. It—"

"Your nose is broken," she said crisply.

"Aye, I know, but—"

"Badly." She reached for his swollen nose and palpitated it.

Nico winced. The doctor turned on a handheld light beam to peek inside his nose. She held his chin between the crook of her index finger and thumb, moving his head this way and that. Jemm was amazed Nico had not ducked away yet. Instead, he let her examine him, one corner of his mouth tucking into a crooked, pleased grin. The dozer, he was enjoying the attention from the pretty lass.

"There is airway obstruction. When did this happen? Today?"

Nico seem to come out of a fog when he realized the doctor was speaking to him. "Aye, but—"

"Someone did a number on you, big guy. Anything else get hit—ribs? Stomach? Was it fists or kicks?"

"Like I said, it ain't no bother."

She let out an exasperated huff. "It does not matter if I am in the Congo or here in space, you men of danger are the same. It never is a 'bother', until the damage is permanent, *tough guy*. Get in line."

"Not tonight, Doctor See-jay. I do appreciate the offer, but I got plans I gotta keep."

A hint of amusement flickered in her blue eyes at Nico's use of her given name. "I advise you—do not wait too long. I am sure you get a lot of attention from the girls. Yes? But girls do not like snoring. But, if snoring loudly is something you want to do for the rest of your life then, please, do not repair the schnoz." She slipped the portable light in her pocket.

"Schnoz?" Nico blinked at her.

"That means nose in Earth slang. When you come back, ask for Doctor Randall." With her quick smile came a mischievous wink. "Or CJ. Whatever will get you to return and be treated."

To Jemm's surprise Nico said, "Aye."

The doctor resumed her examinations of the other Baréshtis in need of care.

"Bring Ma when ya come back," Jemm told Nico, but his attention had followed the young female Earth doctor. "Nico!"

"Aye. I'll bring Ma, too." He reached in his pocket for a vape, sticking it between his lips, then remembered the flycar and returned the smoke to his pocket.

Sir Vedla radiated relief like a radiation glow when they left the site of the Earth-dwellers. He might not know her deepest secrets, but it was clear he had a few of his own. She was dying to know what they were.

CHAPTER THIRTEEN

After they were dropped off at the apartment, Jemm dragged her gaze up all seventeen stories to the top floor, where soft light glowed. "Are ya gonna tell Ma about the signing?" Nico asked.

She gulped. "Aye. You gonna tell her about your beating?"

"Not on your life."

Her heart thumped harder with each floor they climbed. "I'm thinking about what Migel Arran said, about if it doesn't work out."

"If it doesn't, you'll play for me, not for him."

"Aye, but don't ya worry about how the league will react if they find out what I am?"

"Expulsion, most likely," Nico said with a shrug. "But there's no use worrying until ya have to worry."

He was right, but deep down she feared being fined or worse. There was risk in this scheme, no question. But what pathway to a dream came without some measure of risk?

"Button's going to miss me while I'm at training," she said.

Nico kept his gaze trained on the stairs.

"It's time you stepped up to help. It's been three years. It can't all be on Ma."

They climbed up another floor. "I don't know how to be a Da," he said.

"I'm sure ours thought that, too, when he was just starting out."

Nico made a skeptical grunt. "I don't remember much about him, but he was larger than life, Jemm. I ain't."

"In Button's eyes you are."

He met her gaze for a moment, his lips pressed together, his eyes a portal to his inner pain. Would the grief ever leave him? "I'll do what I can, if that makes ya feel better about leaving."

She whispered, "It does, aye."

They climbed the remaining floors, their tongues silent but their minds full. Life would soon change in startling fashion after being the same for so long. Outside the door, in the shadows, Jemm changed clothing and stowed her gear.

Ma was up and Button, too, when they walked inside. "Mum-mum!" Button raced to Jemm, and she scooped her up. Despite her talk with Nico, he made no move to interact with his daughter, although his pensive gaze followed her. Her brother could face down fight club gangsters with more guts than he could his child.

"You good, little one?" Jemm said, kissing her sweet face.

"Aye, but Gramma ain't."

Ma was paler than usual, her eyes watering. She was in the kitchen, sipping water from a cup. "Are ya all right?" Jemm asked, setting Button down.

She waved away Jemm's concern. "The coughing woke me," she said hoarsely. "And woke the child, too." Then she saw Nico's face and her eyes opened wide. "Oh, Nicky-boy. What trouble were ya out getting into tonight?"

"Nothing to fret about, Ma."

"And ya tore your sweater. Give it to me, and I'll mend it." Their mother soaked a towel with water, wrung it, and gave it to Nico. "Put it on ya nose." Her suspicious gaze swerved to Jemm's gear bag before she stifled a cough with her knuckles.

"Earth-dwellers are here," Nico mumbled around the wet towel, handing Ma his sweater. "Frontier folk, like us. They set up a tent in Central. All ya gotta do is show up to get medical treatment."

"I want ya to go with Nico tomorrow," Jemm added. "It's free."

"Bah, nothing comes for free," Ma said with a Baréshti's characteristic suspicion. She examined Nico's sweater with a frown, then sorted through her sewing basket for a needle and thread.

"I think this time it will. They've come to help us. They'll help you."

A coughing attack caused Ma to hack so hard into her fisted hand that Jemm feared she had hurt herself. She wrapped her arm over her mother's heaving shoulders. Button clung to the woman's hand until finally the fit had passed. Tears streamed from Ma's eyes. "I don't know if I'm long for this world," she said, her breath whistling.

Jemm's heart skittered. "Don't say that. Those potions you buy do you no good. Tomorrow, you'll see the Earth doctors, and they'll know how to help. Nico will take you. Right, Nico?" Jemm pulled out the medicine vial Sir Vedla had given her. Ma eyed it with suspicion. "I got this for ya in the meantime. Take it at bedtime. It's a liquid. One squirt in your mouth. It won't cure ya, but it will help ya breathe better, and you'll cough less. The Earth-dwellers can do much more. There are medicines that have machines so tiny we can't see them. They can repair bodies, cure disease..."

"Bah. Upper-class potions."

"But *they work.*" Anything was better than what was available in the city market. Even the gold credit they had earned, that her dozer of a brother had probably spent leasing his club, was not enough to buy the services of a real doctor.

Jemm patted her mother's delicate shoulder, towering over her as she had since she was fifteen years old. Ma was best described as an angelic beauty. Except for their pretty hair, Jemm took after her father in almost every other way. "Sit down, Ma."

"Go on," Nico said. "You need to hear what Jemm has to say."

"Our life's about to change—for the better," Jemm said. Seventeen stories below, a *Vash* nobleman drove away in a flycar, soon to whisk her away to a starship bound for other worlds that she could not begin to imagine. Button stayed close, wrapping her strong, thin arms around Jemm's hips, as if to hold her here, in this world.

Taking a breath, Jemm crouched down to talk to her mother at eye level. "I got a new job—off-world."

Her mother flinched.

"It means I'll have to go away for a little while...to train. It will be immersive. I'll be training all day, every day. So, I won't be able to take ya with me just yet. It's only for a few months. Nico will be here, looking after things. I'll be back for you, Button, and Nico as soon as I can."

"Why, Mum-mum?" Button's piping voice trembled as she crept back to insert herself in Jemm's arms. "Why do ya have to go away?"

Jemm folded herself around the child, her throat thickening.

"Bajha is why." Anger sparked in Ma's narrowed eyes as she spat out the word. She vibrated with fury as she glared at Jemm. "Aye, girl. I know. Don't look so surprised. I know what you've been up to—you and

Nico. It's why ya cut your pretty hair. So ya can play with the fellas. I was willing to go along with it, I was. But now you're wanting more. Just like your Da. He wasn't paying attention like he should have been. He didn't see what was coming; he was too busy planning and dreaming. And it killed him."

"You don't know that playing bajha was to blame. Accidents happen, Ma. People are always getting hurt in the mines."

Nico walked away to look out a dirty window, his shoulders hunched, his hand automatically going to his pocket for a vape before he dropped his fist. Jemm sighed. The dead tiptoed amongst them tonight, turning what should have been a celebration of good news into something somber.

"No. Conrenn's problem was he dreamed too big, that fool of a man, and it took him from me." Ma's eyes filled with bitter tears. "I ain't gonna go through it again, Jemm. I can't."

"I don't want you to go away, Mum-mum," Button said in a sad little voice.

Jemm fought the tears pressing behind her eyes. But if she started bawling, it would be contagious. She wasn't sure she could stand all of them sobbing on a night that should be a joyous one.

She kissed Button's hair and kept her tone upbeat. "Ah, my sweet. It's not for long. When I come home, I'm going to take you on a starship. Won't that be exciting?" The child's eyes opened wide as she nodded. "That's why I'm going away, to get everything ready for that day. I won't be driving tugs anymore. I'm going to play for a bajha team." She spoke to her niece but her gaze lifted and locked with Ma's. "It's called Team Eireya. I'm going to be one of their star players. The owner is a real *Vash Nadah*, a good, decent man. His starship is big enough to fit an entire arena. I played with some other team members there. Champions. Yonson Skeet was one.

You don't know him, but he's galactic famous. And there was a dining room on board. Oh, if only you could have seen and tasted all the food. One day soon, you will."

"A *Vash Nadah*?" Ma raised an eyebrow.

"Aye. In fact, he drove me and Nico home in a flycar." Button leaped off her lap and dashed over to the windows, skipping from window to grimy window to see if she could spy it.

"I'll leave ya enough credits to last ya a while. There'll be more than enough for food and all. Best hide the money in the crock under the floorboards and only keep out what you need."

"Blood money," the woman grumbled, but Jemm knew she would not refuse it.

"I'll be back before ya know it—don't fear otherwise."

"I don't fear ya going, foolish girl! I fear ya coming home. Being in danger *here*. Not paying mind, and winding up like Da."

Jemm blinked at her mother's tormented gaze. "Even if this doesn't work out, and I had to come back to Barésh, I wouldn't return to the mines. I can't. Once ya quit, they won't hire ya back. I'm putting in my notice tomorrow. But I'd come home far richer than I am now. If we couldn't leave right then, it wouldn't be long after. I've thought all of it, Ma. You and Button and Nico are all I think about."

Her mother's anguished eyes lowered as she lifted the rag to her mouth to stifle another cough. Then she thrust out a stubborn chin. "Go off with your *Vash* then."

"He's not my—"

"Don't forget, we ain't nothing to the upper class. Don't turn ya back on them, and don't believe everything ya hear."

The Baréshti blessing. "Aye, I'll be careful. Look, I know that you love me, Ma. I know it every time you cook for me, or mend my clothes, or wait up for me. I see your love in all the things you do, big and small." She took her mother's thin, clammy hands in her strong, dry ones and squeezed. "But, Ma, the problem ain't never been about dreaming too big. It's forgetting how to dream at all."

"I am officially unemployed," Jemm said the next morning, dropping her gear bag, packed with her former work clothes, on the floor of the arena. She knew how futile it probably was, going into the mine boss's office to explain how sorry she was for giving up a job she had loved, but she had tried anyway. The boss-cog laughed at her attempt to quit and told her she was fired. It left her with no palatable options to earn a living if she did have to return, as Ma feared. She would be doomed to freelance laboring down in the caves, or worse. It only reinforced her determination to escape, and to get her family out with her.

"You won't be unemployed for long," Sir Vedla said, handing her a tablet device. "Here are the terms of the agreement." He sat next to her and patiently went over the compensation, her obligations, and notated her request to have an advance on her dazzlingly high salary so she could allocate it to Ma and Nico separately.

Jemm touched the pad of her finger to sign the contract, and it was done. Excitement, relief, and fear whirled inside like a dust devil out on the plains. She had been signed to a pro bajha team. Signed!

"Congratulations, Kes." Sir Vedla's eyes glowed. "Onward to the season ahead."

The two pros applauded. "Now comes the hard part— Practice," Xirri said with a feigned groan as he stretched his arms over his head.

"Let's go!" Skeet clapped his hands. "Into the ring."

The following days were one long grueling session of physical and mental training. Bajha had always been a mental escape, but now she saw the intense conditioning expected of her to be able to compete at the galactic level. There were Skeet's merciless drills, consisting of squats and lunges, to countless push-ups and pull-ups, followed up with actual matches. If not for her high level of fitness, thanks to her job and all the times she had pitched in to help the loaders, she might have had difficulty keeping up. Her favorite part of training were the sessions where Sir Vedla made her try to locate him in the dark while he wore his special glasses and evaded her. It was a chance to use her senses and her mind to focus on the *Vash* without having to pretend she wasn't.

While studying vids of actual matches after lunch the second afternoon, a staffer walked up to Sir Vedla and bowed. "My Lord, you have an incoming message on your private comm."

Sir Vedla helped himself to a cold drink and walked away to retrieve his comm device, the enviable way the galactic elites could keep in touch with each other. Jemm used the moment to ask Skeet and Xirri, "I call him Sir Vedla, but others call him My Lord, or Lord Vedla. Which is right?"

"He doesn't much mind when it comes to us players," Skeet answered. "For the most part, we call him sir. He considers himself a part of the team, and we think the same of him. He doesn't much care if we leave off a few titles here and there. He's an excellent bajha player in his own right, and would have gone pro if his circumstances were different."

"What circumstances?'" Jemm asked.

"He didn't tell you?" Xirri asked. "He's a royal. But not just any royal. He's a full-blooded *Vash* prince, the second-born son of the Vedlas, second in line to the throne of one of the eight royal *Vash Nadah* families."

Jemm blinked in shock at the men. "He never said anything, no."

Holy dome. Sir Klark Vedla was a prince. The son of a king and queen! She winced, thinking about how most of the time she forgot to call him by any formal form of address, even forgetting at times he was *Vash*. He didn't seem bothered by it, of course, but, crat, her manners.

"He wanted to be incognito here on Barésh," Skeet explained. "Maybe he had security concerns. I don't know. He wouldn't say. The entire staff is having a hard time remembering not to use 'Your Highness', or 'Prince' in public."

Sir Vedla returned, the comm in his hand, his regal bearing making sense now that she knew what he was. Not Sir Vedla, but Prince Klark Vedla. Yet the familiar crease was back between his brows as he focused on the screen.

"When are you coming home?" a lilting female voice asked in the same accent as his.

"I am not sure."

Jemm craned her neck to peek at the screen. Seeing an animated, beautiful young woman there made her insides squeeze with an unexpected cold and disappointed knot of jealousy. *Of course he's got a sweetheart or a wife, you silly trill rat. He's a prince.*

The woman's oval face and coiffed hair decorated with tiny gems were stunning. Her *Vash* eyes narrowing at Prince Klark did so with love, even as she fired questions at him. "So, what are you doing?"

"Team business."

Her perfect, pink lips spread in a smile. "Is Yonson Skeet there?"

"Yes, Kat. He's here." His eyes slid sideways to a now grinning Skeet. Then the *Vash* rolled his eyes at Jemm to bring her in on the joke. "My sister," he mouthed at her confusion.

"Ah." A sister, and not a wife. It didn't mean there was no wife, however.

"You still haven't told me why you've called," Prince Klark said. "Is everything all right at home?"

"I wanted to say hello and…" An identical ridge to his appeared between Kat's golden-red brows. "Prince Hajhani is coming for a visit." Her mouth twisted. "I don't want anything to do with him."

"You don't know him."

"I don't want to know him."

"Give him a chance."

"Why? It will only encourage everyone in both families who want to marry me off to him." She tilted her head. The jewels in her hair sparkled. "Can you point the lens at Mr. Skeet?"

With a weary exhalation, Prince Klark did as his sister asked. Skeet nodded at the device. "As always, it is good to see you, Your Highness," he said.

Squaring his shoulders and sitting taller while he did so, Jemm noticed. Great dome, the man was preening! A laugh escaped her.

"Who's that?" the woman asked.

Jemm clamped her mouth closed so quickly she heard her teeth click.

"Mr. Kes Aves," Prince Klark explained, pointing the device at Jemm, who sat frozen. "Our newest player. The one you watched that day on the viewscreen. Kes, meet my sister, the incorrigible Princess Katjian."

"It is an honor to make your acquaintance, Your Highness," Jemm said in her deepest voice. She was not sure it was the proper greeting, but it sounded convoluted enough to meet lofty aristo expectations.

"Be warned, Mr. Aves, my brother is very serious about his bajha. One day, I touched—simply *touched*— his bajha sword, and he went crazy."

Prince Klark's shrug broadcast his opinion that he saw nothing wrong with the accusation. "I would argue that 'crazy' is an accurate description of my reaction, but neither is a fully functional sense-sword a toy." His hooded gaze slid to Jemm. "My sister feels that females should be taught bajha." His thickened voice was a dam against laughter that wanted to spill out.

The pros burst into laughter for him. Jemm bit the inside of her lip to hold back a few colorful swear words to shut the two up. In a heartbeat, the princess noticed. "You do not agree?" the girl asked her.

If only ya knew how much I don't. My Da taught me out of his love of the sport, uncaring whether I was a male or female. But Jemm could not speak her mind. She chose her words with caution. Too much said would raise suspicion. Too little would make her feel like a traitor to her gender. "I think both boys and girls would benefit being taught bajha. Learning to trust your instincts, knowing one's mind, endurance, confidence, persistence—these are traits that benefit everyone."

"I agree," the princess said. "I think some women would make fine bajha players if only they had the chance to be introduced to the sport. It's nice to see that not all men are as close-minded as my brother—and, apparently, his players too. Well, except for you."

Xirri snorted, his eyes watering. "I can't imagine my sister wielding a sens-sword."

Jemm made a mental note to make Xirri regret his remarks the next time she faced him in the ring.

Prince Klark, to his credit, did not join the pro in derisive laughter. "Everything you said is true, Kes, except for the most important point, which I also tried to explain to Princess Katjian. Bajha is more than a sport. It pays homage to our warrior ancestors. Through bajha we preserve and develop the skills the original saviors of our society used to defeat the warlords."

The princess glared at the men then addressed Jemm. "My brother insists that since only males can be warriors, females should not learn the sport."

"There aren't any warriors on Barésh, and yet bajha is played here," Jemm argued.

"Street bajha," Skeet corrected. "And only the men."

Prince Klark leaned back on the bench, his weight on his elbows, the comm held in one hand, his sister's frowning face centered in the bright screen. "The other purpose of practicing bajha is the symbolic expression of protecting and defending our women. The gentler, softer gender."

The princess reacted with an elegant snort. "I won't bring up the rigors of childbirth, dearest brother, but, please, go on. I do enjoy hearing your ineffective arguments on this matter."

"On Barésh gentleness is incompatible with survival," Jemm said.

Prince Klark shook his head. "I can't say I disagree. However, the very idea of females entering the bajha rings of the Trade Federation is absurd. Imagine a female suited up with a helmet, boots, and a sword. Preposterous. What would be next after donning men's clothing—cutting off all their hair?" He winced, making it obvious he found the idea revolting.

The pros hooted.

That smarted. Jemm ran a hand over her shorn hair, where her exposed ears stuck out like stones on the plains that the winds had laid bare. More stinging than the comment itself was the fact that she actually cared what the *Vash* thought—or would think—about her appearance if he knew she was a lass. A few days away from the city in the company of well-fed off-worlders had made her soft—spineless—like the compound-dwelling elites she had never wanted to emulate. "I think everyone should be allowed to pursue their dreams, no matter who they are, noble-born or low-born, if it does no harm."

"Oh, Kes. Yes. Exactly." Katjian's gaze melted, her expression adoring. Jemm instantly realized her mistake.

The *Vash* aimed the comm at his face. "I need to return to practice. Will you be all right?" Jemm recognized a sibling's concern in his tone. It brought out a softer side in the man.

"I think so."

"Don't do anything rash."

"I promised you, Klark. I'm keeping my head above water. But come home soon. I miss you."

They bid each other goodbye, and the *Vash* replaced the comm on the bench, exhaling heavily as he draped an arm across his knees.

"Kes, bud, I think you may have bumped Yonson off his throne," Xirri said, laughing.

Skeet placed his hand over his heart and pretended to be disappointed. But his smile faltered a bit too much. He had feelings for the young princess, the poor man. His hopes of romance with a princess were not nearly as hopeless as Jemm's fantasies of slaking her lust with the *Vash*, but close. "You're the new chosen one, I guess," he told her.

"I hope not," Jemm blurted out.

"Ah, so you have a sweetheart, then."

"No!" This was getting more painful by the minute. "I mean, I don't have time for that."

"You're too shy," Xirri decided. "We need to fix that. Women love a man with confidence." He lowered his chin as he scrutinized her. "Haven't you ever...?" His eyebrows waggled.

"Ever what?"

"Whoa. He really is an innocent," Skeet broke in. "Xirri's asking if you've ever been with a girl."

Instinctively, Kes looked to Prince Klark for help, but his expression was inscrutable. "You shouldn't feel compelled to do anything." He spun a warning glare at the pros. "And you shouldn't pressure your young teammate into doing anything he's not ready for. He's got a lifetime ahead of him for all of that."

"One taste of a woman, and you'll kick yourself for having waited," Xirri said with a wink.

"I ain't inexperienced," Jemm shot back. "But for now, bajha comes first."

"Good answer." The *Vash* pushed off the seat. "Now enough lying around. Yonson and Raff, your ship will be entering orbit soon."

"Back to the goodwill tour for us," Skeet told her. He grabbed her shoulder and squeezed. "We'll see you soon. I look forward to working with you once we all return to the training center on Chéyasenn."

Xirri pounded her on the back. "Chéyasenn City is small, but large enough for our purposes." He winked. "We'll work on your confidence with the ladies. Don't you worry."

She ignored the teasing to tell Yonson, "I want to thank ya for everything you've done, and for showing Prince Klark that vid. If not for that, I'd still be playing in back-alley fight clubs."

Skeet shook his head. "Someone would have discovered you. I'm just glad we got to you first."

"As am I," Prince Klark said.

The pros said their goodbyes to their team owner, and then they were gone.

"Now you're stuck with me, Kes. You'll find I'm even more of a training taskmaster than Skeet. The season is fast approaching and there is much work to do. Let's go." The *Vash* prince slipped his see-in-the-dark glasses over his eyes, grabbed a sens-sword, and strode toward the ring with his usual killer stride. She gathered her gear and followed. It was time for another session of playing track-the-delicious-*Vash* in the dark, but this time they were alone.

CHAPTER FOURTEEN

"D on't think so hard," he warned. "I can feel you."

A tingling across her back alerted her to his presence. Gripping her sens-sword, she swung it around. "Good!" he said. "That's it," he praised when she predicted his next move, too.

He was never really gone for her in the darkness. Like the warmth of a slow fire, the sense of him lingered away from the source.

"Back to Skeet and Xirri—you stood up well to their teasing, Kes. They'll respect you for it, but they won't back off. You're wise to focus on bajha over love interests. It will be taking up most of your time, after all. Moreover, you're playing catch-up when it comes to league rules."

"What about you? Do ya have love interests? Or, are ya married?"

He made a scoffing sound. "Neither."

"Why not?" She ducked when she predicted the arc of his sens-sword. "Don't ya ever long for female companionship?" Why was she pushing this topic? Curiosity killed the ketta-cat.

"If I desire the pleasure of a woman's body, I can have it any time day or night. For anything more than that…finding a wife, for instance, *Vash Nadah* marriages have but one purpose—to strengthen alliances between the clans. Love has nothing to do with it, unless you get lucky, as my brother did, but that is rare. My choices are limited to prospects my family would round up for me. Or, I suppose, marriage candidates I might meet while socializing at court functions—which I quite frankly despise doing. It leaves little opportunity to match with a suitable woman."

Suitable. The polar opposite of her. A girl from the slums who liked the stink and grit and solitude of driving tugs across the badlands. Who, in a heartbeat, would choose the taste of ale over the fine liqueurs she had sampled on this ship. And whose bad grammar and propensity to swearing would likely make any royal faint on the spot. "I wouldn't be wanting to pair up under those circumstances, either. Especially if love had nothing to do with it."

"Actually, I see my confirmed bachelorhood as a public service, a kindness to the royal females of the galaxy. I can be rather intense and serious. I crave solitude. I've also heard it said that I'm a snob."

"You didn't mention protective. I see the way ya look after your pros." And after her. "That's a fine quality in a mate. Even the most capable lasses like to know a man will look out for them. That's what I hear, anyway," she added quickly.

He let out a quick, dry laugh. "My protectiveness is not an asset, I assure you. Let me just say that my protective instincts have led me astray. Besides, my duties keep me far too busy for frivolous pursuits such as wife hunting. As the second-born son, my duty is to support my elder brother, Ché, the crown prince. He's the heir, and I'm the spare."

"The spare what?"

"The spare prince. I'm to step in if anything happened to my brother. It's been my duty to do so since the day I was born. But now that he and his new wife will start producing little princes and princesses, I'll be bumped down the rungs of succession."

"That will give ya less duties, and more time for frivolous pursuits. Problem solved."

He made a sound somewhere between a laugh and a groan. It came from behind her. She spun toward it. "I never thought past being my brother's second," he said. "Until recently." In the ensuing few beats of silence, she intuited a sense of dissatisfaction in him.

He lived a life of unimaginable wealth and privilege, yet he had no real purpose in life other than existing. In contrast, every breath she took had purpose, every step to make a better future for her family. But then she looked survival and starvation in the face on a daily basis. To him they were mere words.

"But in my culture, fidelity, marriage, and family are held in high regard—meaning a *Vash* man does not make the selection of a mate lightly. Since I will not settle in any way, shape, or form, a permanent romantic pairing is not in my future."

"I won't settle, either."

"Ah, Kes." His tone sounded vaguely condescending, as if he were an elder brother advising her. "You're young yet."

"How old *are you*?"

"Twenty-seven, standard."

Only three years' difference. "Ah, Prince Klark," she mimicked. "You're young yet, too. It's too early for ya to give up on romance."

"Romance?"

"Aye. Why not?"

"It's a ridiculous notion, that's why."

She ducked as the rounded tip of his sens-sword whooshed past her shoulder. She escaped him, but only barely. Or, maybe only because he let her get away. After all, he could see in the dark and she could not.

"Great Mother. Why am I telling you all this?"

"I keep asking." Jemm gripped her sens-sword, tracking the sound of his voice as he circled her.

"But I keep answering. What have I not confessed? There can't be much left unsaid. Not even my sister Katjian can coax such natter out of me. Much to her dismay, I can assure you."

"When it comes to interrogation you've met your match."

"Apparently so. Now, be silent."

Disappearing, he sought to engage her on a different plane. She cast her net of awareness wide. In her mind it spun through the air, fanning out over a cerulean sea. He was out there, somewhere. She would catch him, reel him in. The sense of his presence was strong, as it always was; but with the advantage of sight, he evaded her net, reappearing anywhere, and everywhere. It kept her on her toes, mentally, but also a little off balance. That was the entire point of these exercises. The mind, like the body, needed to be worked hard in order to become stronger.

Come, Kes. Find me. I see you. Excellent. Now, try harder. You can do more. See me...feel me. You are better than you know. Yes, that's it. In the silence, they danced in the place called the in-between that only bajha players and those who dabbled in the mystical knew. Jemm felt the lure to delve deeper, to merge with him, but he was skilled enough to keep her at arm's length, until, finally, he burst into her cognizance.

In the blackness, she parried him. Their blades skidded crosswise until reaching the hilts. Their gloved knuckles crashed together. No fountain of brilliant violet light crowned the moment, as the swords were disarmed, only the grate of sword against sword, and then the thud of hers landing on his chest plate.

"Lights!" he called out. "Good!" He pulled off his glasses as she stood blinking at the sight of his handsome face in the rising illumination, as if she had rolled over in bed to find him next to her. "You keep improving, Kes—exponentially. Beyond my wildest expectations."

She bent over to catch her breath, propping her gloved hands on her knees. "Thank you."

He was equally winded. His skin gleamed with perspiration. "You are one of the most talented players I've ever encountered. Taking into account your street-bajha past, perhaps you *are* the best. The kind that comes along only once in a lifetime, if even that." He laughed quietly as he loosened the collar of his suit. "How lucky am I to have found you?"

He wore that wondrous expression again, the same one that took her breath away the first day she saw him. Her heartbeat stuttered, her insides warming, once again she wished it came from a fella who was interested in her as a lass, not from a team owner thrilled about his latest recruit. But she extricated her gaze from his. "I'll work hard to be the player you say I am," she managed.

He surged on ahead, heading to the locker room, and she followed. "I thought a few times this morning that you might beat Raff," he said. "I think you would have had him if it weren't for the poor condition of your gear, the noise of your suit and boots. You came close."

She grinned. "Aye. I did."

"Yonson won't be far behind, what with your learning curve. I'd really like to get you back to the training center on Chéyasenn as soon as possible to continue honing your skills. Before we know it, the regular season will begin. We have work ahead of us. Will you be able to settle your affairs here in the next day?"

"I think so, aye. I already told my family." She swallowed nervously with a now familiar mash-up of anxiety and anticipation. She forced her focus on pulling off her bajha boots and stowing them in her bag, pulling out her work boots to wear. Then one by one she undid the upper fasteners on her bajha suit.

"Very good. They are agreeable to your leaving?"

"My mother would rather I kept my old job—she ain't a fan of bajha—but it's an opportunity beyond our wildest dreams. No one will argue my going off with you, especially now that she's feeling a wee bit better from that medicine ya gave her."

"Good." He absorbed all that, then nodded. "Mothers always worry. If it makes you feel better, you should know that bajha is no mere hobby for me, a way for an idle royal to pass the time. It is a passion, yes, but to see Team Eireya win is a necessity. We will win that cup, Sea Kestrel. The Galactic Cup. This is our year. The Vedlas will reign supreme."

He reached for the hem of his overshirt to change clothes and pulled it over his head, tossing it into a laundry container. His black tank top clung to his muscled shoulders and chest. His coppery skin gleamed. He selected a plush towel and brought it to his face before draping it over his neck. "I want the honor not for me, Kes. I want it for my family. For everything they've had to endure the last few years."

"Did something bad happen to your family?"

"*I* happened." She could tell he had tried to make a joke, but remorse slid over the planes and angles of his face like shadows over the badlands. "Let me just say I am not the most liked, or the most trusted man in my family at the moment. The road back to being liked and trusted will be steep. This—you—the team, it's a start."

Whatever transpired, he was willing to own the blame for it. She admired any man who did.

Not enough to tell him the truth, apparently.

Viewing him through her biased, trill-rat lens, she had dismissed him as an aimless royal. It was a hasty call and it was wrong. He did have a purpose in life: using the Galactic Cup to bring honor to his clan. In the past few minutes she had learned that he had a family he loved and felt compelled to protect, as well as sins for which he felt obligated to atone. This was why he had come to this remote corner of the frontier to seek her out. This was why he had her train with pro players he had pulled away from other obligations, and this was why he radiated unabashed excitement every time he looked at her. Sea Kestrel was the path to his hopes and dreams.

Until she scuttled the entire thing for him.

Her insides knotted up with guilt. Until now she had worried only about herself and her family, but what about Prince Klark and his family? Didn't they matter, too? If her secret was uncovered, the scandal would potentially taint the entire team and sully his reputation as owner. No matter how desperate she was, what right did she have to do such a thing to a man who had shown her nothing but kindness?

"Kes?"

She swallowed. "Aye?"

"Sometimes I get the sense you're keeping something from me." To the sound of her hammering heart, he took a seat on the bench next to where she stood. His expression was even more solemn than usual. His accented words were measured, quiet, his pale golden eyes frank and unsettling as he searched her face for clues. "I want you to learn to trust me. Going forward, I'd like you to feel comfortable telling me anything."

Anything...

I'm Jemm.

Anything...

I'm a lass.

Blood pounded in her ears. She opened her mouth, then shut it, then nodded. "Aye..." She was perched on the precipice of embarking on a journey where the discovery of her secret could cause countless problems, for her and for these off-worlders who had trusted her. What about Skeet and Xirri, and their insistence on ending her innocence? That would not abate, just because she said she was too busy for romance. Not to mention the danger zone of the locker room with not two or three men undressing and showering but an entire bajha team, all of them growing more and more curious as to why she did not join in. Then, when her monthly womanly concerns came, what then? How would she deal with obtaining such personal supplies when she ran out? More, she owned only one cushioned vest to cover her breasts. Eventually, she would need to launder it, or order a new one made, both of which would raise suspicion. The deeper she sank into the abyss of this arrogant sham, the more the lies piled up on top of her. But if she called her own bluff, it meant giving up a future brighter than anything she could have imagined.

Perspiration beaded and tingled between her breasts, crushed behind the vest, as if her own body were calling on her to stop the madness. To confess.

Anything...

He meant everything.

What was she going to do?

"I should wash up." As if she could wash her lies away. She stalked over to the sink with soap and a towel. The face in the mirror did not look like a teenage boy at all. She saw a pale, worried lass with too-short blonde hair with dark red roots. She had cut her hair and quit her job while blinded by wishful thinking she could somehow fool this clever aristo, this prince. Well, she had fooled the man, all right, and maybe she could keep on fooling him. But that did not make it right.

What had she told Princess Katjian? Everyone should be allowed to pursue their dreams, as long as it did no harm. The probability of this ruse causing harm to Prince Klark and his family was high. Because she took this desperate gamble to help her own family, she was able to convince herself of the selflessness of her actions. But, it

made her—a lass who had always valued decency—
nothing more than a con artist.

Da would be ashamed of ya.

That was what she could not live with.

She turned around to face the *Vash*, the truth perched
on her lips, and found him scrutinizing a glint of metal in
her open gear bag: her timepiece, exposed by the sloppy
packing of her work leathers. When he glanced up, their
eyes met, and she knew he had figured her out.

CHAPTER FIFTEEN

That timepiece," Prince Klark said, reaching for it. "I've seen it before."

"It was my great-grandfather's, originally," she explained in a hoarse voice. "My Da wore it every day of his life. When he died, he passed it to me."

"Nico's girlfriend wore this." He cupped it in his hand, testing its substantial weight, reading the inscription on the back—*The Unexpected Brings Opportunity*—maybe even noting that the hands were frozen, because she had never gotten around to getting it repaired. "Details like that, I notice them. Is this timepiece yours, then? Or hers?"

She knew he hoped she would say, "Hers," or, "Mine, but I let her borrow it," so his suspicions could be erased.

"It's both." She cleared her throat. "I'm Jemm."

Disbelief flared in his eyes. "What?"

She stood tall even though inside she was shaking. "Aye, it's true. You came back that night to give me the salve, but I'd already changed back into my street clothes and brushed out my hair. So Nico pretended I was his girlfriend so ya would not recognize me. After that, I went home and cut my hair off."

He leaned forward as much as he recoiled at her words, as if he wanted to believe her admission as much as he wanted to deny it. His gaze slid up her long body, pausing on her chest, her throat, then her lips, before continuing up to her butchered hair. "Great Mother..."

He dropped the timepiece into the bag and shoved to his feet, stalking past her like a large angry predator that might spring an attack at any moment. "I knew it. All along, something didn't seem right." He paced angrily. "I recognized your scent. When I saw you with Nico I thought it was familiar. Then again when you showed up at the ship, I recognized it. But I dismissed it." He paused to scrutinize her then shook his head. "Impossible..."

"I assure ya, sir, I'm a lass, through and through. But I sure ain't stripping down to prove it."

His eyes riveted on her with brief, piercing interest. Her face felt suddenly hot. Blushing—*her*? Crag him.

Then he tore the towel off his neck and threw it into a container of soiled laundry. "I meant a female who can play bajha with your skill. That's what is impossible."

"I've already proved it ain't."

"I'll give you that." His laugh was quick, bitter, and lacking any mirth whatsoever.

"I was a tug driver—for the mines. One of only two females who hauled trailers of ore. It took muscle, aye. That's why more men did the job than women. But bajha is different. The key to being good at it isn't brawn." She tapped her head. "It's the mind. It's more about mental power than physical. Raw intuition over brute strength."

"It's about honor," he said flatly. "We play bajha to honor our warrior past. Not to disrespect it, Kes. Or Jemm. Whatever your name really is."

"I'm sorry ya think I bring dishonor to the sport. I tried very hard to do the opposite."

He rocked back on his heels and exhaled loudly. The crease between his brows was at an all-time depth. His lips formed a grim, angry line as he dragged both hands over his hair. He was not interested in negotiating; his views would not change because she was handy with a sens-sword. In his stuffy, oppressive culture, females were hidden away and protected, as if that somehow atoned for the fact that most of their women were raped, enslaved, and killed by barbaric hoards in the Dark Years. Even now, with the danger of that world long past, their women were not allowed to step into the bajha ring. Eleven thousand years of habit had made some pretty deep grooves in time's road.

"Our agreement is cancelled, obviously," he said, appearing to succeed in a heroic effort to calm down. It turned him into a cool, aloof stranger, and that about killed her. "But, here…" He pulled a pile of credits of various denominations from his pocket and thrust them at her. "Take them."

She recoiled. "Keep it. Time is money, and I wasted yours. I never meant to. I never thought past playing in the clubs. I never thought you'd come along and make the offer ya did. I got swept along in the fantasy of it all. I forgot who I was."

"I would imagine it's quite a lot to forget—that you are a woman." His eyes were stony, his tone mocking.

"I forgot about my principles. That trickery isn't in my nature. I did it for my family. My Da wanted to get all of us off Barésh, but he died before he could make it happen. So, I took over his dream. I knew it'd take years to save up enough to buy starship tickets. Decades. But my Ma, she… She may not have that kind of time. But if I earned extra playing bajha, I figured I could get us all out sooner…" Her explanation petered out when she saw he had averted his eyes, his jaw hardening. "But, I guess there ain't no shortcuts to dreams."

His expression was now so frigid that trying to explain herself any further would be like slamming her soul against a wall of ice. She replaced the towel and the soap and returned to her gear bag, yanking the zipper closed.

Then she paused one last time to soak in the sight of a real galactic royal only inches away, committing Sir Klark Vedla to memory for the long years to come, knowing she would never forget him or the opportunity he had offered. Or, his kind heart. It would be a story to tell Button's children someday, whom she desperately prayed would not have to be born on this festering space rock.

She hefted her bag's long strap over her shoulder. "I hope ya win the Galactic Cup. I'll be watching on the vids. Cheering on Skeet and Xirri. The entire team."

He answered with a dismissive wave, sending her on her way like any other upper-class cog did with a trill rat like her. Hot blood rushed into her head, her heart kicking in indignation. He could blame her all he wanted for her deceit, and she would not argue, but treat her like she was no more than badlands grit?

"Don't do that," she snapped.

Hands on his lean hips, his biceps bunching, he looked down his aristocratic nose at her. "Don't do what, pray tell?"

"Pretending like I'm nothing. Well, *I am* something to ya—more than something. I almost beat your two best players. If I'd had a few more matches to polish up, by the dome, I know I'd have finished them off. Are ya really gonna let me walk away?" She paused for a breath or two, daring him to take a chance on her, but his expression remained aloof, his gaze frosty. "You are, aren't ya? You're gonna let me walk away—your next champion—all because my body parts violate your antiquated Federation dogma. It gets my blood to boiling just thinking about it."

She drew the bag strap closer to her body to give her shaking hands something to do. She was grateful that her husky voice remained steady. "I'd rather have my life than a royal's any day, boxed in by all your rules. I might not have much but at least I've got the hope of freedom. I'll find a way off Barésh. Aye, I'll find a way."

Without a backward glance, she left the locker room to trek back to the city. No boots thumped behind her as she exited the tubes for the docks. What did she expect—that he would change his mind? He was a prince, second in line for a throne. He would be the laughingstock of the *Vash Nadah* if he signed a woman to his team.

Using bajha techniques, she made her mind go blank. It hurt too much to think about what she had lost.

As soon as Kes left the locker room, Klark turned to the wall and slapped his hands against the cold, tiled wall, keeping them pressed there, fingers spread, willing his hands to serve as anchors to prevent him from going after her.

Sea Kestrel, a female.

A woman!

No mere woman, either. He remembered her as Jemm, the errant Nico's alleged girlfriend: her long, strong, lean body and the graceful way she moved; that swaying, tempting bottom as she walked away; her wavy hair wild and loose—all but begging for his fingers to be tangled in it as he made love to her.

Damnation. The mental image alone made his body react and his blood run hot. Yet, this same female to which he was so attracted played bajha far better than he ever could. He had come to respect her as an unbelievably talented athlete, had let down his guard around her as a friend, and now she was a beautiful woman, as well? In his world, such disparate qualities could not apply to any one person. Yet, together, they added up to Jemm.

The ship's comm chimed. Klark shoved away from the wall. "What is it?"

"Your Highness." It was the starpilot Kuentin on the viewscreen. "Mr. Skeet and Mr. Xirri have arrived safely back aboard their tour ship."

"Excellent. Thank you, Kuentin." Klark inhaled a stabilizing breath.

"As well, we just heard from the Barésh Port Control. We are a go for a midnight departure."

"Very good." Klark nodded, and the screen went blank. It was what he wanted, wasn't it? To escape this god-awful space rock?

Not without *her*.

He yanked on fresh clothing and hurried from the locker room. His stride radiated purpose, even though on the inside he was still spinning like a faulty navigational gyro, struggling to realign himself with the bombshell dropped on him. The inscription on Jemm's timepiece read, *The Unexpected Brings Opportunity*. It was one of the more important teachings of the Treatise of Trade. Jemm Aves, AKA Sea Kestrel, was nothing if not unexpected. But also an opportunity.

Like hell if he was going to let a player that good slip through his fingers.

The arena was silent, save for the muffled thuds of his steps. Usually, he could find peace there, in the solitude, but as he followed the railing encircling the ring, he envisioned Sea Kestrel shadowing him as he paced around the perimeter. She had displayed so much natural instinct and powerful intuition in the ability to track him that Klark sometimes wondered if she could see in the dark.

Or into his dark soul.

He set his jaw and plunged on ahead. In the dining room a server was in the midst of setting the table with an afternoon tock service for two: a pitcher filled with piping-hot tock, the ubiquitous caffeinated beverage, along with breads, fruit, pastries, and a pair of mugs. But in his mind's eye he saw a platter of ice chips containing

live seafood, and the memory of Sea Kestrel's—
Jemm's—green-and-gold eyes opening wide at the sight.
He could hear her swearing as Skeet smashed a runaway
dab with a plate, and then all of them laughing. But as he
bypassed the dining table it seemed so empty of life and
energy it was hard to fathom the moment ever happened.

But indeed it had. He had spent two solid days with
Jemm with only the few short night hours apart: sharing
meals, training her, joining her on the mats to push
themselves to the limits of their physical endurance,
studying vids of pro bajha matches until their eyes were
bleary. Two days laughing with her—and at her, pushing,
goading, encouraging, demanding the best from her.
Telling her things he had never admitted to anyone else.

"Well, I am *something to ya—more than
something..."*

Her observation was truer than she might realize. Now
that he knew she was a woman, it made sense why their
developing friendship had felt like more. He had never
experienced anything like it.

"Will Mr. Aves be joining you for tock, Your
Highness?" the server inquired, surprised to see Klark
about to exit through the glass doors.

"No." Klark's tone was clipped. "Nor will I be
partaking. Offer it to the crew."

He cut through the flight deck area. "Possible schedule
change," he alerted the starpilots. "I'll be in the city, and
may be late returning." Many curious eyes told him the
whole crew must have wondered at Sea Kestrel's sudden
departure.

The impacts of Klark's boots resounded on the
gangway. By the time he exited the tubes he had
accelerated into a lope. It was growing dark. Foul smog
and moisture blurred the city's harsh edges. He came to a
winded halt in the center of the port, turning in a slow
circle to scan the busy area. Jemm was nowhere to be
seen. If he knew her like he thought he did, without her

driving job to provide a source of income, she would waste no time returning to the clubs and a money stream. He started toward a fleet of hovercars for hire when, on the far side of the port where the wide road narrowed, he spied a tall, slender bajha player in a baggy suit.

She wasn't walking. She was racing.

He would have to sprint to keep her in sight.

This was the moment of decision—to turn around, to let her go. He was supposed to be abiding by the terms of his early release from house arrest. He was fairly certain "good behavior" did not include dashing through a hardscrabble neighborhood in the slums of a mining colony to chase down a female dive-bar sword swinger.

To hell with that.

Every molecule in his body told him that going after Jemm was the right choice. It was like playing bajha and knowing your opponent's chest plate would be there at the completion of your blind thrust.

As he predicted, she turned toward Ore's Head, the club Nico had leased and now spent much of his time. The gaudy glow of those blasted Earth-dwellers' medical tent but not the tent itself was visible behind the buildings. But other than that, being back in the noisy, bustling neighborhood of arcades was unchanged from last week. It brought thoughts of the first night here with Skeet and Xirri, the anticipation so rich, and then the reality of Sea Kestrel's talent being far better than he could have imagined.

Not to mention the reality of the woman herself. She was, in a word, incredible.

"Kes!"

She froze at the sound of the name, her spread hand on the club's front door. She spun around as he jogged to a halt in front of her. "I would like a word with you." At her bewildered nod, he took her by the upper arm and ushered her inside. He steered her through the pounding blare of thump music and a restless early evening crowd, wishing he could grasp her by the hand instead. But he must remain cognizant of the fact that everyone except Nico thought she was a male.

He found a nook in an area of fewer bodies if not less noise. Wedged inside, they were alone. Her skin gleamed from exertion, her questioning, wide-open eyes caressing every inch of his face, her lips parted—only because she was eager to hear his excuse for being here, not because she anticipated the taste of his. Yet, the proximity of her soft mouth made his heartbeat stumble.

"I erred," was all he would allow himself to say—or even *to think*. This plan, to work as he intended, required precise execution. Reckless romantic feelings had no part in it. "You'll play as a male, but with one difference. This time I'll know your secret. That's how we'll make it work…the only way it can work."

"You were so against females playing," she ventured.

"I never saw one play! More than that, I've never seen anyone who plays like you—male or female. I'll be damned if I allow bias to deter me from seeing you reach your potential. Bias ruled my actions too many times in the past. I've learned my lesson." He kept his voice very low in the dark corner where they were crushed close. Her scent muddled his thoughts. He wanted to drink it in, to drink in all of her, but such longings threatened to distract him from business and turn this encounter into something far more personal.

He summoned every bit of discipline that his upbringing and bajha had given him to continue his proposal, his tone brusque. "I'm not naïve enough to believe a female player will be greeted without controversy. Nor am I stupid enough to let someone with your talent get away. As for the religious aspects of females practicing bajha…it will take some delving into the Treatise of Trade to see what guidance it offers, specifically. But, I'll bear the responsibility of the research. All of that said, are you willing to give this another try?"

"Aye. What do ya think? I'm gonna win us that Galactic Cup." Her earnest expression made his chest ache. "Where will I train—the main team arena?"

"No." Great Mother, no. Throwing her into the lusty clutches of his pros was not something he wanted to think about. It was still the preseason. He would figure it out. He was making this up as he went along, and did not like it, being a habitual plotter and planner. He felt most comfortable knowing what was next and preferred deciding how he would negotiate a matter in advance. In this, however, he had gone off the charts. All he knew was that he did not want to lose Sea Kestrel. "I'll find a facility that allows us—*you*—some privacy."

They were standing even closer now to keep their whispered conversation from reaching prying ears. Her rapid pulse throbbed in her neck, visible above the collar of her bajha suit. A lock of hair had flopped onto her forehead; the urge to smooth it aside was powerful. He imagined his fingertips brushing across her forehead, the pad of his thumb tracing the swell of her cheekbone... *Damnation.* He wanted to kiss her, to feel her yield to him. To lose himself in her.

"Above all..." He cleared his throat to disguise his hoarseness. "You're a pro, and I'm your coach. No matter what insanity may have gotten us to this point, we must respect that relationship."

He saw comprehension wash over her face and, faintly, disappointment. Then, as she nodded, a defiant glimmer sparked in her gemlike hazel eyes. Or had he imagined it?

He hoped so. Otherwise, they were going to be in trouble.

CHAPTER SIXTEEN

F irst, we will see to your fittings with the tailor, then practice with your new sens-sword. Lunch afterward, followed by technique analysis of Teams Dar and Lesok this afternoon." As Prince Klark set out the day's schedule, striding at his usual pace, Jemm slowed, reluctant to tear her gaze from the bank of windows inside the training annex overlooking a breathtaking view of a forested valley. The air on planet Chéyasenn was so fragrant with moist earth and thriving plant life that she drank it in as much as breathed it. No wonder the world had been chosen as the team's home base. Millions of trees went on endlessly, hill after covered hill until they ended in a blue-green blur on the horizon, where two huge pastel crescents dominated the sky—plump, sleepy cousins to Barésh's feverish, always-in-motion moons. To the west, a compact city gleamed— Chéyasenn City. Its white and silver buildings were manmade spires amongst nature's spires: the trees. Somewhere hidden in the forest there was the sprawling main training center for Team Eireya.

"Jemm," he said as they walked. "No dawdling. We have much to do today."

"I'm sightseeing. If ya didn't want me looking, then ya should not have chosen such a beautiful place to train."

He cast her a long look. They arrived on Chéyasenn that morning after many demanding days traveling on *Chéya's Resolute* to a transfer station, where they picked up the starspeeder that Prince Klark himself had piloted here. Each day's schedule had been packed full from dawn until she collapsed onto her bed each night. The pace did not look to be easing anytime soon. Since landing at the training annex, Prince Klark had kept her on the move. The man was on a mission.

She was the mission.

Casting one last hungry glance at the scenery, she pivoted to tread after him in soft boots on the polished wood-plank floor. During their travels, he had made sure to supply her with a selection of comfortable and loose men's shirts and pants. If he was put off by her wearing men's clothing, he did not show it. In fact, the more her feminine form was disguised, the more relieved he appeared. She was his secret, and he wanted to keep it that way. "Do ya get to explore much while you're here? I think I see hiking paths."

"No, I have not had the chance to dally when here. But since much of the world is a wildlife sanctuary, I'm sure many who stay at the retreat center take advantage of the grounds."

"Retreat center. So, this isn't technically a training annex."

"We will use it as such. But no, it's an Eireyan warrior retreat center." He waved a hand at unfamiliar runes carved into a towering stone fortress of a fireplace, the focal point of a cavernous space that seemed to pay homage to masculinity with its rugged furnishings, muted colors, and soaring walls constructed of whole logs. Each log was wider than she was tall. She could not imagine any living thing could grow so big. "There's the warrior's code, in case you forget it," he said dryly. He read the giant words to her, "Fealty, fidelity, family."

"Is that written in Eireyan?"

"It is. Basic will always remain the official language of the Trade Federation, as it facilitates trade between worlds that use individual dialects. We highborn *Vash* also learn Siennan, the language of the B'kah clan. However, Eireyan, my clan's ancient tongue, is cherished, but rarely used anymore."

His family had their own language. It was another reminder that he was part of something much larger than she was. Whereas her family history went only as far back as the great-grandfather who came to Barésh from off-world and got her great-grandmother pregnant. A story that was vague at best. But anyone who might be able to clear up the details was dead.

"Kind of ironic, me training for bajha in a virtual warriors' hub. Considering females aren't allowed to be warriors, or play bajha."

"Thus the reason I brought you here—to hide Team Eireya's secret weapon in plain sight." He used the cozy tone of a coconspirator, but with a defined distance between them that had not wavered since leaving Barésh. She could hardly believe he was the same man who had pulled her in the only private space they could find in that club, standing so close together they were almost embracing. Almost kissing. "Now, come. We have much to do."

He left her under the gigantic runes, walking away so swiftly that it generated a breeze. He had used a different soap this morning, and she liked it. It was spicy, a mix of ingredients she would never be able to guess but that she liked with her first sniff. Heated by his warm skin, it left a faint scent trail behind him as his long, athletic strides carried him away.

"I have summoned a female tailor to fit you for your team uniforms as well as new clothing," he said when she caught up. "It may be temperate here now, but not this winter. You'll need warmer clothing."

"My measurements won't add up as a man's. Won't the tailor be suspicious?"

"She is bound by confidentiality, as are all the retreat center staff. None of them know the real reason you are here, anyway. They live and work at the center. Their lives are dedicated to looking after it and the warriors who visit, and have been for countless generations."

"So, they'll probably assume I'm your paramour." That was the word a *Vash* royal might use, wasn't it? The Baréshti term "bed warmer" did not sound quite as glamorous.

Hearing the word, he broke stride, the slightest hitch in his step, before he resumed his pace. "They are not paid to assume, Jemm. They are paid to serve."

True, that in the short time since arriving she had noticed the staff flitting in and out of sight like shadows. They had laid out a welcoming snack of beverages and fruit, but unlike the staff on the starship, they did not linger or interact.

Prince Klark allowed her to precede him into a round room with windows made of thick, curved glass, open to more stunning scenery. Jemm turned in a slow circle to take in the views around her. An intricate woven round rug provided a luxurious cushion for her boots.

A very tall, very slender and angular woman with *Vash* coloring entered after them on silent feet and seemingly out of nowhere. "I am Saffrenn. May I take your measurements now?" She set a basket on the rug.

"Aye, of course."

"Raise your arms." Instead of using flexible fabric tapes to measure like Ma did, the tailor aimed a hand-sized rectangular box at Jemm. She lifted the hem of Jemm's shirt, exposing her stomach, sliding the device over her bare skin until it beeped twice. She slid the device higher, underneath her shirt and over her bra with a tailor's indifference, measuring her breasts, her rib cage, her waist. "Turn around please."

Jemm rotated, and locked gazes with Prince Klark, whose pale eyes seemed to drink in the sight of her standing there, her hands over her head, her shirt askew, her bare skin visible to him. She sucked in a breath. His penetrating gaze made her feel as if she wore far less. "Say something in Eireyan," she said on impulse, her voice a little thicker.

The sudden heat in his intense, searching gaze made her toes curl. "*Enajhe a'nai.*"

She felt the barrier they had erected crumbling. "What does that mean?"

He snapped his attention away, and she sensed him reeling in his emotions like a poorly cast fishing net. "Eireyan can be learned after you master Basic." His words were clipped and brusque. He turned his back to her, his hands clasped just so at the small of his back as he appeared to admire the scenery he had shown so little interest in observing earlier.

Master Basic? What was that supposed to mean? She was itching for the tailor to finish so she could ask him. Aristo cog.

Then it hit her why she was so mad—not at him but with herself. It was not the comment so much as what led up to it. Before he learned the truth about her, she could gawk at him or tease him from behind the barrier of her disguise. Things were different now. Ever since that night in Nico's club, they had been dancing around an underlying attraction that transcended any mutual interest in bajha. Flirting with each other had as much explosive potential as a tank of fuel left out in the sun too long.

Saffrenn ran the measuring box down one of Jemm's long legs then the other. Then she bowed to Prince Klark and retreated with her device and basket.

Prince Klark wasted no time exiting the room. Jemm wasted even less time catching up to him. "What do ya mean—when I've mastered Basic? I know Basic, through and through."

"Baréshti Basic, perhaps. But the dialect, the swearing, have you ever heard a pro on the news vids who sounds like you?"

Taken aback by his candor when she was expecting to bicker, she frowned. "No. But I've never seen anyone who looked like me, either."

He winced. "True. However, being a pro-player is more than just good moves. You'll need to be the whole package. Galactic League pros are expected to be ambassadors of the sport, to be able to hobnob with the lords and ladies of the realm and also chat with a starpilot's little children. You'll travel everywhere, representing the Trade Federation wherever you go. It's best not to swear at all when in the public eye, but if you must—as we all do at times—say blast instead of crat. Or some such term."

"Blast…" The word sat so strangely on her tongue that she made a face. "No matter how much I practice fancy speech no one's ever gonna believe I'm a noble-born lass." She winced. "A noble-born *lad*." Or maybe a lad at all. She had escaped the burden of having to fool Prince Klark only to be reminded she would have to dupe the entire Trade Federation while touring countless worlds and meeting untold numbers of people. How was she ever going to pull that off? Expectation bias could only go so far.

"No, Jemm. My intent isn't to pass you off as a noble. I'll be working hard enough as it is passing you off as a male."

Reminded once again of the enormity, *the insanity*, of their scheme, they both cringed.

"Besides, everyone loves an underdog. I don't want to see all of your dialect scrubbed away, only some of the rougher edges."

"Aye, I have a few of those."

"We'll work on that while we're here. By the time I present you to the public, you'll be ready." He glanced over at her silence. "I hope you know I'm not criticizing." "I know. You're crattin' right, though. I mean—*blasted* right." He did not want to change the essence of who she was, but he had come to Barésh looking for more than a back-alley fight-club entertainer. He expected her to be able hold her own in any arena, while trusting her not to embarrass him outside of it. She owed him that and more—a lot more.

They walked fast, too fast, past more endless views. Prince Klark did not seem to notice any of it. He was as hell-bent on reaching the arena as a tug driver speeding to the city at dome-set. It was his reaction to their flirting in front of the tailor. She forgave him his single-minded focus.

Outside the windows—many of them flung open to the outdoors—was a sweeping deck made from more planks. Groupings of rough-hewn wood chairs were placed here and there. A circle of boulders looked to be another place to start a fire. Above, the sky went up, up, up toward floating puffs of clouds and beyond. No smog-filled dome held anything in, or kept anything out.

Then, something soared by overhead. "A bird." Jemm burst through the open doors and trotted across the deck to watch the little thing swoop away to where it disappeared into the canopy of trees. Birdsong told of others hiding within the branches. The prospect of seeing them lured her to the railing. Her soft boots were silent on the deck's rugged planks as she crossed its expanse.

The *Vash*'s heavier footfalls sounded behind her. Beaming, she turned around. "Did ya see it? A bird flew over. A live, flying bird." Her smile faltered when she saw the telltale line had formed between his brows.

"There are many birds on Chéyasenn. You'll be used to them by the time you leave."

"I'm not used to them yet." She turned back to the railing, scanning the sky while shielding her eyes from the sun that was this world's parent star.

"I want to get in a practice before luncheon," he said. "Luncheon is to be served at one."

"There—another one!" She pointed at the sky.

He scraped a hand over his dark coppery hair, a gesture of frustration she had come to recognize. A few locks of hair stood up crookedly, little rebels in his otherwise immaculate appearance. Sunlight played across his sculpted profile, thawing some of his impatience, but not all. "All right. We'll take the stairs. We can reach the arena from the lower level, as well."

On silent boots they descended...into paradise. As they rounded the landing, the stairs spilled out into a vast area of greenery. She knew it was a lawn from vids she had seen, but in reality and up-close a lawn was a lush blue-green carpet of tiny individual plants with soft flat, triangular leaves. It was springy under her boots and under her palm when she crouched down to feel it. The fragrance made her lightheaded with pleasure.

The lawn ended at a pool fringed by boulders and carefully tended plants that was much longer than it was wide. A waterfall tumbled over the boulders on one end, bubbling where it entered the pool. Her reflection undulated on the surface, a stranger's short-haired silhouette, as she kneeled down to dip her hands in the water. "This sure ain't what they pump into the mines. That foul brew is reclaimed, and it stinks. This is fresh and real." She scooped some water into her cupped hands, with reverence. It drained out from between her palms, and she scooped up more, standing and turning back to Prince Klark. "Is it drinkable?"

He stood several body lengths away to watch her, his hands behind his back. It was as if there were an invisible line he had drawn, and he damn well was not going to cross it. "It wouldn't harm you, but I'm not quite sure how it would taste. The purpose of the water feature is for recreation."

"Like swimming?"

"And meditation. Plus, the fish swimming in it may not want to share."

She laughed, finally seeing silver and gold fish darting beneath the surface. Her hands were still cupped, water dribbling down her arms. "Will you teach me to swim?"

Eagerness then dismay—the emotions had flickered in his eyes before he could hide them from her. "At some point, perhaps. We have dallied here long enough." He turned to go.

"Wait." She curled her damp hands into fists and pressed them to her chest, drawing air in through her nose. "Before we go, take a moment just to be. To feel the humidity. To smell the living things. The soil, the woods, the leaves. The air here makes me dizzy, but a good dizzy, not Barésh smog, lung-clogging dizzy."

His deepening frown and impatience to go back inside irked her. Didn't he ever take time to pause and enjoy life? Was he all business, all the time? "We are here to train."

"Aye, I know. But do ya have to be such a cog about it?"

"A cog...?"

"Aye. A cog. A sourpuss, an unpleasant person to be around." She walked to him, her loose fists still pressed below her collarbone. "I will train hard, aye. I swear it, and you know it. My family depends on us succeeding. Your family does, too."

Discomfort flickered at the edges of his mouth.

"But, before we leave Chéyasenn, I'm going to learn to swim, whether you teach me, or one of the pros does—"

"A pro is not going to teach you to swim," he pronounced as if issuing a royal decree. "I will."

She smiled a grin of victory, and took another step toward him. "I want to hike on the paths, too. I want to smell everything, to taste everything, to see the birds, and the trees. All of it. In my wildest dreams I couldn't have imagined a place like this. I feel like I've been caged all my life and now I'm finally free. So don't ya go acting like a cog about it—"

His warm hands molded to her head to silence her, his slightly roughened thumbs sliding over her cheekbones as he brought his face close to hers. "Jemm..." His whisper was harsh against her lips.

"What?" she asked weakly.

"I have to act like a cog. Else, I'll kiss you, and I won't want to stop."

They stood there, frozen to the spot. The taut muscles of his chest flexed against her fists, his heart thumping hard. "Holy dome," she said on a sigh. "I might not want ya to stop."

"We have an agreement, Jemm. To be coach and player."

"Aye. I remind myself of it every hour of the day."

"Sometimes, I find myself thinking, are we crazy, doing what we've set out to do?"

"Sometimes? I think that all the time."

"Damnation, Jemm. Why did you have to be so talented?" He tipped her head up, his lips so close. "Why did you have to be so gorgeous?"

"In my short hair? In my men's clothes?"

"It was an ignorant remark. You've proved it so a thousand times over." His mouth grazed over her jawbone to her ear. "You're a beautiful woman," he whispered. A shiver zoomed across her skin, raising bumps on her arms. "I wish I had met you outside of all this. Then we could have had more."

"As a *Vash* lady of the court? With no knowledge of bajha? You'd have found me boring."

"If I met you in Narrow Margin, then."

"Then I'd have found *you* boring. Some stuffy, uppity elite, looking for a one-night bed-warming with a trill rat girl. No thanks."

He shook his head, his laugh quick and quiet. "And so, here we are, and who we are. In this quandary..."

Her stomach fluttered as he brushed his smooth, sun-warm lips across hers.

"About our agreement," she whispered, "You're not making it any easier, by doing that."

"I know."

She flattened her hands on his chest, brushing her thumbs over his pectorals and the nubs of his nipples hidden beneath the fabric of his shirt. His body gave a single tremor, his fingers convulsing around her skull as she ran the pointed tip of her tongue across his lower lip. She never made it to the corner of his mouth before he tipped her head back and kissed her fully.

Her knees almost gave out, but he held her upright, bringing her to her toes. Her lips parted, his tongue searching out hers. Heat coursed through her, her hands caught between their bodies, his fingers buried in her short, soft tufts of hair. He smelled of spice and the musky, masculine scent that was uniquely his. Combined with the sweet heat of his kiss, it was downright intoxicating, warming her deep, deep inside. She imagined them tumbling down to the soft grass, making love to the sound of the waterfall under a domeless sky...

But as quickly as the kiss happened, he ended it. She swallowed a moan of protest as he dragged his mouth from hers. Taking a deep breath, he slid his hands to her shoulders and moved her back. "I take full blame," he said, a little out of breath, too, his golden eyes dark and regretful.

"No. I do."

"I let it happen, Jemm."

"Aye, ya did. But it was mighty good as kisses go."

A hint of amusement and also pleasure at her remark glimmered in his eyes. "Which is exactly why, from now on, we have to be strong."

She nodded. "With what we're trying to pull off, me fighting as a lad, it wouldn't be a good idea to be making yipwag eyes at each other."

He gave her a startled glance. "What are yipwag eyes?"

"It's a Baréshti expression for when you're soft on someone. Yipwags are the shaggy little creatures you see running loose all over the colony. Wagging tails and wet noses. Cute little dozers with big brown eyes."

"No, it would not be a good thing to have yipwag eyes for each other. Soon I have to start playing you against the other pros on the team. I'm good; I can teach you the league rules and whip you into shape, but I'm nowhere near the level they are. I'll invite them here, one or two at a time. It will get you the practice you need, while protecting your privacy."

And their secret.

"I think it's time to get back to work," he said. "Do you agree?"

Smoothing her shirt and then her hair, she took off after him before he got too much of a head start across the lawn. The focused, all-business *Vash* was back in all his aristo glory. But this time she knew it was his valiant effort to protect them both. She was not on Barésh anymore, where any impulse could be acted upon. No, she had entered a new world. With that came responsibility, and willpower.

It meant playing this game by their agreed-upon rules. But it was not going to be easy.

Over the next few days, Prince Klark was a taskmaster of training. They both knew why he drove them both so hard, but neither of them mentioned it.

Jemm learned to play with her new gear: a beautiful brand-new sens-sword and custom-made helmet and bajha suit. She demanded so much of herself that by the end of each day she ached from head to toe. When they were not practicing, Prince Klark coached her on table manners, terms of address, proper etiquette, and readings from the Treatise of Trade, the Federation's holiest document. It would take a person years to slog through it all. He had been at it all his life, and still he did not know everything it contained, a fact proven many times over when she saw him studying it late at night or early in the morning. In fact, she caught him reading the book every free moment he had.

The Book of Everything, she dubbed it. It contained the entire, eleven-thousand-year-long history of the Trade Federation, as well as what little knowledge survived the war of the Time Before and, prior to even that, the scarce details about the Ancients, the long-vanished civilization whose priceless legacy was the gift of advanced technology: most importantly worm hole space travel. Besides the rules regulating intergalactic trade and commerce, there was a virtual forest of *Vash* family trees, fusty, old-fashioned views on men's and women's roles in *Vash* society, detailed (and illustrated!) passages of instruction on sex—which Prince Klark briskly avoided showing her—politics, etiquette, rights of ascension, rights of passage, rights of way, human rights, and nearly everything else imaginable.

Her head spun like a loose ore canister with all there was to learn.

Yet, despite all their efforts to pretend otherwise, the memory of The Kiss lingered like the scent of a snuffed-out candle, suspended in the air between them, yet ignored with diligence by two expert bajha players who were trained to resist distractions.

"The speeder is standing by to fly you here," Klark told Torii G'Zanna, the pro he had handpicked to face Jemm in a practice match. Torii was happily married with three children. His book-perfect technique in the ring was admired across the galaxy. Both aspects made him the perfect choice for the first candidate Klark invited to the annex. "You'll play Sea Kestrel then join us for dinner."

He smiled. "Yes, sir. I look forward to it. I've heard a lot about young Sea Kestrel."

Suddenly, Xirri's face popped into the screen with G'Zanna's. His eyes were alight with mischief but he wore a pout. "We all feel sorry for you, Kes, trapped over there at the monastery."

In the corner of his eye, Klark saw Jemm put down the ionic beverage she had been sipping as they relaxed in the anteroom to the gym. He did not miss the annoyed twist to her mouth as Xirri waggled his thick brows.

"Don't despair. Life will be more fun once you get over here."

Klark heard other players' laughter in the background, although G'Zanna shot the off-screen pros a quelling glare. "Leave it be, chaps. Kes is about the same age as my eldest, and I wouldn't want him hanging out with the likes of you."

"Raff, get back to practice, or I'll trade you to the Lesoks," Klark growled.

"Sorry, Your Highness." Chastened, Xirri bowed out.

"See you shortly, sir," G'Zanna said.

Klark closed out the call and erased the screen with a flick of his hand. He leaned back in his chair and drummed his fingers on his knee. As always, he was torn between wanting Jemm to blend in and his powerful need to protect her from the testosterone-charged pros. "You're a slum-bred youth battling culture shock," he thought aloud. "Thus, you require a chaperone wherever you go..."

"I've got this. I've worked with fellas most of my adult life." Jemm had finished her drink and was now stretching, using the mind-calming, flexibility-enhancing moves he had taught her.

"Not as a woman disguised as a man."

"Aye, that's true. Still, I can handle them." On her stomach, she pushed up on her arms, throwing her head back as she arched her back. Her black T-shirt clung to her torso and the curve of her spine. The muscles in her strong, bare arms flexed as she lengthened the stretch even more. It pulled the fabric of her shirt taut across her small, jutting breasts.

The instant he imagined their warm weight in his hands he was rock-hard. He shifted in the chair to stare outside at a far more harmless view, trying, and failing, to think his body into submission. He had never in his life wanted a woman as badly as he did Jemm, the one woman he must not have. Was it because she was forbidden fruit?

If only that were the reason. It was far too easy of an explanation for the way she dominated his thoughts and made his body react to her with a mere glance. He was a *Vash Nadah*. The unique combination of discipline, self-control, and intimate skills strengthened by the guidance of fealty, fidelity, and family, the warrior's code, defined a male *Vash*. It was an integral part of his education as a male of his culture to be sexually knowledgeable and skillful in bringing intimate pleasure to a female, whether she was a wife or a palace courtesan. But, his sexual education also included being trained from a young age to exercise mental discipline as well as physical. The fact that he found himself having to work on his basics all over again proved that Jemm had less to worry about from Xirri and his cohorts than she did from him.

Two standard hours later, Torii G'Zanna tore open the neck fasteners of his bajha suit as his team owner applauded with a slow clap of his hands. "That was an excellent match, both of you," Klark said.

"And a fast one. I don't recall ever being defeated that quickly. In fact, I know I've never been." The big man blinked the stunned look off his face and turned to Jemm. "I'll say it again, and this time with meaning. Welcome to the team, Kes."

With utter humbleness, Jemm took his offered hand, her voice husky from being forced deeper. "It is an honor to have played against you, Mr. G'Zanna."

"It's Torii. And the honor is mine." The pro shook his head slowly, reaching for a towel and a drink. "How about we rest a bit, and try again?"

"Sure," Jemm said.

Klark shrugged. "That's why we're here."

He returned to the spectator bench outside the ring, took a seat, and let out a soft, victorious laugh.

CHAPTER SEVENTEEN

Jemm could not help grinning the next day as she watched another defeated pro soar away on a speeder back to the main training center. Not only had Torii G'Zanna failed to beat her in any of the sparring matches the day before, but today Garlan Muse fell to her—repeatedly.

When the speeder disappeared beyond the trees, she asked Prince Klark, "Who's next?"

He consulted his tablet. "Tomorrow is…Xirri."

Ah, Xirri. That should be interesting. "I'll be ready for him."

Prince Klark's grin sparkled. "I know you will be. I hope he's ready for you."

He seemed a different man since she beat the two pros. He was so buoyant with enthusiasm it made her heart sing. Her fine performance in the ring was the cause of it. The better she played, the less likely someone would question who—or what—she was. So she had doubled up on her mission to be the best, pushing herself to her mental and physical limits, knowing any loss, however small, would bring doubt—doubt that she could prevail against the men who dominated the sport, doubt that

Prince Klark's decision made to sign a female-in-disguise to his team would be worth the terrible risk. In the jaded view of the Federation no female could possibly be as good as she was. Ironic that the very opinion she wanted to see changed was the one that would protect her secret.

"However..." She placed her hands behind her back in an imitation of Prince Klark at his Mr. Serious worst. "We should address an emergency situation first."

The appearance of the crease between his brows was instant. "I know of no emergency situation."

Jemm tried hard not to laugh. "I'm in danger of drowning." She loved the way he blinked at her as he tried to make sense of the mischief in her eyes coupled with the seriousness of her tone. "As a galactic pro, I'll soon be visiting other worlds. What if I stumble into a body of water? It could very well be fatal." She paced in front of him. "Then there are the bathtubs I may encounter, or even heavy downpours. The likelihood of my drowning is very, very high, all because my coach never found time to teach me to swim."

His lips twitched. "I see your point. We must make learning to swim a priority. After I've put so much work into you, to lose you in a bathtub just doesn't seem right."

"Cog." She pushed at him.

He laughed merrily and it was contagious.

After changing clothing they carried towels down to the pool. Chéyasenn's nighttime sky lacked the ever-moving drama of Barésh's dome, but it was beautiful in a stately, dignified way. Billions of tiny stars flung across the indigo heavens like grains of crystal-sand. It seemed to magnify the bite in the air. While it was still summertime on Chéyasenn, on an instinctive, elemental level Jemm knew that autumn was not far off. It was as if her DNA that originated on other worlds never forgot the seasons.

Small lights lining the path flickered like candles. "These lights remind me of the apartment, and my Ma.

She lights candles to save money on utilities, but I always loved the way it made the apartment look at night. Soft. Not so run-down."

"You miss your family very much, I know."

"Something awful, aye. But more than missing them sometimes, I worry." Had Nico taken Ma to the Doctors Without Borders as he had promised? Was he trying to be more involved in his daughter's life? Maybe Jemm's absence had encouraged him to step in to fill the void.

"My offer still stands, Jemm. I'm happy to transport your family off Barésh at my expense. I'll see that they are settled anywhere in the Federation—even right here in Chéyasenn City, where many of the team families live."

They both went silent at the thought of that. The reality. It was not fair to force her mother and her niece into the situation of having to pretend Jemm was male.

"Never mind on that last suggestion," Prince Klark said, intuiting her thoughts exactly.

"I know you would do all ya could for us." His kindness and generosity were a constant, and never failed to tug at her emotions. But she feared Nico would not want to go yet. If she were to sever father and daughter, they may never recover the relationship. Plus, Ma and Button would feel lost and alone if she was not with them. "But it's best this way." The weeks were flying by. Soon she would be reunited with her family, and they would begin their new life.

She tipped her head back to see the sky. *Da, I know you're up there somewhere in the Ever After, watching over me.* Spreading her arms wide, she could imagine soaring overhead like the Sea Kestrel for which she was named.

This time it was Prince Klark who had to speed up catch her. Shoulder to shoulder, they walked in companionable silence. She yearned to slide her fingers inside his warm hand.

Then she wondered if his sudden silence meant he regretted surrendering to her badgering for swimming lessons. They would be in wet, clinging clothing, and little of it. Plus, she assumed there would be some actual touching involved with the lesson. Neither of them had forgotten what happened the last time they touched.

It had all the hallmarks of trouble in the making.

"Con, ready the pool for swimming," he told the outdoor controller. In an instant the lights in the pool illuminated, sending startled fish darting in all directions. A net motored over them, drawing them into a separate section, before steam rose from the main pool into the chilly air. "The heat would harm them, but behind the nanocrylic, they're safe." He unbuttoned his shirt and removed it before pushing down his trousers, revealing skintight black shorts underneath that extended partway down his muscled thighs. Drawing hard on her bajha skills, she pretended not to notice the noteworthy bulge of his royal jewels, his rounded biceps, the ripples of his flat stomach, the planes and angles of a body kept in peak physical condition by its ruthless owner.

She stripped down to similar black shorts, but with a tight black midriff-length tank covering her on top. It had been a long while since she had worn so little clothing around a man.

"I'll go over the basics." He talked about kicks and showed her how to cup her hands and tuck her thumb, the two of them practicing strokes in the air. He acted eager enough to be giving her a lesson, using the same friendly, confident tone as when he instructed her in bajha tactics; but unlike in the arena, he would not look at her from the neck down. Then he sat at the edge of the pool and pointed to a spot next to him, but without removing his gaze from the bottom of the pool.

What a pair they were. She stifled a laugh. The dozer was having just as hard of a time as she was.

She dropped down next to him, sitting hip to hip, their legs dangling in the warm water. The instant her bottom landed, he slid down into the water. Pushing off the wall with his feet, he stroked across the pool. At the opposite, deeper side he somersaulted and streaked back to her, a sleek dark form under the water, only to explode to the surface in front of her, his grin a flash of white teeth, water sluicing off skin as shiny as glass. He was as at ease in water as he was on land.

"I want to do that," she exclaimed.

"Do ya now?" he replied, mimicking her Baréshti accent with affection. "Well, lass, you soon will." He was tempting her terribly by sounding like one of her own. It reminded her of her secret wish to ruffle him up and take him out to the Barésh City clubs for an evening of ale, thump, and her.

He propped his folded arms on the pool's edge next to her calves. His dark lashes were clumped in peaks, his irises gold rimmed, his smile gentle, all his harder edges softened. "The most difficult part of learning to swim is getting over the fear of it. Or so I am told. I don't remember being taught to swim. On my homeworld we learn to swim before we learn to walk."

She kicked her feet slowly in the water. "I ain't afraid at all. Not a speck."

"Why does that not surprise me?" He covered her hand with his and gave it a squeeze. "My fearless one."

His fearless one? They stared at their joined hands in the sudden silence.

Klark felt his breath stagger at the lustful heat of that simplest of hand-to-hand contact. How could such a thing be? It simply was not in his sphere of experience. But when he saw Jemm's questioning eyes and the pulse throbbing in her throat, a powerful urge to kiss her again boiled up inside him.

He withdrew his hand, trading her warm skin for the cool stone of the pool's edge. When Jemm tried to tuck strands of hair that no longer existed behind her ear, he knew she was as flustered as he was.

To be so unsettled by a brush of hands was crazy, he thought. No question. When he was supposed to be abiding by his promise—their promise—to keep their relationship platonic, he was thinking of anything but. He was a highborn *Vash*. A prince of his people. He could teach her to swim without resorting to reckless behavior and undisciplined thoughts, could he not?

"I'll show you where I learned to swim," he said. "Con, display Eireya." A shimmering rectangle display rose from a seam adjacent to the pool. It displayed water so blue that it made him ache from the beauty of it.

"You learned to swim there? How lucky ya are. That's just beautiful." Captivated, Jemm took in the sweeping views of the sea, a lavender-blue sky, and wave-swept beaches as white and creamy as foam in a glass of ale.

Klark took as much pleasure in her reaction. "We Vedlas are indeed the lucky ones to call Eireya home. But, it was because we were exceedingly unlucky during the Dark Years."

"'The Original Warriors chose the most forbidding places to call home in order to lead by example, to prove their willingness to sacrifice for the good of the many.' Aye, my Da used to make me recite that. I'm lucky he saw to my education. I know that six of the eight *Vash* homeworld are harsh desert planets, yours is a paradise, and one is a grasslands world that gets scoured by craggin' horrendous windstorms."

"Mistraal," he said. The name stuck in his craw. But he did not reveal why. Jemm knew nothing of his misadventures with the Dar princess, his brother Ché's former promised bride. She knew only the good side of him. He had shielded her from the rest. "It's the homeworld of the Dar clan."

"Still, winds and all, it's got to be better than my home rock. The wide-open spaces. When I was a small lass I remember thinking that because Barésh was so awful, it must mean I was making a sacrifice for the good of the many. But without the benefits of being *Vash Nadah*." Her laugh reeked of cynicism.

"You were one perceptive little girl. We *Vash* are always so quick to point to millennia-old reasons why their homeworlds are bleak. But, the palaces on those worlds are lavish when so many others across the galaxy who live on equally harsh worlds are forced to go without." Like Jemm and the colonists of Barésh. "What kind of sacrifice is that? How is that leading by example?" Such thoughts were wildly sacrilegious, he knew. He could not afford to make them public. It would only rile the clans that accused him of far worse.

He pinched his fingers and moved the image of Eireya farther out until it displayed a planet that resembled a polished lavender-blue and white glass ball speckled with green against a backdrop of stars. "We're an ocean world. Water covers most of the surface. There's only one continent. The rest is broken into islands. The scenery is equaled by no other place, Jemm. Especially out on the wild outer islets." The mere thought of the outer islets made him yearn to return. When was the last time he had visited? It had been too long. "I'll take you there one day."

"I'd love that," she said.

Then reality once more landed with a weighty thud.

Klark regretted his impulsive invitation. It had slipped out before he had the chance to censor it. Inviting Jemm to the islets, the place he loved the most and had never shared with another soul—was he mad? They could not visit the islets, not the two of them alone. Not as platonic coach and player, and certainly not as a couple. Jemm was not a palace courtesan, nor a woman of the royal court. There was no other category that permitted them to be together romantically. None.

Yet, it was easy to imagine Jemm lying naked in his arms on the powdery white sand, frolicking in the warm, azure sea together, eating sweet, ripe mangans and laughing as the honeyed juice ran down their chins. Him, kissing that juice off every last square inch of her body.

The sensual image jolted him to the core.

"Con, close display." He could teach her to swim without making a mockery of discipline and self-control, could he not? He would prove it now.

He pushed off the wall, gliding backward and away from Jemm.

"Show off," she called out to him. "I didn't come down here to watch ya swim—unless I can do it with ya. I'm coming in."

"Not without me." He stroked back to her. "I need to protect my investment."

She scooped water into her hand and splashed him in the face.

He burst out laughing and splashed her back. She yelped as water sprayed her body, her laughter musical when added to his. He had thought himself incapable of being playful or lighthearted. He had accepted long ago that this deficiency was a deep and inoperable part of his personality. But here he was, Prince Klark Vedla, having…fun.

"That disrespect will not go unpunished." He almost pulled her into the water with him, but caught himself just in time. Roughhousing would lead to passion, a fact his body recognized before his brain had. Remembering that Jemm did not yet know how to swim yanked him back from the precipice of going too far.

But he was staring straight into the abyss.

"Come in, I'll hold you," he said.

Jemm scooted forward and lowered herself into the water. He curved his hands around her waist, slowing her descent. Her skin was warm and smooth under his palms. A bare thigh brushed against his, her knee against his other leg. Then their gazes lifted and fused.

I am a warrior. I live by the warrior's code. Self-control. Discipline.

The inner monologue failed to cool him off. Perhaps if he gave in to his desire, it would be like scratching an itch. It would take his mind off Jemm, and direct it back to where his attention should be in the first place—winning the Galactic Cup, and the pride it would bring the clan. But he had already accepted that Jemm Aves was no mere itch. She was everything he could possibly want wrapped in one utterly irresistible package.

Her hands landed on his shoulders for balance. Her gaze turned pointed, even mischievous.

Warning, warning.

"I told ya, I ain't afraid," she said.

Did she mean about the deep water? Or taking up with him? He was dying to ask, but was equally worried about the answer. Steam floated around them. Her gaze was as dark green as the nighttime forest. The reflection of the water created dancing lights on her lips. He fought the roaring impulse to wrap her strong thighs around his hips and claim her mouth in the kiss he had been thinking about all evening. But then she would feel quite intimately the full consequence her proximity had on him. That would send him careening past the point of no return.

And scuttle the swim lesson, too. He had promised her that swim lesson.

"Once you are able to put your face in the water, you can float." He kept his tone casual and upbeat. Although he wondered who he thought he was fooling. When had he been able to hide his intentions from her? She could read him as easily outside the bajha ring as she could inside it.

Standing where he could feel the bottom, he positioned her crosswise in his arms, her face above the water. "I'm ready," she said.

"You'll hold your breath, then just let yourself go."

Her face dipped into the water, her cropped hair fanning out, her arms floating. The strong muscles in her shoulders and back flexed then she went still, as calm as could be. She was doing so well that he released her. She remained in place, her body buoyant until she needed to breathe and made the mistake of drawing her knees to her chest. He had forgotten to warn her about that. He caught her before she floundered, taking her by the hands and pulling her along to lengthen her body as he walked backward. "Instinct makes you want to move into a fetal position. Keep your legs extended this time. Pedaling your hands and legs will help you tread water, but that skill will come in time."

Her face was alive with joy. "That was crattin' fantastic—I mean, blasted. Let's do it again."

He wanted to hear those words after he made love to her. It took a steadying breath to counteract the mental image of her naked in his arms; nonetheless, he was hard in an instant.

He concealed it all as they repeated the floating maneuver. This time she recovered without flailing. "That's it, Jemm! Just like that." He laughed at her triumphant whoop, took her by the hands and pulled her upright. Momentum carried her to him, her legs loosely encircling his hips. She appeared to realize her mistake and tried to splash backward. But without enough experience in the water to counter her movements, she wound up pitching forward.

He caught her arms and looped them around his shoulders, bringing her chin and soft lips so close they filled his vision. Water lapped around their necks, her breasts brushing his chest.

Neither of them moved, or wanted to.

"This could be a problem," he said.

"I don't think so," she whispered back.

He skimmed his knuckles over the side of her face, and erased water droplets from her cheekbone with his thumb. Then he bent down to give the lightest of chaste kisses on her cheek. It made her shiver. That honest response nearly made his knees buckle. *She wants you, too.*

The realization came with a heady rush of desire. In his world, the risk of rejection was never an issue; the answer was always yes. The women he had enjoyed over the years were employed to please him. While he had gained a vast amount of sexual know-how to draw upon with which to pleasure Jemm, his experience being with a woman he cared about was nil.

There was no rule book, no prior personal relationships to reference, no passages of ancient text to guide him. Damnation.

He was on his own. Just him, his instincts, and the drop-dead-gorgeous star player of his bajha team. Luckily, he trusted the instincts that now urged him to kiss Jemm Aves senseless, and then some.

He cupped her bottom with both hands and walked forward until her back bumped gently against the side of the pool. He used the leverage to draw her to him, seating himself firmly between her wide-open thighs.

Her eyelids fluttered half-closed, her breath shuddering, her hands contracting on his shoulders. "Klark..."

She had never called him by his given name before. Was she warning him off or pleading for more? He clung to his last shreds of control.

More, he decided, when their mouths came together in a crushing kiss.

CHAPTER EIGHTEEN

Jemm returned the kiss with all the pent-up desire she had collected for him since the day she first laid eyes on him. If he had any doubts as to what she wanted from him, by the time she was done, well, then not a speck of passionate blood rushed through those veins of his.

But he was right there with her, his hungry hands stroking, his kiss fierce, reckless, and nothing like their first. This time he embraced her like he meant it to go somewhere, and to hell with the consequences.

Like a true Baréshti. Savor now, worry later.

With a gush of water, he lifted her out of the pool, hoisting her into his arms to carry her across the lawn, steam coming off their damp skin in the night air.

She was not a small woman, but he carried her as if she weighed nothing as he swept her away in his arms. "You'd better be taking me somewhere to finish this," she teased.

"Finish this?" His *Vash* eyes blazed with heat. "I'm taking you somewhere to start it."

Her body reacted immediately to the utter carnal confidence of his statement. It was just what she had imagined a *Vash Nadah* prince would say, and how he would say it. Deep inside, she clenched with anticipation of making love with him, while at the same time her mind whirled with runaway curiosity. "Good. Because if ya were planning on changing your mind, I was gonna—"

They plunged down to a cushion under a slatted roof that allowed peeks at the stars and the lights of the nearby building. His hard, wet body followed her downward.

"You were going to *what*, beautiful Baréshti lass?" he whispered against her lips. Their uneven breaths mingled as he smoothed a hand over her hair, pushing it off her forehead, his gaze expectant as he gazed down at her. "Hmm?"

"I was…"

At that precise moment, he slid his hand between her thighs. Tremors of pleasure stole away her ability to think let alone form full words. His clever fingers moved over the thin fabric of her shorts to trace her inner curves. He seemed to know exactly what he was doing, and exactly how to do it. "You haven't answered my question, Jemm."

"I was gonna tell ya what I want ya to do to do me, and what I want to do to ya. But we both have too many clothes in the way."

"Hmm. I can help with that." He ran his thumb around the inside of the waistband of her shorts then rolled her onto her stomach. It left her feeling deliciously vulnerable. His lips were on the back of her bare neck now, well-placed kisses and the scrape of his teeth sending shivers down her spine. He kissed his way along the curve of her spine down to her tailbone; then he tugged off and discarded her shorts, exposing her bare bottom.

He came up on his knees behind her, looped a strong arm around her hips and lifted her to him. Her bottom pressed against his hard thighs as he moved her knees apart. His cool fingertips collided with the hot flesh between her bare thighs and set off an explosion of need. Moaning, on her knees, she arched her back and pushed backward—into him, into his caresses. Gripping the cushion beneath her hands, she clung to it as if it were the edge of a cliff. Klark took her to that edge, again and again, only to ease off and start the cadence all over again with his clever touch. His mouth traveled down the side of her throat, behind her ear, nuzzling the nape of her neck. All the while, he kept her flush against his body, his hold on her firm, possessive, as his fingers slipped inside and out. "Come for me, sweetheart."

She muffled a cry as her body clenched deep inside. He held her until the pulsing waves of pleasure had subsided, then he eased her down to the cushion on her back. "Are you protected?" he asked, his accented voice low and adorably husky.

"Aye…" Breathless, she reached for him.

But first, he nimbly stripped off his shorts. Then her hands rode his to her tank top, and they pulled it off together, freeing her breasts. They were puckered and damp, and aching for his touch. A soft moan escaped her, and he had not yet touched her.

Sitting back on his haunches, he looked at her, all of her. Then he swallowed, his gaze merging with hers. "You're perfect," he said. "Strong, gorgeous, and perfect." With their fingers laced tightly together, he bent down to lavish attention on her body.

Only after he had rendered Jemm breathless all over again did Klark seek more. She raised her hips to welcome him, her hands molding to his shoulders, her gaze caressing his face. In the cast-off light from outside the hut, her eyes were so luminous and green with desire that they shimmered like jewels. Her open, unguarded gaze and the candid emotions crossing her face made his chest tighten with emotions he could not name, because he had no experience with anything so intense.

As he slowly entered her, a look of pure bliss stole over her face. He pushed deeper, savoring every contour of her wet inner walls, every contraction of her muscles, learning her body in the most intimate of ways. Drawing on every last bit of his bajha-honed control, he kept up the slow, measured, erotic entry until he was sure it would kill him unless he let loose and plunged deep. But, he reaped the reward for his patience a thousand times over when she sheathed him fully, and gloriously.

They went still, bonded together, her hands gripping his shoulders, their gazes fused. Rocking his body slowly, he brought one hand to her lovely heart-shaped face, "*Enajhe a'nai,*" he murmured in Eireyan. *Body and soul.*

Her eyes hazed over with pleasure. She moaned, pushing against him, deepening his deliberately slow, sensual strokes. It took everything he had not to explode. This was always the place where he would lose himself in the act, the end goal being maximum physical release— his. But this time it was different. This time he wanted the woman he was with to hold him close, to *be with him* every moment along the way.

He wanted no less than all of her as they moved together. He wanted the emotional and mental connectedness they shared in the bajha ring to be here, too.

And then...there she was. He felt *her*. In his mind, under his skin. In his soul. Coupled with the physical sensations, it brought the sex to an indescribable new level of ecstasy.

Enajhe a'nai.

They swayed together, move and counter move, anticipating and magnifying each other's desire. His loins clenched with a heavy, potent, pleasure-pain warning he would not last much longer. But he held on, held back, his breaths slowing as he opened himself to her, opened his mind. *Feel me, Jemm. Feel me, sweetheart.* Her body responded, clutching him with each one of his fierce strokes. On and on…

Until at last her inner muscles convulsed. She let out a soft, throaty cry of delight and surprise as she climaxed, her nails digging into his shoulders.

Instead of pushing up on rigid arms, retreating into himself in that moment, Klark bowed his body to her quaking one, his head falling to hers as he looped one arm under her thigh to press her close. He jolted inside her, once, twice. Then he groaned into the crook of her neck and let himself go. His release shuddered on and on, and eclipsed anything he had ever experienced before.

He sagged to his side like a dead man, and took her with him, drawing her tight to his spent body. Dazzled by what he had discovered in her arms, he kissed and stroked and nuzzled her, holding her close until their bodies stopped quivering. "I was right," he said in a very low, intimate tone. "You are indeed perfect, my gorgeous Baréshti lass."

She smiled up at him, a soft, wondering smile. "You're pretty perfect yourself, my sexy, fine-looking aristo."

They laughed and a feeling of lightness swept through him. "Me? Perfect? Hmm. You may very well be the only person in the Federation who thinks so."

"Tonight, I'm the only person who matters."

He placed his bent index finger under her chin, his tone firm. "If I thought you would matter for only one night, we never would have gotten this far."

At that, she made a small sound of happiness and hunger, and reached for him, pulling him back to her mouth.

Jemm cracked her eyes open in the soft early light of morning. She was lying on her back in the softest of beds. It rained overnight but had cleared. Filtered by tall trees, sunshine streamed through a huge bedside window. It was real, remarkable sunlight—incredible after having spent a lifetime under artificial illumination. She imagined little Button running out from the moist fragrant forest into the sunshine, the brightness warming her bare arms. It was easy to picture the child giggling as she scampered in the soft grass. This was the life Jemm wanted to make for her. This was why she had dreamed.

The dogged pursuit of that dream led her here, to this bed, to this man, only the latest in adventurous twists her life had taken.

She came up on an elbow to savor the sight of her lover sprawled on his stomach, his arm flung over her belly. His muscled back was one long lean line of smooth, bronzed perfection. She followed the defiant curve of his spine to where it ended in a pair of firm cheeks. This man had been blessed with one fine backside.

After they had moved inside to his bed last night, they made love again. She had not thought her body capable of the things he somehow was able to coax from her. Her two previous lovers were not inept by any means, but they could not compare to Klark. He was strong, skilled, and patient. Surprisingly tender, too. She had not expected that. But watching his eyes, seeing his look of awe the first time he was inside her was something she would never forget.

She slipped out from under the dead weight of his arm to scoot to the edge of the bed. His hand shot out and snatched her wrist. He grumbled something sleepily into his pillow.

She lifted her brows at the no-escape grip he had on her then narrowed her eyes at him. "I ain't one of your concubines."

He blinked awake. Then he let out a husky groan and rolled onto his back. "Come here, you. And, no," he added emphatically. "You are not." He pulled her close and kissed her soundly then pressed his lips to the inside of her wrist. "Forgive me. This is all new to me. I have no idea what I'm doing."

She snorted.

"No, really." A sly, sleepy grin dented his cheeks, but she did not miss the hint of doubt in his eyes. He skimmed his knuckles along her jaw, pausing to touch the pad of his thumb to her lower lip. Her breath caught, and she shivered from the tender touch. "A *Vash* prince is either married, or he uses the services of the pleasure girls. There is no…this."

"This…"

"Inviting a woman I care about to my bed."

She touched two fingertips to his lips as if she could feel the echo of his words. She assumed this prince of the realm would be as smooth and debonair socially as he was skilled at lovemaking, but it was not the case at all. With all his barriers down, he actually seemed quite uncertain underneath. Even shy. It added a whole new dimension to a man who displayed so many unexpected angles as it was.

He stroked his hand over her bottom. "So, allow me to start over. Good morning, gorgeous."

"Mmm. That's better. Good morning." She gave him a pleased, sideways glance as she snuggled closer. "So, they must know all about sexual techniques and such," she said, tracing swirls with her fingertip from his chest down the center of his torso, and lower.

"Who?" He stopped her hand before it got to where she was aiming: a very sizeable morning hello.

"Them."

"The palace courtesans, you mean? That's what they're trained to know."

Her face felt warm. "I ain't trained. But ya probably already figured that out—"

He had her on her back in a second, his hands gripping her wrists, pressing the backs of her hands into the disheveled sheets. "Nothing I've experienced compares to you." He laced his fingers with hers, and her insides contracted with a wave of desire. The intensity in his eyes assured her he was telling the truth. "Nothing."

Quietly, she said, "Same here."

A hint of satisfaction passed over his eyes.

"But, you've only been with courtesans," she pointed out.

"You've only been with miners," he countered.

"Loaders," she said. "For the sake of accuracy."

They looked at each other and laughed. It was a joyful sound she was getting more and more accustomed to hearing. Then their laughter faded into sounds of passion as they made love so thoroughly that the ghosts of lovers past faded permanently.

Before breakfast, they showered together in the huge stone enclosure connected to Klark's bedroom that was half the size of Jemm's entire apartment. Multiple heads gushed water down on them. They were laughing, kissing, soaping each other, kissing some more. Not a player and coach, not a tug driver and prince. They were two young lovers acting as if they did not have a care in the world. In that brief moment, at least, they did not.

CHAPTER NINETEEN

I cancelled the match with Raff Xirri," Klark said that afternoon. He knew she was as sore and spent as he was, after much lovemaking and too little sleep. They had kept to the rest of their schedule, but planned only some light sparring.

"Why'd ya go and do that? I would have been fine against Xirri."

"I thought it best not to overly exert you. Due to your nocturnal activities."

She scoffed at that. "I think you're worried about Xirri seeing ya making yipwag eyes at me." She buffed her sens-sword with a cloth. Squinting at a scuff, then buffing it some more, she said, "You could have worn your see-in-the-dark glasses to hide your eyes."

Klark took hold of the unfastened collar of her bajha suit and drew her to him. "Maybe you ought to be the one wearing the glasses. Pretending to clean your sens-sword won't fool anyone."

"You think I'm making yipwag eyes at ya?"

"I know you were last night."

"I did a lot of things last night," she said, softer.

"Yes, you did."

They exchanged knowing smiles.

A rapid chiming noise radiated from deep in Klark's thigh pocket. "A priority call," he said with a sinking feeling, recognizing the distinctive ring. "I have to take it. Priority calls are not to be ignored."

"Your family?"

"Usually." He drew out his comm and wandered away. The screen showed an incoming call from King Rorrik Vedla. Gladness, relief, annoyance, apprehension: he was not sure what he should feel now that his father had finally decided to contact him. For weeks he had waited for the chance to speak with his sire, but to no avail. Now he would rather do just about anything else.

He sat on a spectator bench in the arena and opened the comm. The screen displayed a fit man with the palest of golden eyes, rich bronze skin, and sideburns frosted with silver. "Father," Klark greeted, doing his best to mirror his cheerful smile. "What a pleasure, sir. I trust you are well."

"Yes, very well. And you?" Before Klark could get a word in edgewise, the king continued. "Look, I'm engaged in some tricky trade negotiations at the Wheel, and have only a moment to chat. Katjian spoke with me earlier, and that's the reason for my call."

"What has happened?" Klark's stomach knotted. Had the girl broken her promise and fled before Prince Hajhani's visit?

"What? No, nothing happened. She's all atwitter over your newest bajha recruit." His lips spread into a brilliant white smile. "I never took your sister for a bajha fan."

"It seems to be a new interest," Klark said dryly.

"She tells me you've flown off to the far reaches of the frontier to recruit a young mystery player. A teenager of common birth." The king leaned forward, his expression eager. "So, he's quite talented, then?"

Klark shifted his focus to where Jemm warmed up with stretches, bending forward with willowy grace to hug her calves. A memory from last night of those calves draped over his shoulders exploded inside him. He tightened his jaw and made a fist on his thigh. "Yes. The best I've ever seen, sir. A potent addition to a very strong team—Team Eireya has a very real chance at winning the Galactic Cup this year. It is my intent to make that happen." There it was. He had revealed his intentions to his father. When before he had only imagined doing so, this made it real.

His father's expression echoed pure delight. "Councilman Toren told me of your confidence regarding the Cup. Excellent, son. I can't tell you how welcome this news is after...the events of the past few years."

The *events*. Was that what his father called Klark's transgressions now?

The king's tone took on a quieter, more confidential tone. "I cannot suffer another season seeing the B'kahs or even the Virs ranked above us. I'm proud you've taken such command of the team. The press has taken the good news and run with it. The prospect of a new and talented unknown has only intensified the interest."

Only Katjian had known of Jemm—or, rather, Kes. She could not be blamed for telling their father; she did it to present Klark in the best possible light, he was sure. But now that King Rorrik and Toren were aware of Sea Kestrel, the rest of the clan elders at the Wheel would spread gossip faster than a tree full of chatter-crows. With so many ears in close proximity covering government happenings at the station, the seat of the Trade Federation, the news would make the jump from political commentators to sports reporters at light speed. This time of year there was always rapid speculation about the coming season, driven by impatient fans. Before long, all the major sports news venues would run the story, if they were not already doing so.

There went anything resembling anonymity. From this point forward the media would be relentless trying to learn more about Jemm.

"I couldn't be more pleased, son. I've not seen such positive buzz about our clan in some time. Keep up the good work. Make me proud. Hope to see you soon."

"Yes, sir. Me, too."

After the call ended, Klark stared at the comm he gripped in his hand. It felt like a tether dragging him back to the life he had left behind these past few glorious weeks. The communication from his father served as a firm reminder that his life was not one able to be left behind. He was still second in line for the throne to the longest-lived dynasty in known galactic history. He was still expected to abide by the duties and responsibilities that position required, and to maintain his loyalty to his clan above all else.

Make me proud.

Klark's stomach churned like it used to do at the palace. A heavy weight settled down to roost once more on his shoulders. The sense of not being good enough returned to the back of his mind, of being a very distant second choice, of being prone to making blunders that resulted in harming the two men he most loved and respected. The sense of happiness and accomplishment he had only recently come to enjoy dimmed as the cloud of his real life passed over it.

His plan to train a star player of unbelievable talent to propel Team Eireya to the championships was not unsound. However, it was risky due to the secret involved. He had been poring over the Treatise of Trade every spare minute to bolster his argument why Jemm should be permitted to play in the open as a female. It was a daunting undertaking made more so because the word "bajha" was not mentioned in every section possibly related to the sport. His ancestors had an exasperating way of being overly broad to allow interpretation. Over the years some of those interpretations had come to be seen as law when they were obviously not meant to be. Or, sometimes it was the opposite when passages that were very specific were used as metaphors. But if the answer was in there, he would find it. It had become a quest.

Now, every sharp eye in the Vedla Clan would be on him—and on Sea Kestrel. It necessitated a much higher level of caution. And what was he doing? Frolicking in the pool with her. Taking her into his bed.

Never be complacent. Be vigilant in all things.

An unstable mix of anger and shame boiled up inside him. Jemm Aves was not his for the taking. She was the Vedla Clan's star player. His duty was to protect her, and to protect their plan. The closer they came to the start of the official season, the more critical that became.

The Galactic League would hang them both out to dry if they found out. But Jemm's situation was far more critical than his quest to repair his family's standing. Her success as a player was vital to her family's welfare. He had no idea how the league administration would react if they learned of her identity, or, perhaps worse, how the Federation fans would react.

"Are ya all right?"

He jerked his head up at the sound of Jemm's voice. She approached him, her steps growing hesitant as she absorbed the sight of his face. "What happened?" Neatly combed away from her face, her red-and-blonde hair revealed her small, feminine ears, and also the need for a haircut to trim the girlish curls at the nape of her neck. Without the body padding she typically wore, her unfastened bajha suit revealed the tempting silhouette of her body.

It drove home the precariousness of their plan.

"That was His Royal Highness, King Rorrik," he said, his voice ruthlessly brusque. "My father. It's been discovered that Team Eireya has a new recruit.

Apparently, rumors are flying about a talented new teenage discovery of common birth. On one hand, it gives us an excuse to keep you out of the public eye—your youth. On the other, you must be prepared to play at the highest level, and you are not. In mere weeks you'll be playing pro matches. You're not ready. Hear me, Sea Kestrel. You are not ready. Not even close."

She flinched, then scrunched her eyes at him. "I may not be fully ready yet, but I will be." Her narrowed eyes did little to hide her glowing determination, and a flash of pain.

"You have to be stronger than this," he lashed out, knowing his words had hurt her. But she had to be able to deflect such verbal blows, or there was no hope. "Weakness in you translates to weakness in our plan."

"What's gotten into you—?"

"We didn't come here for a vacation. Obey your coach. Gear up and get in the ring."

He felt her scandalized glare on him as he strode over to his sens-sword case and opened it.

She fastened her bajha suit and sealed her boots. "I won't let ya down, coach."

Her earnest conviction brought back the night in Nico's club. The night he should have let her walk out of his life. Then, when his father called, asking about a commoner player of stunning ability, Klark could have answered honestly: it simply had not worked out. From there he could have gone on with his life. There would have been no repercussions. His father's baseline opinion of him as a distant-second son would not have changed.

"It's just reality setting in. I feel it, too. The pressure. I'm going to win us that Galactic Cup. I told ya before, and I meant it."

"Words will not make you the best bajha player in the galaxy."

"But *heart* will. I've got the heart to go the distance."

Her heart was a prize most definitely out of his reach.

"Keep it up, young Kes Aves—the fans will gobble up such inspiring clichés," he said to stoke the fire of her anger. "However, words are still words, no matter how pretty. It's time you threw some weight behind them. Arm your weapon and prepare to fight."

"Swords armed? But you never play with—"

"Armed, I said."

He heard the faint whine of her sens-sword going active as he slid his light-glasses over his eyes. Hefting his weapon in a gloved hand, he joined her in the ring. They donned their helmets.

With her headgear masking half her face, she faced him with her legs set apart. "You're acting like a cog," she said quietly. "You know that, right?"

"As a female, you'll have to be better than every man you play," he growled. "Every blasted one."

"That ain't nothing new for me. I've had to be better than every man I worked with since the day I first sat behind the wheel of a tug."

"If you think because you beat G'Zanna and Muse so handily that other pros will fall as easily, you are incorrect," he shot back as if her assertion carried no merit.

Her chin came up in defiance. "Maybe I ain't gonna ever lose another match. Did ya ever think of that? I have. All those nights, lying in my bed alone, I thought of it. That maybe Skeet was the last one ever to beat me. I agree ya should have let Xirri come. I would have proved it to ya."

"Words, nothing but words. If you want to prove anything, you'll have to prove it in the ring."

A few heartbeats thumped by. "You're on," she said.

"Lights," Klark called. The blackness was all-encompassing.

"What did your Da say to get ya so worried?" she asked in the dark. The blasted female could see into his soul. Doing so in the midst of lovemaking was one thing;

but when he wanted to shield his thoughts it was entirely another. "Whatever it was, it was wrong," she said.

"So, you're smarter than a king now, are you?"

"That's not fair."

"Since when is life fair?"

"It was fairer to you, *Vash*, than to me."

Truth. It doused some of the riled-up heat inside him. He could not deny her humble origins, the hardships she had faced at too young of an age. One glimpse at the ragtag colonists waiting to be seen by the Earth-dweller physicians told him others on her world faced even worse difficulties compared to Jemm.

"Focus on the match," he snarled.

Her form was visible to him in the darkness, a dark red seething shadow in his glasses. He could feel her emotions pulsing off her in waves. Those waves battered him.

"You want to fight me, coach? Is that it? You want to show your champ what's what? Hmm? Skeet told me that you're an excellent player. You could have gone pro, if it weren't for being a prince." She was able to track him no matter where he walked, intuiting his presence. *Feeling him*. Inside and out. "But those are just words. Words prove nothing. Let's see how good ya really are. Take those crattin' glasses off."

"Concentrate!"

"Ah. I see what it is. You don't want to fall to Sea Kestrel. You don't want a mere female to beat ya."

He flung off the glasses. The sound of them impacting the nanocrylic wall echoed in the silence.

He did not need his glasses to know she sported a satisfied smile on her face and a deadly glint in her eyes. Better players than he had fallen to Sea Kestrel. But not any who had upset her to this degree, or, who had touched or kissed every conceivable part of her body. Would the distraction cost her the win she was so certain was hers? Could he expose her vulnerabilities as a player and exploit them? If he did, then she was not in fact ready.

Muscles tense, his warrior instincts vibrating in readiness, he held his sens-sword in front of him in a sure, two-handed grip. "Bring it, Sea Kestrel."

Jemm attacked, and he evaded her. Pivoting, he swung in a return strike. But she was not where he thought she would be. He caught himself before he stumbled. Her sens-sword skittered across his abdomen, leaving behind a comet's tail of violet sparks. Then the rounded blade whooshed past somewhere close in the dark, too close, enough for him to feel the breeze of its passing.

"Not good enough, Kes. Not good enough."

He felt her wounded fury from the tip of every hair on his body to the marrow of his bones. The match was fierce, punishing, and more strenuous than any he had ever played before. They swung and parried, swerved and lunged. It was exhilarating. But that was not something anyone facing her in actual competition would likely express. They would be too worried about losing the match.

Only now did he understand how unsettling her command of the ring must feel to those who faced her. But he soon saw he had an advantage they would not. The emotional bond he and Jemm shared did not evaporate in the bajha ring. Their connectedness was an advantage that helped him hold his own against her.

But their vivid awareness of each other went both ways. She would have figured out by now she was not immune to him. That the rout she had expected to hand him, and rightly so, had not materialized yet. It left her vulnerable, and that unnerved her.

I feel you, Jemm.

She attacked. He swung his sens-sword to deflect hers. The crack of the batons colliding reverberated in the silence. Violet energy illuminated the air between them. For a fleeting second he glimpsed her masked face, the intensity there, her bared teeth, the slits of her eyes. She looked like an avenging goddess from ancient times, frightening and beautiful.

Determined to see him conquered.

He blinked away the ghost of the image as he swung his weapon in a ruthless arc from left to right. Again their sens-swords collided. The power of her parry did not carry the sheer force of a bigger, heavier combatant, of course, but the surprise of finding her there was worse than the impact. He had guessed her to be on his opposite side. The very instant his mind alighted on that recognition, the blunt tip of her sens-sword landed in the center of his chest plate.

A fountain of brilliant violet energy erupted at the point of contact, and through his suit he felt the vibration, signaling a dead-on hit.

With a soft grunt of effort, she shoved her weapon at his chest. "Give?" she said through her teeth. "Well? Do ya crattin' give, ya stubborn aristo?"

"Give." He disarmed his sens-sword and lowered it. The tip of hers remained pressed to his powerfully beating heart.

Her breathing tore through the silence of the arena. "What your pros said about ya is true. You're good. Really good. Last week you might have beaten me." She finally pulled back and disarmed her weapon. "So. Was I good enough for ya?"

"That's the understatement of the year."

Her sens-sword dropped to the padded floor with a muffled thud. His followed. Then his gloves. And hers. Their helmets too.

He snatched her by the fabric of her suit and tugged her close. His knuckles came in contact with the hot skin of her jaw. He paused there in the total blackness, his lips almost touching hers, feeling her body heat, her pulse, and the bob of her throat when she swallowed. He felt her react to the feel of his hand skimming over her cheek, his breath, the intensity of his desire. "I'm sorry," he said. "My protective instinct tends to run away from me."

She pressed a finger to his lips. "I know," she whispered in the dark.

He closed his hand around hers, moved it to his chest plate where her sens-sword had landed moments before. "I needed to face you myself to realize just how good you are. I needed to offend you, to unbalance you, so that I could believe that no distraction will topple you. None can. Not even me. You are ready, Jemm. Even if I am not." He paused, then said, "I allowed my father's call to exacerbate my doubts. There's history there."

He squeezed her hand, forcing himself to admit the dishonor of his past. It was not right to hide it from the woman whose opinion of him mattered at the deepest level. "I've been a disappointment to him, you see. I interfered in a political and family matter that led to my arrest. I believed my brother Ché wronged when he lost both his succession rights and his promised bride to the B'kah clan. Most in my clan felt the same way. So, I set out to defend Ché. It seemed like a good idea at the time, like all ill-conceived notions do. But it went horribly awry. No one was killed, and no one was hurt—thank the Great Mother—but my public humiliation made headlines across the Trade Federation. I served my time, two year's worth, but it'll take more than that to atone for the trouble I caused. Now, the chance is finally within reach to prove to my sire, to my family, that I'm more than the clan embarrassment."

"Crag them, Klark. I mean it. Really."

A second of astonishment ticked by, then he barked out a laugh. Months back, her Baréshti bluntness would have shocked him, but now it merely made him laugh. He loved the way she took his side without hesitation. No one had stood by him like that before. Well, aside from Katjian, but she worshipped him and Ché blindly. Jemm was not in the least bit blind. She would turn and walk away if she felt he deserved it, as she had done once before. He respected her strength and also dreaded it. In the short time he had known her she had done more to help him become a better man than the Warrior's Code. "But," he continued, "as much as I don't want to fail my father, I don't want to fail *you*."

She came up on her toes to kiss him. "You won't."

As her lips lingered on his, he unfastened the top few fasteners of her bajha suit. "It's why I've been poring over the Treatise of Trade day and night. I cannot stomach someone of your talent being held back because of an unnamed rule. I'm determined to find a way for you to play openly as a woman."

Her voice gentled. "You'd do that for me?"

He would do just about anything for her. "If it's in there, I will find it, Jemm. I want to find guidance that would allow you to compete. Or that prohibits it. In the meantime, our training cannot let up. You can't stop improving."

"Ya know I won't."

They tugged at the remaining fastenings of each other's bajha suits.

"Ya can't let your Da or anyone else make us doubt. Doubt will tear this apart. We either believe in our dreams and move forward, or we walk away from this."

"I'm not walking away from anything. I'm seeing this through to the end." He had never been so sure about anything in his life. He shoved her bajha suit down over her shoulders.

"Seeing this through to the end," she breathed, arching into his caresses. "I like the sound of that. How about you see *this* through to the end first?"

"That is exactly my plan, sweetheart." He pushed up her T-shirt to lavish attention on her two, perfect little breasts. Her sighs were his fuel as he stroked her body. The utter darkness magnified the scent of her clean musk, the silken texture of her hair, her strong athletic body and the feel of her sleek muscles moving under his hands. He had never caressed a woman who felt like she did. She was real, and she was his.

More clothing scattered. He pulled her down on top of him on the padded floor in the midst of a tangle of half-discarded clothing, gloves, helmets, and boots. He was inside her seconds later. In his rush to have her he had forgotten all about orchestrated foreplay and every other rule about lovemaking he had been taught to follow from day one of his adult life. Instead, he had followed his instincts. But she was ready. The pleasure of being inside her as she straddled him was beyond belief, the darkness intensifying everything. It was like bajha, and lovemaking, mixed together; the physical plane, the mental, all at once. He felt her inner pleasure as if it were his own. He was awash in it, his entire body, from his toes to his scalp.

It was frenzied, and fast. When her peak overtook her, she bent forward and sealed her lips over his. He took her moans into his mouth as she took in the full, throbbing length of him, until everything inside her was everything inside him, and he came in an unbelievable rush.

On the arena floor, they lay in the dark as their breaths slowed. He rested a hand on her soft hair, sifting his fingers lazily through the short locks as she lay on top of him, her cheek pillowed by his chest. "The bajha is for our families, Klark," she said. "And, maybe one day, to prove something larger than we are. But this...this is for us."

Us... He had never been part of a couple, nor had he ever imagined he would be. But here he was. No—here *they* were. "For us, yes." He was still inside her, and growing hard again.

She let out a low laugh. "But ya really do need a warning label on that body of yours."

He considered her words with hooded eyes then proceeded to prove her exactly right.

"Don't get too low. That's it. Steady now." Klark's voice sounded a bit tight as they soared over the trees in the speeder. Jemm had been training so hard, day after day, week after week, that they had taken to hiking the surrounding countryside as an outlet for relaxation. But today after breakfast, at almost the midway point of their time at the retreat center, Klark had suggested intriguingly, "Let's fly to the other side of the world," and off they went in the speeder.

Once in the air, she pleaded, "Teach me to fly." It turned into the thrill of her life. Klark was not as relaxed instructing her to pilot a speeder as he was coaching her in the bajha ring, but his composure impressed her nonetheless.

Skimming the treetops with breathtaking velocity, Jemm gripped the control stick, grinning so hard that it made her cheeks ache. Her stomach flipped as the treetops rushed by below. A laugh of pure joy almost escaped her, but she did not want to crash, so she kept her laughter inside.

"I'm not going to let you kill us," Klark said dryly. "I assure you."

"Am I that easy to read?" she asked.

"I'd like to say yes, but I can tell by the way you're squeezing the joystick." Sun-shaders with very dark lenses hid his gaze, but she knew his eyes crinkled with his smile. "Don't squeeze it so hard. It may break off."

"Break off?" The blood drained from her head at the thought.

"Kidding."

She glared at him. "Kidding? Holy craggin' dome. You'll pay for that, Vedla."

"I look forward to it. Now, keep your eyes outside and not on me—although I realize that's hard for you."

"Cog." She threw him another sideways, sassy glance. "I do like looking at ya, it's true. Like last night when you—"

"Since you can't keep your eyes outside, and you won't make sure my mind stays on flying, you're done. My turn." Laughing, she allowed him to take over. With his hand curved around the control stick located in front of his seat, he banked the speeder. The right wingtip dropped as the left one came up.

Watching the craft pivot so steeply over the forest, she felt her insides jump. It was the same kind of giddy rush she felt when he kissed her. "I love this," she breathed. "I love flying."

"I also love to fly. When the season is over, we'll have more time to polish your pilot skills. In the meantime, hold on."

Before she had the chance to ponder enjoying any part of the offseason with Klark, she asked, "Hold on to what—?

Klark leveled the wings and pulled back on the stick. Jemm's hands instinctively snatched the armrests. "First, we need a little more altitude." All she saw in front of her was blue sky. Then he leveled the speeder. "We're going to roll now," he informed her, then did exactly that, offering thrills as masterfully in the air as he did when they were in bed.

As the speeder rotated in a full circle, trees took the place of the sky; then the world righted itself, all at Klark's command.

"I want to do that!" she exclaimed.

"This is not the same as learning to swim in the pool, fearless one. But why not?"

Her heart jumped. She didn't expect him to give her the chance. But then why wouldn't he? This was the same man who had cleared his mind of a long-held bias about females and bajha after seeing what she could do in the ring. His ability to adapt, to take opportunity and run with it, was one of his more endearing qualities.

She listened intently to his brief instructions, then followed them—a little side pressure on the stick to get them rolling, then more pressure, holding the stick all the way to one side as the speeder flipped, side over side. She righted the craft with a bouncing jolt.

They whooped at her achievement. "Again," she said, then laughed. "By the dome, I sound like Button when I swing her around by the ankles."

She practiced a few more rolls before Klark finally said, "We had better head for the valley before it gets too late." He banked the speeder toward a broad, deep valley in the endless sea of trees.

The entire uninhabited side of the planet was designated as a nature preserve. Aiming the speeder at a narrow strip in a clearing, he landed. The speeder quickly rolled to a stop.

The speeder's canopy motored up, allowing fresh air to flood in. As the whine of the craft's engine faded, the silence all around them intensified. It seemed to press on her eardrums like pressure.

For a moment, they did nothing but sit and listen. "Such peace and quiet," she said in a hushed tone.

"It's the trees," he said as if equally awed. "They create a silence all their own."

Occasional bird song shattered the stillness as they gathered their day packs. From the horizon, a distant thunderstorm rumbled. It was easy to imagine that the conversations of the staff at the retreat center or the din in Chéyasenn City many hundreds of standard clicks away would be audible, too, if she listened hard enough; it was that quiet.

Klark armed himself with a pistol, and they both attached knives to their belts. Swinging their packs over their shoulders, they headed toward the cover of the forest. The scent of thriving green life intoxicated her.

"Are there many predators on this side of the planet?" she asked, checking for her blade as they left the clearing.

"Not many. But a few bajha players do go missing every year—"

"Lying cog." She pushed at him, and he laughed as he looped his arm around her waist to draw her close.

Side by side they hiked along a dirt path. "No, nothing large enough to hunt humans," he explained. "The planet is carefully managed. The landing strip is kept cleared, year-round. The hiking paths are maintained. Invasive species—both plant and animal—are dealt with. But, when out in the wild, it's always smart to be ready for anything."

"I know. 'Never be complacent. Be vigilant in all things.' The Vedla view of the galaxy is rubbing off on me."

That generated another laugh, this one as surprised as it was delighted. "I don't think I want you to become too Vedla."

"No?" She moved in front of him, curling her fingers behind his neck as she pressed the length of her body against his.

"No," he replied. His hands landed on her back, the caress tender but possessive. "I'm Vedla enough for the two of us. Besides, I very much like the Baréshti in you." He pulled her into a lazy, lingering kiss that warmed her from head to toes.

Somehow, his hands ended up on her backside, stroking and kneading, lifting her to his hardening length. If he kept that up, in another moment, they would be turning the forest floor into a makeshift bed.

He must have arrived at the same conclusion. "Refrain from distracting us, Jemm," he joked, his golden eyes darker as he moved her to arm's length. "We can't dally for too long."

"Aye. I know. Skeet flies in later." Klark had scheduled a dinner meeting with her and the team captain to get her prepped for an upcoming press conference, the first of several planned via vid feed from the retreat center.

"But first, let's enjoy this." He laced his warm fingers with hers to lead her deeper into the forest.

The farther they traveled, the dimmer it became—a greenish dusk that somehow existed in daytime. With it came a much heavier stillness. "It's like being in nature's bajha ring," she whispered.

"That's what I have heard from others who have been here," he whispered back.

"You never came here before?"

"No. I never felt like bothering."

"What changed your mind?" Jemm asked.

"You." His hand clasped hers a little tighter. "Now we'll experience it together."

"But what is it?"

"If I say, I'll spoil the surprise." His eyes twinkled as he shot her a grin.

"I get to ask questions, though. And you'll answer them."

"Just like you to set the rules."

She ignored him. "Is it animate or inanimate?"

"Animate. Sort of."

"Dead or alive?" she asked.

"Alive."

"Hmm. Animal or vegetable?"

He stopped, cocked his head. "Do you hear it?"

She also stopped walking. Using her senses, she searched outward, as if she were in a bajha match. Very faintly, an almost musical sound whispered then ebbed. "I think so." A slight movement of air rustled leaves on low-hanging branches, but that wasn't it. Then it started up again. She tipped her head, aiming an ear toward the sound. As it grew louder, it seemed familiar. "It sounds like...flutes. Aye, flutes. Nico had a wooden flute as a child. It almost sounds like that."

A soft, hollow sound.

"Exactly." Klark snatched her hand and led her farther along the path. The sound faded then increased again, almost as if the planet itself held its breath before exhaling musically.

Suddenly, they emerged into a glade nestled in a narrow valley. Shafts of sunlight illuminated thousands of pale green flowers, spreading out as far as she could see. The flowers, shaped like tubes, grew on on stalks reaching as high as her knees.

Klark spoke with reverence. "When sunlight warms the air, it collides with the cooler, damper air of the woods and moves through the valley like a funnel—and through thousands upon thousands of these little tubes."

Creating a green, breathy, ethereal orchestra, she thought, rendered speechless with wonder. "It's like being in a dream," she said finally.

Klark smiled down at her, his golden eyes shining. "It's marvelous, isn't it?"

"Aye. Little flute flowers."

"The official name is wind stalks, but I like your name better." His hand squeezed hers. "I worried it might be too late in the season to catch them. That's why I wanted to take you here today. Soon they'll die off for the winter."

Brown and yellow discolored some of the plants. The brownest ones created a rustling papery wheeze. Klark moved behind her, and she leaned back against him, pillowed by his body and encased in his strong arms. They laced their hands together over her stomach and listened to the ebb and flow of the wind stalks. The rumble of thunder was closer now, punctuating the music. "I hope it doesn't rain," she said.

"It won't. It's farther away than it sounds."

Unlike the start of the official pro season, she thought. Beginning with the news conference, things would accelerate—and soon their idyll at the retreat center would end.

Klark's muscles tightened as if he had intuited her thoughts. "We are going to be all right," he said ever-so quietly in her ear.

Her heart skipped a few beats. Did he mean them as the unlikeliest of lovers? Or was he simply uttering a reassurance about her looming entry into the world of high-stakes competitive bajha?

Did it matter? Both prospects carried personal risk and just as many unknowns.

"Aye," she said and stood a little bit straighter. *We will be all right*. She was tough, and she was ready—for whatever came barreling toward them next.

CHAPTER TWENTY

The season opener was days away. Team Eireya would go up against the Lesok clan's team. Klark was in Chéyasenn City—seeing to "team business", he said, leaving Jemm to do as she wished. After a long run along the scenic trails in the forest behind the retreat center, she stripped down to her swim shorts and midriff and dove into the deep end of the swimming pool intent on completing as many laps as she had the stamina to swim. The exercise helped quell her nerves and blunt her nearly constant giddy anticipation.

She was excited.

She was also terrified.

The water enveloped her like darkness in a bajha arena, soothing her, steadying her, before she surfaced and stroked to the far end. *I am ready*. Klark had told her the same, many times. No one on Team Eireya had been able to beat her, not Raff Xirri, much to his boggled dismay, and not even the fan darling Yonson Skeet, her team captain. She had studied the players on the Lesok team with Klark, and also alone, when he was immersed in scouring the Treatise of Trade. He had not stopped his relentless hunt for the elusive guidance that would allow her to do with the Trade Federation's blessing what she would soon do without it: being the first female to compete in Galactic League bajha.

Only, no one but he would know it.

At the far side of the pool, she flipped heels over head as Klark had taught her and swam back. Back and forth, she stroked, entering a trance of sorts, the swimming soothing her mind and body. With the noise of water rushing past her ears, she missed the whine of the speeder until it soared low over the retreat center.

She stopped, treading water in the center of the pool as the craft cast a shadow over the pool and lawn. Klark was back early. She dried off, snatched her shirt and trousers off a hook, and skipped up the stairs to the main level. At the back door, she collided with a staff member. His arms were as full of bulky clothing as his eyes were with concern. "It is not His Highness in the speeder."

"What?" Instantly, her heart kicked hard in her rib cage. "Who then?"

"Your teammates, Mr. Aves. Five of them."

Which ones? What were they doing here? She riffled through the day's plans in her head. No matches were scheduled with Klark away from home. But voices and laughter from inside told her that the pros had already invaded the building. There was no time to make it to her quarters without being seen. Then she understood why the servant unloaded the bundled clothing into her arms.

"I'll be in the meditation room, changing," she said. "Don't let them outside. Distract them with snacks and drinks."

"We already are, Mr. Aves."

She thanked him with a curt nod and hurried to the hut where she and Klark had made love the first time. The servant's quick action and genuine concern reflected the entire household's understanding that her identity as a woman was not known by anyone outside the household. Nor could it be. Their loyalty lifted her.

She layered on padded underclothing and combed her hair away from her face. By the time she tugged on her boots and returned to the house, Raff Xirri was at the back door, eating from a handful of shimmer chips. "I found him," he called over his shoulder.

Yonson Skeet and Garlan Muse appeared around the corner. Two other players, Arlo Heddad and Sorrowman Li came from other areas of the great room. All five players were dressed for an evening out on the town—dark gray trousers and boots, stylish shirts of various colors with crisp high collars and pointed cuffs nipped at the wrists with Team Eireya cufflinks—ebony gemstones inset with the team emblem of a raptor in silver metal, probably trillidium. Some had styled their hair with iridescent cream. Heddad's neck displayed subtle sea-blue glow-tats in an intricate, undulating design depicting a breaking wave. Most of the Eireyan players sported tattoos of either the sea, raptors, or both, somewhere on their bodies, although conservative league rules did not permit any to be visible during play. They smelled like soap, cologne, and men. Her teammates were a handsome crew.

Servants wandered amongst the pros, offering bowls of croppers and shimmer chips. The massive runes denoting the Warrior's Code loomed in the background, punctuating the prohibition against Jemm playing bajha (while ironically permitting these men she had defeated to do so).

"Hello," she said. "I didn't know you were coming today. Sir Vedla isn't here."

"We know." Xirri's thick brows wobbled as he winked at her. "While the ketta-cat's away, the scampers will play."

Jemm's uneasy gaze swerved to Skeet, her anchor when it came to Xirri's unpredictability. Skeet gave her his most charming smile. "We've come to rescue you from your monkish existence while our esteemed owner socializes with the city's elite."

Socializes? She supposed that fell under the classification of team business. Nonetheless an image of Klark suavely sipping expensive drinks while making small talk with Chéyasenn's ruling class flitted through her mind. He was comfortable in a world she did not belong to, or ever would. No wonder he had gone without her. "He had team business to see to in the city."

"He's at the governor's reception," Xirri explained.

Klark had told her nothing about it. She nixed her miffed expression before any of the men saw it.

"But we're here to take you out for a real party," Xirri said and smiled.

"We promised to show you the city, and that's what we'll do," Muse added. "Get changed and let's go."

"Your nicer duds," Xirri advised.

Jemm was suddenly aware of her loose, off-white shirt hanging over her baggy trousers. While the fabric itself was costly, she knew, the style wasn't going to turn heads. "I thank ya for thinking of me, but—"

"You can come willingly, young Kes, or you can resist," Xirri said. "Either way, you're coming."

Crat. This was going to be an invitation she could not decline, or she risked revealing her secret before the season had a chance to begin. Yet, this was as much of a rite of passage as her first match against the team's players. She was one of them now, these men. Her teammates. They liked and respected her. They had played many matches against each other, and shared a number of dinners. She had no choice but to go out with them.

Maybe she wanted to. She grinned as the smart-alecky Jemm of old surfaced. She had worked hard at refining herself, her speech and manners, to suit Federation expectations, but nowhere did it say she could not have a little fun with the team now and again. "I'll go, but with one condition. If Sir Vedla returns to find me missing, there'll be hell to pay. He'll think I've been kidnapped."

There was a ripple of chuckles. "We are kidnapping you," Xirri said. "We'll leave a ransom note," he joked to more laughter.

Skeet patted her on the back. Again she thought of how much he resembled Nico, but in a clean and wholesome way. He dropped his voice low. "The staff would let him know, but I'll send Sir Vedla a message, personally. Don't worry, we would never leave him to think something bad happened to you—or any of us." He was the voice of reason in all this. He was the leader and team captain after all. He would make sure nothing truly untoward happened to her.

"Aye, then. Wait here." She stalked to her quarters to change. She had not slept there in weeks, spending the nights with Klark in his huge, soft bed, making love, then falling asleep wrapped in his strong arms.

Socializing was he? A governor's reception? Well, well. It must be pretty swanky if the pros were left out. And her, too. But she was good enough to warm his bed, apparently. Funny how that worked.

She bolted the door to her room to keep out any wandering teammates. The deadbolt was massive. It clicked heavily into place, as if it were designed in the Dark Years to keep the warlords out. Perfect.

It did not feel as strange as it once did, donning men's clothing. She selected one of the fancy outfits for which she had been fitted but had not yet worn, choosing what best matched how the pros were dressed. She might as well get used to it. There would be soirees aplenty in months to come, but Klark would be running cover for her at them, helping to keep their secret safe. Tonight, she was on her own, and it felt like a new adventure. On Barésh she enjoyed the occasional night out with ale, music, and dancing. As long as her teammates had discarded their plans to set her up with a woman, the evening should prove enjoyable, a respite after so many weeks of hard work.

She checked her appearance one last time in the mirror then returned to the great room. They greeted her with brotherly applause, whistles, and hoots.

"Look at you! The ladies won't be able to resist our handsome young Kes tonight." Xirri's declaration produced a round of hearty, testosterone-laden male laughter—and ended for good her hopes that other females would not be part of the night's events.

Klark was the star attraction in a manicured garden full of people who were important to the team and to him as the owner but with whom he did not enjoy being around. They were pleasant enough, and supportive of the team's presence on Chéyasenn, but they were dull. After so long away from his palace life, he had forgotten just how mind-numbing such events could be.

Despite his dedication to duty as the team owner, and understanding that the governor's reception was a much-anticipated annual event, he found himself noting the crawl of time before he could return home to his sweet Baréshti lass.

Luckily, he was able to go through the motions in robot fashion. He had been trained in such affairs from birth; good manners and small talk were rote and second nature. Ingrained in his DNA. He laughed in the right places, said the right things, chose the correct utensils from a daunting array of them, nibbled the polite amount of hors d'oeuvres, while commenting expertly on the fine wines and liqueurs offered. He knew how to use charm to deflect flirtation and, sometimes, bold sexual interest from the females in attendance, while not causing offense. But when it came to the topic of the phenomenal newcomer, Kes Aves, he ventured into uncharted waters.

Training center rumors of her talent had spread into the city and reached the fans. Everyone wanted to know more. It just so happened it was Klark's pet subject. He felt himself come alive as he regaled the invited sports reporters and *Vash* society columnists alike with descriptions of the young commoner's talent. It was the thrill of the sport that gave him a certain rush, yes, but his feelings for the woman behind the masquerade blended with it all. It lit him up from the inside out whenever he spoke of her. The striking change in his demeanor translated to enthusiasm. Theirs. He had never thought of himself as a promoter, but he had become exactly that. The press conferences he had conducted via vid feed from the retreat center with Jemm, Skeet, and assorted teammates to appease them had served only to hone their curiosity. They wanted to see the new player in the flesh. But when it came time to finally take Team Eireya's slum-bred secret weapon public, he wanted to set the time and the place.

Jemm and her escorts from Team Eireya piled out of a speeder in downtown Chéyasenn City. "We'll take care of you, Kes. Just relax and have a good time," Xirri said. His walk was a bit unsteady as he slung his arm over her shoulders. He smelled of cologne, new leather boots, and "hooch". She could smell the sharp scent of the liquor on all the pros, but Xirri had probably consumed more than the rest of them on the speeder ride over, passing around the bottle as they soared low over the forest.

Jemm's mouth still tasted of the foul brew. At least this drink was not known to be fatal (as far as she knew), but it was potent. What little she had sipped left her slightly lightheaded. She was careful to leave her teammates under the impression that she had imbibed more than she had. She knew how to swill without actually doing so. It was one more useful skill learned from her hardscrabble life growing up on Barésh that helped her survive then, and would help her survive now.

Skeet deftly removed Xirri's arm from Jemm, and draped it over his shoulders instead. "No more hooch for you."

"Aw, you're getting old, my friend."

"Maybe so, but if you want to help show Kes a good time, you don't want to pass out before all your plans come to fruition, do you?"

Plans? Fruition?

But the questions dissolved in her excitement for everything she saw: the lights, the sounds, the smells. The peace of the trees, she loved it. But the cells in her body seemed to awaken and vibrate with the smells and sounds of urban life.

The white buildings of Chéyasenn City were even more beautiful up close. Free of grime, broken windows, and clotheslines of tattered laundry hanging limply from every available spot, they were towering spires of pearlescent perfection. They glowed, literally, from within, thanks to tech embedded in the building material. At night they made the city glow as in the light from full moons.

Local citizens filled the streets with the same happy, bustling energy she had first noticed on Klark's ship. All noticed the bajha athletes in their midst. This was a team town, but the presence of galactic celebrities like Yonson Skeet was thrilling nonetheless. Women flirted with the pros at every opportunity. It left Jemm to observe her own gender from behind the blind of appearing male. It was funny and fascinating at the same time—until a pair of teenage girls fell in step with Jemm. "You're new," one said, walking too close for Jemm's liking. They smelled of perfume, and their garb was finer than anything she had ever owned on Barésh.

"He's the new one! The new player. Kes Aves," said her friend.

Together the girls squealed, drawing more attention. Fans swarmed around Jemm like processors around freshly delivered ore.

Then suddenly her teammates were there, placing their bodies between Jemm and the fans. The soft press of lips landed on Jemm's cheek before her teammates propelled her away.

"They're too young for you," Muse said.

"Kes is too young," argued Sorrowman Li, a big, round, fleshy man who was somehow as swift and nimble as a scamper in the ring. "For everything!"

"Save yourself for the real prize tonight, Kes," Xirri said with a chuckle. "Unless you prefer threesomes."

Jemm glared at him. "No one needs a threesome when the one you're with is good enough."

The men whooped at that. "That is true. Nothing compares to a good woman who knows how to take care of her man," Muse said, pounding her on the back. He sniffed at her. "What do they have you using for shampoo over at that monastery anyway? It smells like flowers."

Her heart almost catapulted out of her chest. Into her mind burst an image of Klark kissing her, his fingers buried in her hair, then his lips, his voice passion-roughened. "You smell like flowers…" She had to dress in menswear, aye, but the servants in their kindness had stocked soaps and creams for her that were exquisitely feminine. She would have thought the pool water washed away any residual scent. But it had not. Luckily, Muse moved away, and in the next instant seemed to have forgotten all about it.

The men bore the arguable burden of the fans' attention. It left her free to ogle myriad goods and food items in the store windows, tempting the hungry Baréshti girl that lived inside her. She wanted to press her nose against the panes to stare at the culinary delights behind them. It was surreal knowing she had enough credits to her name to buy anything she wanted off those shelves.

More than once her teammates turned to find her slowing to gaze at the wares of one store or another. "You're showing your frontier roots, Kes," Heddad said with affection, being the one to gather her up this time. His glow-tats grew brighter as dusk crept over the city.

"Aye. We don't have stores like this where I'm from."

"We need to get you out more often."

I feel like I've been caged all my life and now I'm finally free. But she wasn't really free, was she? Not if she couldn't walk openly with her lover. To hold hands with Klark, their fingers laced together, as they explored every corner of this vibrant jewel of a city. He had been at her side for nearly every other "first" she had experienced in her new life. It felt strange not to be with him now.

But, no, the cog was off with his swanky friends about whom he had revealed nothing. Team business, her eye. He was attending to *upper-class* business. A governor's uppity reception, whatever that was. Not only was she unwelcome at the function, she was too lowly to know about it.

That was the crux of her irritation, his not having told her. Well, she had friends of her own. They might not be commoners like her but her teammates were not *Vash Nadah* royals, either. If they wanted to show her a good time, she was more than happy to oblige.

CHAPTER TWENTY-ONE

At sunset, Klark escaped the reception. The governor himself escorted Klark to his speeder, chattering on about this or that, encouraged by Klark's cordial smile. The press hounded him outside, asking after all the players but in particular Kes Aves. "I just held a press conference," he told them. "Nothing has changed."

"Except that no one has seen the young star in the flesh," one reporter said.

"Only a few more days," Klark promised with a laugh.

The first moon loomed in the sky. Last night at sunset Jemm had said she thought it resembled an overripe marmelon with its orange hue and pockmarked surface. Smiling, he realized how impatient he was to see her, to hold her, to hear her laugh. To make love to her. It was hard to believe that they had spent so many weeks together, only occasionally in the company of others, and yet their time together seemed not nearly enough. This was not an opinion he ever expected of himself, especially after wondering how his brother Ché had endured spending months on a honeymoon alone with his new wife, Ilana—months—without going mad. At one time, the prospect of anyone's long-term company, let alone a female's company, sounded tedious to the maximum degree. That had all changed. He wanted Jemm in his life, for the rest of his life!

You cannot have what Ché has. Your situation is different.

Because Jemm is different.

Klark had put the options through the grinder of his inner logic many times of late. Being with Jemm versus upholding his clan's reputation, personal happiness versus family embarrassment, forging a true relationship with Jemm versus decimating her chances at success as a professional bajha player. But no answers came of it.

He did not like it. In life he wanted logic and a plan of action. In this he had neither.

Klark and the governor stopped in front of the speeder. He made sure his facial expression did not reflect any of his inner thoughts. This was no time for doubt to come to roost. Not this close to the season's start.

"Where is your pilot, Your Highness?" the governor inquired, seeing the empty cockpit.

"I prefer to fly myself, when the opportunity presents." He shook the governor's offered hand. "Once again, thank you for your hospitality, Governor. I will see you on opening day."

Klark settled into the snug interior of the personal speeder and pulled the hatch closed. It sealed and his eardrums popped as the craft pressurized. He noticed for the first time the icon on his personal comm telling him of a message of routine priority. *Yonson Skeet: Sir, if you're looking for Kes, I've got him. Don't worry, he'll be fine.*

The private club was luxurious by Jemm's standards. Crat, by any standards. The stink of swank and body odor was absent. No underlying funk of smog or sewage clogged her nostrils. The music was not the thump she loved, but the banging beat was a mild imitation. The urge to move to the beat was strong, but she danced like a lass and didn't dare.

Female gazes followed her as she walked with her companions to a table. Jemm fought the impulse to jerk away when a few of the bolder women trailed fingertips along her chest. If anyone detected the padding she used to disguise her breasts, it was game over.

But no one seemed to suspect anything. Expectation bias was on her side once again.

Soon drinks came, and then food. Her teammates were irreverent and raucous in the relative safety of the private club. Jemm laughed with them and joined in the banter. But her high spirits nosedived when Xirri brought an attractive woman in a short, red, skintight dress to the table. "Kes, meet Theeran. Theeran meet Kes."

Jemm mumbled a hello. Theeran was beautiful in an exotic way with fair coloring, high rounded cheekbones, and flared brows that twinkled with minuscule purple lights at each end, each one as tiny as a grain of sand. The lights complemented her eye color, an unnatural but striking shade of lavender. The curves of her body were so precise they seemed engineered, and probably were.

An expensive sex server.

"Welcome to the team, Kes," Xirri said, his hands wrapped around the woman's tiny waist as he pushed her toward Jemm. "Enjoy your gift."

"That's all right, I—"

The woman settled onto Jemm's lap. Her perfume hovered around them in a cloud. Jemm recognized some sort of musk. She had heard about chemical pheromone attractants, and guessed it was present now.

"What a sexy man you are." Theeran smoothed back Jemm's hair and kissed her chastely on the lips, pulling back to search Jemm's face with subtle, amused affection, making it clear she assumed she had been hired to woo a young, inexperienced, even skittish lad into bed.

Jemm's teammates applauded, throwing back their drinks and enjoying the show. Meanwhile, Jemm wondered how best to remove Theeran from her lap before the sex server noticed the utter lack of arousal generated by her shapely backside or, more specifically, the lack of any body parts that could provide such a reaction. "I'm in a relationship," she said. "I'm sweet on someone."

Jemm winced at the touch of the woman's hand stroking over her cheek. "Shush," Theeran crooned. "She's at home, and I'm here."

Jemm glared at Xirri. "Raff," she warned and mouthed, "No." But the player was tipsy and beyond convincing. Next, she pleaded silently with Skeet. But while his gaze seemed somewhat more sympathetic than their laughing teammate, Jemm guessed he didn't see the harm in the situation. What fella in their right mind would argue at having a confection like Theeran plopped in his lap?

Jemm couldn't even argue it. Refusing Theeran could call into question many other things. Doubts had a way of coalescing into truth. It was the last thing she needed to happen this close to the season opener. Her family was depending on her. Klark was depending on her.

I can play this game, too, fellas. Aye, it was the same as bajha; she had to be sly and unpredictable to throw her opponent off-balance. Same game, different arena.

She stood, setting Theeran back on her spindly heels. "Where can we go?"

"Someplace private." Theeran tucked herself under Jemm's arm; not difficult to do as Jemm was a full head taller.

Xirri and Muse applauded. Skeet seemed to approve. Only big Sorrowman looked unhappy for Jemm, lifting his foamy glass of ale to Jemm in a toast. "Good luck, kid."

Theeran snuggled close. "You smell like flowers," she said.

Crat. Jemm winced.

"Were you with another girl before me tonight? Naughty boy." Her fingers slipped between Jemm's.

"Kes has beat us all," Xirri told Theeran. "But he won't be able to beat you," he added to more laughter.

Theeran blew them a kiss and led Jemm away.

And directly to a reserved private room. Theeran pressed her fingertip to the entry pad, opening the door, then touched an icon that changed the display from *RESERVED* to *OCCUPIED*.

The instant the door sealed behind them, she spun to Theeran, who had wasted no time removing a gauzy overwrap from her bodice. The swell of the upper half of her ample breasts glowed in the room's soft light. "How much is your tip?" Jemm asked.

Theeran slinked toward Jemm like a ketta-cat toward a tasty morsel. "Not your concern. Everything is taken care of."

"Whatever Xirri said he'd give you, I'll double it." Jemm dug cards out of her pocket and counted out silvers from a thick wad.

The sight of all the silvers stopped Theeran cold.

"I'll triple it," Jemm said.

"Five. That's what most clients tip. The ones who want to see me again, that is."

"I'll give you fifteen." Jemm counted out the thin cards. "But, we're not going to have sex. We're not going to do anything. The tip is for keeping that our secret."

Theeran's luminous lavender eyes reflected her willingness to take the bribe. She had been hired to do a job, but in the end she was just another working lass who needed the money. She hiked up the hem of her dress and slipped the cards into a money purse inside the garter on her thigh.

"Have a seat." Jemm gestured toward an empty chair opposite a plush chaise. Only now were the details of the private room coming into focus, now that she did not have the immediate survival needs of thinking she would have to fend off Theeran.

Theeran gave Jemm another perplexed look then arranged herself in the chair.

Jemm perched on the edge of the chaise. "So, where are ya from…?"

They chatted for a while. Then, when a reasonable amount of time had passed, Theeran stood, finger combing her hair and wiping off her lip tint. She pinched her cheeks to give them color, and then her lips to make them appear well kissed, before reapplying the tint. "I can't look as if I've been slacking off."

"No. I need Xirri to think I got his money's worth." The dozer.

Theeran reached for Jemm to pinch her lower lip a few times.

"Ow."

"Job security." She turned Jemm's collar askew then left the room ahead of her.

Back in the noisy bar Theeran undulated past the team with a dazed air about her, and heaved a dreamy sigh. "I have to say, boys, that Kes Aves remains undefeated."

Their wide-eyed gazes followed her all the way out of the club then shifted back to Jemm, who swaggered back to the table to join them.

Jemm expected Klark to be waiting for her like Ma used to do when she came in late from a night out. But

Klark was nowhere in the main house. She moved outside to the deck, under the vast and starry sky. The sound of churning water came from below.

He was swimming? Surely, he had heard the speeder overhead, both incoming and departing. But he chose to remain in the pool.

She descended the wooden staircase in her expensive dress boots, stopped at the edge of the pool, a female trill rat dressed in fashionable menswear, watching a *Vash* prince swim laps. In the back of her mind she decided it had to be one of the most incongruous scenes imaginable. And one to which no one but the trustworthy staff of this household could know.

He exploded to the surface at her feet, water sloshing over the ground as he propped an arm on the edge of the pool. Steam rose from his shoulders and the heated water. Droplets of water thrown onto her new boots glittered in the moonlight. "I thought you would come looking for me," she said.

Out of breath and tired from the exertion, Klark smoothed his hair back with one hand. His gold eyes were intense. "I wanted to. You have no idea..."

"I sure do. I know how ya are."

At that, he barked out a laugh. "I didn't see Skeet's message until I was about to leave the city. My first instinct was to protect you. To control. But, I reasoned that if you couldn't handle a night out with teammates, then you'd never last in the league. You did the right thing, going out with them without me hovering around, as much as I hated being left behind."

"So, you went swimming."

"Yes." Self-deprecating humor pushed his concern out of the way as he swept his gaze over her. "I've been swimming for quite awhile now."

She tipped her head and grinned. "Help much?"

"Hardly. Come here." He reached for her, but she skipped backward, out of reach.

"New clothes. Don't I look handsome?"

He snorted and pushed up and out of the water, mist rising from his sculpted body, until he smothered it with a towel. "You'll look incredible and delicious once I undress you."

Smiling, she evaded his damp embrace. "They set me up with a sex server. A high-class sex server."

"Xirri," he muttered and she laughed.

"I paid her three times her tip and we chitchatted about our families and such. Afterward she pretty much told Xirri I was the best she ever had."

"The sex server and I share something in common, then. You're the best I ever had, also." Again he said, "Come here," and extended his arm, his desire revealed in his face.

She almost walked the last few steps into his arms, every part of her begged her to do it, but she couldn't let his hot, damp, half-naked body and his sexy earnest self distract her. He tipped his head. "Is there something amiss?"

"How was your...business?"

"My business in the city? Fine. Uneventful. Until I got Skeet's message."

She didn't share his smile. "Skeet knew you were at the Governor's reception. The entire team knew except me. A garden party ain't business. It's pleasure."

"It was not pleasure."

"Maybe it was, maybe it wasn't, but you didn't think to tell this trill rat about it. You could have shared what you were doing. We share everything else." Admitting it and revealing her wounded feelings rekindled her anger. It boiled inside her, but she did her best not to let it show, and failed.

Startled, he blinked at her. "I do not see you as anything less than myself. Nor anyone else."

"Would ya take me on your arm to a swanky affair...if I weren't supposed to be a lad? Would ya?"

Klark scraped a hand over his face as he tried imagining Jemm in his world, at the palace. "Boxed in" by all the rules, as she had once so vehemently and accurately described it the day she walked off his ship and returned to Barésh.

The sound of her boot heel scuffing dragged him out of his thoughts. "Jemm..." He caught her in an instant, pulling her toward him. Thankfully, she didn't resist, but the hurt in her eyes about killed him. "You had to think about it?" she accused. "I saw you. I can't say I blame ya. I—"

He crushed his mouth over hers, the kiss angry at first, until he poured his love into every stroke of his tongue, every caress, as he held her head between his hands, so that she would not run away again. When they finally separated, they gasped for air. "If I were lucky enough to have you on my arm at some 'swanky' affair, I would be the most envied man in the room."

Their lips almost touching, he held her too close to see her eyes, but he felt her reaction to his statement in the slightest softening of her body. *I love you.* He yearned to reveal all that he felt in his heart aloud, but it would serve no purpose other than to make the course they had chosen more difficult. "I didn't share the specifics with you about the reception because I didn't consider them important. It was not at all meant to offend, or to leave you out. I didn't see the event as pleasure. It wasn't pleasure. Once there, I went through the motions and did what was necessary for the team. As you did tonight." He brushed his thumbs over her cheekbones. "We, too, are a team, you and I—in a different, more meaningful sense. It's how I see you, and will always see you. I couldn't have more pride in you, my stubborn little trill rat. I couldn't possibly think more highly of you than I do already. Ah, my beautiful Baréshti lass, if there were any justice in this galaxy, you'd be able to play openly and be on my arm in public wherever we went."

She sighed. Her hands slid up his back, over his shoulders, and up the back of his neck and into his hair, generating an outbreak of tingles. "If there's any justice in this galaxy, your lass is going to make love to you until ya can't walk anymore." Then she proceeded to prove the truth of those words, many times over.

CHAPTER TWENTY-TWO

A nd so the season began. True to her word, Jemm won her pro matches, and continued to win them. Klark had stopped pacing with fists clenched in suspense while she played. Well, mostly stopped. He had started cheering along with the rest of the fans. No one could defeat her.

The winning was contagious, of course, and the excitement buoyed the entire team, which was his fervent hope from the beginning. Everyone played better than in previous years. Yonson Skeet had his best scores to date. Xirri won against a player for the Dars who had defeated him for years.

"The Kes effect," Skeet dubbed it, and Team Eireya soon climbed in the rankings to third place of the eight clans. They had work ahead of them before they caught the true powerhouse teams of the B'kahs and the Virs, but that day would come; Klark was certain of it.

"Kes! Kes!" the audience chanted as Jemm appeared ringside to face Tatam Lesok of the Lesok clan's team, the fifth highest scorer in league history. Not since Tatam finished playing at the university level had he lost a match.

Klark rested his hand on Jemm's shoulder, standing behind her as she viewed the ring. "You've watched the vids. You know how he plays. You've got this."

"I know. I'm ready for him. I hope he's ready for me," she said, as she always did, for good luck.

He squeezed her shoulder and left her to pace (he couldn't help it), allowing his coaches to do their job. Head Coach Kailarrenteyareiliann, known as Coach K, conferred with Kes ringside before sending her into the ring. The arena was the Lesok clan's home turf. But the fans loved Kes, loved an underdog. Loved a commoner like them. While he expected Eireyan media to cover their fans' favorites, journalists loyal to other teams wanted a chance to interview Kes Aves, AKA Sea Kestrel—the Champion of Barésh.

As the lights in the arena dimmed, allowing the nanocrylic to better display the match taking place inside within its protective circle of blackness and silence, Klark rehearsed how he planned to assuage Jemm's spirits after the loss, her first since the long-ago day on *Cheya's Resolute* when Skeet had beaten her. "Tatam Lesok has been at this for many standard years," he would tell her. "You can take pride in how well you played against him, and perhaps one day you will defeat him, too."

A roar of cheers dragged his attention back to the ring in time to witness her sens-sword crashing into Tatam's chest plate.

"Holy craggin' dome," he muttered, because he knew Jemm was thinking the same thing. She beat Tatam.

Team Eireya surged toward the ring to congratulate Jemm. Her helmet was off, her hair messy. Her face was flushed and alive with exhilaration, her eyes gleaming with happiness as she found Klark's. Then well-wishers engulfed her and took her from his sight. His heart squeezed. It reminded him of how she so often looked at him. No, they had not once exchanged the word "love" but he hoped it was what she felt for him, as he certainly did for her.

"Team Eireya's new young superstar Kes Aves decimated Tatam Lesok tonight," a reporter announced on live galactic feed reported from the sidelines. "The many-times-over Galactic Cup champ and Lesok team captain, Tatam Lesok, appears stunned by what only can be called a rout."

Tatam, a tough, compact-sized man, flashed a deadly glower at the reporter thrusting a mic-rod at him. He mumbled something then disappeared with a bevy of coaches and Lesok team staff for their locker room.

In the meantime, Jemm was at the eye of a storm of attention. Skeet and other players joined her for photos. Jemm smiled and waved, a natural at pleasing the fans and the press. But she was also tired; he could tell. They had spent many days on the road. His protective instincts urged him to spirit her away to where he could indulge her a little: a quiet room, a bath, dinner just the two of them instead of with the team, and then he would make sure she got a solid night's sleep.

When the coaches urged her toward the locker room, Klark joined her. "Well done, Kes! Well done." He gave her a brisk, brotherly hug, punctuated with a few bangs of his hand on her back. But he wanted to swing her over his arm for a victory kiss to remember.

They walked to the locker room, where no one ever questioned Sea Kestrel's preference for a private changing area. She wasn't the only pro on the team with an odd habit, and this was her particular quirk. Klark had seeded it as such in the minds of her teammates, and there had not been any problems.

Then Skeet found him. "Sir, Coach K needs you." He motioned with his chin over to the locker room entrance, where the head coach wore an unhappy expression in the midst of what appeared to be a heated discussion with a gaggle of officials.

"What's going on?" Jemm was back at his side.

"No idea. Wait here." Unease invaded his gut as he walked up to the group.

"They want to test Kes for PET," Coach growled.

"Performance enhancing tech?" Klark turned his infamous Vedla glare to the men. All of them visibly recoiled. "What is the meaning of this?"

"The Lesoks have lodged a formal complaint, Your Highness," an official answered. "Mr. Aves will have to give a blood sample."

Klark sensed Jemm watching and listening from farther back in the locker room. By now all of the team had stopped what they were doing to pay attention. Angry rumbling and muttered swearing simmered amongst them.

"This is an unspeakable insult to be thusly accused—to my team and to my clan."

The officials had no choice in the matter, however. If the Lesoks raised the protest, it had to be investigated immediately, as PET left the bloodstream within a short time.

Klark and Coach stepped aside to allow a league medical assistant into the locker room. Jemm looked ashen. "What are ya testing for, exactly?" she asked.

Will it reveal I'm female? That was the real question in those words.

The assistant swabbed the crook of her elbow. "PET only."

"They're looking for the presence of illegal performance enhancing tech—bots—in your body," Klark explained.

"I don't blasted believe it," Skeet blurted out.

"Tatam Lesok needs an attitude adjustment," Xirri growled. "Loser."

Klark waved a hand at the players to quiet them.

Jemm remained silent and grim as the blood was taken. Was this how it would end? Klark wondered.

Everything they had worked so hard for demolished by a sore loser?

Meanwhile the med assistant ran the blood through a small machine. The room went silent as everyone waited for the results.

Using bajha skills, Klark attempted to empty his mind of mounting dread. Not a gender test, he told himself. PET bots only. He knew Jemm was free of those.

"He's clean," the med assistant said. "No presence of PET in the blood."

Klark exhaled and exchanged a thankful glance with Jemm as cheers and some foul language exploded from the direction of the appalled and now relieved team. To be accused of using PET was rare, and an insult. It showed just how much Jemm's wins were shaking up the league. Well, they were going to have to get used to it. Champions like Tatam Lesok would have to adjust to a changed world of play, now that Sea Kestrel was leading a resurgent Team Eireya as a real contender for the elusive Galactic Cup.

Team Eireya racked up more victories. Two weeks after the debacle with the Lesoks, excitement peaked when the team hosted the B'kahs in the home arena on Chéyasenn, and scored enough for the cumulative scores to go in Team Eireya's favor. They were celebrating in the locker room when Klark announced, "A special word from His Majesty the King," and displayed the call from his father, King Rorrik, to the large viewscreen on the locker room wall.

Jemm's heart swelled with pleasure as she savored the sight of Klark beaming as his emotionally distant father congratulated him, and the team. She saw the resemblance between the men, but whereas the king was relaxed, Klark seemed to be bracing himself. Jemm could feel the tension in him from where she stood. It angered her. Did this *Vash* king not realize the level of man he had raised? Sure Klark may have stumbled in the eyes of his clan, but who hadn't made mistakes? He was a hero in her eyes.

"You're doing a great job with the team, son. All the Vedlas stand behind you and look ahead with much hope to the remainder of the season." Then the regal-looking man cast his gaze around. "Where are you, Mr. Aves?" he inquired.

Several teammates' hands landed on her back to push her forward so King Rorrik could better view her. Jemm bent forward in a bow. "Your Majesty."

"You are the most gifted bajha player I've seen in a lifetime of following the sport. Your teammates are certainly a fine and talented group on their own, but with you at the helm, the Galactic Cup is in our grasp."

Jemm answered with a bashful nod. "Thank you, Your Majesty. I am nothing without the rest of the team." She did not like being singled out. No player alone could win the Galactic Cup. Although it could very well come down to her in the final, Cup-winning match against a yet-unknown opponent, it took a whole team to get there. But who was she to correct a king? She could not believe a king was speaking with her, and in such a familiar way. She couldn't wait to tell Ma, Button, and Nico.

The king's voice boomed. "It's just what we Vedlas have needed. Now, carry on and get ready for those Dars next week."

She bowed again, and then the screen went blank.

"Sir Vedla."

Everyone turned at the sound of Coach K's voice. Jemm saw his sour expression and the two officials dressed in suits and cloaks standing behind him. Her heart filled with dread.

"More complaints have been lodged," Coach said, his face red with anger. "Accusations of PET usage by the team."

"This is an outrage," Klark said, glowering at the officials. "Who lodged the complaints? The B'kahs? After being trounced?"

"Not only the B'kahs. The league has been fielding complaints from several teams about Kes Aves and PET."

"But you tested Aves, and he tested clean," Klark pointed out.

"I know, Your Highness." The official sighed. "But, the controversy is growing. I've asked the league surgeon to do a complete physical exam. That will put the matter to rest once and for all."

Jemm's legs gave out. She sat down hard on a bench, her body quaking with adrenaline.

Klark was silent. There were no words. No defense.

There was no way out.

"If your player is clean, sir, and I have every confidence that he is, then you have nothing to worry about."

Nothing could be farther from the truth.

"Sir Vedla, if you would accompany me please," Jemm said, her voice remarkably composed.

They left the main locker room with the league official and physician, headed for a private area with a lockable door that was used to treat injuries. After feeling the outrage and sympathy radiating from her teammates as she passed by, Jemm felt as if she were being marched to her execution. She kept her head high, her face free of emotion. She did not need to look at Klark to know the nature of his thoughts. She could feel them hitting her like grit blown across the badlands.

She and Klark had one chance left. If the physical exam did not require her to undress, they were in the clear.

The door closed, shutting them inside. Jemm stood awaiting further instruction. Her bajha suit was unfastened at her neck; her hair was matted from wearing her headgear. She avoided meeting Klark's gaze for fear of setting off a chain reaction of emotions.

First her blood was taken and sampled. Again, she was deemed clean. Then the league surgeon donned a pair of skin-tight gloves. "All right, Mr. Aves, if you will undress now we'll make this as painless as possible."

Klark's vivid gaze collided with hers. He gave his head a single subtle shake.

"We have the right to refuse the physical examination," Klark told the officials.

"Why, yes, but why would you?" the physician asked.

"Your player tested clean," the official added. "This is just a perfunctory check to confirm there is no physical alteration to the body of any kind. Then I can sign off Mr. Aves, and dismiss the protests. For good."

"Yes. I understand. However, as this player's chaperone and the team owner I cannot allow the examination to proceed."

Crat. Jemm braced herself and winced as her heart kicked against her sternum and her pulse pounded in her head. Here it comes.

"It is for her modesty, you see," Klark said in a cool, measured tone. "Kes Aves is a woman."

CHAPTER TWENTY-THREE

Jemm faced a wall of muscle as the players closed ranks around her. She had never stopped thinking that the risk of discovery was real, but she never imagined it would happen like this. Her success in the ring had caused suspicion. Not her manner, her voice, her eyes, her body.

While coaches and staff secured the locker room, Jemm huddled with her teammates. Klark loomed like a block of trill at the perimeter, his arms folded hard over his chest, as if it were a physical struggle not to jump in and deliver the bad news himself.

I'm doing it, she told him with her eyes. It had to come from her. "I've been banned from competition," she began to say.

Grumbles and questions drowned her out. "But you're clean," Skeet argued.

She thrust up one hand and the men quieted. "Aye. I'm clean. I'm banned because females ain't allowed to play professional bajha. I'm a lass. A woman."

She never heard a hush so deep in all her life.

Then Xirri's raw laugh shattered the silence. "No, Kes. Really. What's going on?"

"I'm telling ya the truth, fellas."

Many pairs of eyes bored into her now, all of them different—looks of disbelief and denial, a few glares hinting at egos bruised by the realization that a female had beaten them, and, lastly, amusement from some of her good friends like Xirri who thought she was joking.

She reached for the fasteners on her bajha suit. An explosion of thrust-out hands stopped her. A collective protest of, "Don't."

Jemm bowed her head. "I'm sorry. I let all of ya down, and I feel awful about it."

Klark spoke up. "Kes informed me that she was female before we left Barésh, but I signed her anyway. It was never her intent to reach beyond street bajha. What started out innocently enough on her part led to something none of us expected. Gentlemen, if there's any blame to bear, it's mine and mine only."

"Blame? For winning every contest so far this season? For the other teams being afraid to face us? For me to be eying the Galactic Cup for the first time since I've been on this team?" G'Zanna blurted out. The fatherly man was usually an island of calm. "Don't be ridiculous, sir."

Anger contorted Xirri's angular face as he added to what G'Zanna said, "Those B'kah bastards better not use this to lay claim to the games tonight. We won, fair and square. Thanks in no small part to Sea Kestrel here."

"The Kes effect!" Arlo Heddad bellowed.

More cheers followed Heddad's cry. The hullabaloo was louder than a North City dive bar on an Eighthnight. "That's enough, gentlemen!" Skeet shouted, and the noise simmered down some. He cast a pleading look in Klark's direction. "They're right, sir. Tonight we won fair and square. We won our past contests the same way. It's not like Kes was using PET. In fact, anyone who hasn't seen her in action would consider her gender a handicap. We're going to protest the decision, right?"

"We absolutely have to protest the decision," Xirri chimed in. "We're in third place in the league now. After tonight we're probably in second."

"And on our way to the top!" Muse yelled, triggering yet another wave of outraged roars.

"There aren't any rules against women players," Klark said when the uproar had eased. "I will say so when I file a formal protest. But we have eleven thousand years of precedent working against us. I've scoured the Treatise of Trade for anything to support Kes competing. But so far I've come up empty."

"This is sport, not religion." Skeet had never looked so frustrated. "If a player is as good as Kes, it should make no difference if they're male or female."

"She can be a purple-spotted Lyrian bog-boor for all I care," Sorrowman Li said, his double chins wobbling. "She won. We won!"

"Team Eireya! Team Eireya!" Muse chanted their battle cry at the top of his lungs.

Everyone else joined in. The noise was deafening.

Jemm and Klark exchanged helpless glances. Jemm tried to smile through an upsurge of emotion. "You gotta keep it going, fellas, straight to the top. With or without me."

"It won't feel like a team until you're back." Skeet rested his hand on her shoulder. "And you are coming back. We're behind you one hundred percent. We're going to hit the media on this and hit hard. We'll take it to the people. What happened is not right. If there are others like you out there, then it's never been right."

Once, she feared the team would reject her if they were to learn the truth. But, after recovering from the initial shock, all they cared about was the injustice of her being thrown out of the ring. She was their teammate first, a female second. It was either the beginning of something wonderful, or it was the beginning of the end.

The next day, a speeder waited to carry Jemm from Chéyasenn to a transfer station, where she would board a privately chartered starship for the long journey back to Barésh. Klark gripped her hands as if he had no intention of letting her go. They stood facing each other in the morning sunlight on the speeder pad, serenaded by birdsong, a scene wholly at odds with the hollow feeling in her heart. She was outfitted like an upper-class lass in knee-high brown boots and a green-hued, gorgeously tailored, mid-thigh-length dress. Tiny polished green gemstones decorated the neckline and cutaway sleeves flaunted her toned arms.

"The color of the grass and your eyes," Klark had said when he surprised her with the gift soon after dawn, explaining that he had ordered it made for some unknown future time when she might be able to wear it. Only, they had not expected it would be so soon, and under these circumstances. For his meeting with league officials downtown he was outfitted just as smartly in a crisp charcoal-gray shirt and black trousers—Vedla colors. They resembled a well-to-do young couple about to go out, not one about to separate, perhaps for a very long time.

She pressed her lips together to steady herself as she reached up to caress his somber face. She remembered the first time she saw him, how cold and hard his sculpted features appeared. They had grown hard again, but his eyes were pools of desolation. His sorrowful voice rumbled in his chest. "If only you were accompanying me to Eireya."

"I know…" But with her ban from competition open-ended, and Klark's urgency to return to his home to handle damage control, the best place for her was with her family. More, her presence at the palace might exacerbate a situation on the cusp of spiraling out of control.

She swayed a bit on her feet. They had not gotten a wink of sleep. When they were not making love, they held each other tight, neither of them wanting time to fly by too quickly, as it would have if they surrendered to sleep.

Klark caught her and pulled her close. "Ah, my sweet Baréshti lass. Know that I'll miss you." He embraced her, his strong hand cradling the back of her skull, her cheek pressed to his heart.

She breathed in his scent, her fist a tight ball on his chest to battle the constriction in her throat. *I love you, Klark*. It was what she wanted him to know, words she had never uttered to another fella. But she remained mum. The last thing she wanted was to throw another complication onto an honorable man's already over-burdened shoulders. The story of her ban from competition had not hit the news yet, but as soon as the league made an official announcement, Klark had to be ready to act in defense of his team and family. She could be prosecuted and jailed. Klark could end up back on house arrest. Hefty fines might be levied, and awful penalties. It was horrible how something that started out with such promise had kicked off a chain of events that could cause the man she loved to lose his team, his reputation, and his family fortune. Maybe even his freedom.

"I can feel you thinking, Jemm."

"I'm always thinking. Crag them, Klark. The league. They had every right to do what they did, I guess, but crag them all the same." For tearing her and Klark apart, for crushing the team's spirit, for keeping those dozer B'kahs on top, where they no longer deserved to be. And for holding fast to traditionalist rules born in a dark and dangerous past when a brighter future beckoned. "I won't stop thinking until I see ya again."

Klark moved her back and gazed down at her. "We'll be back together here on Chéyasenn before we know it." A niggle of doubt inside her contradicted his promise, and she knew he had glimpsed it. She may never see him again after this. Although his smile was one of tenderness, his brows drew together, forming a telltale groove between them. In his shimmering gaze she saw that he wanted to tell her something, something ripped from his heart, but she pressed her finger to his lips. Anything like that would only make this more difficult.

"Come here, you sexy uppity aristo," she whispered and pulled him down for one last kiss, a kiss to last the ages, unshed tears exerting pressure behind her eyes. Then she tore her lips from his and ran toward the speeder's open hatch, her throat so tight it left her unable to utter the simple word "goodbye".

"Ma?" Jemm let herself into the apartment—as tiny, threadbare, and tidy as ever, and smelling like candlewax, home-cooking, and cleaning oil. She took the familiar aromas deep into her lungs. *Home.* Ma was in her favorite chair, mending clothes, a basket filled with more clothing lying at her feet. Shock then delight flared in her pretty face. She stood up so fast that she kicked the basket over. Her arms opened wide and Jemm hurried into them like she was a little girl again. Neither were known to be criers, and yet there were no dry eyes when they separated.

"Look at ya." Tearful happiness and wonder filled Ma's gaze as she took in the sight of Jemm and the green dress. "You're a lady now," she said, but with none of the disdain reserved for compound cogs. "A beautiful lady."

"You're the one who's a sight to see. You look so good, Ma." Her mother's skin had lost its sallow appearance. No dark circles appeared under her eyes. A healthy rosy color tinted her cheeks. She had filled out, too, and looked a lot more like Nico in the face.

"I feel good, too, lass. No more coughing. I've been using Earth-dweller potions. I have my own Earth-dweller doctor looking after me," she added proudly.

"CJ?" Jemm asked with a smirk, remembering the encounter between the vivacious young female doctor and Nico.

"Aye, Doctor CJ Randall. She says my lung condition is cured, but I'll need a procedure to help with the scarring on the inside of me when I'm stronger."

"Thank the dome." The apartment was awfully quiet, Jemm realized. "Where's Button?"

"She's at preschool this morning."

"Preschool? What's that?"

"It's school for the wee ones."

Mineworkers' children were home-schooled, if the parents had any education to share, or they gathered in small, informal classrooms with self-taught teachers.

"The Earth-dwellers set up schools all over the city," Ma explained. "They're requiring formal education for all the mineworkers now. Treating us like the compound elites, they are."

A glance toward Nico's bed curtain revealed that her brother was home and asleep. He must have gotten home late. "Nico's still Nico, I see."

A shadow passed over Ma's face and told Jemm all she needed to know. Her brother had not stopped flirting with danger, embracing unpredictability, and remained a stranger with stability. He still ran from his broken heart and the kind of nightmares no man should have to suffer. Nothing had changed.

"He's got his fight clubs to keep him busy," Ma explained, her tone flatter. "Two of them now. He's making good money he says, but I've not seen any. He's not home much. But, he's happy. Who can take that from him?"

No one wanted to steal Nico's happiness.

"I want ya to hide these and keep them safe." Jemm pulled four cards from her pocket.

With awe, Ma took the starship tickets with an unsteady hand. "Are we leaving, then?"

Jemm gave her head a shake. "Not yet." Then she proceeded to tell her everything that had happened.

And just like that Klark landed back in his previous life. It felt as oddly familiar yet uncomfortable as an old jacket donned for the first time in years, and after its owner had changed and grown. He had changed and grown during his time away. His old life no longer fit him.

He tossed his travel bag on his bed then crossed the spacious suite to the balcony to soak in the scenery that always gave him so much pleasure, and that he had missed. *Home.* A pair of raptors soared past, a flash of gray, gold, and black feathers. It was the mated pair he had always enjoyed watching.

He watched, transfixed, as they hunted together, dipping low and soaring over the sea. Two equals—two halves that together formed something greater than one. Many months ago, before Jemm, he had marveled at how the raptors instinctively trusted that the other would be at their side. Back then he had decided that such a bond was something he wasn't destined to experience. But he was wrong. He had found that kind of bond with Jemm.

Enajhe a'nai. Body and soul. His mate, his heart.

For her, he would fight and win this war. He would defend his family, and defend her. The league had issued only a single terse statement on the matter: Kes Aves had left competition due to personal reasons.

Klark knew he had dodged a bullet. By not admitting that a female had infiltrated the ranks of the Trade Federation's elite players undetected—winning every match—the league had spared him from being called in to explain to his father, to Councilman Toren, or to any of the other Vedla elders why he had chosen to embarrass the clan by trying to pawn off a female as a pro bajha player. However, he felt anything but relieved. It unsettled him that the league had released such a mysterious statement. He sensed there was more to come. It was like facing a bajha opponent who did not play by the rules. So far Klark had done everything by the book, but he had better be ready for a crippling body shot.

The fans had not taken the announcement well. When Klark left Chéyasenn the uproar was only just getting started. Skeet was chomping at the bit to leak the truth to the press, but Klark asked him to hold off until he gave the okay. This had to be a coordinated effort.

If only he and his father had a better relationship. Then he and Klark could brainstorm the best way forward. But if he presented bad news and what his father might view as half-baked plans, it would make things worse. He thought of consulting with his brother, but Ché was on Earth with his wife, and sounded busy for some time to come. Klark once again was on his own, trying to defend his loved ones.

He left the balcony to change into workout wear in preparation for a long run, a preferred way to organize his thoughts. The suite seemed utterly empty, his boots echoing on the black slab of a floor. Once, being alone was all he wanted. When he was with Jemm, they were able to exist comfortably in silence, often for hours. It was akin to being alone but better. Infinitely better. He missed her all the more, not knowing when he would be able to see her again. What if he had made a horrible mistake, leaving their time apart open ended? What if she moved on without him? After all, he had exacted no promises from her.

Nor did you give her any.

He reeled in his thoughts, again. News was about to break that could leave his team and his clan in shambles. That needed to be his focus. That was why he had returned home.

A run, yes, a very long run along the coast was what he needed.

He was on his way outside when the sight of the table of creatures entombed in amber stopped him short. Frozen forever, they stared helplessly, their maws open in eternal screams. It was like a relic from a past life— someone else's life. Whatever was he thinking to want this monstrosity in his quarters?

"Bring me a sledgehammer," he snarled at the startled galley boy who had arrived to clear the plates leftover from a welcome snack. Then he squeezed his eyes shut, pulling himself back. "Disregard that." Jemm would think it the height of arrogant elite behavior to destroy a priceless artifact on a whim. "Take it—the table. When I return I want it gone from my apartment. Do you understand? Gone."

It weighed thousands of pounds. Klark did not know how it could be done, but that was not his concern. The boy scurried away to get help.

Outside, it was the most perfect of days. He stopped on the shore path to gaze out to sea for a moment, his hands placed behind his back. The sea was so blue, the sky Eireyan lavender. The scent of sea and sea creatures was intoxicating. All of it stunning. It was a salve for his raw soul. As much as he sometimes sought to escape it, Eireya was in his blood, part of his DNA.

Movement caught his eye. To his right was a fish trawler motoring toward the docks from its daily run. On his left was Uncle Yul, waiting to watch the glistening, rainbow-colored catch spill from the trawler's holding tank. His posture was regal, his profile trillidium-hard, as he stood there with his hands clasped behind his back, right over left, his boots planted at precisely shoulder width.

Klark blinked away an odd sensation. It was like looking down into a tide pool, expecting to find spiral shells and rock crabs but encountering his own reflection instead. Jerking his right hand from his left, he folded his arms across his chest. His sire, King Rorrik, had long since raised his children, including an heir, the all-important crown prince, freeing his Uncle Yul to live wherever he liked. But Uncle Yul chose to hang around the palace like an extra appendage with no real use.

It hit Klark that he was destined for the same thing. But by some miracle, he was given the chance to do more with his life, to be elsewhere, to be someone important to another human being. To be loved.

But he had let her go.

Uncle Yul pivoted to resume his walk, then halted, seeing Klark. "Ah. Klark. You're just who I wanted to see. Don't just stand there, young man. Come here." His eyes were like a fishing line, reeling him in.

Klark closed the distance between them until he finally stood at his uncle's side. It was the closest he had been to Uncle Yul since he was five years old.

Shoulder to shoulder, they watched the trawler unload its catch. "We come from a long line of brooding men who like to stare out to sea," Uncle Yul observed.

Klark frowned. Having his similarities to Uncle Yul confirmed by the man himself did not improve his mood.

"Walk with me," Uncle Yul said. "Men who plot are far less likely to be suspected of it if they're out strolling."

Men who plot? Klark fell in step with his uncle.

"I heard the news today, Klark, about your commoner bajha discovery, our star player, leaving the league.

Personal reasons? Bah. Something doesn't sound right. What do you know?"

For the most fleeting of moments, Klark considered deflecting the question, telling Uncle Yul he was not at liberty to share any information. Then he reminded himself that he needed an ally in the family. "Your suspicions are correct, sir. Kes Aves didn't leave voluntarily. She was banned from competition by the league."

Uncle Yul's steps faltered. "She, you said?"

"That is correct. Kes Aves is female. She was a successful street bajha player, playing in disguise. After tryouts, she admitted she was a woman. She was fully willing to walk away from the opportunity of a lifetime for the sake of being honest. But I wanted her on the team, anyway. She is the single most gifted player I have ever seen."

"The single most gifted player in the entire league. Unequalled talent. I would have done the same thing."

By the time it caught up to Klark that he was chatting about bajha with Uncle Yul, they had actually agreed on something. "I filed a formal protest in person before I left Chéyasenn. Then they came out with that blasted lie. You see why, don't you? The league doesn't want the embarrassment of a female defeating the best players in the league to be public knowledge."

Uncle Yul wore his deepest scowl. "Cowards. I bet the B'kahs are celebrating this decision as we speak. The Lesoks, too. If those bastards haven't influenced it from the very beginning."

"My entire team and I agree with you wholeheartedly, Uncle. Now rumors are flying, including some that connect the decision to performance enhancing tech. The choices are to leak the truth and be forever known as the team that tried to sneak women into the bajha ring, or we allow the rumors of doping to persist. Both have the potential to be damaging to the team's reputation and ours."

Their boots ground against the sand strewn on the path. The sound of the scavenger gulls battling for scraps from the trawler faded behind them. Uncle Yul said, "We need the truth to come out. Then we need to get the decision reversed. Kes Aves must return to the ring, and in time for Team Eireya to win the Galactic Cup."

"Yes." It was encouraging that Uncle Yul, the family's most conservative member, agreed with his plan.

"The risk, Klark, is that forcing the league to admit they covered up banning a female will humiliate them, as you said. Once that happens, we can expect them to come back at us, twice as hard. They could levy enormous fines on the team and our family. Huge penalties that could prove quite taxing on our assets."

Klark's gut knotted up at the thought. Just when he thought he could not cause the family more trouble. "I hope we don't have to weather that storm, but we Vedlas are a powerful family. We will survive. I'm quite frankly more concerned about this coming down hard on Jemm."

"Jemm, is it?"

"Jemm, yes. That's Kes Aves's real name. Jemm Aves. She'd be powerless against the league. No matter what course of action we take, I want her folded into the protection of our clan. I will not stand for her to be prosecuted, or sent to jail. I'll see her protected, no matter what it costs me."

Uncle Yul halted. Silence reigned as Klark held the man's penetrating stare for longer than he ever had in his adult life. "Why, you're in love with her, boy."

Klark's heart nearly stopped. "I trained her as a coach would. She was my player." The words seemed woefully inadequate to encapsulate his relationship with Jemm, and the magnitude of his feelings for her.

Uncle Yul laughed. "Tell the truth."

Klark cast his gaze out to sea as thoughts of him and Jemm and all they had shared cascaded through his mind. "Yes. I'm in love with her. It was the most wonderful and extraordinary thing that ever happened to me." He took control of himself before more foolish words spilled out of him. This was Uncle Yul, after all, and not his teenage sister, Kat. "We both understand the impossibility of being together, however."

"Ah. The impossibility of being together. I used similar words myself once." Uncle Yul's expression reverted back to one of perpetual disgruntlement. "I convinced myself of them when I was about your age. I was the second son, like you are. I had your father to watch over." He sighed, a sound that carried the weight of years. "I was a fool. I let her go. Every day I imagine I see her out there on the water, and pretend she thinks of me."

"Perhaps she does," Klark offered.

"Does not. She's a grandmother now with a large family and a husband-protector who adores her. She moved on."

And I never did. Klark guessed what his uncle had left unspoken.

Uncle Yul's brilliant, pale golden eyes narrowed. "I let the love of my life go because she did not fit the Vash mold. I have regretted it ever since. She was a commoner, as your Jemm is."

Dour, by-the-rules Uncle Yul had fallen in love with a commoner? The same man who had railed at Klark for allowing Ché to shoulder the blame for a spilled garden cart? Klark tried to wrap his mind around the impossible revelation.

"Take a look at me, Klark. Take a long look at this life-long bachelor. This bitter old coot who strikes fear in the hearts of his nephews. This will be you in thirty years if you let that woman get away. And she will. The good ones always do. Go get her and bring her home. And if she doesn't want to come home with you? Well, just go get her. Things will have a way of working out."

That brought Klark up short. "I can't leave now. Not with all this about to hit."

"Bah. Did you not listen to anything I said? You need to go follow your heart, young man. It matters not whether you are at the palace while we work on this. In fact, standing with your shunned champion shows you believe in her, and in your team. I have the best connections to deal with this problem from here. The influence. The respect. I've lived this life for far longer than you. I can also handle Rorrik. You know me, Klark. You know I've never turned away from a fight. I will relish this."

Klark had never seen Uncle Yul look so passionate and full of determination. His instincts told him to trust this new and fervent ally, that together they would solve this debacle. Uncle Yul from the palace, and Klark from Barésh. "I had better tell you what I know, then, sir." He filled his uncle in on his pros wanting to speak to the press, the rising frustration of the fans, and even the failure so far to find supporting evidence for their cause in the Treatise of Trade. "That's everything," he said finally.

They stopped on the path. "Go take your run, young man, as you are dressed for it. I'll get started on this. I expect you gone by morning."

"I will be gone by tonight."

His uncle's hard lips gentled some before he turned back toward the palace, his boots crunching on the surface of the path. It almost could have been a smile.

"Klark!" Katjian exclaimed when she opened the door to her quarters. Her hair was brushed loose and long, and it left her looking very young. Little more than a child, actually. It set off Klark's brotherly protective instincts. He thought of the family's pressure to marry her off. Prince Hajhani or any other hopefuls had better back off, he thought darkly. It would not happen unless Kat was willing. Not on his watch.

"I'm leaving for Barésh," he said.

"You're leaving? Again?" Happiness drained out of her expressive face. "Why? You only just came home. How long will you be gone? What will you be doing? Where are you going? I heard about Sea Kestrel. Why did he leave the team? Please tell me what happened. I watched every match the team played."

And he considered Jemm a master interrogator? His sister would give her a run for her money. "Answers in private." He took her by the elbow and steered her back into her suite. Her lady's maid was tidying up scattered clothing.

At Klark's appearance, she snapped upright. "Your Highness."

"I would like a moment alone with the princess, please."

The maid made a quick exit. Then Klark turned to Katjian. "I need a favor."

She seemed to bloom with his request. "Yes, of course," she breathed.

"You've been researching the Treatise of Trade, looking for answers whether or not females may play bajha. Yes?"

"Yes. I study it every morning. Why?" Her luminous pale eyes scoured his face for clues.

"Have you discovered anything yet?"

She shook her head. "Not anything that specific, no."

Ah, well. It had been worth a shot. Failing to find support in the ancient document would not change the nature of the fight he and Uncle Yul were about to undertake, but it would add credibility to it.

"Actually, there is one thing." Her expression brightened. "In the saga of Queen Keera's flight from Eireya, when she escaped the massacre with the young prince Chéya in the Dark Years, there is much written about her dangerous journey. In book two of the Flight Saga, verse seventeen or eighteen, I can't remember off the top of my head, it says that along the way the queen had to..." Katjian scrunched her eyes in concentration. "'Lay waste to those who sought to deny her a safe haven.' I'm trying to form an argument that those words—lay waste—meant that she called upon her personal warrior skills to fight off warlords. And if she possessed warrior skills, then it follows that other females could possess warrior skills, and thus the practice of bajha is needed in order to hone those skills. But I have more research to do."

Hope ignited inside Klark. "Lay waste..." Only two words in a vast tome spanning untold millennia, but it was two more words than he could claim before—two words that might make all the difference. "The person who saved our family was female. Queen Keera Vedla. If she had been too meek to escape the palace, to fight her way to safety, the entire Vedla line would have ended in the massacre. She survived, and her bloodlines survived, because she was a warrior. A warrior, Kat. I don't know why I never saw it before. You need to go tell Uncle Yul what you've discovered right away."

She looked at him as if he had grown a third eye. "Are you feeling all right?"

"Yes. More right than I can possibly explain." He sighed deeply. "I'm going to trust you with a secret, dear Kat. And you must promise to keep it."

"I promise."

"Swear on the blood of Clan Vedla."

"The blood of Clan Vedla," she repeated gravely. It reminded him of when he and his brother Ché were children. They would get into mischief, and often had to force their little sister to keep secrets after discovering she was witness to it all. She had never once leaked anything to their parents.

"Sea Kestrel is…a female."

The blood drained from her face and returned in a rush, turning her cheeks pink as her eyes flew open wide. Her clever mind was churning with all the possibilities his surprise raised; he could sense it. "That's why she can no longer compete," she said.

He nodded. "My goal is to get the decision reversed and return Kes Aves to the ring in time for Team Eireya to win the Galactic Cup. We don't have a lot of time. Uncle Yul is taking charge of the matter here at home, while I rejoin with Jemm."

"Jemm." She lifted an inquisitive brow, her grin turning sassy. "That's a pretty name. Is Jemm Kes?"

"Yes, she is. Before you ask the question, yes, I've fallen in love with her, and that's why I'm going back to Barésh."

"Oh, Klark." Katjian let out the deepest sigh.

"But she doesn't know yet."

"Why ever not?"

"Ask Uncle Yul." Klark felt enough optimism about the plans that were in motion to let out a quiet laugh at his sister's baffled expression. His team was growing, and so was his hope that they could turn this around. "He gave me some good advice, bachelor to bachelor." Second son to second son. "Come, we'll tell him what you've found. You're a part of this now. You and Jemm are alike in many ways. Now, both of you have the chance to make history. Just as Queen Keera did when she saved our bloodlines."

Then he would go find Jemm to save his chance at love. If his luck held out, she would love him back.

CHAPTER TWENTY-FOUR

A t the frontier border, finally inside the transfer station after a grueling voyage, Klark carried his belongings from a chartered deep space vessel to the starspeeder he would pilot solo to Barésh. A Trade Federation official wearing a tag that read *Department of Earth System and Frontier Security (DESFS)* checked his IDs. "The procedures have changed recently, Your Highness—for everyone, including *Vash Nadah*. You'll have to process through Bezos Station before they'll let you through."

"What in the name of heaven is Bezos Station?"

"It's the Earth-dwellers, sir. Our government has given them a refurbished space station with which to exert their authority in the frontier. That's what they have named it."

Earth had been granted sovereignty over the frontier, yes, but giving the ruffians the hardware with which to do it? Well, he supposed that without the technological know-how to build an immense space station, they would have to accept spare parts and Trade Federation charity for some time to come.

"They are the gatekeepers of Barésh now?" Klark demanded.

"For Barésh and other worlds in close proximity. I apologize for the inconvenience. It should be a routine process for you, and nothing more," the official assured him, and wished him a pleasant journey onward.

But at Bezos Station the Earth-dwellers detained Klark, requesting that he board their station for "further processing". No surprise that his presence set off red flags, he thought gloomily. He was not a fan favorite of Earth's. Certainly not after all that had transpired leading up to his arrest. He knew enough of the English tongue to carry on a conversation, and the personnel on board had a reasonable command of Basic—far better than the Doctors Without Borders who had set up their hasty shop on Barésh.

A pleasant fellow who introduced himself as Mark Vinson escorted him to the commander's office. "I'm sorry about the inconvenience, Your Highness," the officer said in a thick Earth accent. "But every craft except mining and cargo vessels will have to process though Bezos the first time through. No exceptions."

"Does everyone have to make an appearance before the commander?"

"Ah. No." Vinson's uneasy sideways glance told Klark that his earlier suspicions were valid. It may not go well for him with the Earth-dwellers.

Vinson paused outside the open door to the office. "Commander, Prince Klark Vedla is here."

"Ah. Good." The commander stood to greet him. He was a tall, good-looking, very fit brown-skinned Earth-dweller. His uniform was identical to Vinson's, an olive-green jumpsuit with many colorful patches, but this man displayed dark blue birds of prey on his shoulders, not brown leaves like Vinson. Klark made a mental note to learn Earthdweller military rank.

The officer did not round the desk to shake his hand as Earth-dwellers were often wont to do. It forced Klark to walk forward to grasp his offered hand across the desk. But there seemed to be no insult attached to the act. The man wore a smile that appeared warm and genuine. "Denzel Duarte," he said. "Welcome to Bezos Station, Your Highness."

Klark shook his hand. "Klark is sufficient." The Earth-dwellers were famously informal. It would do him no favors to adhere too strictly to protocol. He needed to process through this roadblock to get to Barésh without delay.

"Call me Denny. Please. Be seated." Duarte's accent was not as thick as his second-in-command's. "As my executive officer may have already briefed you, we've been here only one standard week. We're all still adjusting. Earth uses approximately twenty-four standard hour days, and Federation standard is closer to twenty-eight. It makes for longer days than what we're used to. Would you like some coffee?"

Klark almost made a face. The bitter Earth beverage tasted like burnt wood. "No, thank you."

"Tock then? The galley stocks it."

"I very much appreciate your hospitality, but I need no refreshment. I would like to resume my journey as soon as possible."

Duarte lowered himself in a stiff manner into his chair and leaned back, his hands tented on his stomach. "What brings you to Barésh?"

"Bajha."

"Ah. Your ancient form of martial arts is gaining more and more enthusiasts on Earth. Some describe it as a cross between yoga and cage fighting," he said with a smile. "You play as well as own a pro team, as I understand it."

"I do."

"Basketball is my passion. I played college ball. You're tall, athletic. You'd do well, I think. But it hasn't gained the fans in the rest of the galaxy as we had hoped."

"Lobbing orange balls into little hoops." Klark tried for tact. "It may take some time to catch on."

Duarte laughed. "I've watched bajha matches. It's exciting. But I have not stepped in the ring myself to give it a try. I'd probably end up getting walloped with the shock baton like a piñata gets whacked by a stick."

Klark did not recognize all the words, but he got the gist. "They're called sens-swords. More, body hits are not allowed during league play. If they do occur, it's a penalty. If it's deemed intentional, the player forfeits the match. I hope someday to have the chance to introduce you to bajha."

"I'd like that very much. So, tell me…how does bajha relate to your visit to Barésh?"

"A female bajha player of extraordinary talent lives there. She was on my team, but the league banned her from competition last week after they learned she is female."

"I'm sorry to hear that. Is there a women's league? Some sports teams on Earth are segregated by gender."

"Women don't play bajha at all. Until I saw her in the ring, I quite frankly didn't believe females had the capability. She has singlehandedly changed that view. I discovered her out of the Barésh street bajha circuit and signed her to my team. She went on to defeat every pro player she went up against. She was undefeated at the time the league sent her home last week. I'm working on getting the decision reversed. Time is running out before the season will be too far along for it to do much good."

"I would like to see the end of gender discrimination on all worlds. If I can help, please let me know." Duarte's interest in the story seemed genuine. He opened his tablet. "What is the name of the woman player? Maybe she could give a demonstration match here in the station. I think we'd all like that. And if the Federation won't allow women to play, Earth will."

That was a marvelous idea. The league would be assaulted on all sides. "She goes by the ring name Sea Kestrel. Nico Aves is her manager." He spelled the names in Basic for the commander, who noted the information. Then the chitchat ran dry, and Klark braced himself for the real reason for this summons.

"You're probably wondering why I asked to meet with you."

Not wondering. He already knew. But he chose silence.

"Bezos Station has been tasked with protecting Barésh and other neglected outpost colonies in this region, which includes bringing desperately needed improvements to the citizens. You're number one on my Do Not Enter list. Are you aware of that?"

"Absolutely not. I was here a few months ago."

"There are concerns about your criminal record. Why don't we go over it?"

Duarte's expression was quite somber. Klark's forehead prickled with sweat. A cold feeling filled his gut. He would never shake his past. He would never be able to express enough remorse. Never atone enough. He would not be allowed past this gatekeeper, and Jemm would be lost to him. He waited for the bad news, his hands spread on his thighs, the image of stoic neutrality on the outside, and clanging alarm on the inside.

Duarte glanced up. "This is not a short list."

"I'm well aware."

"Let's see, we have obstructing governmental administration, political obstruction, attempted assassination." Again his gaze flicked up to Klark, appearing to weigh him before he read on, "Racketeering, public intoxication—"

"That's a lie."

"Which one?"

"I was never drunk."

Duarte lined through the charge. "Hijacking, resisting arrest, and, finally, escape." He set the tablet on his desk and pushed back in his chair. "That's quite a list."

Commander Duarte would be familiar with the circumstances of Ché Vedla losing both his promised bride and his ascension to the high throne to the new B'kah heir, Earthdweller Ian Hamilton. Duarte would also know that the finale of Klark's attempts to defend Ché and their family's honor played out on Duarte's homeworld Earth, in downtown Los Angeles, in front of billions on the frontier planet.

Ian clocked him good. The memory of that humiliation pained Klark like the dull ache of an old injury. "All the charges stem from my attempt to sabotage Crown Prince Ian Hamilton's ascension to the B'kah throne by interfering in frontier politics, and from when I tried to dissuade Princess Tee'ah Dar from marrying him. I did it to defend my family's honor, but I made a mess of things. I regret what happened. I served time for it. I learned from it, and I am doing what I can to make amends. I saved Princess Ilana Hamilton from an assassination attempt earlier this year. She is now my brother's wife. I learned of the threat to her safety while serving time for my previous crimes. I escaped in order to save her life. Now, that I've been freed, I've taken on the fight to end bias based on ridiculously arcane laws that are no longer applicable to modern life." How had Jemm phrased it? "Antiquated Federation dogma must go."

Duarte observed him with a vaguely startled expression, as if he had expected a different response. Most people expected Klark to be arrogant and defiant, he supposed. At one time he was.

"Well. Thank you. You've answered all my questions." The commander pushed to his feet, steadied himself, and walked around the desk. A metal web of crisscrossing struts and tiny blinking lights supported his lower body from his waist to his ankles. The parts made quiet clicking and whirring noises with each of his steps.

"I'm still getting used to the thing," he said, with the slightest of winces. It was clear the apparatus caused great pain, but that discomfort was mostly hidden behind the impeccable bearing of a career military officer. "The medical folks say I'll be able to remove it someday, once my spinal cord is fully fused. It's hard being a patient— or, being patient—when you've been an athlete all your life. But if it means I'll heal and be near-normal again, I'll do whatever it takes."

Something passed over his eyes then, and his gaze became more pointed. "But here's the thing. You've got a helluva rap sheet, Klark Vedla. Despite agreeing with your extremely valid reasons for wanting to be admitted, I'm not supposed to let you in."

Klark's spirits sank as his mind spun with alternatives to getting into Barésh. But, the Earth commander continued to speak, and he had better pay attention if he stood a chance at reuniting with Jemm anytime soon.

"My mother passed away from breast cancer a year before first contact with your people. It was an aggressive cancer that didn't respond well to treatment. Then my sister was diagnosed with breast cancer three years ago— the same aggressive variety. It was going to kill her, no question. She went into the hospital in Chicago on Earth for treatment, and four hours later she walked out— cured. In my family, your civilization's med-bots are microscopic miracles. I have firsthand experience now. I survived a jet crash last year. My aircraft was in an inverted spin when I ejected. It broke my back and it left me a paraplegic. Thanks to your people, my story didn't end there." He patted the bot-web encasing his lower body. "The gift that keeps giving. Why tell you all of this? Because I'm going to let you through today. It's a thank-you for what your people have done for my people.

And for me, personally; for giving an irascible, hoops-playing fighter pilot the ability to walk again. To use an Earth expression, I'm paying it forward." Commander Denzel Duarte smiled. "Don't disrespect it."

"You have my word." Now there would be one more member on his team to reinstate Kes Aves: Earth.

The long journey from Eireya back to the frontier was finally over. In Barésh City, Klark stood under its artificial sky dimming with looming nightfall, taking in the sight of the roiling heavens above and the crushing crowds below. He absorbed the trademark hullabaloo and the stench of the place. *Ah, you festering rock. I believe I missed you.*

At any moment, he could cross paths with Jemm. She would be surprised to see him so soon. He never wanted them to be apart again. Did one simply come out and say so? Or, wait for the right moment? Nerves made his palms tingle. If only life were like bajha, then he would know exactly what to do.

But winning in bajha did not come without a lot of practice and listening to instinct. Perhaps relationships were built much the same way.

By the time Jemm had walked through the apartment door the first day back on Barésh, she had formulated a plan to help persuade the dozers in the Galactic League to reverse their decision. It required immediate execution. With the season moving ever forward, there was no time to waste.

"I want to play bajha for you," she had informed Nico the moment he cracked his bleary eyes open that morning. Then she explained what had brought her home. "You'll play at Ore's Head and at my new club Under Duress," he had said. "Everyone knows about ya, sis. You're the star of the colony."

"I'll only play as a lass, though. And that's against the rules. It means you gotta break gaming regulations just as you're getting started owning clubs. It could ruin ya."

His shock at her proposal was comical. His almost immediate enthusiasm for the crazy idea five seconds later was pure Nico. "To hell with the rules."

Rules never mattered on Barésh anyway.

But rules mattered to the Galactic League. If all went as she hoped, news of her playing openly as a woman would depart Barésh on the lips of the many travelers who passed in and out of the colony and gambled on a little street bajha while there. Just as news of Sea Kestrel had passed from a cargo pilot to Yonson Skeet to Prince Klark Vedla, word of her playing as a female would reach the ears of infuriated fans who wanted Kes Aves back in the ring. They would know that competing as a female was not only possible, it was profitable. Then she would have done her part while Klark was busy doing his.

Now, Jemm and Nico traversed Central City toward Ore's Head. Her belly might be warm and full with Ma's cooking, and her excitement at another evening playing bajha as a lass was high, but her heart felt as hollow as a discarded ore canister. It was hard not to imagine weeks apart turning into months, or longer. Maybe forever.

Being with him seemed like a fantasy now, a beautiful dream, now that she was wide-awake and facing reality. If the ban on her play could not be reversed, she would accelerate plans to resettle the family somewhere she could find work to make the bajha savings last. Klark would still be a prince. She would still be a working lass.

As time went on, he would eventually move on, drawn back to the life into which he was born. They had not made any promises to each other for more.

But, she could not think of that now. It was time to cause a ruckus in the staid world of elite bajha as only a Baréshti could do.

Once at the club, which was packed to capacity, she put on a good show for Nico's patrons, aye, but it was hard not to fight the matches with as much automation as one of the bucket-bots used in the mines. Her opponents were so far below the level of the pros she had played with that she had to fight the temptation to finish them off in mere seconds. They deserved better than a quick dismissal, and so did the audience. Black Hole she was not.

Nico had taken her suggestion of holding weekly instructional classes for a very small fee. Baréshtis did not like paying for things they could not hold in their hands, inhale into their lungs, or ingest into their bellies. But in mere days the signup sheets were full, and the waiting list had filled three times over. Nico would need to hire more staff to handle the workload. Already other fight clubs were planning to imitate them and divert the overflow. But most citizens wanted to learn from the champion herself.

Jemm waited in the ring for her next challenger. Her blindfold was snug, her headgear fitted on top of it. The announcer made the usual introductions. She proudly wore her Team Eireya uniform, but with a strip of fabric cannibalized from the inside of Da's suit tied around her upper arm. In this way she had both her Da and Klark with her.

The match had barely commenced when she felt the energy in the club shift. She cast her awareness toward her opponent, but felt nothing radiating from the man but a sense of nervous, pessimistic determination. She redoubled her effort to concentrate.

She sent the hopeful to his defeat with as much entertainment value as she could muster. The crowd cheered. She kneeled waiting until the referee grabbed her by the wrist—although far gentler now that he knew she was a lass—and tugged her to her feet. Off came her blindfold. "The winner, once again, is the infamous and infinitely lovely, the invincible Sea Kestrel! Let's hear it for our very own Champion of Barésh!"

The stomping and howling rocked her eardrums. The stench of sweat and vapes thickened the air. But Nico had installed ventilation that helped…some. Wearing a brilliant stage smile, she mentally counted down how many more matches were left to go when another weird hunch drew her attention back to the mass of spectators. She scanned the crowd, and almost turned away when her gaze snagged on someone who did not seem like the rest.

In the dim light, she could make out the silhouette of a tall nobleman outfitted in dark off-worlder finery, his hand curved around a cup of ale. The back of her neck tingled. When she met his familiar, penetrating golden eyes, the tingle of joy slid down her spine and made her shiver. Klark!

Holy dome. What was he doing here?

Her spirits levitated and whirled like the heavenly bodies in the nighttime dome. It took a massive effort not to leap out of the ring and into his arms, and to refocus her attention on her next opponent, who trotted with cocky hope into the ring.

An assistant wrapped a blindfold over her eyes then Jemm put her headgear back on. She was so rattled by Klark's unexpected appearance she could hardly form coherent thoughts. She wanted to run into his arms. She wanted to run away. She wanted to rail at him for letting her go, and for coming back. She wanted to pound her fists on his chest, and to kiss him to within an inch of their lives. She wanted him inside her mind and deep inside her body. Because with that one glance, she knew the maddening aristo was stuck inside her heart for good.

Quiet your mind. Glad for the darkness, she sucked in a shuddering breath and distributed her weight equally between her boots. Her gloves curved around her senssword as the crowd roared and stomped, drowning out her pounding heartbeat. It had never taken more discipline than it did in that moment to gather her self-control to complete a match. But she did, and she continued to play until she had run through the entire slate of opponents for the night.

She tore off her helmet and blindfold, handing them and her sens-sword to her assistant, before she jumped down from the ring and pushed through the roiling crowd of well-wishers. "Good going, lass! "That's our girl!" All of them were elated she had made their pockets a wee bit heavier while providing an evening of entertainment of the likes never seen before in their hard lives on this world.

At the same time, Klark shoved his way toward the ring as she continued plowing ahead in his direction. The patrons parted, allowing the champion to pass, likely seeing the intensity in her face, and the fire in her eyes indicated that she was a force they might not want to reckon with.

Player and prince finally collided halfway between the ring and the bar.

With a tender smile curving his mouth, he stood still, taking in the sight of her as if she were all that mattered in the world. It was the kind of heart-stopping gaze she had waited a lifetime to see focused on her...and for all the right reasons. "You crazy aristo," she said, her voice thick.

"I know." He hauled her against his hard body. The toes of her boots skidded over the dirty floor as he lifted her into a deep and dizzying kiss. His wonderful and familiar scent intoxicated her; his hot mouth even more so. She was only somewhat aware of cheers and laughter as those milling close by reacted to the show.

"How the dome did you get here so fast?" she demanded. "It hasn't been a week yet. You must have turned around and left as soon as you got to Eireya."

"I did. I wasn't there for a single night."

"But, why? What about your family? When this scandal hits, you need to be there."

"No," he said. "I don't. I belong here, with you. My uncle is well equipped to handle matters at home, and I'm able to do my part from here. Especially now that you've laid the groundwork by playing as a female."

He kissed further questions from her lips before she could ask a single one.

"Come to the back," she told him, breathless, when they drew apart. She looped her arms around his waist to keep him close. *I can't believe you're here.* This time it wasn't for the bajha. This time it was for her.

Clinging to each other, they burst into Nico's office.

"Sir Vedla," Nico called out, grinding out his vape, wiping his hands and dingy gloves on his pants legs before greeting Klark with a hearty man-hug.

"From now on, it's Klark."

"Aye." Nico beamed. "All right then."

"Jemm is playing as a female," Klark said. "There's been no backlash?"

Nico laughed. "I'm making money hand over fist. I don't have enough seats in the club to accommodate everyone who wants to come see Jemm play. I have a second club but I need more players. Female players welcome."

Jemm nodded. "I'm planning to teach a bajha class, open to all. Then we'll hold tryouts for the club team— also for anyone who wants to give it a try. Fellas, lasses, trill rat or compound cog. It doesn't matter. Everyone's welcome. Except, we won't have room for everyone. It's been too popular."

"This is brilliant," Klark said, his excitement surging through her. "Word will get out about what's happening here. As Barésh goes, so goes the galaxy."

"I kept waiting for the scandal to hit, and for you to be dragged through the mud. But it never did, and you never were."

"Not yet," he said in an ominous tone, and shared the details of his unlikely alliance with Uncle Yul, of Katjian's discovery in the Treatise of Trade, and how he planned to use the information to bend the league to their will. Then she peppered him with questions about Skeet and Xirri, and the rest of the team, and asked if the rumors of a fan rebellion brewing were true. All this while Klark's hand stroked up and down her back, a possessive and affectionate gesture that seemed like so much more because he could do it in public for the first time.

"Nico!" Someone from her brother's staff came into the office and stopped to give Klark a long and awestruck look. "I gotta go," Nico told them. "I'll see ya after."

As soon as he was gone, Klark drew her into his arms for another kiss, and then another, his hands all over her. They couldn't get enough. If they were in private, their clothing would have long since hit the floor.

Then they clung to each other, neither willing to let the other go. He stroked her hair, holding her close. Her body molded to the hard planes of his. "I missed this, Jemm. I missed you. I used to think that needing others made me soft, and weak. But meeting you has made me strong." His callused thumb brushed over her chin, and he tipped her head back to look into her eyes. "You can thank Uncle Yul for helping me get my priorities in order. Who knows what would have happened with us if I got sucked back into the mire of clan politics and let too much time pass. All I know is that losing you would be something I would regret the rest of my life."

"You wouldn't have lost me."

"I didn't want to take that chance." He skimmed his fingertips over her temple, cheek, and jaw. "I want a life with no regrets. That's why I came back, my sweet Baréshti lass, because you deserve a man who would cross the stars to be with you—and damn the consequences."

She slung her arms over his shoulders. "You sound more and more like a Baréshti every day."

Thump music swelled, filling the club with its addictive, pounding beat. "I've wanted to take you dancing for the longest time. We need to celebrate. Do ya like to dance?" She swayed her hips against his in time to the beat, and felt his instant reaction.

His gaze turned dark. "If it's with you, the answer is always yes."

She discarded her bajha gear and left it under lock and key. She had only a simple T-shirt and pants to wear, but with Klark she always felt attractive. He took to dancing the Baréshti way with very little instruction. He was the kind of person who instinctively knew how to move his body. And moved it very well. With his hands on her hips, on her bottom, and everywhere, they swayed and rocked, and she soon wished they were doing something a whole lot hotter and with a lot less clothing.

Later, lightheaded from ale, desire, and the thrill of their reunion, they walked out the front door of the club to head home to the old city. Arm in arm amongst people who didn't care or give them a second glance, except if it was to compliment her bajha playing, was freedom of the best kind. She would never again take for granted the simple act of being able to stroll in public on the arm of her lover.

The street was more crowded than usual. It could be because of the proximity of the Earth-dwellers' medical facility, or the success of Nico's clubs. A glimpse of a red beard caught her attention. She blinked, and it was gone. Her heart lurched. Red Beard? Migel Arran's gangster?

Or only someone who resembled him? Nico claimed he and Arran had maintained their truce ever since Klark had reprimanded the club owner. A second look around reassured her that none of the people milling around looked familiar...or sinister.

"Sea Kestrel!" A female voice came from behind them. "Miss Aves!"

They turned around. A tall lass, a young teen, thin, with smudges on her arm, her clothing mismatched and badly mended, pushed her way past several large miners to stop in front of them. "Ever since I heard you're really a lass, I knew I had to meet ya," she said, breathless. "I've dreamed of playing bajha all my life, but I'm a lass, and I'm poor. But seeing your success made me believe I can, and one day be like you."

"Aye, my sweet. You can be like me. Or, ya can be better than me. If ya work hard, there's no limit to where you can go. Have ya ever played before?"

"With rods and sticks, things from the trash, but never a real sens-sword." The girl was so nervous talking to her that her hands shook.

"There'll be tryouts soon. Add yourself to the list. Do you think ya can come?"

"Aye," the girl breathed. "What do I do? What do I wear?"

"Come just as ya are. Bring your big heart and the hunger to learn."

"Thank you, Sea Kestrel. Thank you." She gave Klark a fleeting nervous glance then scampered off into the night.

Jemm exchanged an incredulous glance with Klark. "Did ya hear that? She said I helped her believe in her dreams." It felt as if the world had shifted beneath her boots that night. Instinct told her that everything from that moment forward would be different. "Winning the Galactic Cup for Team Eireya is my goal. But, this is my calling. Inspiring people to dream, the way my Da inspired me."

As they walked, he wrapped her in one arm and reached for her wrist, her great-grandfather's timepiece. "Remember...the unexpected brings opportunity." He tapped the watch with his finger, indicating the engraving that said the same. "Everything that's happened with us has been unexpected. It's brought us opportunity. Whether or not we prevail against the league."

Nagged again by an odd sensation of being watched, Jemm glanced over her shoulder.

"What is it?" Klark's entire body went taut. "Brigands?"

"Not sure. I keep sensing someone following me. I thought I saw the gangster that beat up Nico that day. Migel Arran's man. He has a red beard."

"I told Arran to back off, or I'd see his clubs shuttered," Klark growled.

"Nico says they coexist. Arran hasn't interfered since."

"It could change. You put Barésh on the map, Jemm. Now you're back, and causing an upsurge of business for your brother. Arran can't compete."

"But I don't intend to stay here. I want back in pro bajha. I want to finish the season."

"Arran didn't get where he is by being meek," Klark argued. "If he feels threatened, no matter how temporary your stay is here, he could start trouble all over again."

Jemm hoped not. But hoping that something did not happen was not enough. Baréshtis were born to fight. If Arran tried anything, she would make sure he regretted it.

Klark drew her close again, but they kept to the main streets and away from the alleys where pirates lurked. By the time they got home, the feeling of unease had faded, but she could not help thinking there was something more to it.

CHAPTER TWENTY-FIVE

Jemm grabbed hold of Klark's hand outside the closed door to her apartment. He was still catching his breath after seventeen flights of stairs in the thin Baréshti atmosphere. "Are you ready?" Her golden-green eyes were full of anticipation.

Klark laughed. "I am."

Jemm pushed open the door and pulled him inside. Unlike the somewhat foul odors permeating the stairwells, a montage of pleasant scents filled the small space. This apartment where four people lived, slept, ate, and bathed, was not much larger than his closet at the palace, but the sense of love in the small space was strong. He saw it in the smallest details, from handcrafted items to the pieces of many times repaired furniture.

"Ma, look who surprised me tonight. Klark! He's going to be staying with us for a while."

"I hope he's hungry. I made stew."

Klark's stomach growled at the mere suggestion.

Jemm's mother, Marin Aves, was a tiny, pretty, and feminine version of Nico. She greeted him with delight, "Jemm's *Vash*, at long last." Then she insisted he call her "Ma".

A shriek of "Mum-mum!" startled him as a little girl launched herself into Jemm's arms. She wrapped her skinny legs and arms around Jemm, her head burrowing in the crook of her neck. Suddenly, his star bajha player who had brought previously unbeatable galactic champions to their proverbial knees had transformed into a maternal figure, cuddling a little child.

Mum-mum. A name for mother. Was Button Jemm's daughter? Klark realized they had never talked of Button outside of Jemm's worries for the girl. He had assumed the child was a younger sister, but this girl was in fact very young. Young enough to be a daughter. Shame on him for not knowing such details about her life. That changed tonight.

"My niece, Button," Jemm said, grinning as Button hid her face shyly, taking curious peeks at him.

A cataclysm of unexpected feelings hit, relief chief amongst them. Relief that this child was a niece, that Jemm had not borne another man's child and all that went with it, and that if they were to have a baby together, the experience would be the first for both of them. All these thoughts were from a man who had never seriously considered marriage, or children, or any of that.

Until that moment.

He realized that both females waited for him to do something. He reached for Button's tiny fingers, and incredibly, she accepted his gentle squeeze, although all he could see of her from behind Jemm's shoulder was one wide, thick-lashed, curious eye. "It is very nice to meet you, Button. I look forward to getting to know you better." Is that what one said to a small child? He was not sure. He had not interacted with a child of any age since Katjian was young, and he had received no training on the subject.

"She's a little shy at first, but she'll warm to ya, and then you'll regret it," Jemm said.

Ma rounded them up for dinner amidst heavenly aromas. At the palace, dinner was a communal affair—a noisy gathering of family, acquaintances, visiting officials, with palace servers swirling around, attending to every need. Numerous courses were served, and afterward, liqueurs and sweets. This was something completely different.

And completely wonderful. With Nico staying behind at the club, it was only their small group of three at the table, a tiny knot of a family. Button sat on the floor, absorbed with color sticks and paper. Ma fussed over him as if he were her own. On the table was a single main course in a crock—a thick brown broth laden with chunks of some sort of meat and vegetables.

"He normally only eats seafood," Jemm warned.

"I eat other foods," he insisted. "Not often, but I do."

"He actually does," Jemm said, and squeezed his hand with affection under the table.

"I've never eaten anything from the sea," Ma said. "I've never seen a live fish."

Klark offered, "I will endeavor to change that as soon as possible."

"Shoal dabs." Jemm laughed. "They're alive when you eat them, Ma."

Ma made a soft snort. "I don't know about that..."

"Well, this smells heavenly, and I am telling the truth." Jemm and Ma watched him expectantly as he took his first taste from a bent and ancient-looking spoon. The bite contained myriad subtle flavors, and was so delicious he sighed with pleasure. "Incredible," he said, and scooped up another spoonful of the broth he knew had cooked all day. It was one thing dining on a gourmet meal prepared by the finest chefs in the galaxy. It was quite another savoring a dish home-cooked for loved ones.

A sleek brown shadow shot through a door flap installed in the wall and disappeared under the table. Klark leaned sideways to peer at the intruder.

"That's Ditsi," Jemm explained. "I can't say she's our ketta-cat, because she lives her own life that corresponds with ours only at meal time."

A soft paw tapped his shin.

"Ditsi thinks ya may be Nico," Ma said and made a soft kissing sound. "She prefers men. There are too few for her liking around here." There was some exchange made under the table, then the ketta-cat launched itself to a shelf from where it could survey the scene and study Klark.

Button appeared at his side. "Klark," she said in a breathy, pint-sized voice. Somber, she handed him a drawing of a lollipop-shaped tree, a round yellow sun, and a light blue sky containing a single white puff of a cloud. A stick figure of a girl stood on a strip of green grass in the middle of it all.

"Thank you, Button. It's a beautiful work of art."

She averted her eyes shyly and returned to her color sticks.

"She's been drawing such things ever since she started schooling with the Earth-dwellers, I never saw anything like it." Ma said. "They're filling her head with things she doesn't know."

"Filling her head with dreams, Ma," Jemm put in.

"Who is the mother?" Klark had not heard mention of Nico having a wife.

Ma put her spoon down. Jemm's hand slid onto his thigh with a caress of warning. He had breached some protocol, but was at a loss as to why.

However, this would pale in comparison to the so-called dinnertime protocol of an ancient dynastic clan of staggering wealth and privilege. Just wait until Jemm met his family and experienced a meal with them for the first time. Little intimidated his Baréshti lass, luckily, but the thought was enough to make him sweat.

"We don't talk about that," Jemm said under her breath. Then, even softer, she added, "We don't talk about a lot of things around here. I'll explain later."

She made good on that promise after they descended seventeen stories after dinner to put the trash out for Ma. "Kish, Button's mother, and Nico were best friends since they were about two standard years old. It was instant. They grew up together. They were never not together. You couldn't imagine one without the other. They were made for each other."

They tossed their bag of rubbish into a bin that stank so badly it made his eyes water. Then they began the long trek back up. "Nico proposed to Kish when they were eight. He planned it all out. He made it official by giving her a button he had found somewhere. Popped off of some compound cog's finery, we guess. Kish kept it with her from that day forward, pinned to her clothes. When they grew up, Kish got pregnant. They married. Many people don't legitimize that here, but they wanted to. It was important to them. They named their baby after that button."

They rounded another stairwell, then trudged up more stairs. No wonder she was so fit.

"Nico and Kish both worked. They were skull collectors. Their job is to drive into the mines and collect the AIs at the end of the shifts—the bucket-bots, the auto-diggers, and other mechanized what-nots—and transport them from one place to another, or to be repaired. Ma always watched Button while Kish was at work. Button was about four months old when it happened. Kish was gathering up some bots while Nico repositioned the cart. The brakes failed. It rammed a support beam. The ceiling caved in on her. He had to dig her out with his hands. Through all the dirt and rocks. He found her crushed. And it crushed poor Nico's heart."

"Great Mother," Klark muttered under his breath. "Heaven keep her."

Jemm's eyes grew noticeably brighter with emotion. "Then, on top of that, mine bosses held him accountable for her death, and the damage. They fired him. Losing the love of his life, his other half, blamed for what he probably blamed himself for anyway, an infant at home... He was lost to us for a long time."

On the tenth floor, where a pavilion opened out onto the city below, they stopped to catch their breaths. Or, rather, he stopped to catch his breath in the insufficient air, while Jemm continued the tragic story. "Years," she said. "Nico would get drunk on the least expensive swank he could find, or he'd smoke hallucivapes. They're laced with sweef, powdered swank, the kind that kills ya. He wouldn't come home, and Ma would send me out after him. I'd find him near-dead in a North City bar, or in an alley. I'd get him home somehow, only for it to happen all over again. It was a bad time. He got better after a while, but never could hold a job for long. It left me to support the family on my own, because Ma was sick and needed to look after Button. I brought up the idea of disguising myself as a fella to make extra money playing bajha. He took to it like a scamper to cheese, and here we are."

Yes. Here they were. Klark stood with Jemm looking out over the smoggy sea of lights. Distance muted the roar of the turbulent colony, but not by much. "I see the sadness in his eyes. It makes sense now. To lose the love of your life in such a gruesome fashion, and to be blamed for it." He swallowed, and tightened his hold on Jemm's warm hand. "At least he has Button."

"I know. I wish he saw it, too. But, all he can see in her is Kish, and what he thinks are his failings as a Da. He won't talk to her. He won't hold her. I thought it would get better when I went away, but nothing changed. He contributes money now, at least. I've wanted to take them all far away from here. But I don't know if I'll ever get Nico to leave. I think he feels if he leaves Barésh, he'll be abandoning Kish. It's why he wears those grubby gloves. They were what he was wearing the day he carried her broken body out of the cave. He says they're the last thing that touched her, so…"

"They'll come off when he's ready to move on."

"If he ever is. But the bajha and the clubs have changed him. So, maybe he will."

After a bit, Jemm inhaled deeply, as if the horrible air were a salve. "This is where my Da taught me to play bajha." She extended her arms and turned in a small circle with her eyes closed. "This is where all my dreams began."

"Take care." He reached for her arm, but with bajha-honed instinct, she evaded his grasp. His heartbeat skittered. "There's no railing."

"I know." She twirled, and he grabbed her.

"No, you are not falling to your death tonight." He pinned her to him so she could not escape. "No wonder you're so good. Since this is where you learned to play. One false move and…"

Both of their gazes shifted to the chaotic city scene below. She pointed to the edge of the city, hazed over in brownish air. "See out there? Where the buildings end, the badlands begin. That's where I used to drive every day. The smelters are out on the plains. I'd get my trailer loaded up with ore and drive it to the processing plant down by the docks. I'd make the roundtrip many times in a day, and a few times, after dark." She sounded bittersweet about it.

"You miss it."

"Aye. Sometimes. I grew up out on those plains, you can say."

"Were you ever in love, Jemm?"

She swiveled around to look at him. "No."

"Good. Then I'm the first." Before she could say a thing in favor of his observation or against, he pulled her close for a kiss, and loved her mouth so thoroughly that by the time he was done she was putty in his arms. "I love you, Jemm Aves," he said. "I love you, and I want you in my life. Somehow. Some way. I do."

"I told ya, you're crazy." She beamed up at him. Her multicolored gem-like eyes blazed with emotion. "I love you, too," she said, her voice huskier, as her fingertips traced the outline of his jaw. "I love ya truly, and madly."

He kissed her while he could still taste the words on her lips. "Say it again," he murmured.

Smiling, she did, and he kissed her again, standing in the very spot where she told him all her dreams began.

They returned to the apartment, hand in hand. Button was put to bed, requiring Klark to sit patiently with Jemm on a couch while Ma knitted a sweater. He wanted Jemm. Badly. But there was little he could do about it with Ma keeping a watchful eye over all. Planning ahead, as he was wont to do, he took an accounting of the sleeping areas. Thick curtains provided privacy, but not at the level he would like.

Jemm's fingers were wrapped in his. He lifted their clasped hands to his lips and kissed her knuckles. He saw Ma's lips curve into a smile, her attention supposedly on her knitting. It fascinated him: the yarn, the clicking of needles, the emerging creation. "It's a new vest for Nicky-boy," she explained.

Klark had never seen such a thing done. Clothing came to him in its final form.

Seven of the eight original *Vash Nadah* warriors had been commoners like Jemm's family, yet in the centuries since, they had become insulated in their palaces, enjoying lives that were far removed from what the rest of the galaxy experienced. Both commoner lives and those of the highborn had their advantages and disadvantages, but could they be straddled?

He was going to blasted well try.

"It's time for me to say good night." Ma placed her knitting in a basket and stood, yawning. After everyone bid each other good night, she disappeared behind the curtain on the far side of the kitchen, drawing it tightly closed.

As soon as she was out of sight, Jemm slipped her hot hands under Klark's shirt. "I've been waiting all night to get you and your body alone," she whispered.

"This," he mumbled as she started to kiss him. "Does not seem very private."

"My bedroom is over there."

The opposite end of the apartment from her mother's, thank heavens. But privacy was still going to be an issue.

They took turns showering in the tiny washroom. Then, Jemm's fingers lightly held his as she led him to her small, narrow bed. She set a candle on the bedside table and worked at making sure the curtains were thoroughly closed.

He walked up to her from behind, slipping his hands under her T-shirt to discover, much to his delight, that she wore nothing underneath. "The Earth-dwellers on Bezos Station—did you know there was such a place? I didn't— almost didn't let me in today because of my prior convictions. They demanded an explanation, which I gave them. Apparently, I topped their list of individuals who aren't allowed to enter. Now, unfortunately, everyone knows I'm the bad prince." He smoothed his hands over her clean, hot skin and bare breasts, savoring the exquisite, unequaled feel of her—and the way her body responded to his touch.

"Bad prince, I like the sound of that," she breathed, arching into his caresses. "How bad?"

"You know the details already. I told you."

"That's not what I meant."

"Ah." He chuckled as his hands moved under her T-shirt on their exploratory mission. "I am a very bad prince, then."

She moaned. Then bit back the sound.

"This is going to be a challenge," he said in a quiet, passion-roughened voice. "The proximity to the rest of your family."

"You're not the type to let a challenge frighten you away, are ya?"

He pulled off her T-shirt. He loved her breasts; he loved everything about her body. He ached to be inside her. The week apart had seemed an eternity. She turned and kissed him hungrily, until her body molded to his and she sighed into his mouth. With his thumbs inserted between her hot skin and the waistband of her pants, he popped the fastener there, tugging her pants down over her rounded bottom. He slowly lowered himself to his knees, kissing his way down her flat, toned stomach. He moved her thighs apart to lavish attention on her pliant, wet folds, while she held on to his head for balance. By now, he knew what pleased her. Her hands convulsed around his skull as he brought her higher, and higher. Then she stiffened, coming up on her toes. "Shush," he warned as she shattered for him. He groaned quietly himself as she pulsed and bucked. With one last shuddering sigh, she sagged against him.

"Holy craggin' dome. I hope Ma didn't hear me," she whispered.

"I'm sure she did not. However, she might have felt the tremors and thought it was quake."

She pushed at him playfully, and he muffled her giggle with a hand. She snatched his hand away, pulling him with her down to the bed, where they kissed and caressed with pent-up need, all while he stripped her of every last stitch of clothing.

"Wait here," he said, at last, and stood.

"I ain't going anywhere, I assure ya." Nude, she stretched out on her back on the narrow bed and watched him strip off his clothing. Her parted thighs offered a glimpse of wetness between them that tempted him to the limits of his restraint. If only they were in the big bed on Chéyasenn, and he could take her rough and hard, plunging inside her until she cried out in pleasure and he lost himself in her.

But it was always good with Jemm, no matter what they did, hard and quick or sweet and slow. He could not believe he had gone all his adult male life not knowing lovemaking could be like this. He had assumed himself an expert on such things, but he had been woefully mistaken.

He joined her in the bed, straddling her, his knees almost off the edges of the mattress. He kissed her, knowing she tasted herself on his lips. He was throbbing so hard by the time he pushed inside her that he nearly exploded then and there.

The lovemaking was unexpectedly erotic, having to be so silent, so restrained. They made it a game. She moaned, and his fingers moved over her lips to quiet her, and she suckled them, nipping him. Then it was his turn to groan. "Shush," she said, teasing him. He withdrew almost all the way, only to sink deep inside her, an exquisite invasion, just so he could hear her soft cry.

He missed this. He missed her. The way she felt, the way she sounded, her taste, her scent, every blasted thing about her. They laughed, panted, swore, and loved as they rocked together. When they peaked, she muffled her cries against his shoulder, and he hissed in a sharp, swift, indrawn breath.

Sometime after that, he curled up with her on the narrow bed, across from a window permanently scoured by centuries of bad air, in an ancient building at the edge of a slum.

With the woman who had won his heart.

Tomorrow loomed, and with it all that could possibly go wrong, but for those next few hours, nothing else mattered.

CHAPTER TWENTY-SIX

The next day it all began. They launched tryouts for the club teams as well as instructional lessons, doing so days before they had planned. Every day lost would be one less for Jemm to participate in the pro season. They could afford to waste no time getting their plans underway.

They wanted a wave of proof crashing across the Federation that bajha was for anyone with the aptitude for it, and would no longer be a game reserved for only the highborn. They wanted that wave to sweep from the outer reaches of the Frontier to the wealthy homeworlds of the *Vash Nadah* and everywhere in between.

Nico split his times between his clubs, doing an admirable job of keeping the chaos to a minimum. That night Klark volunteered to compete in the ring at Under Duress as Jemm held sway at Ore's Head. The tryouts had netted a few promising hopefuls. Using his pro gear, he sent his challengers to their defeat, but sought them out afterward to offer pointers. It was an investment in the future of the sport.

Galactic media took the story of what was happening on Barésh and ran with it. Not only in Eireyan-loyal affiliates, or sports news sources, but all of them. If the league had expected Klark and Jemm to go quietly into the night, they had erred badly.

Sure enough, by the end of the second day, the scandal broke in a wide and very public release. As they predicted, their actions on Barésh had pulled the league from its cowardly stance of silence like an angler lured a fanged sea-eel from its reef den. The Galactic League announced that a female had infiltrated the lofty ranks of professional bajha, and that this denigration of the sport must not be tolerated. Then, in private, via a comm-call to Klark, they came back hard, threatening fines and penalties, and also expulsion for most of the players on Team Eireya, all spiked with the additional threat of barring him from further activities in the sport if he persisted in defying the decision.

Defying. He rather liked the word.

He shared the details of the call with Uncle Yul, traded updates, and pressed on. He recalled how he used to run scared when his clan was threatened, lashing out in panic, but he greeted each turn of events with a deep sense of rightness and calm.

One outcome that brought immense relief was the reaction of the fans. The *Vash Nadah* elders might keep a conservative grip on galactic-level bajha, insisting on tradition over common sense, but most of the Federation citizens who made up the viewing audience were commoners. They cared little about who played for their teams, as long as they won. Klark intended to capitalize on that sentiment.

He and Jemm accepted an invitation to hold a news conference. They wore their Team Eireya bajha gear, and sat on chairs Nico had arranged in the ring at Ore's Head. All around them stood a motley group of bajha trainees, including the teenage girl, Farra, who had sought out Jemm on Klark's first night back on Barésh. The group also included an upper-class woman who hailed from the compound and was descended from Barésh mining royalty. The only prerequisite to learning bajha was hard work, good instincts, and the heartfelt desire to play. Klark shared this view with what was estimated to be an audience of billions watching the feed at various times and locales on the many worlds across the Trade Federation.

"Yes," Jemm said answering a question in her best Basic, harkening back to the lessons Klark had given her on Chéyasenn. "I'm aware that the fans are upset with the ruling. They have every right to be. Banning players willy-nilly on some teams and not others is akin to having the matches fixed. We don't even do that here on Barésh in street bajha. No one here would stand for it. What's next? Prohibiting an athlete because of the color of their eyes? Or because of where they were born? There is no rule in existence or any reason I can't be permitted to finish out the season. I hope the Galactic League reconsiders their decision, as well as the threat to expel my teammates, including everyone's favorite, Yonson Skeet."

Klark tried not to smile. It would be unsportsmanlike. But he had not expected Jemm to mention the threat the league assumed would be kept private between him, his clan, and them. But just as Jemm was known for her dazzling, unexpected moves in the ring, she played one now that could very well end up defeating her much larger challenger.

"Do not forget that Miss Aves has brought in a whole new audience," Klark said. "Hundreds of millions of women are watching bajha now who didn't before, a number that's expected to skyrocket once more females enter the league. As we have seen here on Barésh, the wider audience will generate unprecedented profit. And is not profit one of the founding principles of our Trade Federation? The future is bright for the sport that we love...unless the Galactic League flatly refuses to listen to the fans and athletes without whom our professional teams cannot exist." Klark paused, changing the tone of his voice to a more serious one. "We owe the survival of our civilization to the Eight Great Warriors. However, the mother of one of those warriors, the original matriarch of my clan, the Vedla Queen Keera, was a warrior, too. It is written in the Treatise of Trade." He paused again to allow that shocking statement to sink in. "But, sadly, this has been overlooked. The legend of our warrior-queen has been tamped down. Boxed up. Put away. We as a civilization recognize that society is stronger when both genders are strong, and that men and women each have their roles to play. But, by the Great Mother, if a female is able to compete and win in bajha, then she should be allowed to do so. What do you think?" He posed the question to both the audience with them in the bar, and to those listening on myriad worlds.

A chant turned into a roar. He could only hope the thunderous voices filling the club in which he sat with Jemm found an echo across the stars. "Bring back Kes! Bring back Kes!"

Klark turned his gaze to meet the glowing eyes of his dive-bar sword swinger, his star player, the love of his life, and smiled. They reached for each other and stood, raising their clasped hands in a show of strength as the chanting continued all around them.

Exactly two hours later, while they were all still at the club, tucked away in Nico's office, Jemm saw Klark jerk and reach into his pocket. He pulled out a vibrating comm. "It's Uncle Yul," he told her.

She held her breath, seeing Klark's face turn somber. Each time he nodded and said, "Yes, sir," she died a little bit inside. Then his eyes lifted to hers, and the most astonishing smile lit up his face. "Thank you, Uncle Yul. Yes, she's here with me. Yes, I will."

He closed the call and held the comm unit between two hands.

"Well?" she almost squealed. "Are ya gonna keep secrets now?"

"We did it." He threw back his head and laughed. "We crattin' did it!" He jumped to his feet and grabbed her, spinning her around. "It's a mixed victory. The league refused to budge on allowing females in the league—yet. But, we were able to negotiate an exception for you. Your ban was rescinded. You're going to be allowed to finish the season!"

She whooped, pumping her fist, then kissed him until he practically begged for mercy. "What happened?"

"The news conference did it, Uncle Yul said. It was the final blow. The league knew what they were up against. Half the teams were ready to refuse to play. There was even talk of a new, fan-based league forming."

"We have to get back to Chéyasenn."

"Yes. Tomorrow, I think. There's no time to waste."

Klark's comm vibrated again. He glanced at the identifier. "Ah. It's the league commissioner." His mouth tilted into a sly, lopsided grin. "I can't wait to hear him grovel."

The artificial sun was on its end run to the horizon by the time they made it back to the apartment. It had been a long, exhausting, and very successful day. Klark had even fielded a call from his sire, King Rorrik, to congratulate him on a job well executed. "Son, I might not be fully used to idea of females playing bajha, but I'm anxious for our Kes to pick back up where he—she—left off." The king went on to say that both he and his mother were proud of him. The entire clan was proud, in fact. Klark was glad to know it, but, whereas he used to be starved for even a single kind word in passing from his father, he now had other sources from which he could expect regard, love, and support: Uncle Yul, Jemm, and even his sister. Climbing out from the lowest point in his life, he had assembled a team for life.

Nico said they needed to go out and celebrate. "I found a new restaurant. You'll love it."

While the thought of eating unregulated Baréshti street food was somewhat troubling, Klark estimated he had been here enough days for his digestive tract to build a suitable defense.

"I don't think Ma will want to go out to eat," Jemm warned. "She probably cooked something."

Klark's stomach clenched with hunger at the mere suggestion. "I could eat Ma's cooking day and night," he admitted. "Despite the fact it doesn't include seafood." Fish was available on Barésh at the market located behind the walls of the compound, but at a steep price. Jemm no more wanted to give her business to "upper-class robber cog" compound merchants than she wanted to overpay. They decided that Ma would enjoy her first taste of seafood once they took her off-world, and could obtain it fresh.

Nico laughed. "We *do* eat Ma's cooking day and night. But we had a major victory today, you're gonna go off-world again, and all that needs celebrating." He was in high spirits. Yet, it was clear the prospect of a night within the apartment's close walls troubled him. He probably saw Kish in every chair, every spoon, and that was why he spent so little time there.

They carried their high spirits and laughter into the cramped space. Ma rushed at them, her hands wringing a dishtowel. She tried to peek around their much larger frames. "Is Button out there?"

"No." Jemm scanned the apartment. "Button!" No answer. "She wasn't with you, Ma?"

"She was..." Panic flared in Ma's eyes, and Jemm felt the echo of that dread course through her body. "She was coloring her Earth pictures." She pointed a trembling finger at the scattered color sticks on the floor. "I went to fold laundry on my bed. I came back at the sound of ya at the door, and she wasn't here."

"Button, this ain't funny," Jemm called out. "If you're hiding, come out now. You're scaring your gramma."

Klark stalked around the tiny apartment, lifting blankets, peeking in baskets.

"Button!" Nico yelled, louder.

"She ain't here." Ma pressed a shaking hand to her mouth. "What if someone took her?"

"Not from under your very nose, Ma," Jemm assured her. Then she remembered her periodic unease of the past few days. "I thought I saw Red Beard the other day," she said, low, to the men. "Arran's gangster. The one who went after me and Nico."

"Gangster?" Ma almost shrieked.

"Crag it." Nico's face darkened with an urgency she had not seen before. He pivoted on his heels, armed himself with an illegal knife slid in a holster inside his shirt, and shoved back out through the door.

Jemm, Ma, and Klark thundered down the stairwell in hot pursuit, calling out for Button. But the child was nowhere in sight. Jemm's mouth felt so dry she couldn't swallow. It horrified her to think she had brought the perils of street bajha home. Her loved ones would suffer because of her ambition. Her dreams had put them all in danger. Her deepest fears had come true.

"I knew this would happen," Ma said, making Jemm wince and hammering home her fears. "I knew the bajha would be back to steal away what's mine. It's what happened to your Da."

"Da did not die because of bajha," Jemm snapped as they rounded another landing.

"Aye, he did. He was an up-and-coming player. A real star here in the colony. Everyone loved Badlands Fire. He wanted to play for another club and quit the one where he started. The next day, some men accosted him in the mines. They broke his shin bone with a metal rod to punish him and teach him a lesson."

Their steps faltered. "How do ya know that, Ma?" Jemm asked carefully, exchanging a distressed glance with Klark.

"Your Da told me. He said he would never let any club gangsters hold him back. He intended to go back to playing as soon as he was healed. He was determined to take us off-world, that fool. That fool dreamer of a man. But infection set in, and no potion, no amount of love, could bring him back."

"Oh, Ma..." This was why her mother despised bajha. Who could blame her? "Why didn't ya ever say anything? Why'd ya keep it secret all these years?"

She shook her head, her lips pursed with old pain. "It doesn't matter. I'm telling ya now so ya know what you're up against."

Nico flew down the stairs so fast now that Ma lagged behind. The sound of their boots was explosive in the stairwell. After five floors, they reached the building's midsection and spilled out into the open air. "Button!" Klark called out, then Nico did the same, their shouts reverberating from column to column across the enormous round terrace.

The answering yowl of a ketta-cat echoed across the space. Ditsi darted past the frantic group, leading their gazes to the small form of a child standing near the edge of nothing, the breeze strong as it lifted her hair. In a pair of tiny but strong hands was a sens-sword as long as she was tall.

Da's sens-sword.

Jemm almost collapsed with relief. Klark's comforting hand found the small of her back and steadied her. "Thank the Great Mother," he murmured.

In Button's wide-open eyes was a twinkle of defiance to go with the fear and guilt there. Jemm had always seen Kish in her, but in that moment, she saw her brother, too. "You're going away, Mum-mum. If I play bajha, I can go with ya."

"You thought if ya played you could come along?" Jemm managed, her throat thick.

"Aye!"

Jemm started forward but Nico pushed past her. He closed the distance with purposeful strides. He snatched Button up, stripping her of the sens-sword. Their joined form was silhouetted against the expanse of the city spread out below, the edge only steps away. Nico's hard back and shoulders quaked. "I'm sorry, Button. I'm sorry." A single, raw sob pierced the quiet as he held her to him.

Button was stiff in Nico's arms. Her confused and anxious eyes found Jemm's over her father's shoulder.

Jemm encouraged her with a nod and a tender, teary smile. *He's your Da. All ya have to do is love him back.*

On Chéyasenn, Jemm emerged from the pool after an endurance-building swim. From where she stood, drying off with a towel, she glimpsed Ma sitting on a bench next to the hiking path, where she had taken to looking out at the sea of trees daily, her gaze sometimes sad. She wished Da were with her, Jemm knew.

Family members from both sides had gathered temporarily on Chéyasenn—Klark's sister Kat, Ma, Button, and Uncle Yul. Only Nico stayed behind on Barésh, out of necessity. He could not yet trust anyone to manage his clubs in his absence. He never found an explanation for the red-bearded man, but it led him back to Migel Arran, and ended with them deciding it was time they joined forces. Jemm could not believe Nico wanted to work with that dozer dandy. His name alone was enough to get her hackles up.

But Nico had convinced her to stand down, saying that Arran was not interested in flexing his considerable muscle. Arran even came to bid her farewell the day she and Klark left, along with hundreds of other well-wishers—a rowdy and unlikely crowd of trill rats, compound cogs, and Earth-dwellers.

The iridescent pomade Arran used on his hair and brows was more subdued than she remembered, and he appeared just as fit. But his high starched collar and trill-threaded ear were just as gaudy. "I watched all your matches, Sea Kestrel. Seeing you play galactically, watching you take down those elites, it was a sight to see. If I hadn't discovered you, where would you be now?"

"Discovered me?" she had scoffed. *Ya couldn't discover your nose if it were pasted to your face.*

"Joking," he said, his shoulders coming up in a self-effacing shrug. "I know the true story. But I still like knowing I paid you your first silvers earned playing. I like that my club Rumble is known as the place you started your career. Black Hole still plays for me on Fourthnights. He bills himself as Sea Kestrel's first bajha opponent, and draws crowds because of it. Look, I'm sorry we were at cross purposes for a long time. If we can put that in the past, I'd be happy. I come from humble beginnings like you and Nico. Once a trill rat, always a trill rat. You know us Baréshtis, we're born to fight. We're born fighting and we fight to keep from dying."

"And fight every day in-between," she said, reciting the old saying.

"Like everyone else I've had to fight to hold on to what I have. It's not to say I've made mistakes along the way. Twelve clubs. It's not easy." He had looked to Nico then. "I hope you'll consider my proposal. A partnership would make us unbeatable in this colony."

A grin creased Nico's face and the two former adversaries shook hands on whatever they were soon to cook up. Then Arran nodded at Jemm, his smile charming in the way it never was when he thought she was a lad. "I'll watch for you in the Galactic Cup finals, Sea Kestrel. Good luck."

"Thank you, Mr. Arran."

"I have the feeling this is the start of a beautiful friendship," Nico said as Migel Arran walked away in the false Barésh sunshine.

"I hope you know what you're doing."

"Jemm. It's time you worked up some confidence in me. Have I steered you wrong yet?"

He hadn't. She owed so much of what had happened to Nico. And now, she hoped, he could find as much happiness in his life as she had found in hers. The love lighting up his face when he was around his daughter was what she remembered seeing when he used to be around Kish. Maybe now that he had broken down the barrier keeping him from growing close to his little girl, he would not be so closed off to new possibilities, like the pretty Earth doctor, CJ, the only one to catch his normally disinterested eye.

Nico's transformation was not the only one Jemm had observed. Uncle Yul had taken to walking along the forest paths, always holding his walking stick clasped in both hands, his knuckles pressed to the fabric of his cloak at the small of his back. He now came around a bend in the trail, slowing as he spied Jemm's mother sitting on the bench as usual, her pensive gaze fixed on some infinite point beyond the horizon.

He stopped a few paces away and also contemplated the sea of trees. "We're waiting for ghosts who will never return."

A beat of silence. "I suppose we are." Then she tilted her lovely face to look up at him.

"Good day, Mrs. Aves."

"Good day to you, Prince Yul."

"Please. Call me Yul."

"I'm Marin."

He gestured with with the walking stick at the bench. "May I, Marin?"

"Aye. Of course."

As he sat, he snagged his cloak on one of the bench's posts.

"Oh dear." She withdrew a pouch from the folds of her coat. Filtered sunlight warmed the red highlights in her hair. "Give me your cloak so I can mend it."

"That's servants' work," he said, but did as she asked anyway.

"No, it ain't. Why let a stranger do for ya what a friend will do? Go on. Give it here."

As she sewed the tear in his cloak he sat rigidly, looking somewhat shy. "A friend," he said, appearing to enjoy the sight of her bent to the task of doing him a kindness, and with such focus and care.

"Aye. Friends, we are."

Yul aimed his smiling face into a shaft of warm sunshine, and his hard, lean frame seemed to melt like a cake of marl-butter left in the sun.

Grinning, Jemm wrapped a towel around her shoulders and left the garden area to allow the pair some privacy.

As everyone close to the sport of bajha had predicted all along, Team Eireya would face the B'kah clan's Team Sienna in the finals. The tension and anticipation was palpable in the locker room on the desert world Sienna, the B'kah homeworld. Klark would have enjoyed the glory of seeing the Galactic Cup Games hosted on Eireya instead, but they had lost the all-important card toss.

Jemma was to face Reeglan A'nnar B'Kah, who was also undefeated. While the media cheered her advancement to this point, most seemed to agree she would finally meet her match in the ring. Some already praised her for taking second place in the league, and what a wonderful accomplishment that was, for a female. Opinions were that she would be eliminated, and maybe even quickly. To Klark, it seemed premature.

Klark took a moment with her before she left to confer with the coaches and then to enter the ring, where he could follow only in his mind. As always, he hunted for flaws in her bajha suit, checking the seams, her boots, her gloves. Her hair was longer now, curling in reddish-gold waves around her neck and jaw.

"How do I look?" she asked.

"Beautiful."

Her tight expression melted with a laugh. "If only that was an advantage in the ring."

A security officer approached them with a porta-note card in his hand. "Miss Aves, there's a message for you from the king."

"Hmm, why would my father message you in this manner?"

"Not your father, Your Highness." The security officer sounded a bit awestruck. "The King of Kings. His Majesty Romlijhian B'kah."

Startled, Klark and Jemm leaned in together to read the note.

Security level: Private

Miss Aves, Queen Jasmine and I are fans of yours. For obvious reasons, we cannot say that we will be rooting for you, but draw your own conclusions if you will. Good luck. RB

"RB? The king of the entire *Vash Nadah* Trade Federation signed a note to me with his initials?"

"And wished you good luck."

"Crag me."

Klark tipped his head back and laughed. "I love you."

She came up on her boots and kissed him. "I love ya, too."

He held her there for a moment longer, while she was still his and not the fans', as she would soon be. His hand lingered on her back as he willed her to know that he would be with her in spirit in that ring. Then he dropped his hand. He had done all he could to help her reach this point. Now it was up to her.

To the deafening thunder of a capacity crowd numbering in the hundreds of thousands, in one of the most awe-inspiring arenas in the galaxy, Klark emerged into the open with Jemm, Coach K, and the team's staff. He watched Jemm exchange nods with Skeet and Xirri, and her other teammates, and with some league officials. What pressure she must be feeling now.

On the other side of the ring stood her opponent, waiting. The B'kah champion. Fit, capable. Ready.

Jemm paused for a moment before entering the ring, turning her head to cast a glance back over her shoulder at Klark. He waited, questioning, as he tried to read her. Was there some doubt she wrestled with? Second thoughts? But her glittering gaze was sure and steady as one corner of her mouth lifted in an impish hint of a smile.

He smiled back. *You're ready.*

I know. Then she was off, striding into the ring, and he knew the Galactic Cup was theirs.

CHAPTER TWENTY-SEVEN

T he reaction to Jemm's victory was explosive. Even before the lights came on, she heard the crowd roaring. When the referee pulled her to her feet and the helmets came off, the defeated B'kah champ congratulated her—graciously—and she thanked him, complimenting him on his fine playing. It was a long, brutally exhausting and well-executed match that left her limbs feeling rubbery.

As she always did, she went still and closed her eyes for a second. *Thank you, Da.* Then, dispensing with protocol, she thrust two triumphant fists in the air.

Holy dome. She craggin' *won* the Galactic Cup.

If only she could see Klark's face. She knew he was out there, wishing he could be with her, but enjoying the win and celebrating with their families and the rest of Team Eireya. He would tell her this was her moment. It was! By the dome, she had seized it.

Hundreds of thousands of strangers cheered as she kept her fists high, turning in a slow circle as a gesture of appreciation and respect for all who came to see her play. Her grin was so wide that it made her cheeks ache. Her vision blurred with tears, even as she let out a laugh of pure joy. The win was so much more than just her senssword hitting her challenger's chest plate, more than putting Team Eireya on top. It was a victory for commoners, and for females, a reason for every person who had ever looked hopelessness in the face to keep on fighting and never give up.

To never forget how to dream.

In winning, she brought honor to Barésh and also Eireya, to the Aves family and the Vedla clan. She could not have wanted anything more, or wished for anything harder, than winning the Galactic Cup. Except to see the joy of it reflected in the face of the man she loved.

With fireworks exploding overhead, refs and league officials ushered her from the ring to where her teammates and coaches waited to mob her. They swept her up into a storm of hearty hugs and shouts. Xirri kissed her loudly on the cheek then Skeet started the chanting, "Team Eireya." They all shared in the victory. Bajha was a sport of individuals in separate matches, but it took a team to win the games—and the Cup.

Finally, she fought her way free to search for Klark. She saw him heading for her, his expression of exultation and love powerful enough to make her knees go weak.

He threw her backward over his arm, dipping her low for a very public victory kiss. They had never before displayed their affection publicly, although the entire team knew they were together. But now, in the flashing lights of the media crush, it would never again be a secret. Owner and pro, coach and player, prince and trill rat: they would be the leading story across the vast Trade Federation for days to come.

Laughing, Klark hauled her back into his arms and spun her around like she weighed nothing, letting her slide slowly down his long, hard body to her feet. They grinned at each other, needing no words, never needing words. Everything they could ever desire was in each other's eyes. She could not have done this without him, and he could not have done it without her. "I told ya I'd get ya the Galactic Cup," she said, grinning.

Love glowed in his golden eyes. "You did."

"So, now that we got that out of the way, what's next?" she asked with an air of mischief.

He gave her a quick hard kiss on the mouth. "The rest of our life is next, Baréshti lass."

"*Our* life, aye."

For those few seconds, there was only them. Then their families swarmed in.

"Mum-mum! You won!"

Nico had arrived with Button riding high on his shoulders. Her little face shone with happiness, her thin arms linked around his neck. She sure loved her Da. Nico swung Button down, and Jemm hugged them both at once, laughing with happiness. Then Ma was there, followed by Uncle Yul, joining in the celebration. Jemm noticed how the tips of his fingers brushed across her lower back, ever so lightly. The gesture was all at once respectful and intimate, and spoke volumes about the developing closeness between the two. *Well, well.* Jemm winked at Ma, and the woman glowed.

"Jemm!" They turned at the sound of Katjian's voice. Klark's sister embraced each of them. "I'm so happy. I'm so proud. You did it."

"We did it," Jemm corrected. Klark's little sister was so adorable, Jemm always told her she wanted to pack her up and put her in her pocket.

Then the princess stepped aside to reveal a regal couple approaching. Klark's parents, the king and queen, led more family and a bevy of staff toward them. Klark's other sister, Princess Tajha, was there, as well as the Crown Prince Ché and his Earth-dweller wife Princess Ilana.

They exchanged warm, sisterly grins. Jemm had felt an instant bond with Ilana when she first met her. They were both outsiders led into the Vedla inner circle by the men who loved them.

As his parents approached, Klark wrapped his arm around Jemm with a definite message of possession. It was not the clasp of a team owner, but that of a lover. His message to his parents was clear. *She is mine, and I am hers.*

Jemm was not sure how his parents would react. The king seemed to be a bit stiff and at a loss for words with his son. It made her heart ache for Klark. But, upon a closer look, she saw he did love his son. He was lacking only in the ability to express it. "I'm proud of you, son, and admire what you did here. The entire clan is grateful."

Klark's tight expression gentled. "Thank you, sir."

"Congratulations, Jemm," Queen Isiqir told her, surprising her with the use of her first name. "We're so very proud of you and of the entire team." In her lovely face Jemm saw warmth, even a welcome.

"Yes, we are proud," the king said. "Well played. Well done."

"Thank you, Your Majesties." Jemm bowed to both.

"From the Earth-dwellers," Nico called out and set Button on her feet so he could wrest a cork out of a green bottle with explosive force. Foamy, sweet-smelling liquid poured over his hands and splashed onto the floor. "They had me deliver an entire crate of the stuff—champagne, they call it. Courtesy of Commander Duarte and the crew of Bezos Station."

"And Doctors Without Borders, too?" Jemm asked slyly. "Maybe even a doctor named CJ?"

Nico's cheeks reddened and he rolled his eyes, which told her everything she needed to know. There was hope for him with the pretty Earth doctor. And if not CJ, then another woman as worthy. Life had been a rough road for her brother at too early of an age, but he had won his daughter back, and it had begun the process of healing his heart.

Fireworks lit up the sky as more corks popped. The sweet, foamy Earth beverage filled everyone's glasses. It packed more of a punch than anyone anticipated. Their group was well on their way to becoming tipsy when a contingent wearing the B'kah coat of arms arrived.

"His Majesty King Romlijhian B'kah and Her Majesty Queen Jasmine B'kah request your presence in the royal viewing box for the presentation of the Galactic Cup," said a royal staff member who eyed Jemm with no small amount of awe.

But it was Jemm who felt awed. Who ever would have imagined someone like her would meet *Vash* King Romlijhian B'kah and his Earth-born Queen Jasmine?

Jemm slipped her fingers in Klark's warm hand. He beckoned to the rest of the team. Yonson Skeet smiled at Katjian, and she smiled back. Then he, Xirri, and the rest of the men fell in step with Jemm and Klark. As one, they walked together toward the royal box.

Jemm stored away the moment, knowing she would come back to it again and again. Life had its twists and turns. Some were wonderful, some were awful, but she had a good feeling about her life to come—a very good feeling. Her family was happy, the love of her life was at her side, and the Galactic Cup was theirs. Klark had returned honor to his family, and she had made a better life for hers. But for now, she would do as Baréshtis always did: savor the moment. On that remarkable day, under the orange-tinted sky of a desert planet, a lass from a backwater world was on top of the world.

EPILOGUE

LONELY GALAXY TRAVEL GUIDE
http://lonelygalaxytravelguide.com

Travel Alert: The Department of Earth System and Frontier Security (DESFS) advises against nonessential travel to Barésh. Check with your applicable national government for the most up-to-date information.

Introducing Barésh:

Take a Brazilian *favela*, cross it with a coal mining town and the tawdry glitz of Vegas, add a generous layer of Beijing smog and you'll better understand what to expect on the dwarf planet Barésh. Once on the surface, you'll encounter a teeming mass of humanity sealed inside a poorly ventilated terrarium. If Barésh is your introduction to galactic tourism, prepare yourself (and be sure to stock up on antibiotics before you go). The colony isn't a hostile place but its manic energy, punishing pollution, lack of police presence, public transport, or basic sanitation (or much of any infrastructure at all) makes it a challenge for visitors.

With Barésh home to one of the galaxy's trillidium mines, it comes as no surprise that the entire colony of drudges, miners, sex-trade workers, gangsters, pirates, and stray animals revolves around the industry. Don't be mistaken, there are some positives to be had in a visit here. The heart of Old City contains some of the oldest surviving structures in the galaxy. Explore a little more and you'll uncover an energetic (albeit sketchy) club scene, home to more virtual reality arcades per capita than downtown Seoul, where you can spend an evening grooving to thump, the colony's unique techno-dance music, and sampling local ale. (Steer clear of the beverage swank if your brain is an organ you value.) While out on the town be sure to do as the Baréshtis do by betting on a bajha match in one of the many fight clubs featuring street-gladiators duking it out in a slum-dog version of the popular sport. Just keep your wallet close, a face mask handy, and stick to bottled water.

Editor's Update: There have been significant improvements to the conditions on Barésh since the aforementioned section was published. Securing accommodations can be tricky for travelers from Earth destined for Barésh during the annual Dream Games. But if you can get in, the experience is unforgettable. The games were founded three years ago by former Galactic Cup winner and retired athlete, Jemm Aves, and her husband, Prince Klark Vedla. The couple, tireless champions of Barésh, split their time between Barésh, Eireya, and Earth, but you can sometimes find them out and about enjoying the city's unique nightlife. They were recently awarded the prestigious Starward Prize for their efforts to help disadvantaged boys and girls achieve their dreams through playing bajha.

DEAR READER,

Thank you for taking the time to read *The Champion of Barésh*. If you enjoyed this story of galactic royals matched with commoners in exotic, star-spanning locales, you might also love *The Star King*, Book 1 in the Star Series. *The Star King* is the story of the Crown Prince Rom B'kah and fighter pilot, Jas Hamilton. Together they embark on an adventure of a lifetime. But soon old enemies threaten to tear them apart and leave their worlds in ruins. In Book 2 of the series, *The Star Prince*, you'll meet Klark Vedla for the first time. His story and that of his brother Ché continue in Book 3, *The Star Princess*. While *The Champion of Barésh* is a stand-alone launch of a new series, it follows *The Star Princess* in direct chronological order.

If you love action, space adventure, romance and consider *The Champion of Barésh* a 5-star read, please:

1. Help other readers find my books by writing a review on the retailer's website where you purchased this title.
2. Find out when my next book is available by signing up for my newsletter.
3. Love to arm-chair travel? Sit down, strap in, and visit my Come Fly With Me blog.
4. Follow me on Facebook, Twitter, and Bookbub.
5. Add my books to your Goodreads shelf, recommend my books to your Goodreads friends, reader's groups and discussion boards.
6. Learn how to become a member of my exclusive ARC Team and receive a FREE advanced copy of new releases in exchange for an honest review.

BOOKS BY SUSAN GRANT

Star World Frontier Series
The Champion of Barésh

The Lost Colony Series
The Last Warrior

The Borderlands Series
Moonstruck (RITA finalist)
The Warlord's Daughter
Sureblood

Otherworldly Men Series
Your Planet or Mine?
My Favorite Earthling
How to Lose an Extraterrestrial in 10 Days

2176 Series
The Legend of Banzai Maguire
The Scarlet Empress

The Star Series
The Star King (RITA finalist)
The Star Prince
The Star Princess
The Star Queen

ABOUT THE AUTHOR

Susan Grant is a *New York Times* bestselling author who enjoys being able to indulge her love of travel and adventure by piloting jumbo jets around the globe. Her careers as a commercial pilot and air force pilot have provided endless inspiration for her books. Susan is the author of *The Star King*, launch book of her popular Star series about a spacefaring Earth family, as well as the RITA-winning novel *Contact*. Her new series debuts in 2016 with *The Champion of Barésh*. Susan and her family live in the scenic foothills of northern California.